Mer... T-Shirts

EVE KEOGH

MENTOR

This Edition first published 2000 by

MENTOR BOOKS
43 Furze Road,
Sandyford Industrial Estate,
Dublin 18.

Tel. (01) 295 2112/3   Fax. (01) 295 2114
e-mail: admin@mentorbooks.ie
www.mentorbooks.ie

ISBN: 1-84210-026-2

Cover Illustration: Slatter-Anderson
Typesetting, editing, design and layout by
MENTOR BOOKS

Printed in Ireland by ColourBooks

Dedication

For Shaun and Hannah

Chapter 1

With my feet no fella would ever fancy me. Mind you, this assumes two things of course. First, he wouldn't see my arse, thighs or boobs. And second, if he did, that he wouldn't faint. I'm quite used to the size of my bum, the weight of my thighs and the tendency for my boobs to wobble and make me feel like a sofa. But as for my barge-like size sevens? Skinny women, hairy spiders and other people's children apart, there was nothing I hated more.

But between you and me, it's not something I'd mention on my CV or at a job interview. Let's be honest, it would put off any discerning or squeamish human resource manager now, wouldn't it. However, I do consider my name (Gina Birkendale) perfectly acceptable. And as for the customary information required? Well, I'm an Irish female, just about to turn twenty-three and, wouldn't you know it? Cursed with more than a passing interest in the opposite sex – though I probably wouldn't mention that either.

Mind you, I don't think it does any harm to have a discreet pinch of suggestive info mixed in to enhance one's sales pitch. You know, in case the poor sod wading through the umpteenth CV is bored shitless and loves to read anything even slightly revealing about the applicant, as he trawls through looking for the elusive one with enough talent to organise the eleven a.m. coffee break. I wonder if 'engaged to an accountant' is in my favour or not? I know. Don't say anything. But Ralph's not that boring, honestly. Even if I am of the opinion that if accountants were a town, they'd be twinned en masse with some obscure Siberian place built on seventeen feet of permafrost miles inside the Arctic Circle.

And there's no harm in stirring in a good dollop of experience either, is there? (Though maybe I won't refer to that awful incident with the architects I used to work for. I'm still getting over my shock and blazing embarrassment after my Wonder Bra padding slipped silently out of my blouse and under the table at the Christmas do, where it then accurately placed itself beside the managing director's left foot.)

Oh, and I mustn't forget to whisk in a few details of my various talents and qualifications (flirting, chocolate and, oh God, men I suppose, tall ones preferably, if you don't mind).

Somehow though, 'Gina with the feet as rough as a dog's backside' isn't exactly the icing one would prefer to plaster on the cake of successful job applications, now, is it? But I suppose I've never been very good at introductions. In fact, it's one of my bad points; along with my passion for swanky shoes and (you'll never guess!) gorgeous fellas.

There are moments when I truly believe that maybe my parents are right and I shouldn't be let out unless accompanied by a chaperone. (Unfortunately a bit of a fuss ensued the night of my sixteenth birthday, you see, so Dad would prefer me to spend my weekends at the bingo hall with Granny, instead of all tarted up and out with an alarmingly handsome bloke.)

Even the weekly trip to the supermarket can lead to situations where my parents must wish for the millionth time that they'd given me up for adoption. Or to the circus. Or stuck me in a nunnery once I'd reached puberty. Well, my dad in particular.

Only last week, my long-suffering father labelled me a social outcast and a burden on society. I didn't take a blind bit of notice of course. I knew he was only being snotty because he was missing some bloody match or other that he was desperate to see on the TV, instead of being dragged around by the hair and made to watch my mother and me spend a small fortune at the cosmetic department. In fact now that I think about it, both Mum and I were tarred with the same brush so to speak. Which was very unfair as I seem to remember that she was the flirty one, off chatting up the fruit-and-veg bloke, having hysterics laughing and picking fluff off the poor fella's shirt.

Anyway today is my twenty-third birthday. Oh, and I'm also considering moving. You know how it is, I'm the eldest child and at this stage I'm convinced that my parents, Stephanie and Ted, are aliens and I can't think of a word to describe my brother, Tommy, though my little sister, Jessie, is OK, as long as you ignore her fascination for anything weird. Well, I happen to think that washing your hair with a concoction of tomato juice and bananas is somewhat strange and she is forever saturating our homely atmosphere with smelly incense sticks and reciting her own poetry while lazing in the bath.

My father has an addictive personality and my mother (God love her for marrying my dad) copes very well on her diet of watching the various TV shopping channels and deafening us all with her Frank Sinatra collection. It's not unusual to enter our family home to find Dad popping a few paracetamol while mother sings 'My Way' to herself in the loo. She really does adore that man. Frank that is. (Oh, and she occasionally likes Dad too.) So much so, that between the ages of zero and four I could have sworn she was married to him. Isn't that terrible? I was convinced Frank Sinatra was my father. And every time he was crooning on the radio I'd belt around the estate to ensure everybody knew that it was my dad singing on the radio and hope they'd be consumed with jealousy.

Which of course they weren't. They simply thought I was mad. Because although my dad did indeed sustain a fleeting resemblance to the real Frank, he was no artist. Other than possibly being a piss artist, Mum would declare.

So, poor me! I was devastated when one day, just before I started school, she kindly took me by the hand and gently explained (with the aid of a packet of chocolate buttons) that Frank Sinatra was only the fella on the telly, whereas Dad was just the fella who watched the telly. It was the first time a man had broken my heart and I did cry a bit. Until I realised that chocolate is a vital remedy when it comes to dealing with bastardly men who have bruised and battered your feelings without a second thought. (I think Mum thought so too, as she polished off at least half the bag.) Anyway, that's enough childhood reminiscing for now.

My two best friends in the world are Roisin and Lotty (as in Charlotte). Roisin is a ferocious cabin crew attendant, while Lotty is a mild-mannered aromatherapist. Our last full-scale manhunt together was a few summers ago. (Isn't it terrible, we've only just met and already we're back to the subject of men?) As the three of us set out for our first night on the tear in Corfu and marched briskly into the usual dodgy disco place I seriously had to consider going home a week early. I mean how do people end up in these horror zones? I'm damned if I know but thankfully the first thing that I registered once I got over the shock of the wallpaper peeling down in front of my eyes and the smell, was all the sailors – millions of them. Thank God! We were saved. I wouldn't have to fly home on my own and be persecuted by some mindless old bag who would insist on telling me her entire life story over a bag of boiled humbugs and a flask of cold tea. I had never seen so many blokes in my life (OK I was only twenty but you get my drift).

Mind you Lotty certainly gave us a run for our drachma. Apart from the waiter bloke with the personality of a bucket, and the helicopter 'blond bombshell' fighter pilot who couldn't speak a word of English, she did rather well, and she'd only had six drinks and it wasn't even ten o'clock. As for me, as usual I fell madly in love with a 'jet fighter hero' type. He was gorgeous and came nicely packaged, complete with a melting accent that made me feel all wobbly.

Now, here I am only a few years later. Almost on my way up the aisle (with baby tucked under my dress, knowing my luck), and probably a million paper clips and Velcro holding my cleavage up and my bum in, finally about to acknowledge the huge panic attack I'm convinced is going to finish me off. Why am I merely dropping in a story of a long lost love that's past its sell-by date? Well, I'd better fill you in instead of warbling on like some old timer.

Just after my Corfu love fling with the black-haired hero (Leo Di Caprio, forget it) I came home full of passion and longing for a romance filled with flowers and drink and sex of course. I'd spend hours in work daydreaming of my prince who would undoubtedly come and rescue me soon from my non-existent love life and my life in general. My Leo Lookalike even kept in touch (well, for about two weeks).

I was twenty-one when I met Ralph and at the time he seemed to fill this hole in my social life and occasionally he kept me warm on cold winter nights (now that I realised my jet fighter hero wasn't going to land in the back garden, get me rat-arsed on tequila and whisk me off to strange new lands where we would spend our time frolicking naked on a beach and I'd spend hours getting sand out of you know where).

But since then something terrible has happened. I've suddenly realised that, well, Ralph is slightly on the boring side of the fence. Yes. I admit it and it's frightening. Now that I'm being honest with myself I might as well tell you that I can't stop staring at other men. I know, it's awful. I feel so bad. It's become a reflex action no matter where I am. It's quite embarrassing really and I can't find a self-help book on the subject of 'how to stop mentally undressing men in the local chippie' anywhere. So I'm feeling very sorry for myself and terribly guilty.

Here I am on my twenty-third birthday, waking up to what? It's not that Ralph isn't nice and thoughtful. Or maybe there's something wrong with me? Most women want everything he is — reliable, kind, 'a set your watch by him' type of bloke. Not the most dishy man in the world but ecstatic about me to such an extent I feel like punching him in the face and demanding an argument. Obviously I'm simply a cow who is so ungrateful and wicked that I don't deserve him, or so my sensible nineteen-year-old sister, Jessie, tells me. On a very regular basis. I decide she's probably right and make a conscious guilt-ridden effort not to throw up next time I see him. Which will undoubtedly be some time today.

Oh did I mention I lost my job as well? Maybe this is somehow related to my growing dislike for my lover. Something about him reminds me of a ferret. And I do, well did, until last week, work full time in a pet shop. Not that it was big time exciting, in fact there is only so much tweeting and chirping and cleaning out of cages a girl can do without going absolutely bonkers. And that doesn't include dealing with the customers.

You know the type: little old dears coming in to buy high-class gear for their budgies, or coming to buy another budgie because they discovered Mickey or Tricky feet up that very morning. Never mind the weird crusty blokes coming in and buying cat litter by the skip full and mumbling at you strange things that sound like 'Wouldn't mind some of that, missus.'

But I did love the easy hours and the money wasn't too bad, not that I ever managed to actually save any of it. How could I with all those clothes to buy? And what kind of woman would I be if I went on a manhunt (or dinner with Ralph, should I say) without a decent plunge bra?

It was last Monday as it happened when my boss, whom I actually quite liked, delivered the bad news. Shop was being shut down, no money, thanks for all the fish etc etc. I couldn't blame him I suppose. I mean how many people want a tarantula on Valentine's Day? And let's face it a bunch of millet spray doesn't have quite the same effect as a dozen red roses now, does it? So that's life and I've duly signed on with our local recruitment agency. God spare me from agencies; if I ever see another form I'll crack up. But what the hell. Working in an office won't be all bad news I surmise.

I'm fantasising long and hard about a great big salary and a nice nine-thirty to five job typing the odd letter (I'd better brush up on the old keyboard skills) and flirting on the phone – fab! I'm drooling at the thought of lunchtime shopping sprees and I won't have to wash rabbit poo out of my hair every two hours. (How it even got there was beyond me.) Things were looking up after all, I decided as I lazed in bed – if only I could get a job with a dishy foot doctor, now wouldn't that be cool?

Shaking off the guilt cloud trying its best to smother me in thoughts of how horrible I'm being to Ralph, I actually decide I'd better get out of bed. Yes I will be nice to him today, I decide, whipping off my nightshirt. Definitely. He's a lovely bloke really, I resolve as I jump into the shower. The best. He has the kind of good points essential for keeping any girlfriend smiling and content: excellent credit rating, expensive car, charge card for Marks and Sparks – all the important must-have stuff, not that I'm completely materialistic minded or anything. My mother adores him. My dad thinks he's gay. I hurriedly dismiss that one. Any bloke who wears a blue shirt and tie isn't a 'real man' according to my dad and all his colleagues in the light bulb factory. I'll do my very very best to act like a proper fiancée, I conclude quite firmly, and not some cheap tart that can't stop eyeing up everything from the weatherman on *Sky News* to Jeremy Beadle

'Who's in the shower? Get out, will you, for God's sake. I have to have a shave.' Meet Tommy. I suppose most half-decent sisters like their brothers. I do have a relationship with him, make no mistake about that.

'I'll only be a minute, you'll have to hang on,' I shout back angrily.

Now, what was I saying? Oh yes, my relationship with Tommy. I suppose we should bury the hatchet really. After all, he is twenty-one and I'm not that far ahead. It's simply he's so repellent and nauseating. I know that sounds dire, and blood is thicker than water, but everytime I see him I can't get past those playful childhood incidents that forge the lifetime bond between brother and sister.

Oh silly things come to mind. Like on my fifth birthday for example, when he pulled the head off my Cindy doll and buried her hideous headless torso in my birthday cake. I was inconsolable. Or how about the time he painted 666 on the back of my furry new white kitten which I'd wanted for ages, and told me it was the devil's messenger. I was devastated! Not to mention scaring the living daylights out of me in bed at night pretending to be a teenage vampire or jumping on me at four in the morning simply to make me scream. I know I should like him really; it's only that he's so horrible.

Even now at twenty-three he can almost make me cry. He spent his childhood making me miserable and I returned the favour by hating his guts. Plus, he always got away with murder. My brother's fascination with uniforms and his homophobic tendencies went unnoticed in our house of course. All Mother would worry about was Tommy's backpack knocking her pictures off the wall and his possibly frightening the postman.

'How come it's OK for Tommy to traipse around the house in full army gear and with two stone of camping equipment on his back trying to light fires in the back garden, pretending he's lost in the bloody jungle while defending his country and chanting to any who might listen "Please, please, please can I have a military funeral!"' I argued hopelessly on the night of my sixteenth birthday

when Dad wouldn't let me out because I was
wearing a belly top and no bra. Even worse, all
Tommy had to do when he fancied playing Action
Man around the house was to nod to my dad, hand
over a couple of cans of Guinness and it was
anything goes. It was OK for Tommy to go around
the house switching off lights and worrying that the
military police might come calling for him.

'And don't come back here with any Eco-
Warriors or vegetarians or any other fecking eejits,'
was the final warning for me that particular evening
when Dad did eventually agree to let me out.
Honestly! Men and their double standards.

'Never mind, Gina,' Mum would say. 'You know
what he's like when there's no sport on the telly.'

Well, he's not going to spoil this birthday, I decide
as I take all his shaving gear out of the bathroom and
dump it in the linen basket on my way back to my
room. Pathetic isn't it? That's families for you and it's
another reason I can't wait to move out. Don't get
me wrong. We're not that dysfunctional but I think
it's about time I had some space of my own and let
my parents have their front bedroom back.

There's absolute chaos going on as I walk through
the kitchen door. The radio is blaring, the toaster is
belching smoke and Mum is singing Frank Sinatra
songs in the back yard with the door open, oblivious
to the fact that the house is practically on fire. As
usual she's 'showering the plants' (did I mention that
she's a bit of a gardener?). As for her Frank fetish,

apparently my parents fell in love while listening to old Blue Eyes strut his stuff on her little pink stereo way back when. They were married within three months, or so the story goes. Three months? It takes me that long to buy a pair of shoes never mind get married. Still, they seem blissfully happy together in that sort of disgusting way you don't associate with parents, if you know what I mean.

My dad's obsession with addiction doesn't seem to bother Mum for some strange reason. He really is one of these people who will 'try anything once' and every week it's something different. In the last month it's been Mars bars and squashy cakes from Tesco. All washed down with a litre of coke. I'm so fed up with sitting on the sofa and finding a squashed Mars bar wrapper has attached itself in a death-like grip to my arse. But he does have some really good points (in between the packets of biscuits) and also an unnatural fetish for sport. (I don't care what you say – it is unnatural to watch a bunch of blokes run around a field/garden/next door's driveway chasing a ball/an empty beans' tin/the cat and whacking/kicking the life out of it. Not to mention the two-nil, two-nil! chanting and getting hysterical/pissed/tearful in the process.) Which means that he is the best man on our estate to coach the under-twelves football team. The poor loves. My heart goes out to them, especially the little ten-year-olds, when I hear my father yelling at them about dignity and pride and then insisting they wear their stupid jerseys or he won't let them play the following Saturday.

'Happy birthday, pet,' Mum says as I wander into the garden.

'Thanks, Mum,' I smile back. I think my mum may somehow be responsible for my love of men. She invested many hours in teaching me the importance of flirting properly. She's actually quite liberal in her own way.

'Be bold! Be adventurous' is her usual line to female friends suffering from stale sex lives. And the advice for women having affairs with married men? 'He'll be on the next bus home with his curry chips and cans of beer before you can put your undies back on, dear. It'll be her credit card he'll be paying this month not yours.'

And she does love my Ralph. But by the same token I know she'll understand how much I despise him at the moment. Funnily enough I'm comforted by the fact that Dad really has taken a dislike to him, completely unjustified when you think about it. I mean Ralph's hardly an axe murderer and Dad doesn't have to go to dinner with him and listen to him spout on about trial balances and debtors lists while enduring his unsuccessful attempts to feel my knee under the table.

'He's an eejit! For Christ's sake, what kind of a fella likes calculators and wears pansy suits to breakfast? And he doesn't like the Grand Prix either! (Dad's very animated at this stage and is waving his arms around quite a bit.) You want a real man who'll get his hands dirty and plant spuds in the back garden. Bloody poofter!'

I know. Not exactly PC but there you have it.

'Let's have a cup of tea,' Mum says waving furiously at Dad to see if he wants a fix of anything sweet with his cuppa.

'Some of those Jaffa Cake things,' comes the reply via loads of funny hand signals which could mean anything from 'I've got my hand stuck down the toilet,' to 'Yes please,' or 'Has the milkman got his pants on?'

Mum is obviously an old hand at this game and steers me back in the direction of the kitchen.

'I was going to make you a cheesecake for your birthday,' she suddenly states as she unplugs the toaster, which is now shaking violently and sending burnt crumbs cascading around the kitchen like bullets. I heave a sigh of relief and smile back.

Mum's cheesecake killed the dog. We all know it but it's now a 'Family Secret'. Never to be spoken of except at funerals. In fact I can't believe she's even mentioned the 'C' word. In public venues (like next door's garden) my mother blames Pedigree Chum. 'It was the fishy one, he didn't like it at all!' But we know the truth.

'Any news today, Mum?' I enquire, cunningly trying to change the subject. She looks lovely in her autumn-coloured trouser suit, but somehow the yellow wellies don't quite go.

'Go and make us some tea, dear,' she instructs Tommy, who has finally emerged from the bathroom and enters the kitchen scowling viciously and making very rude gestures in my general direction.

'Stop that, Tommy,' chides Mum merely to add salt to the wound. 'And get us some of that fruity thing I made last night,' she continues, gesturing me to sit and pushing Tommy towards the kettle, 'after all it is your sister's birthday.'

Mother can't cook, or bake (hence the dead dog) but to her advantage she can drink, abuse several haircare substances at the same time and spend money even quicker than I can. She's a regular agony aunt on our street and it's never a surprise to find her in a neighbour's house mopping up tears, encouraging gossip and rumour or advising on how to dump one's husband in a quick and painless fashion and move in one's lover before the marital bed is even cold.

'Any news? Not really, Gina, though Loretta next door finally got her husband to have the snip after I gave her my magazine article on it. It's very popular you know,' she said matter of factly while pulling off her wellies. Tommy finally brings over the tea and I'm rescued from any more of his filthy looks by the phone ringing.

'That's probably for you, dear. Ralph I expect,' says Mum with what I swear looks like a dreamy glaze in her eye.

'Mum!' I shout. 'You fancy him, don't you?'

Before she has a chance to defend herself my darling sibling shouts some obscenity at me along the lines of 'It's for you,' but not anything as polite as that. And before I can say, 'Sod off, rat face,' all the joys of not going to work, the laughing viciously to myself at the thoughts of avoiding a packed train, the hooting loudly at my memories of all the bad smells that accompany commuter transport these days, are shattered. You've guessed it. The agency from hell with an assignment for me. Throwing the tea into me as fast as I could, I donned my best flirting-on-the-phone gear, and off I went.

Thank God I missed the rush hour. They said I wasn't expected at the office until the afternoon.

'Young dynamic company looking for long-term temp with a variety of skills willing to fit into a busy environment.' That was it, no further information available other than an address.

'Keep left when you get off the train, dear. You can't miss it; just follow all the men in dirty T-shirts.'

Intriguing.

Of course the only information that registered with me was 'all the men' bit. Dirty T-shirts didn't bother me as long as I didn't have to wash them or use them as pillowcases. But believe me pillowcases were the last things on my mind when I actually saw the place. I mean have you ever seen a portaloo outside your office door? Not even a clean one. At first I thought it was a telephone box but closer inspection and the smell that strolled out and shook hands with me told a very different story. I was horrified. The only place I've seen a loo like that is at one of those music events that the entire WORLD goes to during the summer where you throw muck at the person next to you, smoke joints, get drunk and eat suspicious-looking hot dogs and not give a damn.

Throwing caution to the wind, comforted and encouraged at the thought that maybe there would be a Brad Pitt lookalike in the office who would be thrilled to show me around, I made my grand entrance. (Well I tried to make my grand entrance but the door jammed and I sort of fell into the place.) I picked myself up off the floor and as my body caught up with my brain I could feel my facial muscles start to twitch and launch into a performance that deserved a standing ovation. My first near coherent thought went something like: Oh shit! What am I doing here? Can I have a drink? Oh he's nice! What's that thing on the floor? Oh! Lovely bum, like him, don't like the other one. I miss the rabbits. Can I go home now? Wait till I tell Roisin and Lotty about THIS!

There were men everywhere. But not the type your above-average intelligent twenty-something woman would be willing to trade her self-respect for and happily make the leap from Good Catholic Girl to Willing and Desperate Tramp.

I'm afraid not. This lot belonged in a circus. Mad,

bad and very smelly. I got a couple of goofy smiles
and a lot of raised eyebrows and, my God, builders'
arses were on view everywhere. This was intolerable,
I thought, feeling slightly panicky as I realised I had
forgotten how to breathe. Surely I was in the wrong
place. OK I admit it. Yes, there were one or two nice
bums but overall . . .

Before I had a chance to clear my throat and
announce my arrival some strange man approached
me and enquired whether I had ordered cement and
if I hadn't could I do it now and not to forget the
sand either, not just any sand mind, rabbit sand.

'Rabbit as in hop, hop, bunny?' I replied,
chastising myself as soon as I had said it for sounding
so utterly thick, and at the same time trying not to
stare at his well-endowed hairy face.

His reply was one of those looks you get when
someone thinks you're either very stupid or possibly
foreign. As I usually do in situations requiring
combat gear and lots of deodorant I smiled back
with my 'of course I know what you're talking
about' look, and hoped he'd be as confused by my
feminine charm as I was by his scary grunting. Then
I hurriedly made my way into my office. Or what I
presumed was my office.

Well it has a desk and a chair. Or at least I think
it's a desk and a chair, I thought to myself. It's a bit
hard to tell under all the dust. And is that concrete
on the floor in lumps the size of tennis balls? Oh
and a PC terminal where someone has being

playing solitaire and decided to leave the remains of a six-pack of Budweiser.

Where the hell am I, anyway? I can't remember the name of the place, I thought, as I dumped my handbag on the dusty desk and started rooting around inside it for the piece of paper with the address of this godforsaken refuse heap. Oh, here it is (written of course on the back of a very crumpled A Wear receipt): Benjamin Ryan Construction Ltd.

But I didn't remember anything about being told to bring a gas mask and a newspaper to sit on. At that moment a tap sounded on my door and a funny looking bloke popped his head around.

'Are you all right there, dear? I'm Joe Butler, the site manager. You must be Gina. Have a seat won't you and I'll get one of the lads to make us a cuppa.'

Before I could say 'don't forget the dettox and rubber gloves', he'd gone again and I heard lots of laughter from somewhere outside the building. Well, it wasn't exactly a building. I don't want you under any false pretences here. It was a sort of portacabin. Bigger than a portaloo but equally aromatic. And damp. I nearly jumped out of my shoes when suddenly another big hairy head appeared around the door. Honestly, I wasn't ready for any more shocks.

'Yes,' I squeaked nervously, trying to pull a scary face myself.

'Joe wants to know do you take sugar in yer tea?' growled the hairy head.

'No thank you,' I replied, hoping that the shy

timid voice I heard wasn't mine.

Hairy Head disappeared as quietly as he arrived leaving me at last to gather my wits about me and wonder if aliens had abducted me. I mean you read about it all the time and it was on *Richard and Judy* last week. Lotty told me at length all the gory details about how they strap you to a big shiny operating table and remove your ears without any anaesthetic and then dump you back on Earth where you're doomed to wander around forever telling anyone who'll listen to you about your terrible ordeal. Oh God, I thought, I promise never to make fun of old ladies again who witter on about absolute crap. Just get me out of here!

Joe Butler appeared unannounced with the tea and I got such a fright I dropped the contents of my bag all over the floor. Cursing wildly, but thankfully incoherently under my breath, I scrambled amid the lumps of concrete and empty beer cans to retrieve my belongings while silently giving out yards to myself for being so stupid.

'Are you all right down there? Can I help you with something?' said Joe, a twang of concern in his Kerry accent.

Standing up quickly (not particularly wanting to be seen with my bum in the air and the rest of me under the table) I typically walloped my head on the desk and immediately put on my best idiotic smile in an attempt to pretend that I hadn't almost sent my brain matter splatting across the room (as you do during rather embarrassing situations like this).

'No thanks I'm fine,' I lied, resisting the urge to rub my forehead and blink back those 'God, that hurt' tears forming in my eyes and instead took the chance to observe the non-hairy and very grey middle-aged man standing looking at me with that 'Christ, we've got a right one here' expression on his face.

He placed the tea on the desk and eyed me cautiously, presumably in case I was about to spontaneously combust or maybe it was simply that I was the only person in sight without a willy.

'Don't mind the lads, they're a bit boisterous at times. It's not often that we have female company here, you know,' he said, sounding as if I'd landed in a remote all-male colony where they'd just discovered how to use a knife and fork.

I'll bet, I thought to myself. What woman in her right mind would want to spend her days in a dirty hovel surrounded by shaggy foul-haired and filthy-clothed blokes who can't speak properly and who go to the loo outside the main door?

'There was someone here a minute ago looking for sand and cement to be delivered,' I said nervously to Joe.

'That'll be the general foreman,' replied Joe. 'We call him "The Legend".'

Chapter 2

Don't get too intrigued. I didn't have five minutes all day after that to find out why scary bloke number one was called 'The Legend'. I drew my own conclusions on that one and put it down to the good old male ego. And it's a bloke's thing anyway, isn't it?

'Yes, my lovely, I'm The Legend and shall I tell you why? It's because I can fu—'

Sorry, Joe interrupted my train of thought. He plonked himself down opposite me and was taking great big twenty-five decibel slurps out of his tea.

'So Gina, how about I give you a little background to the place so you don't feel too lost on your first day?'

'Fine,' I replied, gingerly rubbing my head in such a way that I hoped he'd think I was only fixing my hair whereas I was really massaging the enormous lump that was about to make an appearance any minute.

'That would be very helpful of you, Joe, and by the way, should I bring a top-to-toe set of plastic clothing with me tomorrow just in case, you know, what with all the mess. And God knows, I thought, our late dog needed a bath and a haircut but you and your set of merry men really take the biscuit.'

No, sorry I didn't really say that to him but I was very suspicious of the mug my tea arrived in. It was one of those 'six for a pound' jobs with a very rude photo of a naked woman on it and enough germs to kill an entire community no doubt. I opted to keep my mouth shut for the moment and sit back and listen to what Old Joe had to say.

'You'll be meeting Nicola tomorrow.'

This was said in a very hushed sort of tone, and I didn't like the way Joe threw a quick look over his shoulder. Why in the name of God was he acting so weird? And the whispered phrase was accompanied by narrowed eyes and a contorted facial look (quite like one I would have gladly made myself after the whacking my head on the table incident).

'Nicola?' I replied. 'And she is—?'

'Well, she's our lady in charge of personnel, health and safety, as well as being Mr Ryan's business partner of course.'

'Of course,' I echoed, giving him the 'come on tell me the rest, she's really a bitch isn't she?' look.

Oh no, he's glancing over his shoulder again.

'I would advise you to keep on the right side of her though,' Joe continued, fiddling with his tie. 'She can be a little bit . . . demanding . . . at times.'

'Demanding?' I was feeling the urge to glance over my own shoulder now.

Joe didn't need any more encouragement. In very spirited tones he told me a horror story about the most menacing woman ever born.

'She makes the lads work weekends and bank holidays, doesn't let any of them smoke on the job and for God's sake don't mention the outstanding VAT returns or she'll start to weep hysterically and call us a shower of no-good bastards.' And if that wasn't enough to make you slightly hesitant about meeting her, she is a healthy six-foot-two with heels to match.

'Oh! I see. Is there anything else I should know?' I asked, as if it wasn't enough to learn I was going to be working hand in hand with Alexis Carrington.

Then came the boring bit. They were apparently building a bypass. And a bridge. The only thing I knew about bypasses was that Granny had one the year before and ever since carried a bottle of holy water with her, which she liberally drenched my family with on a regular basis (and anyone who wore skimpy shorts). Oh and she developed a fondness for Mr Kipling Bakewell Tarts afterwards as well. Though I decided not to mention any of this to Joe.

'Have you any experience of the construction industry, Gina?' he asked.

'No, I'm afraid not, Joe,' I replied timidly. (Silly

me, I forgot to mention on my form for the recruitment agency that I had no experience working in the hole of Calcutta with the dirty dozen.)

'Never mind, you'll pick it up quick enough. Later on I'll introduce you to our other office staff: Jason Ward and Danny Stone, a couple of our site engineers, as well as Mr Ryan himself. He'll probably drop in on his way back from the airport. He's off drumming up business in Europe, you see.'

I smiled back my 'of course he is' smile and accepted Joe's offer of a quick tour of the 'building'.

Sitting on the train on the way home I decided it wasn't too bad though I wished my nose would stop running. It always happens when I've been bawling my head off for ten minutes or more. God knows I'd probably get the hiccups next. I'd scrubbed my hands in the loo on the platform but I couldn't quite shake off that yucky feeling as if I'd been cleaning toilets all day. I'm sure I'll get used to the place, I thought to myself, and maybe I'll suggest to Nicola the Vampire that perhaps a cleaner wouldn't be out of the question.

After all she sounded like the type of woman who wouldn't be happy sharing her loo with thirty blokes. Especially as it was outside, hidden by bushes and beer cans and draped in soggy newspapers. And as for the kitchen. My God. I'll never know how lucky I was with only the rabbits and gerbils to worry about. On the plus side there was a fridge and a microwave and plenty of cups and plates. On the minus side all of them looked like they'd been stolen from a skip and were either chipped or cracked with little host families of *E-coli* and *Listeria* bacteria happily populating their surfaces.

At least one good thing happened today, I decided, comforting myself with a large bar of Cadbury's Wholenut from the vending machine: I don't like men anymore. I'm cured. It's a miracle! In fact, the thought of eyeing up anything testosterone related is giving me the shakes and I'm going straight home for a bath.

I hugged myself as the train slowed down and pulled my pink woolly scarf closer around me. Even the thought of Ralph waiting for me at home with a big smile and a dozen red roses didn't make me want to vomit anymore. In fact, it was quite a pleasing notion after the day I'd had.

I can't wait till Friday, I thought. I'll treat myself to a sauna and a facial and hopefully it'll be sufficient to get rid of the film of grime that will undoubtedly have become my new best friend by the week's end. Otherwise I may have to consider a power wash from Statoil but hopefully it won't come to that.

As soon as I got in the door I picked up the phone to ring Roisin. Thrilled to be in a place where it was a safe option to use the loo I quickly dumped my coat on the floor and stuck the phone under my chin while I excitedly opened the small selection of birthday cards that had arrived while I'd been away.

'Hello,' said a chirpy voice, 'sorry I can't come to the phone but I must be off in some fabulous European city having fun with an array of wonderful people. Do leave a message.'

'For God's sake, Roisin, that's the worst one yet.' I giggled to the machine. 'Ring me back. And guess what? I've gone off fellas.'

I hung up feeling somehow liberated and in a way free of the terrible cross I'd been carrying the last few months. Just think, now I'd be able to walk down the street like a released woman no longer hostage to my awful notions of what it would be like to have sex with the bloke cleaning the windows at number twenty-nine. Or making excuses to chat up strangers in the supermarket. And to think that morning I'd practically been clinically depressed.

Of course my new views of the male gender would also pave the way to my moving out of home sooner rather than later. I'm embarrassed to admit it, but I knew Lotty and Roisin would be thrilled to share a flat with me now the threat of my accosting strange men in public was totally diminished. Gone. Forget it. No chance. Not even Ben Affleck (well maybe Ben Affleck but that's it). I swear. All their fears of coming home from aromatherapy or Rome to find a partially-clad male doing the washing up or finding a gorgeous hunk dressing in a hurry when

they brought their mums over for a cup of tea
would be dissolved.

Not that I'd actually ever brought home a
stranger, or any bloke for that matter (besides Ralph,
but he didn't count). I'm not shy about admitting
the idea of it sent me into dreamy spasms which
inevitably left me up to my ears in face masks and
shaving foam just in case I'd meet 'the one' on my
way to Spar for a pint of milk.

I felt genuine remorse when I remembered how
Lotty went into that awful depression the last time
the three of us went to a twenty-first together.

'Please be good tonight!' she had begged me. 'I
know what you're like. I really fancy that petrol-
pump attendant and I don't want your reputation
arriving into the function room ten minutes before
we get there and grabbing him by his essentials.
Please, Gina, just this once!'

Honestly, I wasn't that bad was I? Well, maybe. But
no more. I'm a traditional one-man woman now, I
decided, feeling very proud. Maybe I should set up
a helpline for other women like me, I pondered, as
I made my way to the kitchen. Maybe I should
write that self-help book I've never been able to
find, and my current job will be a sort of hands-on
opportunity to help me with my quest.

'How was work, dear?'

My fantasies of saving the planet's female
population from the realities of men and the fact
that I now knew for certain that they can't iron

(never mind wash) were gate crashed and I was brought back to reality with a thud.

'Em . . . different,' I replied sitting down at the kitchen table, not realising what I'd said before it was too late.

Mum all of a sudden forgot about the poor chicken she was viciously stuffing with a seasoned mixture of Lord knows what and plonked herself down beside me looking very intense and focused. A bit like Jack Nicholson in that movie *The Shining*. You know the scene where he's stuck his head through the bathroom door with that psycho manic look about him. Either that or he's just sampled Mum's Sunday roast.

'What do you mean, different?' she asked suspiciously with one eyebrow raised so high that it's almost engulfing her hairline.

I knew she was hoping I'd say I saw next-door's youngest snogging the boss or a brick fell on my head and I was going to sue. Anything juicy to tell her best friend, May.

I could just hear her: 'You'll never guess what, May. Our Gina's working for him. The fella your next-door neighbour swears was only fixing the plumbing on her washing machine that day.' Or: 'My God! Gina's working for the richest firm in the country! And she's so popular even the boss's son can't take his eyes off her. I'm hoping he'll propose; it's obviously on his mind what with all the milkshakes he keeps buying her from McDonalds.'

She was giving me that other look now. You know the one mothers are famous for: 'It's OK, you can tell me and I swear I won't say a word. The things I know about people and I've never said anything!'

'It's OK, Mum, there's nothing scandalous going on, I'm just working with a bunch of blokes,' I said, yanking a Chocolate Kimberley from the packet on the table.

'You're working where?'

Oh no! Granny had arrived.

'You never said Granny was coming over,' I hissed at my mother.

'Nothing to do with me, Gina, I couldn't stop her!' she replied feigning innocence.

'Did I hear you mention men?' queried Granny plonking down beside me and filling the kitchen with the pungent smell of that weird scent she insists on making for herself. It's a bit like week-old yoghurt mixed with squashy bananas.

'Well, yes—' I attempted to explain.

'God help you, child! Oh I can't believe it, my own granddaughter surrounded by evil-thinking men with only one thing on the brain. How will I cope?' she wailed, sprinkling me very enthusiastically with her ever-present bottle of the Lord's juice taken from her overflowing handbag.

'Surrounded by men!' my mother echoed frantically.

'Well, if you'll let me explain—' I tried to get in edgeways but it was a bit like reversing up the motorway when these two got together.

'What about the bloody chicken?' My father, who was standing and staring at his half-stuffed dinner temporarily rescued me. 'Jaysus Christ, when you women get together the rest of us suffer even more than usual,' he said rather too loudly while stamping over to the counter to inspect the aforementioned bird. 'You haven't even peeled the spuds yet,' he continued in his 'I give up. I've done my best' defeated sort of tone.

'Oh for God's sake, Ted, you get on with it. We're very busy over here listening to Gina telling us how her life is in ruins,' explained Mother, tutting at him very loudly and throwing a filthy look in for good measure as if to say: 'You men are so pathetic.'

Beaten and vanquished, Dad started peeling in a 'bit too loud to be polite' fashion and once again I was under the spotlight.

'I have to go and ring Lotty,' I said pushing my chair back and smiling innocently. 'We're going flat-hunting tonight . . . and my life is not in ruins.'

'Haven't you any self-respect left?' yelled Granny after me as I made my way to the phone.

'None,' I replied, picking up the phone and dialling Lotty's number.

'Don't be long on the phone, dear. I have to ring the church,' yelled my mother after me.

Lotty answered straightaway.

'Happy birthday,' she sang down the phone. 'And have I got a present for you. I think I've found it.

The perfect place!'

'Where?' I couldn't believe it.

'Not far from Clarkes.' She was so excited I thought she might have a coronary.

'Is it big?'

'Yes. '

'Is it clean?'

'Yes. And Mr Tibet said the kitchen is huge with big pine cupboards and there are brand new carpets and three bedrooms, one en suite, and loads of wardrobe space, so we won't have to rob one from your house after all.'

This was too good to be true. A big clean state-of-the-art furnished flat in twenty-something paradise. I simply had to find the catch. Lotty was too innocent and trusting for her own good. And she'd obviously had her head turned by this 'Mr Tibet' bloke. We'd probably move in only to find next-door's cat dead under the floor and a bathroom straight out of *Midnight Express*.

'Does it have a shower, washing machine, microwave, all the usual things, Lotty, like a roof and a flushing loo?' I continued, my anxiety looming over me like a giant thunderstorm.

'Yes, yes, yes. It's perfect and we've got first refusal!'

Oh no. That was it. Why would any grungy old landlord give us first refusal? We hadn't even seen the place and for all he knew we could be a coven of new-age witches who'd never pay the rent and only go shopping on a Sunday. Obviously he was a maniac. Or a murderer.

'Lotty,' I said apprehensively, 'are you sure about this?'

'Trust me,' she practically screamed down the phone excitedly. 'We're going to see it at eight o'clock.'

'OK.' I gave in, reminding myself to stay calm but deciding it would be a justifiable move to bring a hatchet and a blowtorch with me just in case. 'I'll meet you at seven-thirty at your house,' I continued. 'I have to go now. Mother's still on about getting the local parish priest to let her help with confessions and if I don't get off the phone she'll kill me.'

'See you later,' laughed Lotty still clearly delirious and thrilled with herself.

In Mother's ambition to be the queen of anything slanderous and sordid her latest excuse for pursuing this particular avenue really took the biscuit (wafer or otherwise). 'I'm not God, but information in the right hands can work miracles,' was her line of defence.

Granny was thrilled to bits naturally. It would mean she had a 'woman on the inside' to keep her supplies of holy water freshly blessed and well topped up especially now that Christmas was coming. We would all undoubtedly be drenched in the coming weeks what with parties and all. The sexy underwear adorning our backs and bums to help us celebrate the Lord's birthday would have

Granny and her Zimmerframe booting along the road after us like a mad thing.

Now I have only one other thing to worry about, I pondered as I went to get my coat. Well sort of. And that's Ralph. You see he was enamoured of the thought of the two of us living together now that we were engaged and all that and he simply couldn't get his head around me living dangerously with two of my best pals. In fact he was positively horrified at the idea.

'Look what happened when the three of you went to Greece,' he had wailed at me the last time we had an 'adult discussion' about the subject.

'Oh, for God's sake, Ralph!' I'd snapped. 'That was years ago. And this isn't Greece.'

Mistake number one. You know the scenario only too well I'm sure. You think you've fallen passionately in love all over again with your new boyfriend. And on one of your cosy nights together, after he's kissed you in all the right places and convinced you that you're the most beautiful and intelligent person he's ever met, and no it doesn't matter that you didn't have time to shave your legs sure he loves you anyway, you then feel safe enough to spill your guts in a moment of coupledom togetherness.

In my case it had been all the funny details of our 'girls in Greece' holiday. I'd gleefully recounted all our wild escapades and listed by name and colour the cocktails we had demolished on our first night, and of course all the men we had met. (Not that we had acted like three complete and utter whores or anything but we did have a ball.)

While Ralph was sipping his wine rather silently and picking specks of dust off the carpet I'd happily reiterated our favourite one of all. The tale of the infamous 'Johnny Wanker' as we had labelled him. The one and only bloke Lotty had brought home in a drunken stupor. I did feel sorry for her. It's really not her fault, you see. It's the way she's made, perfectly happy to offer unconditional love to the first bloke who looks her way. Whereas Roisin on the other hand is blessed with an extraordinary perceptiveness that should be rewarded with some sort of scholarship. She can spot the bad ones a mile away. As for Lotty, well, this was another one of those times where she didn't get a chance to see if he had a tattoo under his right thigh even though it had taken her three hours to do her hair.

Both of them as pissed as newts had fallen in the apartment door sounding like a couple of newly weds. While he was shedding his clothes between the bedroom and the loo, Lotty, as usual, had raided the fridge to ease her drunken state and had sufficiently sobered up in time to realise she had made yet another terrible mistake.

Through floods of tears she had stood in the middle of my bedroom and told us, 'He's English and he said I was beautiful and that he'd get me a brilliant job as a model.'

'So why are you bawling your head off then?' snorted Roisin from a yoga position on the floor.

'Because I can't get rid of him.'

'Well do you fancy him or not?' asked Roisin, forever getting straight to the point.

'No! Yes! Maybe,' snuffled poor Lotty, kicking off her silver sandals and almost sending one of them soaring over the balcony. 'I did at about one in the morning after he said I'd be indispensable on the catwalk and because I thought he looked like Tom Cruise in that movie where he's always wearing a suit,' she continued, wiping her nose with the back of her hand.

'Hang on a sec, is that *Jerry Maguire* or *The Firm*? I mean he lives in a suit that guy, and anyway he's so small, Lotty, shame on you!' threw in Roisin sounding absolutely outraged to be in the same social circle as someone who had the nerve to fancy anyone under five-foot-eight.

'Oh shut up, Ro! He's in there, in MY bed getting very intimate with his you know what, warbling on about men's sex drives being like roller coasters and asking me where we keep the frozen yoghurt. You have to help me. My life is a wreck and it's only our second night here.'

'Honey,' said Roisin giving Lotty that 'now don't be stupid' look. 'According to you, your life has been a wreck ever since that lady in Marks and Spencer's said you'd never get past a 34A. Not to mention your uncontrollable habit of picking the wrong guy. Just kick him out and forget the whole thing.'

I know it sounds awful but Roisin was right. Lotty was great at getting in a panic over the smallest things. Although full of good intentions and great at handing out motherly love to everyone but herself, she's bought every single Mind Body Spirit book on the planet but is still convinced that no one will ever want to marry her (written in stone since the episode in M and S).

'The shame of it, Gina!' she had whimpered at me from the crowded dressing rooms that fateful day. 'Two fried eggs for the rest of my miserable life.' Not to mention the fact that her parents' enormous wealth is usually the only attractive thing about her (or so she keeps telling us). Roisin and I have spent hours, days, nights telling Lotty how wonderful she is but as soon as we've gone home she's always back to square one.

'You're not being fair, Roisin. I'm asking for your help and all you can do is remind me how useless I am, you horrible bitch,' yelled Lotty, hopping around the room in circles in a vain attempt to yank off skin-tight white trousers.

'Come on you two, this is getting us nowhere,' I heard my voice pipe up from under the bed sheet. 'Anyhow, I have a brilliant idea!'

I thought it was about time I intervened. And as I had had a drop or two to drink myself I thought that my brainwave was too good to keep quiet about.

'What?' the other two snarled at me as if to say 'you better have a shit-hot magnificent idea, lady, after daring to interrupt us as we were just about to tear strips off each other.'

Not willing to be subdued by two jarred and dangerous women I innocently continued. 'Well,' I said, standing up and trying not to wobble, the sheet draped over my head making me look somewhat like Madonna in her 'Like a Virgin' video. 'It's quite simple, girls. We'll all go into the room in our bikinis and scare the wits out of him,' I suggested smiling madly.

Lotty and Roisin merely stared.

'And,' I went on, ignoring the vicious glares from the other side of the room, 'we'll say, "Thanks, mate, for getting us all pregnant, up the pole, with child" and I bet he'll leg it. Simple,' I finished, toasting myself with a large swig of my new friend – duty-free Smirnoff.

They were still staring.

'You're crazy, do you know that, absolutely barking mad,' said Lotty, eyes wide open and looking terribly tearful and woebegone now that she realised she was asking to be rescued by two half-cut women.

'Oh, I see,' I muttered humbly, devastated that she didn't whoop for joy and slap me on the back for saving the day or her entire life for that matter. I mean she was the one who had brought him back to the apartment in the first place.

'No, hang on a minute,' whispered Roisin, suddenly looking very visionary and, well, dangerous. (She definitely had that 'I'm totally invincible' look about her.) 'You might be right, Gina! Three hormone-wild women might be just what we need.'

Oh God. I'd forgotten. After Roisin's had one too many she's quite convinced even the Lord Jesus would drop his pants for her.

'I know what we'll do,' she whispered, rising from the lotus position frighteningly fast for my liking.

'What!' whispered Lotty suddenly looking rejuvenated and no longer forlorn and pitiful.

'You two stay here and leave him to me. Just make sure you empty his wallet before he leaves. I see he's left his jeans in the loo,' she hissed, grabbing her camera as she flew past us.

Doing exactly as instructed Lotty and I huddled together like two lost waifs and watched as Roisin made her grand entrance. Choking back giggles we went to listen at the door.

'Well hello, gorgeous!'

We heard a gruff and slurred voice purr in reply, just before Roisin shut the door. Slurred or not this guy had one of those accents that just oozed charm and would make even Granny consider abandoning her religion for.

'Quick, Lotty, get the money out of his jeans, will you?' I whispered a bit too loudly pushing her into the bathroom.

'How could he?' she whinged. 'He doesn't even care that it's not me in there. Oh I hate him. And after all I told him about myself. I don't believe it!'

'Just get the money!' I hissed, grabbing a very nice pair of Calvin Klein jeans out of her arms, if nothing else just to stop her hugging the bloody things as if George Clooney were inside them.

'I didn't really want to sleep with him, not until we had known each other for a full forty-eight hours at least. It's just that he seemed so lovely . . .' she gushed dreamily, fiddling inattentively with the top of a shampoo bottle.

'I'm quite sure you'll meet someone else, someone really nice tomorrow night,' I assured her in a beamingly trusting tone, giving her a little convincing hug and begging God to forgive me for being so optimistic in case Mr Wonderful didn't appear.

'You cow!' Mr Melting Accent suddenly screamed from behind the bathroom wall, then a funny scuffling noise then a bang.

'He must have fallen on his bum,' giggled Lotty, momentarily distracted from being miserable.

The sudden jolt as the bedroom door was flung open nearly sent us into another spasm of laughter which was soon forgotten as there he was, all six-foot-two of him, looking very dishevelled and very annoyed. Lotty in an instant was silent and staring. I was silent and staring as well but for other shameful reasons. Well done, Lotty, I thought, he's gorgeous, an absolute God! I was astounded but didn't say this out loud. It isn't the done thing to admit your friend's conquest is rather fabulous after all. And that no, you wouldn't mind a quick look at his bum, if she doesn't mind that is.

Anyway I didn't have to wish. I had the perfect view as he whipped his jeans from my hands and practically spat in annoyance on his way out the door, calling us a crowd of 'Irish tight-arsed bitches' who didn't know a good thing when we saw it, or something along those lines. I couldn't really make out the rest of it with Roisin laughing so much and Lotty simply standing there looking bewildered and still a little tearful.

'What did you do to the poor chap?' I laughed, the apartment still vibrating from his rather loud slam of the door.

'Oh my God, I haven't had this much fun in ages!' roared Roisin in reply. 'All I did,' she continued suddenly in a very matter-of-fact tone, 'was take an instant Polaroid of him in all his glory and tell him I was going to post it to his wife,' she beamed.

'His wife! What wife? His wife? He didn't tell me he had a wife! Jesus!' wailed Lotty throwing herself onto the nearest bed. 'I'm so stupid!'

You guessed it. Lotty was getting hysterical again. So being the good friend that I am I offered her my bottle of Smirnoff, which I was very attached to but willing to share under these vile circumstances in which she had nearly sold her heart and body to a bloke with a wife.

And especially because she had nearly sold out on only our second night. And because he was delicious. And a loss to any hormone-ridden/drink-driven/miserable/horny woman. And because I didn't want to be hugging her and making false promises for the rest of the holiday. But mainly because I had forgotten to pack a ventilator.

'How did you know and I didn't?' she whimpered at Roisin, finally taking a huge slug of my best friend.

'Honestly, Lotty, didn't you see his ring mark?' she tutted. As if to assume that no it's not impossible in a dark night club while melting from the affections of a sumptuous bloke, to say in the middle of a heart-stopping kiss: 'Hold yer hand up there, mate, till I check that yer not married and trying to get me home for a quick shag—'

I had suddenly stopped mid-sentence, so 'quick shag' came out sounding a bit like 'quicksand'. Why? Because Ralph appeared to be pacing the carpet and practically wearing it out, and God knows I didn't want Dad coming in saying 'Calculate that per square foot, you, and I want every penny and no cheap crap either.'

From the look on Ralph's face I had realised that maybe it wasn't the most intelligent thing to blab on about long nights spent belly and flamenco dancing with wondrous looking blokes. I had smiled idiotically and taken a few swigs out of the bottle of white wine Ralph had left on the fireplace and quietly suggested a game of Scrabble. Our night of coupledom togetherness had come to an abrupt end.

'Mum, can you keep my dinner for later on?' I yelled into the kitchen.

'OK,' yelled Mum, and all I could hear from Granny was 'Filthy nails, filthy minds and filthy arses.'

I can't be responsible if Ralph decides to blow a gasket when he finds out I'm moving in with the girls, I thought. I'm not worrying about his precious feelings today of all days. Especially since I haven't recovered from the shock of my new working environment.

For now, though, sod the lot of them, I decided quite resolutely. First things first. See the flat and take it from there. I'll worry later about Ralph, the deposit for the flat (thankfully Lotty owes me a mint) and the fact that I need to shave my legs before tomorrow.

Chapter 3

I arrived at Lotty's about fifteen minutes later. And
no, I didn't stare at any men along the way, not even
the alarmingly gorgeous bloke in the newsagents
who was wearing a very cool jacket and couldn't
take his eyes off me. (Much to my delight but alas it
was too soon. I still couldn't get out of my mind the
terrible sight of the loo at work and all those smelly
bums walking around freely without a care in the
world.) Talk about aversion therapy. I could make a
fortune bringing women, oblivious to the hard
truth, on day trips to my office.

'Here it is, girls. He may have the face of an angel
and the body of a Greek god but do you really want
him doing that in your bathroom? (I thought at this
stage, maybe I could wave some second-hand loo
roll around for effect.) Or putting those clothes in
your washing machine?' The plentiful supply of
positively vile and unwashed boxers which would
obviously have been floating around for months

would no doubt impress them too.

Nevertheless, I still closed my eyes nice and tight as I passed Gorgeous on the way out of the shop just in case I had any indomitable withdrawal symptoms.

Roisin's little Nissan Micra was parked practically in the middle of the road outside Lotty's front door. As usual the poor car looked somewhat abandoned and lonesome. Not to mention rusty. I was sure all that held it together was a bit of spit and some old tissues. As if begging the first person that passed it to please steal it in the hope it might end up with a devoted owner, it simply sat there. Miserable. Perhaps it was an omen, I speculated, as I swished past it and up the driveway feeling a little bit excited about the evening ahead in spite of myself.

'Roisin, are you ever going to get rid of that car out there, it's such a heap,' I heard Lotty say as her mum, Mrs Jeffers, let me in and wished me a happy birthday.

'I know I know but how do you convincingly spell 'knackered' in a small ad?' replied Roisin with a long drawn-out sigh.

'F –U- C- K- E- D,' was the reply from the sitting room. That meant only one thing. Roisin had brought her little sister along.

I haven't told you about Ruth yet, have I? I actually really like her, but she drives Roisin mad. I think it's because they're too alike. Outspoken, witty, skinny (the bitches) and both as fierce and fiery as a hairdryer that's been dropped in the bath. Not unlike Mother when her credit card won't work and she's off to skin my dad, I reflected, as I waltzed in and join the happy group. Lotty was already busy packing. I was horrified. We hadn't even seen the place.

'What on earth are you doing? Are you mad—?' I gasped, my jaw almost on the floor. After all it was a wee bit premature surely.

'Get a grip on yourself, Gina!' commented Roisin laughing at me. 'Lotty does her Christmas shopping in February for God's sake. She'll have unpacked and even sterilised the kitchen while the rest of us will be getting in a knot looking for a clean pair of knickers. And what's all this about you going off men?'

So I told them in great detail all about my first day at work. But I didn't quite get the reaction I was hoping for. No great intakes of breath followed by, 'Oh my God! How did you cope?' or: 'Jesus, I'd have fainted.'

'You lucky bitch,' was the one and only remark from Lotty. In fact she practically snarled at me. 'It's not fair. You're engaged as it is and now you get a job most women would die for. Surrounded by men for ten hours a day. And you're whingeing about it. I wish I worked there . . .' she trailed off miserably.

'Oh, fine,' I replied, glad she was sober in case she decided to stab me for being lucky enough to be working hand in hand with the filthiest men in the country.

'Come on, you guys, let's go. Lotty I'm sure you can wait until tomorrow to finish packing your make-up bag. You're hardly going to need it tonight,' said Roisin, ushering us all towards the front door.

'OK, Ruth, we're ready. Buy Mrs Jeffers.'

Ruth had been waiting patiently at the front door with a right face on her.

'Hurry up,' she moaned, 'I'm going out later and at this rate I'll be drawing my pension before we see this bloody place.' She finished with a sigh. We all piled into the Micra, me in the back with Lotty, and Roisin and Ruth up front.

'Bloody hell, Roisin, what am I sitting on?' said Lotty trying desperately to yank something from under her bum. On her third attempt out sprang a purple push-up bra.

'Brilliant! I've been looking for that for ages,' beamed Roisin in the rear view mirror. 'I never thought of looking there.'

'What's it doing here anyway?' I asked trying to ignore the fact that she was driving in the middle of the road at three times the legal speed limit.

'I think it's there since the last time I saw that geek from the library,' she replied, tuning in the radio and stuffing her face with a Mars bar.

'Which one was he then?' enquired Ruth, busily painting her nails and waving her hands around madly like a chicken waiting to be plucked.

'Em, the guy I met at the barbecue I think,' Roisin continued, wiping mouthfuls of gooey chocolate off her chin.

'Stop! Stop! We're here!' yelled Lotty quite suddenly from behind Roisin's head, almost frightening me into an early grave. This was quickly followed by my nearly having a coronary as Roisin literally stopped bang in the middle of the road, leaving the driver in the car behind honking and cursing wildly.

'Where?'

'There, park just there,' suggested Lotty pointing at a bus stop.

'OK,' replied Roisin, finishing her Mars bar and stuffing the wrapper under her seat.

Glancing up at the building Lotty was pointing at so enthusiastically, I have to say I was gobsmacked. The place was amazing. Just what we wanted. Well from the outside that is. We all piled up the driveway, Lotty and Ruth ooh-ing and aah-ing at the little cute shrubs adorning the generous lawn. I half expected the duo to start fertility dancing in the middle of the garden, chanting little nature-related ditties about how wondrous flowers, plants and fallopian tubes are.

Eventually, after she had picked a handful of half-dead daffodils and waved them around to show us, Lotty rang the doorbell which was answered by a very respectable looking man. Unfortunately his taste in aftershave was wicked and I nearly fainted cold as I passed him on my way in.

'Well girls, this is it. I'll give you a quick tour and

you can wander around yourselves for a bit then,' he said pleasantly, giving us a generous group smile. Which was obviously a ploy to make us feel relaxed, cheerful and very trusting. Well, it wasn't going to work on me, I decided, giving him a filthy look as I quickly glanced around the hall. Not a hatchet or balaclava to be seen anywhere. But that didn't mean he wasn't a lunatic only waiting to murder us all in cold blood and steal the clothes from our barely chilled backs simply so that he could prance around in them listening to Jim Reeves in the privacy of his own home. Oh no, I wasn't going to be taken in by him. I let him know by issuing a few snarly grins whenever he looked my way.

Room by room we followed him, Lotty and Ruth continuing on their quest of touching every little thing and squealing with delight at the sight of a brand new washing machine and the fact that the milkman would deliver three times a week if he wasn't en route to the bookies for a quick flutter.

They gasped in amazement at brand new beds and two-seater couches as if they were gold dust. And as for the bathroom – you'd swear it was full of half-naked Chippendales what with all the shrieking going on. Not to mention Lotty practically wetting herself over the skylight. Roisin seemed quite pleased with the place. And I had to admit the atmosphere was becoming infectious.

Our only gripe was the meters, one for the gas and one for the electricity. The two old-fashioned boxes of plastic-coated steel graced a small spot outside the loo.

'As long as we keep a decent float of fifty-pences going we should be OK,' Roisin whispered to me as we stared at them.

Lotty meanwhile was getting more and more ecstatic. 'It's really nice!' she exclaimed.

I couldn't help but agree. It was lovely, and really bright and cheerful. Maybe I was being a tad paranoid. After twenty minutes or so Mr Tibet left us to look around ourselves.

'Isn't it cool!' screamed Ruth as if she was actually going to be living there with us.

'What do you think?' pleaded Lotty, staring at Roisin and me with big wide eyes as if we were complete meanies and she was trying to convince us not to run over her favourite kitten. 'Isn't it fab, and so big!' she continued, giving us that 'don't kick up a fuss and be selfish bitches' look.

'Heads might roll if we don't say yes,' grinned Roisin looking at me for approval.

'Well OK but I'm not doing any hoovering for at least a month. And if any of you steal my underwear or dye it pink I'll kill you!' I laughed as Lotty jumped on me and gave me a big hug. And so that was it, I was moving whether I liked it or not.

I don't know how we got home in one piece. It must have been Granny's holy water and all those years of praying. What with the babble of excited women in the car, all yapping at the same time, and

Roisin driving like a lunatic. Even more like a lunatic than usual but I didn't really care. I was as thrilled to bits as the rest of them. We all landed in my front door talking nineteen to the dozen and already arguing about who would do the washing up and who was more entitled to get the en suite.

'Definitely I should get it,' stated Roisin. 'After all, my social life is much more hectic than yours, Lotty. Especially now that I'm going out with Jack. And I'll need to be able to jump in and out of the shower at a moment's notice when I'm on standby, instead of spending twenty minutes yelling at you two to get out of the bathroom.'

Jack was Roisin's new love. Well, not love exactly. Shagging partner would be more like it. Typical of Roisin (or rather, blessed and fortunate cow). She had gone out one night with 'the geek from the library' and come home with 'the stud from the petrol station near Spar' all delighted with herself. And actually he was quite nice and he adored her. (The luck of her to be adored by a hunk.) Not that it would make the slightest bit of difference to Roisin. She firmly believed and lived by the fact that there were billions of men living on the planet and she wanted a crack at a fair percentage of them before her twenty-fifth birthday. Which was a good time to settle down with, say, one or two of them.

Before Lotty had a chance to argue the toss, we all piled into the sitting room. Chucking coats left right and centre, the girls made themselves comfortable while I made my way into the kitchen to make the tea.

'Hi, happy birthday,' said a smiling face which was attached to a tall body wearing a vile blue suit and hugging a large mixed bouquet to his chest. Christ! Ralph had arrived to see me. Before I had a chance to reply I had two carnations and a prickly rose stem halfway up my nose as the flowers were squashed between Ralph and me as he insisted on giving me a smothering hug and a sloppy kiss. If I had listened to my body language at that moment he'd have been lying on the floor with a broken nose. But I was very good and restrained and stopped myself from punching him in the face.

'I wasn't expecting you this late,' I lied, cursing myself for forgetting all about him again. It was a bad habit of mine, recently formed since I had agreed to become 'an engaged woman' one evening not so long before after rather a lot of drink had been taken. You stupid cow, I thought biting my lip and trying to ignore the fact that I could hardly breathe. I'll simply have to start remembering I have a fiancé, just the way I have to remember to feed the dog when Mum and Dad are on holidays. But worse than that, I hadn't planned on breaking the news about the move to Ralph just yet. No. I had had a better plan in mind, which had gone along the lines of getting him squiffy and telling him at three in the morning when he hopefully wouldn't give a damn.

Now, as they say in Japan, I was fucked. Short of

ushering either him or the girls outside rather
hurriedly with an excuse about cutting my toenails
or steaming my face, how was I going to avoid him
hearing the news tonight? Already, I could hear
Roisin and Lotty in the sitting room making out
lists about pots and pans and whether Lotty would
be able to pinch her mother's duck-down duvet
without getting caught. Roisin, meanwhile, was
determining what great crack it would be to get in
a dishy window cleaner for the laugh.

'There's a gorgeous bloke who does our office
windows and he has a twin brother. We could have
one out the back and one out the front. How about
that for Sunday breakfast?' was all I could hear,
granted somewhat muffled as my face was still stuck
somewhere between Ralph's shoulder and the top
button of his shirt.

'I'd better make the tea,' I muttered, afraid that I
might pass out or get high from his terrible attempt
at men's eau de cologne.

'I bought you a present,' he said cheerfully, while
I clattered around making as much noise as possible
in a miserable attempt to drown out various house-
moving conversations going on in the sitting room.
(All the while wondering if a quick on the spot
novena would be of any help.)

'Oh, you really shouldn't have bothered,' I
mumbled indifferently, turning my back on him and
forming faces of despair out the window. He
followed me silently and touched my hair gently,

obviously trying to enchant me. It didn't work. I almost head-butted him I got such a fright.

'Jesus!' he said taking two steps back rather quickly.

'Sorry, you startled me,' I replied in a huff.

'I just wanted to give you this,' he said in that sulky way blokes do when you don't drop your clothes on the floor the second you see them or, God forbid, you've 'hurt their feelings'.

'What!' I replied, deciding to get in a bit of a sulky strop myself. 'I'm trying to make the tea!' I said in my most exasperated 'you're an idiot, stop annoying me' tone.

I had hoped he'd get thick with me and slam out the back door. Unfortunately the gods and all the saints were on holidays that night.

'This!' he yelled, thrusting a rather small packet into my hand.

'What is it?' I said tutting as if making tea was more important than accepting a thoughtful present from my husband-to-be.

God knows, it's probably a G-string, I thought to myself, ripping open the wrapping paper. Hopefully it is a G-string, now that would be the answer to my prayers as I could then boot him out the back door with a clear conscience. Slamming the kettle down on the counter I ripped open the little parcel with new vigour. Praying, begging, dear Jesus! Please let it be something foul so I can chuck him out.

Instead I found a little set of keys jangling

between my fingers. Oh shit! They didn't look like car keys and I somehow doubted they opened a surprise safety deposit box in our local bank. I looked at him questioningly. Then I put on my best 'I'm really not in the mood for mind games, honey' look hoping he would simply get frightened and make a bolt for the door (as any sensible bloke would do when their other half looks like they could shoot them at point blank range and enjoy a nice cup of tea afterwards).

Alas Ralph was a lot more stupid than I had given him credit for. He only stood there looking poised and hopeful and obviously about to deliver some sort of speech, I realised, wondering if I should be the one planning my escape.

'They,' he said pointing rather wildly at the keys sitting in my open palm, 'are the keys to a new two-bed apartment I've just rented this morning which I was hoping you'd like to share with me. After all we are supposed to be getting married in case you'd forgotten,' he finished rather shortly almost spitting at me.

Full marks to Ralph for being so observant. I had forgotten. But my threshold for hysterical blokes really was at a low ebb this evening. So I had no choice but to do the only thing any woman backed in a corner can do. Especially when a man has backed her in there. And it doesn't matter one bit that he's the one she's supposed to love and cherish and all that stuff.

Taking a leaf out of my mother's book (the one where she goes through Dad for a shortcut because he's fallen asleep in front of the fire with his gob wide open which drives her crazy and leads inevitably to her storming around the kitchen threatening divorce as she's 'not going to stay married to some old fella and if she sees one drop of dribble flowing down his mouth then he's for it!' She'll get him a wheelchair and push him down the nearest cliff and see how fast he can move then etc etc) I went for him.

'How dare you!' I snorted in good old Roisin fashion, slamming the keys on the nearest surface for added effect. 'How dare you assume I'd move in with you just like that,' I said, clicking my fingers right under his nose and trying to look ferocious.

'It's not "just like that", Gina. We've been engaged for six months!' he replied, clearly somewhat taken aback by my outburst.

'You're so selfish, ruining my birthday just because you want to get your leg over more than twice a week,' I continued, fluttering my hands in front of my eyes hoping to create a sort of 'woe is me' effect. 'I'm devastated. How could you?' I mumbled, pretending to sob a little and hugging the kettle for comfort.

'You're not being fair, Gina,' he said very matter-of-factly. 'We talked about this a few weeks ago and you said you'd think about it. I was just trying to surprise you, for God's sake!' he finished in a mournful tone.

The cheek of him to sound mournful after the day I'd just had. And he didn't win any brownie points either by standing there looking all miserable with his hair flopping down in front of his eyes, his appearance somewhat reminiscent of an incessantly annoying mongrel.

'Well I have thought about it,' I replied snapping my head up and staring him straight in the face. OK that wasn't technically true. I stared his hair straight in the face, as I knew I couldn't justly stare him in the eye. Even I wasn't that ruthless.

'I'm moving in with the girls. I've discussed it at length and it's what I want to do. And that's final!' I finished with a slam of my fist on the kitchen table, nearly breaking two of my fingers in the process.

'Fine, at least now I know where I stand,' he glared, making a grab for the keys and stuffing them into his pocket.

'Good!' I lashed back, beginning to wonder why exactly I was being so rotten to him. After all he wasn't that awful. I could do worse.

'Maybe just maybe we should meet up over the weekend sometime and discuss precisely where this relationship is going,' he suddenly piped up, sounding like a right accountant as if our relationship was a profit and loss sheet. The cheeky git. 'If of course such an arrangement will fit in with your packing plans,' he snorted, obviously in a big huff. Which was a mistake really. I just wasn't in the mood for this.

'Fine, ring me on Friday. Here's my new work number,' I barked back, scribbling it on the back of his hand and giving him my 'if there's nothing else on your mind then please fuck off' look. Which I was quite famous for. Which usually worked. Please let it work! And it did. He bluntly grunted a goodbye at me and was gone at last.

I stared mournfully at the now cold kettle in my arms. What was I doing? I'd just chucked my fiancé out the back door on a freezing cold night without so much as a cup of tea or a 'thank you for calling' smile. Evidently the day had caught up with me and I was in some sort of an emotional whirl. It had nothing at all to do with the fact that I didn't really fancy Ralph anymore. In fact I'm not sure I even liked him anymore. I decided my roller coaster emotions regarding my loved one were probably all down to my finding a new home and a new job in the same twenty-four hours. And I still hadn't managed to fit in any lunch, never mind dinner. What I needed was a long bath and a good night's sleep before I could even contemplate my real feelings for Ralph. Not to mention needing a large dose of Valium before I could go back to that bloody cabin (sorry, office) the next day.

'Is it safe to come in?' whispered a squeaky voice from the doorway.

'Only just,' I smiled at Roisin as she tiptoed in with the good sense to wear my mother's riding hat

in case there were any stray pots and pans flying
around.

'Presumably that was yer boyfriend,' joked Roisin
trying to cheer me up.

I must have looked a right state. I was still
hugging the kettle and I could see from my
reflection in the kitchen mirror that I had a big red
face from all the shouting.

'I told Ralph about the flat but not before he had
handed me the keys of a little romantic pad for two,'
I grimaced, as I looked at Roisin and tried not to
laugh. To laugh really would be horrible. Very
inappropriate.   Unforgivable   under   the
circumstances. But I couldn't help it!

'Are you sure you want to go through with this?'
she asked looking genuinely concerned. And why
wouldn't she? After all I was stifling giggles and
looking generally dishevelled yet somewhat
sprightly since Ralph had made his exit.

'Yes! Absolutely!' I practically screamed, while
Roisin merely stared at me as if I'd finally lost my
marbles. All of them.

'What about loverboy?' she said giving me a
funny look.

'He'll get over it. And stop giving me funny
looks.'

'I'm not giving you funny looks!'

'Yes you are.'

'OK, if you're sure.'

'I'm sure!' I yelled, my voice nearly smashing the

overhead light bulb.

Roisin followed me back into the living room where Mother was practically sitting on Lotty's lap in an effort to yank as much information from the poor girl as she could.

Lotty looked panic-stricken as Mother launched into another attack about the new flat, the new job 'with those dirty fellas' and of course the argument with Ralph. All the while trying to bribe the poor girl with a box of Chocolate Kimberleys.

'Oh go on,' she said shaking the box under Lotty's nose. 'Have another one while you tell me all about those dirty fellas in that office of hers.'

Poor Lotty looked terrified and gave Roisin and I a couple of seething looks as we all huddled together on the sofa.

'Lotty said the flat's amazing,' said Mum obviously trying to gain our trust so she could subject-hop to my scrap with Ralph. God, I thought, I will be glad to move. Not that I don't like my mother. She is very lovable and a great shopping partner especially when there's a sale on in Boots. But she has no shame. None. She'd happily ask complete strangers if they've had pre-marital sex and then delight in chatting endlessly about new contraceptive devices.

'We didn't have that Persona thing in my day. Isn't it great!'

And these are only the poor souls at the bus stop minding their own business. Or trying to, God love them.

'We'd better head, come on Lotty,' said Roisin clearly reading my mind and throwing me an understanding glance. 'We can sort out all the details tomorrow in the pub.'

'Isn't it well for some; going to the pub, moving into big flats, working with men all hours of the day. Honestly I just don't know,' Mother trailed off, sounding more than a bit huffy, and waltzed into the kitchen. 'See you, girls,' she yelled.

'Bye Mrs Birkendale,' replied Lotty, Ruth and Roisin while we piled back out to the front doorstep to have a quick whispery conversation.

'What time do you finish work, Gina?' Lotty asked quietly.

'About six, I think,' I replied, shivering a bit with the cold.

'OK, I'll ring you when you get home and we can start making plans for the move,' she said all excited and rubbing her hands together.

'See you so,' shouted Roisin as the three of them jumped into the car, slammed all the doors and blared the stereo.

'Bye,' I yelled at the moving car and quickly shut the front door before the neighbours came out to complain. Deciding I'd have a quick bite to eat and then a long bath, I hurried inside. I deserved it. What a day!

Chapter 4

Trying to organise a bath in our house was not in the least straightforward. First of all Mother insisted we both have a cup of tea so I could tell her all my 'news'. When I finally escaped her clutches and had refused the bribe of chicken sandwiches and cake in return for as many gory details as possible I made my way up to the bathroom only to find Dad had decided to tile the walls (as men generally do at ten o'clock at night when there's sod all on the telly).

He eventually agreed, after much haggling and only after I had promised to bring him home a big chocolate cake next time I was in Tesco, to let me have a quick shower. Men. All I needed now was to jump into bed and find Tommy had left a big hairy tarantula under my pillow or a slug in my nightshirt. Thankfully he must have had better things to do this evening and I was safe at last to cuddle up to my pillow and think about the day.

I didn't know what to feel. A new flat. Yes, I was

excited about it! Once I'd finished all that packing
and unpacking business which would be an absolute
curse. But hopefully I'd get off lightly, though mind
you, there's only so much stuff that will fit in
Roisin's car. And God knows it'll probably cave in
just as it's my turn to move my gear. You're being
negative again, I chastised myself, while plumping
up my pillow and settling back down.

And what about Ralph? I used to think I was
quite a nice person. Thoughtful, willing to
compromise, put the other person first and all that.
Now I felt only guilty. I had been a bit mean to him.
He only wanted us to live together like any normal
couple does before getting hitched. And what had I
done? Chucked him out like an empty pizza box
gets dumped in the bin, and you're left wondering
why you ate the bloody thing in the first place
because you don't even like pizza.

I honestly didn't know why I'd shown him the
door. Well, maybe I did. But now wasn't the time to
admit anything to myself. Once it was out in the
open then I'd have to confront it. And I'm willing to
stick up my hand with the rest of the cowards in the
world and joyously admit I'm proud not to be a
heroine. I like the simple life.

I sighed, thinking that my birthday was nearly
over. And now I was beginning to feel even more
miserable than I did when I woke up this morning.
All my resolutions about being a good little wife-to-
be were shattered and it was only eleven o'clock and

I hadn't even had a birthday drink.

Now I was starting to toss a bit in the bed. You know the feeling I'm sure. It's definitely not a good sign. It usually means I'm trying to escape from one of three things: guilt, a full bladder, or the dreaded head spins. You guessed it. Guilt was starting to follow me around the bed. A bit like your kidneys do when you've been drinking for three days on the trot and never find time to go to the loo because you have much more exciting things to do. Like slamming three more tequilas before heading to the local nightclub, not in the least bit bothered that you have to get up in two hours time and head to work where you have to pretend to be sober and professional in case you get fired/sick/obnoxious and tell your boss what you really think of the company.

I shut my eyes really tight and pretended to be asleep while Guilt tried to have a conversation with me.

'Fuck off!' I mumbled into my pillow.

But it didn't. All I could see was Ralph's face when I slammed down the keys and started roaring at him. Hurt and confused.

'It's not working,' I grumbled out loud. 'It was his own fault. I win. One to me. Ha Ha!' I replied gleefully, quite determined that I would not give in. I had nothing to feel guilty about!

'I have nothing to feel guilty about,' I chanted to myself, a bit like Judy Garland in *The Wizard of Oz* as she warbled on about following the yellow bloody brick road.

I was still chanting away at three in the morning when Tommy banged very loudly on my bedroom wall and told me to 'Shut the fuck up'. Which of course woke up Mum and Dad. And one thing led to another. Before I knew it, there was a civil war or rather uncivil war going on outside my bedroom door.

'What in Christ's name are you at now? I thought we were being burgled, you eejit!' my father positively roared at Tommy.

'It's her,' disputed Tommy pronouncing 'her' in a very exaggerated manner as if he were trying to spit battery acid out of his mouth. 'She's been talking in her sleep for effing hours now, and I'm up at six to practise those outdoors survival skills I saw on the telly last—'

'What are you on about?' seethed Dad, hopping up and down in a rage outside the loo. But before he could go into a full swing kill there was a rather loud knock on the front door followed hastily by an urgent ring on the bell.

'Jaysus Christ, what now!' bellowed Dad, slamming down the stairs and landing with a bang in the hall after losing his footing on the carpet.

I sunk lower into the bed deciding that hell hath no fury like one's father when one's father has gone arse over tip to the bottom of the stairs with only a pair of black Y-fronts on.

'Who is it? It's three o clock in the bleedin' morning you know!' hollered Dad, cursing under his breath and loudly rubbing his behind.

'Stop that noise, will you? Do you not know what time it is!' yelled a voice in the letterbox.

Shit! It was Mr Markham from next door. He of the vasectomy fame. I sunk even lower into my bed.

'Is that you, Markham?' shouted Dad with a growl.

'Yes, it is. You'll just have to keep the noise down in there. We've been thoroughly disturbed because of that son of yours yelling and screaming like a hooligan,' he continued.

'Well, at least he hasn't been neutered. Now sod off and stop shouting in my letterbox!'

Dad charged back up the stairs like a raging bull and Tommy quite sensibly locked himself in the bathroom.

Mother tutted and mumbled about what a holy disgrace her family were and how ashamed she was and how she wished for the millionth time that she'd married that fella with the yacht. He had lovely manners and a very healthy bank account and he hadn't tried to shag her in the back of his car or yacht or garden like Dad had.

'I'll see you in the morning,' promised Dad rather threateningly to the bathroom door before finally slamming back into his own room with Mum still giving out yards behind him.

'Bloody hell,' I whispered to my pillow. 'Dream

flat, here I come!'

I was supposed to be in work for eight fifteen the next morning but I couldn't get my head off the pillow. Jesus, even the nuns don't get up this early. All the same I decided to be cheerful. It might not be that awful. But then I remembered Nicola. Oh God! First hysterical men and now I had a dictorial tyrant of a boss to deal with.

I very reluctantly plonked my feet on the floor and stared at the clock. At least it didn't try and have a cheery conversation with me. It only stared back. So I sat there until my eyes began to focus, under protest may I add. It was seven forty-five and I wasn't even dressed never mind awake. At least I didn't have a hangover. Now it was seven forty-six I realised with horror, as something inside me finally kick-started my brain into action.

Like a woman possessed I threw on the first thing I saw. Which was a repulsive jumper Granny had knitted me for my birthday. Screaming at my own reflection in the mirror, I yanked it off as hastily as I could, nearly taking my eyelashes with it and grabbed my favourite black top instead.

I laddered my tights, spilt tea on my top in the kitchen and wrenched my ankle on my way out the front door but finally made it to the train station by eight. I was exhausted by the time I got off the train at eight twelve but managed after a lengthy sprint to arrive at last, red in the face and hair like a mangy mat at eight twenty. I let myself into the office, my

senses on alert. What was wrong? It was so quiet.
Not a scruffy fella to be seen. No colourful
conversations radiating from the kitchen. In fact all
I could hear was the hum of my office computer
and a muffled discussion going on in Joe's room. I
was beginning to feel a bit like Janet Leigh in *Psycho*
just before she gets stabbed. I could just see The
Legend popping out from under my desk, wielding
an axe and wearing nothing but a dirty eye patch.

Berating myself for having such absurd thoughts,
I shuffled into my own office and turned on the
heater. It was freezing! I mean, he might be a nice
chap. You never know, I consoled myself, still ready
to bolt for the door if so much as a scrap of paper
moved. My attention was suddenly caught by a large
A4 piece of paper lying in wait on my desk. I
approached it with caution. After all you can't be too
careful when you find yourself in life-threatening
surroundings, now, can you? Written in large
reclining, lazy letters it said or appeared to say:

'Dear Lady,'

I picked it up.

'Please get me some Mickey wire and a rubber
duck for tomorrow.'

I sat down.

'Dear Lady,' I spat at the heater, which was
making some sort of grunting noise. I looked
around half-expecting Roisin to arrive in and roar,
'Ha, ha! Got ya!' But she didn't. Stunned. I
continued to read words, which were practically

striding off the page to greet me.

'And I need a portaloo sent up to the lads by the motorway. Ask Joe to tell you where and be quick about it.' And that was it. No signature. No please or thank you. And what in the name of fuck was Mickey wire? Obviously it was a joke. It had to be! Anyway I was damned if I was going to ring up anyone and ask them for a rubber duck.

The absolute bastards! They were picking on me because it was my first day and I was the only girl in a world full of intimidating blokes. Well I'll show them, I decided, rolling the paper into a ball and aiming for the wastepaper bin. I was not going to give in to their obscene sense of humour. I needed to command some respect if I was going to survive here. So by eight thirty I was feeling very proud of myself and on top of the situation. Until the phone started to ring.

Well it didn't exactly ring so I didn't exactly answer it. Because all I could hear was a sort of hooting noise that went on and on forever. And it was only when Joe flung open his office door and made straight for me that I began to wonder what I had done.

'Gina, Gina, can you please answer the phone for me? I'm up to my eyes in here,' Joe said breathlessly looking rather annoyed, his hands full of photos and scraps of paper.

'What phone?' I stammered feeling like a complete eejit. He gave me that look again. Like the one I got yesterday when I whacked my head on the desk.

'Oh you mean the hooting noise,' I continued hopefully, trying desperately to grab at any available straw so he'd think I had a brain.

'Yes. The hooting noise,' he repeated, staring at me as the phone started to ring again. Talk about being saved by the bell. Or the hoot in my case.

'Of course,' I smiled and if I could have run for the door I would have.

Joe disappeared like lightning leaving me to deal with the incessant hooting. Terrified, I picked up the phone and tried to sound like I knew what I was doing.

'Good morning, B Ryan Construction,' I said in my best cheery Dublin accent which I was quite proud of really.

'That's Benjamin Ryan Construction,' came the reply. Well not reply really. More like a snarl. Or a Rottweiler. A snarly Rottweiler that's been half starved. And is very pissed off. I nearly dropped the phone.

'Oh sorry! How can I help?' I asked starting to rattle but not beaten yet.

'Get me Joe,' continued the snarl now sounding none too impressed.

'And who's calling?' I snapped back, deciding the best form of defence is attack. As you do when your life is being threatened by a crazed bloke on the phone.

'Mr Ryan,' the voice replied very slowly. As if to suggest I had a hearing problem. The ignorant bastard!

'Mr Ryan?' I echoed. Obviously it was Mr Ryan. Who now thinks I'm a dumb blonde with a hearing problem.

'Do ya want me to spell it for ya?' Now he thinks I'm a dumb blonde with big boobs, a spiralling credit rating and more than likely couldn't change a plug if my life depended on it.

'No. Just hold a moment please,' I squeaked.

I pressed the hold button, realising that this man not only believed that his new receptionist didn't know the first thing about answering phones, but it was also quite possible that she didn't know where ice cubes come from either. Now what? I hadn't the faintest idea which of the squillions of other buttons on the phone was Joe's extension. Feck! I thought counting the seconds and staring at the flashing red light. That must be him. The traveller. Pity he wasn't in bloody Antarctica, I thought, panic beginning to grab hold of me in record-breaking time.

'Joe!' I yelled, trying not to sound like I'd completely lost the plot or was having my leg amputated. No reply. Unable to stare at the flashing red light any longer and in case the phone exploded which it probably would knowing my luck, I legged it into Joe's office and breathlessly informed him that Mr Ryan was on the phone. I didn't mention the snarling bit as the poor man looked hassled enough as it was. Even more hassled than I felt, if that were possible.

'No problem,' he smiled obviously grateful that I'd managed to answer the phone at all.

Thankful to be back at my own desk I sat down and tried to unruffle myself. After all it was only an office job. And I'd had thousands of them. Millions! I'd spent days, years out of my life dealing with absolute pigs on the phone. And that was the key, I smiled knowingly to myself. On the phone. They were only on the phone. It wasn't like they were going to file in to my office one by one to shoot me on the spot.

Feeling much better, I gave Joe a big smile as he came back in to my office and even offered to make him a cup of tea.

'That was Mr Ryan,' Joe said rubbing his hands together as if I didn't know. Suddenly I could feel my heart racing. He had an awful funny look on his face. Or maybe I was over-reacting and the poor chap was merely constipated.

'He'll be here in an hour so we'd better get busy!' he boomed loudly. 'I'll have two sugars in my tea, Gina, if you don't mind. We're in for a long haul!'

You could have locked me in a high security institution and I wouldn't have given a damn. Joe continued to give out stink about Mr Ryan's unscheduled arrival which apparently would leave him 'in the shits' but I didn't bother replying. The last two days had been so hectic and now I had to face the next six hours without the aid of even a single drop of alcohol. The Devil was en route and would undoubtedly want to know who the thick receptionist was. I was terrified and needless to say would gladly have drunk every last drop of Granny's holy water if I thought it would help me now. Joe was still standing in front of me. Worse than that, he was sort of jittery and hopping from one foot to the next in perfect rhythm.

'I'm going to need Matt here . . . and Jason,' he said staring into space and tapping his index finger off his chin. Honestly he reminded me of one of those fellas outside the bank who plays the flute, the bagpipes and a guitar all with his little finger and probably have a harmonica stuffed up his arse for good measure.

Joe was beginning to drive me crazy with all his tapping and hopping and jitteriness. Jesus! I was seriously debating whether or not to slap him across the face or yell loudly in his ear when he suddenly prodded the air and started staring at me. Oh no. What now? I could feel my tights (which were one size too small as it was) getting even clingier as if they knew what was coming. At this rate I wouldn't be able to walk as far as the train station because the blood supply to my nether regions would be completely cut off. I held my breath and waited.

'OK, Gina, you ring Matt and Jason and tell them to get here straight away. Warn them that Mr Ryan is due in an hour so he'll be arriving before ten.

Hurry now! We need all hands on deck!'

All hands on deck! Was I now working for the
Navy? Were we about to set sail to foreign parts? I
was trying to calm myself down and Mr Butler here
was more hyper than a small child who's been
drinking coke for a week. I wasn't going to panic –
I wasn't going to panic – Oh shit! I was chanting
again and look what happened the last time I did
that. I didn't want Joe falling down a pothole or a
manhole or anything else with a hole for that
matter. I scanned my desk as quickly as I could
searching for anything that looked remotely like a
telephone book.

I eventually unearthed a very scruffy office
telephone book where someone had been busy
doodling on the cover. I flicked through it with
lightning speed which surprised even me. I came
across Matt's mobile number. Though it didn't say
'Matt's mobile number'. It said 'Chicken's mobile'
with 'Matt' written in brackets. What in the name of
God did that mean? Did I ring and ask for Chicken?
Did I ring and ask for Matt's chicken? Did Matt
have a fondness for chicken legs? Did Matt have
chicken legs? I paused as I picked up the phone but
catching sight of Joe practically doing the
Riverdance outside my window I shut my eyes,
quickly dialled the number, held my breath and
crossed everything I could. Including my bra strap.

'Yeah?' a gravelly voice answered.

No. It's OK. I didn't hang up. Though I wanted to.

But not as much as I wanted to boot out the door at a hundred miles an hour.

'Is that Matt?' I stammered. Perspiring, hyperventilating and generally feeling on the verge of collapse.

'Yeah.'

I gulped. Obviously this bloke had a way with words.

'Can you come down to the office? Joe said Mr Ryan will be here shortly and he'd like you to attend as soon as you can please.'

I held my breath again, straining to hear his reply (which would hopefully consist of at least one syllable). The phone line was terrible. And what was that noise in the background? Was he in the middle of a war zone?

'Who's that? I'm on the throne.'

'It's Gina in the office and—'

'Howareya, Gina, can I ring ya back? I've no toilet roll.'

Jesus! For the first time in my life I was really stuck for words. What should I do? Demand he get up, there and then, and walk his soggy arse the hell back here? Or should I provide possible solutions on how one wipes one's bum without the aid of loo roll? I couldn't believe it. On the toilet! Speaking to me while he was on the toilet and we hadn't even met. Thank God we'd never met. I hoped we'd never meet. As I hung up I wondered if he'd wash his hands when he'd finished.

Men in Dirty T-Shirts

Joe was still dancing outside. I started to smile and point enthusiastically at the phone, trying to say I'd been cut off. He didn't look convinced. He was giving the Walls of Limerick his best shot and if he didn't slow down I was sure he'd impale himself on that shovel thing hanging off the roof.

I reached again for the dog-eared phone book, this time searching for Jason. Joe's life and future career, it seemed, depended on me successfully getting through this time. Thankfully Jason didn't have any letters after his name (other than a-r-s-e-h-o-l-e, scribbled by some juvenile young fella no doubt). Again I held my breath while the phone rang out, praying 'please let this one be at least fully dressed and able to speak English.'

'Hello?'

'Is that Jason?' I asked quietly, not betraying my state of mind one bit.

'Yes. Who I am speaking to?' a brusque Welsh accent demanded.

'It's Gina in the office. Can you come in please? Joe and Mr Ryan wish to see you.'

'I see. Be there shortly.' And he was gone.

I started breathing again. I gave Joe the thumbs up and he stopped dancing.

'Oh that's great!' he said coming back into the office and wiping his brow. 'I was getting worried there for a minute. Any chance of that cup of tea now? I'm done in!'

Typical, I thought as I slammed around in the

kitchen looking for the kettle. I was so rigid with annoyance I felt like I had rigor mortis in both my legs. I found the kettle and dusted it off and eventually managed to make Joe his tea.

'Cheers, Gina,' he said, saluting me with his cup.

Cheers yourself, I felt like saying, but I didn't. I really felt quite put out. I hadn't been in the place for ten minutes and I'd had obscene notes left on my desk and been forced to converse with people in need of serious psychiatric care. I looked cuttingly at Joe as I walked back into my office. He could bloody well make his own phone calls in future.

I settled down behind my desk now that the panic was temporarily over and for the first time had a chance to really take in my surroundings. Jesus! It was filthy in here. But worse than that, my desk was an array of invoices and dockets and other bits and bobs nobody had bothered to file away. I gingerly picked up a sheet labelled 'Plant on hire' and skimmed down the list of items. It looked like an itinerary for a Bruce Willis movie. 'Muck skips and bogeys' it said on the first line.

'And they are what?' I asked my now growling heater. I gave up straight away and started to try and sort out the mountain of paperwork which was reproducing on my desk before my very eyes. Most of it had been used as coasters or napkins and I had to tug a little to free them from the surface. It was quite a struggle. But I won.

I spent the next hour or so watching the door and

kept myself busy pulling, yanking, sorting and filing until eventually it was done. By the time I filed the last docket I felt like I'd just finished a two-step aerobic class. I glanced out the window. It was raining of course. And then at the clock. Eleven and still no sign of Rottweiler Ryan, Matt or Jason.

'No sign of the lads yet then?' said Joe, his head suddenly appearing around my office door. I looked straight at him with my eyebrows raised. This popping his head around the door business was getting a bit out of hand. I'd have to start training him and his habits, I decided with a sigh, if there was going to be any reasonable chance I could work with him. But before I had an opportunity to do that or to make any sarcastic comments about the difference between men and boys, a car pulled up outside with a screech. And then a bang. And then the cabin swayed just enough for me to hang on to the sides of my desk. Now what? Joe flew to the nearest window and had a quick glance outside.

'Oh damn! It's Nicola!' he groaned, waving his hands in the air in a wonderful display of death throes. He really was exhausting work. What a wimp, I thought, toying with the idea of joining in and creating a Mexican wave effect in order to slyly gain his confidence and then – whack! a good slap in the face and a prescription for Prozac might do the trick, I fantasised, all ready to jump out of my chair there and then and give him a good thump. But I wasn't quick enough. Nicola had flung open the cabin door and was making her entrance amid a cloud of very expensive perfume and several colourful scarves. The spoilsport!

'Well hello there, Nicola!' Joe said, all nicey nicey and full of smiles. I thought I was going to puke.

'Yes hello,' she retorted indifferently, thoroughly celebrating the possession of power and eyeing him up as if he were something nasty she had just stood on. Or maybe she simply wanted to stand on him in general. Which wouldn't be hard as she was so tall and he was only four-foot-something. I, in the meantime, wasn't really sure what to do with myself (now that my 'slapping the boss in the face' plot had been foiled). I sort of shuffled a few bits of paper around on my desk, straightened my skirt and waited for Joe to introduce me. And waited. Just as well I wasn't in a hurry.

'Nicola, this is Gina by the way,' Joe eventually said, still gushing smiles and flashing a set of teeth my granny would have killed for.

By the way! The cheeky bastard!

'Gina!' Nicola said whipping around very fast and facing me. She looked me right in the eye. She was blonde and completely terrifying, I'll grant Joe that. And she was dressed to kill. Which was something she was obviously quite good at, I thought, as I observed the large mink coat adorning her figure and her furry gloves that had once been a couple of cute trusting moggies. (She was now slapping them neatly off Joe's obliging head while she stared at me.)

I gulped. I felt completely inadequate in my Marks and Sparks knickers. Not that she knew I was wearing Marks and Sparks knickers. But I was sure she probably had X-ray vision and could tell at a glance that my tights were from the sale in A Wear and my shoes from the depths of Lotty's wardrobe. Whereas Nicola was dressed head to toe from the catwalks of Paris. How dare she! I must admit I did feel a bit put out. My favourite black top and I had been completely upstaged. Utterly inadequate and not in the running at all. No Marks and Sparks January sale bargains adorned the body of this woman, you can be sure of that.

Nicola was still looking intently at me. Dissecting me. With a little smirk on her face. The bitch! Naturally I was obliged to do the same even though I was apprehensive to the point of sheer collapse. But in doing so I was surprised to see that Nicola was one of these women, who, yes, dress to shame all of us normal Miss Selfridge's/Dunnes/bargain basket women. But (and I was so delighted when I realised) she was also one of these woman who was a size fourteen (nothing wrong there) who insisted on pouring herself into a size ten so all the blokes would think she had huge cleavage, massive boobs and no bum.

And she knew I knew. Which was becoming life threatening. You could hear a pin drop until Joe, clearly unable to cope any longer with the silence or the possibility that one or both of us might pull out a Braun hair curler from our handbags and demand a duel, offered shyly to make Nicola a cup of tea.

'I'd prefer it if you'd organise one of the men to paint the outside of the cabin. It's a disgrace. Have you even looked at it recently? Mr Ryan will be frantic if he sees it. Actually Joe, he can't make it today. I expect you'll see him first thing tomorrow.'

'Of course, yes I see,' mumbled Joe, virtually bowing down in front of her.

I shut my eyes. This was deplorable. I couldn't watch. He was doing his utmost to please her and she loved every minute of it. At least I had stared back at her, bravely taking my chances and ignoring the fact that she might poke both my eyes out with one of her long red fingernails. I felt betrayed by Joe in some way I couldn't quite put my finger on. I simply couldn't explain it. One minute he was normal and now he was acting as if he had undergone a partial lobotomy. Anyway Nicola wasn't hanging around. She did another one of her little twirls and marched into the office next to mine.

'Don't disturb me unless it's urgent,' she said and slammed the door.

'You'd better help me get the painting organised so,' Joe said, at last sounding some way unruffled and rather pleased that Nicola was no longer flicking her gloves at him. 'Hand me over that order book and I'll get the paint if you ring Jason back and tell him to hurry up.'

Thankfully Jason arrived before I had to even pick up the phone again. Joe spotted him out the cabin window. I hoped I'd be pleased to see him. He might be normal. I'd even settle for a customary dreary bloke at this stage, who didn't carry a backpack of paranoia, apprehension and anxiety around with him in the presence of an attractive woman.

I looked up from my desk as Jason strolled into my office, immediately extending his hand to me. Mind you it wasn't your average-sized hand. It was more like a shovel. A shovel with the diameter of a galvanised bucket. But as I took his hand in mine (it was quite rough and coarse but warm and comforting as well, just in case you're wondering) I realised he would have looked daft with your ordinary run-of-the-mill hands. For he was at least six-foot-four, his frame completely blocking out the scrap of sun trying its best to squeeze in and smile upon my dreary surroundings.

His striking black hair and generous blue eyes gave him a nice god-like silhouette, I thought dreamily. I'm holding the hand of a god, I realised with genuine excitement, automatically comparing his physique with Ralph's which was more like a streaky rasher with arms and legs in the right places than this tower of manhood leaning over my desk. This Jason was quite a dish.

'So, you're Gina?'

I tried not to blush. 'Yes,' I said, sitting back down

and fiddling with a few more bits of paper on my desk, willing him and his luscious body to go the hell away. No such luck I'm afraid. Not that I'd normally complain if a gorgeous bloke were giving me the eye. But it wasn't like we had met in a pub or some awful disco where I'd gladly devour him and then drag him home and show him off to my envious and resentful flatmates and tempt him with witty chat and a cheese sandwich.

This was different. Why? Because I was exhausted and knowing my luck he was probably a right bastard anyway. Granted a sexy one, but I was definitely doing myself a favour by not falling head over heels in love with him. On the spot. As I have done in the past to my regret and shame. I'd rather settle for the fling that could never be than make a holy show of myself. But let's face it, it wasn't easy.

'I see you've sorted out a good bit of the paperwork then?' Jason continued, picking up files and folders off my desk and having a good poke around. The way men do. As if he was looking for the bloody sports page.

'Yes,' I said in my best, 'bugger off will you?' tone. 'And I'll thank you not to mess them all up again, if you don't mind!' I snarled, snatching them out of his huge hands but at the same time I couldn't help wondering what it would be like to have those hands around me and to get lost in his big woolly jumper. Cute or not, nobody was going to come in here and mess up my desk. And it didn't matter one bit if he had the body of a god and mesmerising eyes to go with it.

'Sorry,' he smirked. God, he was gorgeous! 'Would you like a cup of tea?'

I relaxed, accepting his offer of refreshment. And had a good look at his bum as he strolled out of my office and gently closed the door. I had to decide there and then that I would not under any circumstances allow myself to fancy him. Anyway, I was still an engaged woman. Only just but engaged all the same.

Chapter 5

You'll be pleased to hear that the rest of the day wasn't too bad. Relatively speaking. I only crashed the computer once; and Nicola didn't emerge from her office until well after lunchtime. And that was only because I jammed three phone lines and managed somehow to set off the alarm. And nobody knew the code. So Jason had to phone the security company from his mobile because the phone lines were still jammed half an hour later. But, worse than that, The Legend arrived. Or to those of us who have normal titles, the general foreman arrived. Like fifty bastards. All sweaty and cursing because his rubber duck, Mickey wire and portable toilet hadn't arrived. So as you can imagine by four thirty I looked and felt like a bolt of lightning had struck me.

Seeing The Legend making straight for me, all hairy and flashing enormous yellow teeth, I bolted without a second thought into Joe's office. (Any port in a storm and all that.) I could have given any self-respecting greyhound a run for its money. OK, I still hadn't forgiven Joe for being so utterly rude earlier, when he had overlooked introducing me to Nicola. But he did seem to like me on occasions when he was being rational, which was good enough for me. I flung aside my dignity as if it were one of my dyed green, well-worn pairs of knickers I'm forever finding in my bottom drawer. (That's usually all that's left after Jessie has helped herself.) I felt like apologising, but there was no time for second thoughts and sentimental reminiscing now. If I hung around much longer The Legend was definitely going to dismember me and my life would be over. I mean the lads had been looless all day.

'And no fella can work with his bowels all chockablock!' he was roaring to anyone that would listen. I was defenceless.

I screeched to a halt in front of Joe's desk just in time. Another two seconds and I would have landed in his lap. Which would have finished me off there and then and left me covered in muck and dirt from his top to toe plastic coat and wellie boots.

'Jesus, Gina! Are you all right?'

'I forgot to order the loo for The Legend and he's going to kill me!' I babbled at a hundred miles an hour, pulling myself upright and trying to fix my hair all at the same time. You know, now that it had that sort of electrified look about it.

I managed to make myself look reasonably

presentable – just about. After all, I am good at my job, I told myself while Joe straightened up and threw me yet another peculiar look. (Imagine him giving me peculiar looks. After all he's put me through today.) Well, normal jobs that is, where one doesn't require a bulletproof jacket and huge steel-toed boots for protection. And I do know how to use a telephone, I consoled myself, trying to reassure my deflating ego and plummeting self-esteem. Preferably one that rings, that is.

But I didn't actually want to say any of this to Joe in case he thought I was a complete liability not to mention an absolute halfwit. And I did have my pride to think of after all. (It was bad enough that I had thrown away my dignity willy nilly without so much as a thank you and goodbye not two minutes before. I had to at least try to hang on to my pride.)

'Fuck pride!' something inside me suddenly quipped. Against my entire professional and 'I don't want to look like a plonker' instincts, I heard myself sag into the nearest chair with a washed-up sigh and tell Joe everything. (And so would you if a demented seven-foot man was going to kill you because none of his men had been to the bog for ten hours.) Yes everything, including the bit about how I hadn't ordered a thing scribbled on The Legend's list because I thought he was a complete weirdo who probably kept a spare tyre and a chicken under his pillow. And because I thought he was taking the piss as I was a member of the opposite sex which wasn't fair, etc etc.

In no time at all (about thirty seconds I reckoned) I looked like a bedraggled, hassled, soggy old teabag. All weepy with a tissue stuck up my nose which was running like Sonia O'Sullivan except a lot faster. And neither of us looked the least bit professional or in control.

Joe was very sympathetic about it all. (My novena from last night had been heard. I must remember to put a tenner in the next Trocaire box I see, I resolved there and then. And I promise I won't change my mind at the last minute and buy *Hello* magazine and a skip load of chocolate instead. As you do, especially if you're a lonely woman whose fiancé is an accountant.) And once I had stopped blubbering he patted me on the shoulder, picked up the phone and did all the ordering for me. Which I was so grateful for as time was of the essence. I could hear The Legend on his way into Joe's office. All huffing and puffing like a scalded cat, the torrent of bad language reaching crisis point. Which really wasn't good news for me as we still hadn't been introduced. And here he was planning to kill me before he even knew my first name.

Joe smoothed things over with The Legend and attempted to calm him down. (He obviously hadn't been to the loo either I surmised.) I tiptoed back to my desk and tried to compose myself for the next assault as there would undoubtedly be one if the rest of the day were anything to go by.

I sat down. My heartbeat gradually returned to normal. My pulse slowed to your ordinary 'I'm not having a seizure' pace. My hands stopped dithering.

'Gina, you might as well head home for the night. It's nearly six. I'll see you in the morning. Well done on a good day's work.'

I glanced up at Joe through my two-ply, rather snotty tissue. Was his voice laden down with sarcasm or was he simply being nice? I decided he was being nice and gave him a grateful smile for safeguarding my life and making sure I would live long enough to see the January sales. What a sight I must have been! All tissues, red eyes and a runny nose. I could have been dying with the flu instead of a good old dose of chronic embarrassment and bewilderment. Christ, daft or not, he thinks I'm a right one, I thought, cringing. I dolefully picked up my bag and coat, more than willing to streak out the door before something else happened to make me feel even more witless.

'Gina! Can I see you please before you go?' Oh Jesus! Now what?

Nicola had emerged from her office. You should have seen the face on her. Like a dog with a gob full of wasps. Joe threw me an understanding glance as I unwillingly followed Nicola into her quiet and airy office which was so unlike my dusty grime-encrusted little space. I was a bit scared and nearly fell over when she smiled at me. (I mean wild animals don't usually smile do they? Principally because they've got somebody's arm between their teeth.)

'Sit down,' she instructed, pulling out a chair for me. 'I don't bite,' she said quietly, when I sat but didn't say anything.

I was too busy searching for the wasp-chewing loony I had encountered earlier. That person appeared to have run for the hills and instead all I could see in front of me was a pleasant if now slightly tired thirty-something woman who was handing me a cup of tea.

I felt alarmed but accepted the steaming hot cup as I sat down, or perched more like it, on the edge of my chair repressing instincts that were howling at me to relinquish the tea and defect immediately.

'I'm sorry about all that earlier,' she gushed (and looking as near as she could to . . . embarrassed?). 'You must have thought I was so rude.'

I felt an inner prod, smiled appropriately and shifted a bit on the chair as I tried to smother the non-stop chattering of my inner defence system which was desperate to warn me she was nothing but a crafty and insidious bitchy actress who was (of course) about to machete both my legs off.

'How was your first day, Gina? I hope the lads weren't too noisy and frightening? They really are a great bunch, but all the same they'd get a huge kick out of winding you up given half a chance. Are you all right?' She was smiling still. 'You look like you've had a hard day. Here, have a tissue.'

More smiles and an offer of a box of tissues to mop up my runny nose. My gut instincts were becoming harder and harder to ignore, but I had to admit she did look sincere and concerned as she pushed her blonde locks away from her face and eyed me in a distinctly motherly protective sort of manner. Either that or she had a gift divinely given to fabricate lies very convincingly. I wasn't convinced.

'It was grand!' I boomed with a faint laugh, a combination not easily attained and making me sound more than a bit touched. I think she knew I was planking myself. She definitely knew I was lying my head off.

'It's not easy being one of the boys,' she stated softly as if this were a fact they forgot to tell us in primary school. 'Especially when you realise that sometimes they don't take kindly to being accountable to a woman,' she continued, looking slightly sad and lighting a cigarette.

(I had to agree. They definitely forgot that one in primary and secondary school.)

'Which is why I have to be like that,' she continued, pointing towards the office door with a dramatic sigh. 'You see, Gina, if they all weren't terrified of me some of them would walk all over me and I can't let that happen.' Slight silence as I worked out what she was saying and attempted to ensure I wasn't hallucinating.

'As far as you're concerned,' she said leaning

forward, 'do your job, enjoy your job and don't crack on that I've told you I'm not the mad old bitch they think I am,' she said with a little wink.

The wink confused me. Did she fancy me or was she just trying to put my mind at rest? I know the mind boggles during stress-related meetings like this, doesn't it? But whose mind? Mine or hers? She was talking again.

'I would love you to come to me if you have any problems and not to be frightened. Deal?'

I continued to perch edgily as I looked long and hard at her. I think it was the phone call that finally did it for me. It rang suddenly and Lovely Nicola abruptly turned into Roaring 'Feck Off' Nicola. It was an amazing metamorphosis which was frankly quite terrifying and would have almost made my legs give under me except I was sitting down.

All the same I was captivated watching her every move. I couldn't help myself from smiling as she displayed even more of her divinely endowed gifts by deliberately taunting, angelically demanding and delicately offending some poor creature before finally slamming the phone back in its cradle. Giving me a knowing glance she lit another cigarette.

'Bloody accountants,' she said. 'Should all be shot,' she continued with a sparkle in her eye and a small smile advancing towards the corners of her mouth.

I could learn from this woman. If only I could talk to Ralph like that. The luck of the woman to be the perfect bitch. Maybe some of that luck could attach itself to me?

'Anyway, what do you say, Gina?' Lovely Nicola was back. My instincts furthermore were lulled into a deep, peaceful repose. She didn't fancy me. I delayed no longer.

'Deal,' I replied with a huge smile.

I now know why men think women are so weird. Here were two women who hardly knew one another and in less than ten minutes were chatting away like best friends.

I felt so ashamed. My snarly comments about her attire which five minutes ago were minding their own business at the back of my mind were now step dancing on my forehead. Interrogating me, having a right hooley and thoroughly enjoying making me feel shockingly small.

'You narrow-minded hussy' popped its head up and poked me hard in my stomach. 'Horrible unfair cow' played pinball with my rib cage, as it taunted and cuttingly reminded me that I had allowed Joe cloud my judgement of Nicola before I'd even met her. I had totally miscalculated this woman who was such fun as well as being quite normal and understanding. I begged my emotions to flee the scene; just the way fellas flee the scene. You know, when they've dumped you without warning in the middle of a nightclub and run out the fire exit with your best friend.

Satisfied that I had been neatly reprimanded, my scolding thoughts finally packed up and left leaving

Nicola and me to spend a pleasant half-hour trying to decide what to do for the Christmas Party which was only a few weeks away.

'I presume you'll be able to come,' Nicola said with a smirk, 'and won't mind eating dinner with thirty rowdy fellas?'

Me! Mind having dinner with a heap of brutish and rowdy blokes? As if!

I agreed to take names and numbers in the coming week of all those who would be attending and Nicola would keep in touch with me about venues and ordering transport. I was so relieved when I finally left the office and started to make my way home. It was nice to find a friend, so to speak. And even though she would only be in the office once or twice a week, I was thrilled. But I still felt a bit thick. You know, all that business over the phones jamming and Joe thinking I was a nutter.

I did my best to put the whole episode in perspective on my way home on the train. Admittedly, it had looked like I was incapable of organising anything, was absolutely useless in an office environment and the first sign of trouble and I'm in a heap on the floor. I had coped rather well under such dire conditions, I told myself. Hadn't I?

There was no way I'd let down the entire female working population, I convinced myself. Of course not! Any sane woman would have felt smothered in such a testosterone-laden climate. Hadn't Lovely Nicola said as much?

Plus, I hadn't even been able to escape to the loo for five minutes break because there wasn't one. I'm sorry, but I couldn't bring myself to use the one outside — I'd rather die from internal explosion of the bladder. And believe me, speaking of exploding bladders mine was at detonation point. I was convinced I could hear it counting away the seconds to blast off. Even though I had survived almost being killed over a bloody toilet, not to mention being in dire need of one, I still felt wretched. Humiliated.

I was doused in self-loathing by the time I got home. I had let myself down no matter what Nicola had said. I should have stood up for myself and not run for cover on only my second day. After my premature exhilaration this morning when I had thrown The Legend's note in the bin I was left feeling totally deflated. (Well not totally. My bladder was a mere ten seconds away from eruption, don't forget.)

I felt hopelessly stupid, silly and entirely out of my depth. All this over a rubber duck and all the other strange items one doesn't normally encounter during routine daily office life. Worse than that, after all my pain and suffering I still didn't know what a bloody rubber duck was.

I arrived in the front door like a streak of lightning and flew up the stairs to the bathroom, quite oblivious of Dad hopping up and down in the sitting room and yelling at the TV, 'Get him ya bloody eejit!'

You've guessed it. He was watching 'the match'. And getting very emotional and wound up. The language was fierce. Which meant Mum must be out shopping because even my dad would be terrified to curse in front of her. It drives Mum mad (and believe me the woman is mad enough as it is). She's very particular about things like that, you see. It's perfectly acceptable to go out and run up an enormous credit card bill (preferably your husband's/lover's/toyboy's). But God love you if you so much as squeak, never mind direct a stream of foul emotion-filled hairy language, at the person responsible when the bill arrives.

You have to get your priorities right in this world. Sure you could be dead tomorrow. So there'll be no cursing, dancing on the spot or slamming of doors/tequila/heads off walls, thank you very much. Or hitting the postman because he's the bastard who delivered said bill in the first place. I didn't even bother saying hello to my hysterical father. I was a wreck and quite unable to listen to him grumbling obscenities at the telly.

However I couldn't stop thinking about Jason, I realised with a horrified jump, as I came out of the loo and into my bedroom. (OK, OK maybe not horrified exactly – maybe excited would be closer to the truth.) I know. It's disgraceful. What with me being a spoken-for woman and all that. But I couldn't help myself.

I threw myself on to the bed so my poor bladder and I could have a chance to retrieve some feeling of normality. We'd had a very long day. He was probably married anyway, I consoled my turbulent hormones, as I kicked off my shoes. And even if he wasn't, God knows he probably thinks I'm too argumentative and bad-tempered to be approachable in the first place. I mean I wasn't very friendly or chatty to him, so he could understandably be terrified that he might lose the use of a vital organ if he came anywhere near me again. Which I couldn't blame him for really as I had practically spat fire at him when he arrived in with the tea and presented it to me with a big beaming smile. Which I didn't exactly return – quite the opposite.

God, he probably thinks I'm a right, wound up little Antichrist, I surmised miserably. A sulky bag that grunts instead of conversing like a normal person. I'll blame that one on my father. It's obviously his fault after making me spend years listening to him bark and swear under his breath when Mum was in a huff with him.

At that moment (the precise moment I was contemplating what it would be like to swap ice-cream kisses with my new found hunk) Jessie flung open my bedroom door quite unexpectedly and just about managed to scare the life out of me.

'Jesus! What are you doing?' I yelled at her, sitting bolt upright all ready to fling a well-aimed shoe at her flowing jet-black locks in case she was an intruder who might want to rob what's left of my undies and my favourite boots. (I was half asleep you understand, lost in a heaven filled with indulgent and spine-tingling thoughts.) As it happens there's not much difference between my sister and a barefaced thief anyway.

'Hi ya!' she said quite sprightly as if she hadn't nearly given me a full-blown heart attack. If that wasn't enough to get on my bad side she was wearing my favourite black jeans. I rest my case.

'You're wearing my jeans, you thieving gypsy cow!' I hollered, suprising even myself that I sounded so angry.

'I know, thanks. Anyway how's the job? And what's going on with Ralph? Ma said you had a huge fight and you threw the kettle at him and he had to go to casualty and now he's going to dump you. Or maybe he's dumped you already?' she carried on, looking thoughtful and not in the least put off by the massive dirty look I was giving her. She was like a bloody newsreader, I observed, delivering the goods at ninety miles an hour. The details of my love life, if you don't mind. As if they were up for grabs. Juicy details to the highest bidder. The cheeky bitch!

'She said what?' I couldn't believe my ears.

'That you threw the kettle at Ralph—'

'I heard you the first time,' I snarled at her.

How dare she! Just land in my room without so

much as an invitation and give me a blow-by-blow
account of how my love life is a wreck. And I
wouldn't mind but I hadn't thrown the kettle at
anyone. Though maybe I should have, I reflected.
Ralph might have run a bit faster if a kettle full of
boiling water were chasing him.

'I always knew you wouldn't get married anyway,'
Jessie finished quite firmly, interrupting my
calculations of just how fast Ralph would be able to
run with the threat of said kettle endangering his
life. Jessie meanwhile was looking at me like I
should thank her for sorting out my romantic
entanglements following her wise judgement. The
judgement of a nineteen-year-old, may I add. Who
dresses like an extra for a Wes Craven horror flick, if
you don't mind. And wears shoes that one could
only accessorise with a plastic bag.

'Why? Don't you think I'm the marrying type?'

I would later kick my own arse for asking such a
leading question. In less than five minutes, as it
happened.

'Well, more like you're the type no one would
like to marry really, aren't you?'

'Thanks, Jessie' I said, feeling a bit hurt and more
than a bit like hurting her back.

The nerve of her to be so outspoken and try to
break my already flagging spirit. That's little sisters
for you. Nothing but bitches. Bitches who steal your
jeans and rummage through your make-up bag on
their way out on a Thursday or Friday night and

then try to convince you that you're suffering from Alzheimer's disease when you confront them about it. Even though you had caught them red-handed. The cows.

'What do you mean exactly?' (another leading question – would I never learn?) I asked, all indignant and huffy, interested now and happy to sit up and listen to her gems of wisdom. 'Why wouldn't anybody want to marry me?' I continued in a small hurt voice.

'Because (which sounded like Becaaaause) if you wanted to marry Ralph, you would have by now. Instead of chucking kettles and abuse at him you should be all lovey dovey and happy. But you're not! And that's because you're emotionally off centre, aren't you? Your karma is in a right mess and you can't commit yourself to him.'

We both paused for breath. I was enthralled. I didn't dare utter a sound.

I was immersed in curiosity and braced myself for the next lash of understanding my discreet and tactful sister was about to throw at me.

'So that's why no one will marry you!' She said this quite bluntly. 'You'd be snogging the best man after the wedding. I'm telling you, it's true!' she finished, all smiles, as if she hadn't just ruined my life and battered my now aching head with her theories and suggestions that I was nothing short of a tramp. I was livid. But before I reached to pull her hair out by the roots my stomach churned and I realised that, yes, maybe she was right.

I mean why would any potential mate want to spend the rest of his days with me? All cuddled up in front of the fire sipping drinking chocolate and watching the *Late Late Show*. Which was an insufferable bore of a thing anyway? I mean the humiliation of it. I couldn't even commit myself to buying a new jacket without checking and double-checking that it could last the pace of wild nights out with my friends and me. That it wouldn't be offended if I spilt half a bottle of red wine on it in the middle of a giggling fit. Not to mention the possibility of my throwing it in the back of my wardrobe only to come along and retrieve it a good three years later after Jessie had stolen if not sold every other jacket I owned.

Jesus! Commitment really wasn't my bag in life, I realised, as a wave of sheer gloom and terror descended upon me. I could feel my legs starting to wobble as the reality of my hopeless situation tapped me on the shoulder and gave me a thumping big smile. The Holy Family hadn't been the least bit generous when handing out their supplies of commitment and joyful togetherness. The stingy bastards!

I had been encumbered with a healthy dose of the seven deadly sins (lust and greed being my adored choice). I remembered with a jolt that box of chocolates I had promised to buy Granny for her birthday last year. I had bought them. Yes legal

tender was exchanged. Two pounds fifty I think it
was. But my commitment level was at a famous all
time low (probably because Ralph had taken me out
the night before and had bored me to the brink of
suicide with more stories of bank statements and
Visa bills) so I had eaten every one and stuffed the
empty box under Tommy's bed.

Oh yes! I had also been burdened with an arse the
size of New York City and feet the length of the
Titanic plus enough VO5 mousse to last me a
lifetime. Not to mention my big hairy eyebrows that
gave me the appearance of a half-bred wolf.

Fate had cursed me with endurance when it came
to downing any number of bottles of wine and the
stamina to finish off a whole packet of Chocolate
Kimberleys unaided. Unfortunately when it came
down to the qualities essential in pledging one's life
and promising to stay with only one bloke the Holy
Family had joyously dumped me with the leftovers.
The last biscuit in the tin or the battered can of
beans in the supermarket.

How could They? I'd done quite well with the
blessings of flirtation and dressing up to the nines at
a moment's notice. I had an accomplished and well-
publicised habit of loving a good party. And chatting
up men – any men. Including the unfortunate taxi
driver who'd have to drive me home, carry me in
the front door, sit me on the fridge and then shout
up the stairs so one of my parents would get out of
bed and pay the poor bastard. Shy was not a word

that applied to me. But as for commitment?

The Holy Family had been a bit miserly there, now hadn't They? I was a dirty stop-out destined to live my life alone. I didn't need to probe any further into exactly why nobody would ever want to marry me. It was obvious. And to add salt to my gaping wound my horrible little sister had been the one who'd made me see the light.

How could I have accepted Ralph's proposal? I know I'd drunk the off-licence dry and I will admit I don't really fancy him. Not the way I fancy Jason, let's say for argument's sake. But it had felt so romantic. The soft lighting and glowing candles not to mention the wine and cosy chat all had worked their magic on me.

The poor thing. To think I had chucked him and his keys out in the cold. Slapped him in the face when he was down and drenched from the rain. Flung his mixed bouquet frivolously in the bin on top of the chicken carcass mother had so lovingly stuffed. That miserable bird had been shown more love than I had afforded Ralph. The unfairness of it all. And all he had wanted was for us to be together. Instead he was left wondering exactly when I went barking mad and if we were still engaged at all.

Jessie was right. If I had wanted to be with him then that moment in the kitchen would have been my chance. I would have grabbed those keys and told him he was more gorgeous than Matt Damon. I would have flung my arms around him and kissed

him tenderly. Instead I had nearly head-butted him
and called him an opportunist. Jesus! I'm the most
horrible person I've ever met. I'm nothing but a
selfish cow, I realised with a large intake of breath
that made me feel as if a giant hoover had attached
itself to my mouth. Well sod this for a game of
marbles, I thought sitting bolt upright. If you don't
have it buy it, as Oprah Winfrey once said. (Not that
I was planning to make my way to Spar and ask
them for a bag of commitment and a size ten waist,
you understand. But I had to try to put things right.
My marriage depended on it. I had to grow up.)

There was nothing else to say. Nothing more to
be done. Except to ring Ralph and apologise. Tell
him I now knew that I was a rotten cow. A miserable
selfish bitch. OK so I was still moving in with the
girls. But there I could have space and time to begin
acting like a responsible and engaged twenty-three-
year-old. If I wanted to be a sensitive Ralph-loving
woman I'd have to start learning how. Today.

And the same formula could easily be applied to
my new job. I would learn all about these cursed
Mickey wires, bogeys and whatever else I needed to
help me do my job properly. Instead of running
squawking like a headless chicken at the first hurdle.
I would gain respect and trust in my new
environment. And to do that, the first thing I'd have
to get rid of was my crush on Jason. As devastating
as that would be. The ultimate sacrifice to save my
marriage and my professional career. To give up the

(possible) love of a (likely but not confirmed) married man who had the physique any woman would scratch her best friend's eyes out for. Now if that wasn't turning over a new leaf then I don't know what was.

I kicked Jessie out of my room and ran downstairs to ring Ralph. He was very cool until I told him I wasn't going to behave like a selfish wagon anymore and asked if we could arrange to go out for dinner the following night. He was very taken aback and a bit quiet, but sounded happier than he had in weeks. Sure why wouldn't he? Now he could relax and stop worrying that his future wife was going to take off with the bin man.

I think it had been a terrible shock for him. All that worry and me throwing him out and acting psychotic. He didn't sound too thrilled about the moving bit but he did say he'd keep his flat for three months in case I changed my mind. All of which I thought was very grown up and compromising of him. It made me feel very humble that he would wait for me after all I'd put him through, forgetting I was engaged on a regular basis and dishing him up cold tea whenever he came over to see me.

Now that I had once and for all sorted out my romantic life and made decisions I promised myself I would stick to, my new life beckoned and I thought it was about time I got down to the wretched business of packing. Straight after dinner, while I was waiting for Lotty to ring, I enlisted Jessie to help me sort out my overstuffed wardrobe. On condition that I'd pay her a fiver at least, give her first refusal on anything I didn't want plus come Friday night, lend her my new boots, no questions asked. I agreed.

I didn't care. I'm a great one for putting things off, especially major things like tackling my jam-packed wardrobe. The thought of it was enough to make me want to go to bed for a week. And if I didn't do my packing then and there, it would never have got done. I'd convince myself that it would wait till tomorrow and then suddenly it would be next Wednesday and still nothing done. And before you know it I'd be in a huge panic the night before the move stuffing everything I owned in a black bag which Dad would undoubtedly chuck out with the rubbish.

I heaved a massive sigh and cursed like a sailor. I was dreading it. I tried to motivate myself but it wasn't working. I am only human after all. Jessie came thumping up the stairs carrying two huge suitcases and a million bin liners.

I felt exhausted merely looking at her. My earlier enthusiasm had gone running for cover and was making 'V' signs at me from across the room. I sighed heavily again and looked at Jessie as she lumbered up the stairs with enough ardour written on her face to satisfy ten million horny tomcats. Isn't it amazing what the promise of a fiver and a pair of boots will do for a nineteen-year-old, I thought idly.

'Come on then, lets get started,' she said, pushing open my bedroom door and chucking the suitcases on the floor. 'Where will we begin? Chest of drawers or closet?' she said breathlessly, eyeing up the technical specifications of my bedroom furniture with her hands on her hips, like a bloody surveyor.

'Over here,' I replied with yet another gigantic sigh, reluctantly yanking open the wardrobe doors.

Our eyes were met by a vision not often seen by the human race. My wardrobe looked like it was about to vomit. It gladly thrust forward its contents onto the floor.

It was like an avalanche. T-shirts, trousers, jeans. Leg warmers left over from my leading role in the final school play I had been forced to partake in. Last year's Christmas presents and the fireside poker my father had been looking for over the last ten years (it had craftily disguised itself with a yellow sock). Plus my old school hockey stick (which almost beheaded Jessie as it boomeranged out of the wardrobe in a chivalrous effort to escape the confines of its keep). It all piled down on top of us like nuclear fall-out. Then my once heaving closet relaxed, no longer about to gag. I could feel its nausea lift as it practically smiled at us and wept with relief. I felt a bit weepy myself.

'Jesus,' whispered Jessie in awe of the sight that was lying at her feet. 'This is worth at least a tenner,' she continued, throwing me a look of pure disgust.

It took ages. Years. I had at least four hundred grey

hairs by the time we were half-way through matching my numerous shoes. We carried, heaved and sorted until we were about to pass out. All the same Jessie was becoming more excited by the minute now that she had got over her initial shock of nearly being mugged by a heap of my odd socks. My bountiful wardrobe had suddenly become her Aladdin's cave.

We became submerged in my thriving array of cartooned tights. Leftovers from my eighties Halloween party, I reminisced. The one where a slightly tipsy Lotty fell over the dog, sprained her wrist and insisted she be rushed to casualty in case she got a blood clot. In her leg. Like her Auntie Mary had. Talk about a drama queen.

We were laden down with old summer shorts which were teeming in abundance from the darkest crevices. All stained beyond recognition by layers and layers of sun tan lotion. We chucked all of them in the rubbish bag, well nearly all.

Except for a crumpled little purple pair which I couldn't bear to part with. I had worn them on the beach in Corfu on my last night with the fighter pilot, I remembered with a contented little sigh, hugging them to my chest. But then the grown-up version of me issued a sharp warning which felt like a tap on the shoulder with a mallet and I unwilling flung them aside to join the other discards.

I didn't even have time to say goodbye. I had turned over a new leaf, I reminded myself harshly. I'd started a new life in the last hour, I chastised myself, and couldn't afford to be sentimental about other blokes. Jesus, I was such a martyr. Wasn't I brilliant? A beacon of hope for commitment-shy women the world over.

Jessie meantime was chucking jackets, jeans and all manner of clothing onto the middle of the bed.

'There're mine,' she informed me with her 'don't argue or you can bloody well do it yourself' look.

'OK,' I gave in meekly.

What a pain in the arse she is, I thought mutinously. But I didn't argue the toss too much. I was willing to sacrifice a few leftovers from my brimming wardrobe and give them a new home in my miserable little sister's bedroom if it meant getting the bloody job done. And it was a big job. I could be quite lazy you see whereas Jessie was organised above and beyond the call of duty. The smug bitch!

For another two hours we laboured like brickies. We pulled and sorted every rank, type and variety of clothing one person could possibly own. Then we started on the leftovers. Or should I say what was left after my sibling had robbed me blind and was insisting on fifteen quid or she would jump ship. Speaking of ships we nearly needed a lifeboat to wade through the mounds of suits, coats and even my old school uniform which had made an appearance. I hadn't realised what a hoarder I was. It was sinful the amount of clothes I could have packed away for Oxfam at least five years ago.

Jessie was giving out stink.

'What have you been keeping this old rag for?' she said grimacing as she held at arm's length a very moth-eaten jumper. One that might fit a six-year-old.

'Dillon gave it to me!' I retorted dramatically, snatching it from her before she had a chance to dump it.

'Who the hell is Dillon?' Jessie said looking confused.

'My first boyfriend in school,' I replied sounding extremely defensive. Like a mother protecting her firstborn child.

'You sad old cow!' responded my sister yanking the jumper from my hands and chucking it in the bin.

'What the hell are you doing?' I said, all fired up and itching to kill her there and then as I leapt across the bed in a useless effort to save my beloved jumper and nearly causing myself a serious spinal injury in the process. It was too late. Jessie was guarding the bin like a well-trained Rottweiler.

'No! You're not having it. It's rubbish!' she said sitting on the bin and wrapping her legs around it.

'You're a mean, thoughtless, evil little cow!' I spat at her, terrified to even attempt to retrieve my cherished jumper. Which wouldn't be a good move, you see, as I hadn't paid her yet and she was after all a black belt fully conversant in self-defence. Who didn't get much practice. So you see my predicament. I backed off, hissing at her while she sat there smiling. How could she?

But then again Jessie always excelled at everything. She had a fascination for anything alternative and thoroughly believed in 'mental housekeeping' and chucking out the contents of your home every six months. Dad was forever looking for hats, shoes and coats he'd had since before he met my mother. His searching was futile as Jessie had whipped them all out of the cloakroom years ago and stuffed them into charity bags while he was at work, oblivious to the fate of his much loved and very worn clothes.

Mum on the other hand was thrilled to be rid of 'those filthy dog-eared smelly bags of shite' as she so loved to call them.

While my parents had worried endlessly about my performance or lack of it in school and Tommy's for that matter, Jessie was their whisper of hope. And Dad loved her because for a while there Mum told him it was his fault we were thick. Obviously his sperm had been half-dead the night of conception, the thought of which made him very upset and worried. Not to mention nearly killing his ego and stamping it into the ground.

Jessie had a brain as sharp as an ice pick. Not only was she an academic genius ('She could count before she was ten months old!' Mum loved telling the neighbours), she had a flair for creativity the rest of us Birkendales lacked.

While Mum and I could hardly boil an egg without burning off the water Jessie had been cooking the Christmas dinner since she was nine. And even then the little cow had the intelligence to make sure she got paid for it (and an extra tenner for doing the washing up). So by the time she reached her current age of nineteen she had a bank account balance I would give my left arm for. It simply wasn't fair. She was born with a criminal money-scheming mind and I got a big arse. So that's why I gave up the ghost. Or the jumper in this case.

The wardrobe cleaning continued under a cloud of cursing. I eventually stopped hissing as there was a lovely river of spit running down my chin. And it was very embarrassing and not in the least becoming of a woman my age. By nine o'clock we were finished. I was ecstatic! Exhilarated and overjoyed! And nearly willing to forgive Jessie for being such a pain.

It had been an emotional wrench of an evening rummaging through all my acres of clothes like that and remembering what a good time we'd had together. I suppose you could say it was a bit like waving goodbye to your best friend knowing you'd never see her again.

I was getting a bit tearful by now and an empty feeling of loss and abandonment began sneakily to take hold of me. Jesus! I screeched, shaking it off. Honestly this growing up thing wasn't as easy as it pretended to be. But at least with Jessie being the proud owner of practically everything decent I owned I could pop into her room every now and again and say hello. Share a few memories. Shroud myself in recollections of my young commitment-free days now that I was practically married to Ralph with three brats and a crippling mortgage. And it had taken my mind off Jason and the fact that I didn't fancy him anymore. Or wasn't allowed to fancy him anymore.

'Bloody hell!' sighed Jessie, finally looking done in and pushing her hair out of her eyes. 'You could have warned me,' she whinged. 'I'm going down for a cup of tea, do you want one?'

'Yes,' I smiled at her. Amazed that we had managed to partake in something so bloody time consuming without me pulling her hair out and her telling me what a lousy sister/lover/daughter I was.

'Right! I'm out of here. I can't stand it in here anymore.'

Jessie tramped down to the kitchen complaining very loudly to Mum for a good ten minutes about what an unholy disgrace my bedroom was and how grateful she must be to be finally getting shot of me, before hollering up the stairs informing me to get a move on if I wanted any tea. The cheeky cow. But I would miss her, I admitted to myself. Even though I hated her. Hated her for being so bloody right all the time.

Chapter 6

Thank God it was Friday. I had survived my first week at work (not to mention the packing) and was feeling a lot more in control. Nobody would get away with calling me a worthless and inefficient office clerk now.

I had also met a lot of my new colleagues. And yes, they were a scruffy filthy-minded bunch who loved nothing better than to wind me up and insist that I go out on site with them and learn how to build a motorway. And eat steak for breakfast with them in the canteen. And then call me a snotty, Dublin 4, frigid Bridgid when I refused point blank. And yes I was terrified out of my life by most of them. I had considered bringing holy water, a dozen cloves of garlic and a crucifix to work with me. Instead I brought a litre of Domestos, several packets of baby wipes and a scented geranium which I hoped would mask the all-pervading smell of diesel.

I kept all the boys at arm's length when they came

in to speak to me about hiring pumps and buying nipples and spuds and rams. And what in the name of God are they? I hear you ask. I know. I nearly fell over myself when I realised I was actually going to have to order all these things. I mean I was frantic at the mere thought of picking up the phone and asking another human being to send me twenty nipples post haste. And not because they might think I was mad, oh no. It was in case they thought I was a weirdo which is a very valid reason if you ask me.

It had to be a sex-starved bloke that christened all this gear, I argued with Matt (the Chicken) first thing yesterday morning. We had finally met and he wasn't the least bit embarrassed that I had conversed with him while he was on the toilet. He thought it was very funny and told everyone how intimate we were, seeing as I had spoken to him when he was half-naked and all that. I was mortified! I mean how would you feel if some bloke waltzed into your office and asked you where his nipples were?

But I kept to my promise and pored over price lists and descriptions. I learned by heart the differences between this pump and that pump and made sure I had a good chat with the blokes on the hire desk and in the supply stores who could explain all these things to me. So I wouldn't look like a moron. A moron who didn't know the difference between a male end and a female end, if you don't mind. By the end of the week I could have worked for NASA.

I stared impatiently at the clock again. I only had an hour or so left to go and it was beginning to drag a bit. I was dying to get home and tart myself up, which as any woman will tell you is essential when you're out to re-impress your almost estranged boyfriend.

More importantly I wasn't merely out to re-impress Ralph so he would fall even more in love with me than I thought he already was. Nor was it really truthful of me to say I was getting all geared up simply so I could receive his absolution for being a moody and frivolous bitch. No it was much more important than that. I needed money. Yes you can sit there and accuse me of having no shame whatsoever and of being a no good hussy if you want. But it won't do any good. I'd got myself in a big financial bind and I was quite sure Ralph wouldn't mind helping me out. Considering he adored me so much. And no I wasn't taking advantage of him in the slightest. In fact I was offering him the perfect opportunity to lavish me with love of the financial kind – a bit like an engagement present I suppose you could say.

And why was I acting like a desperate tramp? Well you won't believe what happened in the last couple of days. I'd got rather worried about Lotty because she hadn't phoned me about the move. Remember. This is the woman who was practically doing cartwheels naked in her rush to move in before the next setting of the sun and all that. So I rang her from work when Joe had gone for his lunch (he was in much better form now that Mr Ryan had decided to go off to Germany with his fancy woman instead of calling into the office).

Lotty was in a heap when I finally got to speak to her. She was broke, as in bankrupt, ruined, and feeling very humiliated as a result. The poor girl was wetting herself every time the phone rang in case it was her irate bank manager ready to give her a bollocking. Which left me in a hole the size of a swimming pool in Beverley Hills.

Why, you may well ask. Well Lotty owed me at least two month's wages. I was forever bailing her out now that she had become struck down with 'mail order catalogue syndrome'. And although I was angry I could sympathise. It's a terrible affliction, one that I've been victim to myself. More than once. More than twice. And one that my mother and every woman on our street is currently hooked on as each new day sees their hallways become a grotto full of family album catalogues, *Next Directories*, and special offers from the shopping channel. You name it and our heroic postman with his chronic backache has delivered it.

To rationalise the ins and outs of the scenario and so you don't get confused I'll put it as plainly as I can. I was now screwed too! Lotty couldn't give me the money she owed me so therefore I couldn't use it to pay my deposit for the flat. My share now took the form of one suede jacket, a pair of leather jeans, three push-up bras and several bikinis. But she did get a free fondue set for the flat, she informed me gleefully which was supposed to make me feel better. Apparently I could use it as a toothbrush holder. Or stick a plant in it. Or even wear it to a fancy dress party if I liked. But it wouldn't make up for the fact that I was two hundred and fifty pounds short on the rent.

I would have asked my parents to bail me out but I simply couldn't bring myself to do it. I knew for a fact that Mum was expecting an enormous Visa bill. One larger than the *Irish Times* and its property supplement. She'd arrived home the day before with what I thought was a carpet but actually it turned out to be a massive fur coat with matching shoes, bag – the lot. She loved her coat so much that she wore it at the dinner table and while she was watching *Coronation Street*. Which meant there wasn't enough room for Dad to sit on the sofa. Hence he got in an almighty sulk and started banging around in the kitchen causing quite a commotion and would undoubtedly have kicked the arse off the dog if the poor mutt were still alive. So I didn't dare ask him for a dig out because it would only have reminded him that his subscription for the sports channel was now gracing my mother's back.

I'd hate to ask either of them anyway, I decided, fiddling with my hair. Now that I'm an adult and I'm supposed to be mature enough to deal with my own bills, go to Mass more than once a year without being told and refrain from using my father as a taxi service.

'I don't have any other option,' I confided in the wad of paperwork lazing contentedly on my desk.

'Talking to yourself again, Gina?' a melting voice suddenly enquired from the doorway. It was Jason, I realised with a jump. The god.

He sauntered in looking scrumptious in his dirty blue V-necked jumper and muck-stained jeans. How could he walk in on a Friday afternoon looking so attractive, I thought to myself, wondering what he was doing for the weekend, and if it might possibly involve seducing the secretary from work.

'I brought Danny in to meet you,' he continued, sounding slightly hesitant. Which was fair enough, considering that I hadn't actually answered his question yet as I was too busy staring at him and trying to make it look like I wasn't staring at all but was actually attempting to type a letter with one hand on my PC. As you do. When you're half-mad with lust and longing. And when lust and longing have become your best friends and won't leave you alone long enough for you to have a cup of tea in peace. They don't care in the slightest that you've promised yourself not to encourage wild dreamy notions of him and you lying half-clad under a starry sky after polishing off a bottle of Baileys. Instead you're first on their hit list and you might as well get used to it.

'So anyway, Gina. This is Danny, Danny Stone, our

site engineer from the motorway.'

I forced my eyes to stop looking at Jason and the way his wavy black locks were cascading down in front of his eyes. Affording him a certain Clarke Gable sensual look, I thought, quite distracted.

I hurriedly indulged in a last fleeting glance before deciding I'd better say something coherent and act like a well-balanced sane person in case the two of them thought I was (a) drunk on the job, (b) stoned or (c) menopausal and about to pull out a chain saw and let loose there and then.

'Hi, Danny,' I gushed, shaking the poor chap's hand with such willingness that it was nearly wrenched from its socket.

'Hello,' he replied with a grimace, snatching back his hand and rubbing his shoulder vigorously.

'You'll be dealing a lot with Danny over the phone, Gina. He's running that part of the job for us,' Jason added sounding very serious as if he'd forgotten it was Friday afternoon, that the weekend beckoned and I was waiting patiently to be seduced.

'So he just wants to go over some details with you now, before you go home if that's OK?'

No it's bloody well not OK, I wanted to yell at him. Just as I was settled and comfy in my chair and waiting to bolt as soon as the clock struck half-five. Which was only twenty minutes away (presuming Jason wasn't going to throw me on the desk that is and ravish me in good old caveman style).

'Oh! And I got you a portaloo. Just for you. I'll

put it beside the kitchen over the weekend so you won't have to use ours, OK?' he finished, dazzling me with his eyes and making my legs jiggle uncontrollably. Imagine having to settle for a chemical toilet instead of being captivated by Jason and his wellie boots, I sighed, my heart and hormones flagging with frustration.

'Thanks,' I said, smiling gratefully for the first time since I had set eyes on him and his scrumptious body, which no man should be allowed walk around with willy nilly in the absence of a warning tattooed on his head.

Jason made his exit leaving me with dreary Danny who nearly drove me mad. He spent an entire hour being very serious and boring, and spoke to me in a manner that suggested I didn't know the first thing about bookkeeping or the difference between an invoice and a delivery note.

It was gone half-six before I got my key in the front door and then I had to wait before I could jump into the shower and start the tarting up business because Jessie was in there singing away and not hurrying up one bit. And she took no notice of me cursing like a sailor outside the door and threatening to burn all her clothes (well my clothes really). I resigned myself to wait in the kitchen which had taken on a definite affinity with a war zone.

Granny had come over for her dinner and was arguing the toss with Mum over the holy sacraments.

Mum, you see, was apparently in a big sulk because the parish priest had told her quite firmly that she could not help him hear confessions, not even when he was on his lunch break or busy counselling his housekeeper whose husband had run off with someone half her age. Mum was quite welcome to help clean the church or organise a few flowers every now and then, he explained (allegedly through gritted teeth which was very unchristian of him) but if he heard her trying to give absolution to anyone over the phone he'd kill her. So she was very upset and fired up. And Granny was not too far behind as Mum was now insisting that vasectomy and vodka should be considered sacraments without delay.

Particularly vodka and definitely sex. No matter who you have it with, sure isn't it a gas thing anyway and good for the soul. And if it wasn't for the vodka she wouldn't have known how to do it in the first place and none of her children, whom she loved so much, would be here at all if it weren't for the Russians inventing the stuff. Bless them! Not that Father Murphy knew one relevant thing worth mentioning when it came to sex and vodka. Those fucking priests didn't know what the hell they were talking about anyway, seethed my highly strung mother, putting a lot of unnecessary vim into the f-word.

We should all be pouring the stuff into us and having sex all the time, she insisted quite dramatically, slamming her fist on the table. Which

led to a very hairy conversation regarding the
vasectomy sacrament. All the talk was obviously
making poor Dad severely uncomfortable so he
made his excuses and ran into the garden.

And straight into Tommy. Poor Tommy had been
told in very persuasive tones that he could now live
in the bloody garden. Which was my fault really as
Dad still blamed him for the falling on his arse down
the stairs scenario. So as much as I hated him I did
feel very sorry for him. He'd been there for three
nights and was now insisting that he had chronic flu,
and was going to ring social services and complain.
Dad and Tommy started having a right barney in the
garden before I even had a chance to take my coat
off.

'Oh, let them get on with it!' growled my mother.
'As long as they don't touch my plants I couldn't
care less if they killed each other.'

Oh no! Warning lights started to go off in my
head. The chairs began to back away from the table
all by themselves and practically dig a trench under
the fridge.

Obviously this hoo haa with Father Murphy had
really got to her. My mother loves a good scrap. She
simply adores a catfight and is still devastated that
Network 2 has stopped showing *The Colbys* and
Dynasty every morning. It was very unlike her not
to put on her riding hat and join the party in the
back garden.

'Why don't I make us a pot of tea?' I suggested

brightly, hoping to ease the tension as poor Granny was sitting on the edge of her chair hugging her favourite miraculous medal and looked like she was about to faint or have a stroke.

'I don't want a cup of tea!' Mum yelled at me. 'I need a drink,' she whimpered. 'A proper drink. One which is at least forty per cent proof, if your father hasn't already polished off every last drop in the house,' she groaned with her head in her hands. I glanced at Granny and then at our lovely floral curtains which were starting to curl up and shrink as if they knew what was coming.

'Well I'm not having dinner here now!'

Oh shit! Granny was standing up and waving her walking stick at Mum. 'I didn't bring you up so you could drink all day and curse the church and all it stands for, you know,' she hollered, her blue rinse practically turning white.

'And look at your husband!' she insisted, actually slugging from her bottle of holy water for the first time in living memory. 'He's useless and irresponsible,' she shrieked poking her stick at Dad, who's head was just visible through the patio door, and flinging her beloved medal at my mother. 'Why you didn't marry that Simon fella I'll never know.'

'And your son!' she roared, her little voice cracking slightly as the stick was produced yet again, this time almost bopping mother on the head. Thankfully she had the good sense to duck. 'He's a bloody homosexual!' she bellowed, plunging back

into her chair inadvertently and almost falling out
the back door in a heap.

Pregnant pause. Very pregnant pause. At least a
month overdue pause. With the capacity to carry
triplets, a year's supply of nappies, a christening cake
and the priest's vestments. I felt myself and the
cooker begin to shudder.

'He is not!'

Mother rose from her chair like a Venus flytrap in
heat. It was a terrifying spectacle as she lifted her
head and homed in on Granny. She was livid. Her
face crimson with fury as she got ready to pull out
every hair left on my grandmother's head.

The sight of her reminded me of the cartoon
channel we used to watch when we were kids. You
know the one I'm sure with the Road Runner
revving up his back leg and poised perfectly for take
off. And let's face it at this particular moment in
time I felt like taking off myself. It was a grim day
when two generations of Birkendale women were
about to let rip.

Pity the poor bystander (i.e. me) who had to
witness the wrath of Granny Birkendale especially
when she was gunning for Mother Birkendale after
nearly murdering her with a walking stick. I didn't
know what to do. I was both rigid with fear, and
fascinated at the same time.

Did I jump in there and attempt to restrain them
as politely as possible? Or let them get on with it
and be an unwilling accessory to manslaughter?

Or (and this was definitely my favourite option) should I discreetly boot it.

'What the hell is going on here?'

It was Jessie. I now loved my little sister more than Ralph or Jason, I gleefully decided, as she waltzed into the kitchen wrapped in towels and still dripping from the shower.

'Why has Dad got Tommy's head in the coal bunker?' she asked frowning out the window. 'And what are you doing with your stick, Granny?' she demanded, briskly walking over and whipping the offending article from her hand before the poor woman even knew what was happening. Now why hadn't I done that?

'Your mother's a pagan and I'm going home!' Granny announced, her face like stone.

Oh Christ! Mother was starting to weep very dramatically. 'She said your brother was—'

'Was what?' Jessie encouraged as if trying to prise information from somebody under the age of two. Jesus, talk about role reversal.

'Was gay!' shouted Mum before collapsing into a flood of tears.

'I'm off,' announced Granny before Jessie had a chance to say anything. 'I'm not staying here, you're all mad!' she said curling her lip up. 'And he is bloody gay,' she finished before stomping out the front door.

Jessie immediately took hold of the situation which was very brave of her I thought. But then again I suppose she is a self-defence expert trained to deal with mad self-destructive people.

'Gina, go out to the garden and stop those two halfwits from murdering each other, will you?' she instructed while comforting my mother. 'Loretta Markham is hanging out her bathroom window with a camcorder for Christ's sake!'

Jesus! I'd never get into the shower at this rate. All the same I wasn't going to start another argument. The sooner my family were behaving themselves and pretending to be rational the sooner I could get out and secure the deposit for my flat.

You have to get your priorities right, I informed myself, as I imagined Ralph pulling up in his new car outside the restaurant. Expecting to meet me on time, where we would then delight in the finer aspects of nominal ledgers over a swanky meal and generous amounts of chianti. (He's a whore of a man when it comes to time keeping.)

Even though I knew Ralph would be in a horrible snot with me for being late (tonight of all nights) I would gladly have had all my teeth extracted without an anaesthetic rather than risk my life in an heroic attempt to come between the idiotic and shameless hooligans doing war dances in the garden. But this was important, I encouraged myself hearteningly, while I filled up a huge saucepan with freezing cold water. My success or failure at drenching the two of them sufficiently before one of them might need a transplant would determine without doubt whether or not I would be able to move house.

I glanced out the window. The language was indulgent and terribly nasty for this time of the day and that was only in the kitchen. Outside, Tommy was attempting to climb Mum's cherry blossom tree in a last-ditch effort to get away from Dad who was two paces behind him wielding a peat briquette. Thank God we didn't own a chain saw.

I opened the back door determined to complete my assignment while the freezing cold water slopped all over me from the weight of the saucepan. I can't believe I'm doing this, I grimaced, nearly spilling the whole lot over my shoes. And Jesus, Jessie was right. There was Loretta, agog and hanging so far out her bathroom window she must have had her legs wrapped around the banisters. The nosy intrusive bitch!

I laboured my way up the garden towards the moving tangle of legs and arms that had once been two members of my family. You couldn't tell one from the other now since Tommy had fallen heavily on his arse out of the aforementioned tree and Dad had gleefully seized the opportunity by trying to stick a coal bag over his head.

Thank God they didn't hear me coming. Jesus! I suddenly thought, trepidation stamping all over me. What if they did hear me at the last minute? I'd be caught in the crossfire, a perfect target for Dad and his briquette. Ralph would be having dinner with a sexy tramp with only half a face. Which might be a cloud with a silver lining, I thought slyly. I mean what sort of a fella would he be to turn me down if my jaw was hanging around indifferently waiting to be reunited with the rest of me, and my facial wounds were oozing blood and goo into my soup? I decided my misgivings were unfounded. They definitely couldn't hear me, what with Dad effing and blinding like a madman and poor Tommy shrieking for help and trying to stamp on Dad's feet.

I decided to forget about Ralph for the moment as I knew it would take all my energy simply to sling the saucepan of water never mind ensure it would reach and successfully drench its feuding targets. And not merely land with a giant splash all over me and the washing line.

With great gusto I lifted my arms up, nearly knocking myself out in the process, if you don't mind, and managed to stretch them as high as I could, finally aiming and flinging with enough energy to light up the national grid. I must have looked like a pissed ballerina. I felt like a pissed ballerina. One who'd just given birth. All huffing and puffing and in need of medical attention.

I could hear Jessie and Mum giggling at the back door. While up at her bathroom window Loretta was yelling for her husband to come and see the neighbours behaving like a crowd of knackers. I held my breath and delighted in the sight of Tommy and Dad all of a sudden becoming very still. And confused. Not to mention perplexed. And very very wet.

The coal bag fell to the ground with a gentle whish. The peat briquette landed with a soft thump on the grass. So when the two of them glanced skywards in an effort to figure out where this awful dampness had come from Mum, Jessie and I fell around laughing.

I clapped myself on the back, hung my head and thanked God silently for making me go to those dreadful aerobic classes last year with Roisin. If I got a move on I might, just might, be in time to meet Ralph. After all, as Granny says, God helps those who help themselves. Leaving the men to recover from the deluge I ran upstairs two at a time.

I applied my make-up in a very methodical slap dash, 'sod it, I'm dead late anyway' mode. Not unlike those poor lads tarring the dual carriageway in a wonderfully careless and nonchalant manner on a stifling summer day because all they really want to do is get to the nearest pub before they faint. So while I was busy trying to make myself look radiantly beautiful Jessie popped her head around the door and placed a wine glass and half a bottle of my favourite white beside me on the dresser. The angel. Oh, I needed it! It wasn't easy making oneself look naturally dazzling and heart stoppingly gorgeous in less than five minutes when all one had was two aching arms and barely enough foundation to cover a slice of weightwatchers' bread. Especially as one's sister had been helping herself to said make-up while one was working herself to a standstill in a stinking portacabin all day.

'Thought you might need a drop to help you recover,' she said, smirking. 'Wasn't that gas?' she laughed. 'Dad and Tommy trying to kill each other!' she shrieked, rolling around on the bed and flicking through my *She* magazine. 'It was like *Gladiator*. Jesus, I nearly wet myself. And did you see your woman next door?'

'How's Mum?' I inquired, throwing the wine into me and refilling my glass straight away as it tasted sooo good. Good enough to forgive Jessie for being a robbing little toad, in fact. So good that I decided I'd have another one while I pondered about the night ahead of me and listened to my little sister fill me in on my mother's current mental state.

'Ah, she's grand. Tickled pink at the state of Dad. It did her the world of good to see him drenched like that you know, seeing as he's in a big huff with her over the coat and all that. Anyway good luck tonight.'

And off she went, leaving me and the wine to get on with the job in hand.

The drink was a great idea. I helped myself to a drop more and looked in the mirror, fiddling with the stem of my glass while I decided what to wear. Would I go for the innocent 'butter wouldn't melt' look? Or the dirty 'go for it, tramp' look? I conferred with the wine and we jointly decided on the latter.

Hoping I didn't look too much like a drag queen I threw on my favourite plunge bra, poured myself into a skimpy cornflower blue dress that gave my cleavage a wonderful creamy womanly look which might just sway the evening my way, I decided, and toasted my reflection in the mirror.

Then came the hair bit. God, I hate trying to do my hair in a rush. I yanked, and curled and sprayed until my eyes started to run. (Jesus, I was more nervous than I thought.) Then I pulled and straightened (and drank a bit more wine to calm myself down) until eventually I had managed to create a sort of Cindy Crawford look, all flowing and windblown and natural.

Feeling very proud I swished into the hall to ring for a taxi but the look Dad gave me sort of threw me a bit and made me feel like I had a sweeping brush stuck to my head. So I flew back upstairs for a go but decided to have another mouthful of wine instead and ran back down to the phone.

I was late! I was supposed to have met Ralph in our local Italian restaurant at least twenty minutes earlier and so all my plans to step out of a taxi looking like Kate Moss's sister and saunter in fashionably late had been utterly gazumped. I could visualise him sitting down reading the paper and glancing at his watch every thirty seconds. Cursing me and realising that the stock market is more reliable than I am.

Worse, I couldn't get a taxi. My best efforts at bribing the receptionist with twenty quid failed miserably. I slammed down the phone, cursed her loudly and hoped she'd get piles and crabs and nits all at the same time.

The awkward cow! Couldn't she tell tonight was the most important night of the year? That it would be forever on her conscience if Ralph didn't wait for me? I knew Dad was in no humour to drive me down, so in pure desperation and completely ignoring my instincts, which were yelling 'don't do it!' I jumped on Mum's old bicycle and peddled as fast as I could, thinking that at least my hair might manage to look fresh and flowing by the time I got there.

I can understand why Ralph didn't immediately recognise me. He was after all expecting to have dinner with a reasonably attractive woman wearing reasonably attractive clothes. What he wasn't expecting was to share his prawn cocktail with a filthy, wet, deranged, slightly jarred bag lady.

Filthy because I caught my heel in the spokes of the bloody bike which tilted me slightly to the left, allowing my dress to wrap itself around said spokes in a wonderfully intricate sailor's knot. Leaving it and my nether regions smeared in crusty mud, thank you very much.

And wet because before I had a chance to get over the shock of my dress being sucked into the wheel of my bicycle, I went flying over the handlebars instead, faster than the speed of sound and bang, landed in a huge puddle.

I was mortified. And exactly what I landed in I didn't ascertain other than knowing I was now saturated and had a funny smell in my hair that reminded me of dead fish.

And yes, I did look like a deranged bag lady. A deranged bag lady with bits of twig and moss fluttering down the length of her hair. Each taking its turn to drop lightly onto my shoulders should I have the gall to forget that they had now taken up residence and had duly given notice to my VO5 hairspray and hot oil conditioner.

In short, I could have auditioned for the *Rocky Horror Picture Show*. I looked lovely with my mascara flowing down my cheeks as it blended like a bloody Delia Smith recipe with my blusher.

My tights once a flattering shimmering nude shade were now shredded so badly I'd have done better with grated mozzarella cheese glued to my legs. I was not a pretty sight. In fact you could safely say I looked wicked. This certainly wasn't the evening I had planned.

My beautiful dress which I had once loved now had a slit in it all the way up to my arse and beyond. I was glowing with shame and pure embarrassment. Ralph looked a bit like nosy Loretta Markham had earlier. Agog. His jaw dropping and his eyes bright with confusion.

I could have cried!

I tried to smile and shrug my shoulders in an effort to defuse the situation. Ralph hates 'situations' like this especially ones where I'm ridiculously late and eventually turn up looking like I've been ravaged by a mad dog who has spat me out half chewed so my appearance is now that of a partly digested salad sandwich.

'Here I am!' I said with a swish of my bedraggled dress, wishing for the millionth time I'd listened to my inner child, who obviously had more intelligence than her barely twenty-three-year-old counterpart. And let's face it, I was a bit pissed. Which didn't help because I was also fighting off a fit of the giggles. So it wasn't easy to look angelic under the circumstances, believe me.

Once Ralph realised that no, I hadn't been mugged and yes, I had fallen from Mother's bike in an attempt to get here on time, his face fell. So did mine. His starter was better dressed than I was. Then a terrible silence decided to join us. It was about a mile long hanging in the air waiting enthusiastically to bungee-jump in and gleefully gatecrash our evening.

'I'll just pop to the ladies and clean myself up a bit,' I suggested, smiling with unappreciated enthusiasm, and hoping the silence would have the good sense to bugger off while I was gone.

Poor Ralph simply nodded in utter amazement, his face plastered with shock. I naturally didn't hang around waiting for him to reclaim the use of his vocal chords but fled into the loo like greased lightning.

Chapter 7

Thank God for vending machines. Thank God I had change. You'll be thrilled to hear that I managed to extract a pair of nudey coloured tights and a little emergency pack to which I will be forever indebted because it had a comb in it plus a panty liner that was brilliant for rubbing the mud from my dress. So all in all I began to look a little less frightening than when I had arrived.

I tried my best to ignore the wine which was making me feel ridiculously relaxed, warm and invincible. I was sporting a beaming smile which refused point blank to be wiped off my face. Not the best ingredients required, I'm sure you'll agree, for partaking in a civilised and refined dinner with an unsuspecting bloke (who already thinks you're half mad and doesn't have the faintest idea that you're about to ask him to clean out his current account so you can move in and party with your best friends).

I quickly gave my face a wash, fixed my make-up,

and finally arrived back at our beautifully set table and sat down. Still accompanied by my huge smile which refused to budge. I could almost see my teeth reflected in my wine glass which I hungrily filled and sipped at while I waited for Ralph to finish ordering our main courses.

'It's been ages since we had a meal!' I said in a sprightly way.

'Yes,' he said with a sigh. The miserable bastard.

'So, how have you been?' I said, hoping for a reply full of gusto and news and scandal. Anything to scare off the tension which was now sitting at the table with us swinging its legs and having a great laugh.

'Fine, and you?'

Oh Jesus, I was going to murder him. I tried again.

'Mum was asking for you.'

A grumble. A slight twitch of facial muscles. He picked up his knife, polished it with his tie and placed it neatly by his elbow. I refilled my glass and clenched it tightly but Ralph being Ralph didn't notice of course. Maybe if I stabbed him in the groin with his bloody fork he might be more willing to act like he had a pulse, a heartbeat and was actually sharing a dinner table with his fiancée instead of simply the *Financial Times*? My thoughts were beginning to turn viciously livid and were doing a good job of prompting me to kill him on the spot, until:

'How's the new office job going?'

My God, he had spoken! And would thankfully

never have to know what it is like to attempt reproduction with a fork prong embedded in his genitals.

I jumped on his crumb of interest all the same, thinking 'Don't look a gift horse in the mouth' and all that. I filled him in on the circumstances in which I now laboured, how my boss was lovely but a bit mad and the lads were gas really as long as they behaved themselves and hopefully I'd have a loo to call my own on Monday.

I didn't mention I was almost kind of passionately in love with Jason and couldn't stop dreaming about him and what he'd look like with a dark and flattering tan. Which he could achieve in five minutes if he came on a sun holiday with, shall we say, me, for example.

Ralph nodded and picked at his hair and then his chicken while I recounted my last few days on the job. He had some very annoying habits, I realised. The way he loved to stick his little finger right in his ear every five minutes. And the way he dribbled sauce over his chin. It was all becoming a bit much so I finished off the bottle of wine without offering him any and wondered when would be the right moment to suggest the loan. Would there be an appropriate time in between all the dribbling and picking and fiddling? I mean it wasn't as if I was asking for a kidney or a new car was it? Our waiter arrived with the dessert menu and I don't know what happened next.

Maybe it was the way Ralph grabbed it off him very rudely? Maybe it was the fact that I was half pissed and feeling super sensitive? Could it have been that another five minutes in his company would have driven me insane? I really couldn't say.

What I do know is that he started giving out yards about this client and that client and how awful they were at keeping their paperwork up to date and what a lousy secretary he had. Sure she couldn't even make a cup of tea properly and she definitely couldn't spell. I wouldn't mind but I had met his secretary. Her name was Isabel and God love her but she was a pet. And he was such a rat to her.

I flirted with my cheesecake while Ralph went on and on. But somehow the delicious and sinful sweetness of it was lost on me. I played affectionately with the biscuity crumb base and tried to tempt my taste buds with the gooey chocolate topping. It was useless. My beautiful dessert was trying its damnedest to seduce me but all I could concentrate on was the self-centred prat sitting opposite me. And this was the bloke I was going to marry?

Jesus! I realised with absolute clarity that he was a boring, rude, ignorant, ugly, unappreciative bloke who expected everyone to fit in with his needs and wants. I bet he was a right git when he was a child. I bet his parents had a whore of a time getting a babysitter for their little trog, I told my cheesecake in an effort to excuse my lack of interest. I had been so naïve. There was no way I was going to ask this cheap and nasty bastard for two hundred and fifty pounds. And there was no way that I was going to marry him.

My face must have turned a funny colour all of a sudden because thankfully Ralph paused for a second from his incessant ranting and gave me a distasteful glance. Obviously I had interrupted him. How dare he look at me like that!

'Something wrong, Gina?' he asked very half-heartedly, as if he was dying to get back to his story.

It was now or never.

'Yes, actually there is,' I snorted.

That was it. He was putting on his 'she's off again' face. Oh, I felt like killing him.

'It's you, you and everything about you. How can you sit there and say such cruel things about Isabel? And I don't care one bit about your clients,' I continued getting rather wound up and feeling quite good about getting wound up. I'd wanted to do this for ages.

'You're a mean and useless little worm. You use Isabel every day just like you use me. You don't want a wife. You want someone to organise your shirts and clean your fridge. You certainly don't want me to move in with you because we're getting married!'

I said this with a little wiggle of my shoulders which complemented perfectly a well-timed slam of my fork off the table. Unfortunately it boinged out of my hand and landed under the feet of a nice man in a black suit sitting behind me. He politely handed it back to me with a frightened little smile which obviously meant he'd like to finish his starter please without being terrified that he might find my steak knife buried in his head. I smiled back bashfully and would have apologised except I was all revved up for another go at Ralph. All I needed now was a power suit from Gucci and a beefy hairstyle from Vidal Sassoon.

'I'm just another player in this shitty game of yours, aren't I? Well, I'm not playing "entertain Ralph" anymore. I'm fed up of you treating me like an employee. I'm sick of your petty routines, your pointless rituals and useless writhings in bed. You're a nasty vile man. I hope you never get married.'

Wine glasses shuddered on surrounding tables and that poor chap whom I had almost stabbed with my fork hastily settled his bill and left. As for Ralph? Well yes, he did look slightly bewildered. But the bewilderment passed from his face and was rapidly replaced by astonishment and hot on its heels was blind fury. Oh how I loved antagonising him. I hadn't done this for ages.

'I always knew you were a commonplace tramp,' he spat, slamming his dessert fork into the middle of his blueberry ice-cream. 'I'm ashamed to even sit at the same table as you, especially after you having the front to turn up looking like a rag lady. You're not good enough for me, Gina Birkendale! You have no style, your family is a bunch of total losers and Mother always disliked you from the beginning, from the second she set eyes on you. What a pity I've wasted so much time on a little gold-digging cow like you, Gina. What a sinful waste of time you are,' he finished, smirking and applauding himself silently.

The fucker. I punched him in the face. He went out cold and fell off his chair. I nodded at our waiter, handed him Ralph's credit card and a twenty quid tip. Instead of calling the guards, he gave me a sly wink and a smile. The love! I could have kissed him.

'I'll see your friend home, miss. He's a regular here. Never did like him anyway. You head on home now and I'll clear up the mess.'

I calmly put on my coat and strolled out of the restaurant. I felt wonderful. I stood outside for a moment taking in huge lungfuls of the evening air. I couldn't believe what I had just done. Then I picked up what was left of Mum's poor bicycle and made my way to the off-licence. I was feeling so ecstatic that I bought Jessie two Bacardi breezers and a box of Pringles. And I couldn't forget Mum, so I thought I'd indulge her with a bottle of her favourite liqueur and a box of chocolates from the late night newsagent. I did a lot of thinking on the way home. I really felt happy (except for the nagging pain in my hand). And as for my deposit on the flat, I'd do what any normal person does and get an overdraft which hopefully wouldn't be a problem as Dad had thankfully dropped in a hamper of Christmas goodies to the bank staff last year.

In no time at all I was home. I kissed Dad on the

cheek while he sat watching sports highlights and he nearly fainted. I walked into the kitchen and handed out the goodies to Mum and Jessie. Mum hugged her chocolates like an old friend and then delved into them, showing no shame.

'How was Ralph, dear? You're home early for a Friday.'

I grinned at Jessie.

'Did he give you the money?' she whispered as Mum began rooting around the fridge looking for some ice to have with her liqueur.

'What money?' Mother shouted from the depths of the fridge.

'No,' I replied pretending to look upset and terribly mournful.

'Jesus! Why not?' asked my sister looking heartbroken on my behalf.

'Because I punched him in the face. '

I made my way out to the garden leaving the two of them hanging. Tommy was sitting on the coalbunker looking frozen. All the same I approached with caution in case he tried to shoot me or even worse lasso me with some barbed wire. Funnily enough he was very quiet. No shouting of 'Who goes there?' or 'What rank are you, soldier?' In fact I think I would have been happier if he had tried to take me hostage and keep me locked in the shed until he was admitted into the house again. At least then I'd know where I stood. I had no experience of a subdued Tommy or Tommy not attempting to shoot me on sight with a water gun if I so much as grunted at him. This was very strange.

'Hi,' I said quietly, still keeping my distance in case it was all a ploy to gain my trust just so he could jump me.

'Hi, Gina,' he spluttered. He had a terrible cough the poor fella. 'How was dinner?'

'Fine,' I lied deciding he wasn't that much of a threat and sat on the ground beside him. Christ I was freezing. But I did feel sort of sorry for him so I stayed put.

'Is Mum still upset?' he said sounding a bit tearful.

My brother? Tearful? Never!

'No, she's OK according to Jessie. Why don't you come in and sort things out. You can't stay here forever,' I said, trying to make myself more comfortable which was basically impossible.

Tommy got up and slid onto the ground beside me. He looked awful. Really. I never thought I'd ever care but I did feel a pang of concern when I saw his runny nose and felt his ice-cold hands.

'Everything Granny said was true, you know. The gay thing and all that. She was right,' he said looking straight at me, his runny nose being very off-putting, if you don't mind.

'I know, Tommy, but it's not the end of the world. Mum and Dad are very liberal really. You know that so why not come in and sort this out?'

He didn't look convinced and my arse was practically stuck to the ground with the cold. I'd have to do something else and fast otherwise I'd have a nice dose of pleurisy or influenza to keep me company over Christmas. Which would be catastrophic as I had just booked the venue for the office party. Which Jason would be going to. Which I would be going to.

'I know we haven't exactly been friends recently but you know I'll back you up. Moral support from your big sister and all that!' I smiled, poking him in the ribs and thankfully managing to drag a smirk out of him.

'Thanks but there's something else I have to tell you,' he said, sounding awfully serious.

Oh Jesus, as long as he didn't say he wanted to move in with his gay lover or tell me he fancied Ralph. Actually I wouldn't give a damn if he fancied Ralph. It would be hilarious! Or what if he wanted me to go to the gay clubs with him? Oh Christ, I suppose I could. After all it's no big deal really, is it?

As long as he didn't ask Mum to go or tell Granny the ins and outs of gay sex, if you'll pardon the expression. Sure I wouldn't mind really. I could bring Lotty and Roisin along for the crack. They'd love it.

Tommy was looking at me like a frightened rabbit. The muscles in my bum were beginning to seize up from the cold. If he didn't hurry up and tell me what was eating him I'd be stuck permanently to the ground.

'What? Tell me what?' I coaxed with my best smile.

'It's just, well, you know the way you're always after Jessie for stealing your make-up and stuff. . . '

'Yeeeesss,' I replied, feeling the hair on my arms begin to rise just a little bit.

'Well, it wasn't Jessie who took all that stuff. It was me,' he whimpered. 'I know I shouldn't have. It just happened one day. I'm really sorry.'

It took a couple of minutes for what he'd said to sink in. Having a gay brother was one thing. Having a gay brother who robbed my make-up every weekend was going to cost me a fortune. There was a bit of an odd silence while he waited for my reaction. Then something else clicked with me as I turned to face him.

'And the knickers?' I said with a raised eyebrow, remembering all the times I had rummaged around in my drawer searching for anything I could throw on me that didn't look like the dog had been chewing it for a week.

All those times I'd cursed Jessie while getting more and more hassled because I couldn't find a single pair of decent wearable knickers. I just couldn't believe that while I was rapidly becoming engulfed in terror, and aghast in case I'd be in an accident where the medical staff would snigger and have detailed conversations about what awful undies I had on, my brother was swanking around town in my Dunnes Stores best leaving me and my arse bereft and frozen. I could have killed him.

'Yes,' he whispered shamefully, swallowing loudly.

Beads of sweat were now gathering on his brow even though he had to be frozen.

'And my favourite silver bra that cost me a fortune last summer?' Another nod.

'And a few pairs of your tights here and there as well,' he finished with a coy smile.

'You cheeky git! How dare you rob all my stuff!' I yelled, suddenly feeling quite pissed off with him and standing up to shake off my annoyance.

This was ridiculous. I didn't know how to feel really. Imagine. My snot-nosed little brother helping himself to my most precious intimate items. It was a bit weird really, wasn't it? I felt awful imagining him actually wearing any of my stuff and happily plastering on my favourite make-up before hitting the clubs. Yuck!

I stood there for what felt like years and it must have felt like longer to Tommy now that he had confided in me. I promised myself not to overreact. After all he was still my brother even if I had spent ages hating him. And he was confused and needed my help. But I couldn't afford to keep him in knickers and foundation for the rest of my life either, could I? I let out a huge breath and calmed down.

'OK, what now?' I asked.

'So you'll still stand up for me when I deliver the news?' He was rattling, the poor thing.

'Of course,' I said, swallowing my annoyance. 'As long as you stop lifting all my favourite stuff!'

'Thanks Gina, that's great!' he smiled, relief finally

coming back to his face.

'So what is it you do then exactly, dress up as a woman?' I asked, still curious even though I felt funny about the whole thing.

'Yes,' he shyly replied. 'But I don't think I'll tell them that bit just now, OK?'

'OK,' I agreed as we both stood up and made our way into the kitchen.

Talk about an anti-climax. Usually when you're about to drop a bomb on your family, never mind your parents, it's a safe bet that at least one of them will faint, clobber the deliverer of said news or simply reply with a veil of silence that's hefty enough to kill a horse.

Jessie was totally unfazed. 'It was always on the cards, Tommy,' she said very simply with a pat on his shoulder as she made her way into the sitting room.

Mum was just completely pissed off that her mother was right. 'Oh shit! She'll rub my nose in this for years,' she said with a heavy sigh, before getting up to put the kettle on. 'Tommy, I love you no matter what. Just don't bring too many hunks home to tempt me, I mean look at the fella I'm married to. I wish he were dead and buried! Never mind,' she continued wistfully, 'I'll go to the hairdressers tomorrow to cheer myself up.'

I was stunned. This was going incredibly well. Obviously Dad would be the one to crack up. Dead cert. 'Place your bets now please,' I could hear myself saying silently and praying that he wouldn't.

'Surely you fancy some sort of woman?' he snorted, leaning heavily on Tommy's chair and practically yelling in his face. 'What about yer one off that breakfast show on the telly?' he suggested with a dirty smile and raised eyebrows.

A shake of the head from Tommy.

'But she's lovely! Her with the long legs and I love those skirts she wears in the summer. What about her then. Ah go on, what do you say?'

Something about flogging a dead horse came to mind.

'No, Dad. I don't fancy her or any woman, OK!' growled Tommy, getting embarrassed and shifting around noisily in his chair.

'Not even Anthea Turner? She's the perfect woman. Isn't she the perfect woman, Gina?' he hollered, clapping me on the shoulder and shoving a tenner in my hand. The git!

'You'd love her, I know you would. Go on, what about her then?' he persisted.

'Jesus, Ted, give it a rest, will you? Didn't he just come in here and tell us that he's gay. Are you deaf as well as stupid?' snarled Mother, clearly getting fed up of the whole conversation at this stage.

'All right!' Dad shouted back. At least he had completely forgotten that Tommy was supposed to be banished from the house. 'Just don't tell the neighbours or any of my mates from work. I don't want them thinking I'm one as well, right?' he threatened.

'OK,' promised Tommy throwing me a smile that for once in our lives was genuine and not masking some awful deed he was about to pounce on me. Even though he had once been my archenemy, my cross to bear. Thank God I wasn't the only one who had a healthy interest in men. So finally making my way upstairs and out of my filthy clothes I decided I wasn't that weird after all.

The next week passed and went wonderfully well. I got on great with Danny which was a miracle. And I quite liked the way he rang me all the time and relied on me alone to organise all his hiring and buying for the job. OK he was still overbearing and needed to lighten up but we had formed not quite a relationship on the phone, but a friendly chat line where he was more than helpful when I got confused between orders or if I reminded him that I wasn't his personal assistant when he expected me to get his lunch delivered.

Jason got more beautiful by the day. It was soul destroying and completely distracting. Even worse I'd swear he was flirting with me a lot of the time and no, before you say it, I'm not being paranoid or suffering from a large smothering dose of wishful thinking. He was flirting and it drove me mad. I forced myself not to think about him for one week. Why? Well this was the week I'd been waiting for, and I needed a clear head. We were moving into the flat at the weekend and I was so excited I could hardly do any work as it was, what with all the frenzied phone calls and rushed lunches between myself and the girls.

I had managed to get my overdraft as well. And no, there were no promises of middle-of-the-night punishment beatings or any talk of repossessing my swanky new hairdryer if I messed up my payments either. So as you can imagine this week was mind blowingly hectic enough without Jason busy flirting and making small talk with me from morning till night.

As a ploy to keep him out of my office I reluctantly decided to dump the photocopier and the fax machine into the general office so he wouldn't have to come into me every five minutes. It was an awful wrench but it had to be done. I did feel a bit weepy over it but pledged to myself that I'd bring them back in once the move was over and I was feeling normal again. I had also cleverly discovered from a couple of conversations with Joe and Matt that Jason wasn't married and didn't even have a girlfriend.

The only downside to the week following my punching of ex-lover in the gob and deciding to ignore Jason was breaking the news at home that I was no longer with Ralph. Mother was devastated.

'But why? I don't understand. He was so lovely,' she groaned, looking at Jessie for back up. Which thankfully she didn't get.

'Yeah, well I always thought he was a prick,' she

stated simply. (Mother wasn't the only one who was floored by this calmly delivered declaration.)

'But he's an accountant. He has prospects. His father is loaded. Oh, how could you, Gina? You'll never find another like him, you know. You will regret this when you're older and hopefully have some sense.' Mother said quite defiantly, waving a fork at me with one hand and a leg of lamb with the other.

I kept my mouth shut but it was so tempting to tell her the truth. If I did tell her what Ralph had said about the family I couldn't be responsible for what else she might do with that leg of lamb. But I had to tell someone. So I only told the girls and Jessie who was appalled and so disgusted that she decided to take revenge by inserting a large potato up the exhaust of Ralph's new car. Hence putting an end to the whole episode.

So here I am a week later and my mother is still in denial. But at least she's talking to Granny again. OK they're tiptoeing around each other a bit but the rift is almost healed and Granny leaves her walking stick at home now just in case she has a relapse. Oh and we haven't told her about Tommy. Mum said she'd kill us stone dead if we dared. She'd never live it down and God knows she'd have to buy a new carpet as well as Granny would be pumping holy water into the house and generally driving us all bonkers. For once I gladly agreed with Mum.

Come Friday I was in a heap. Danny was on the

phone every two minutes while I frantically tried to get all my work finished early so I could go home, complete my packing and be ready to move early on Saturday morning. The phone didn't stop all day. I was cursed. Pumps were breaking down all over the place, the carpenters were in screaming for something called a 'Granny's tooth', half a dozen mickey clips, and, dare I say it, a 'Mickey puller'.

I know. I was so close to having a complete seizure that I fell about laughing instead. Then, just as I thought everything was back on track Joe came in all agitated and alarmed to tell me that someone had parked a JCB outside the garda station the night before. I threw him a wary glance over the heap of paperwork on my desk. This had better be good.

'And . . . ?' I coaxed, pleading with him to get to the point right now as I didn't have the energy to cope with any catastrophic out-of-the-blue scenarios today of all days.

'I think it was Martin,' he continued, sounding confounded and wiping his brow anxiously with a well-washed and ironed hanky.

'And Martin did what?' I encouraged with a nod of my head, Martin being one of the RTPs as I called them. Ruffty Tuffty Pipeliners that is. Pipeliners it seems have nothing at all to do with panty liners but you could safely say they have a lot to do with dirty holes, the sort that these fellas I'm spending my days with love to dive into at a moment's notice.

'He went to the pub!' Joe shrieked, the momentum of his voice gathering speed at a startling rate. 'And of course he got himself completely drunk and fell asleep in the JCB and was still drunk at seven in the morning when he decided to drive the bloody thing on to the job to meet Danny!' The poor man was practically foaming. And as much as I liked him he was obviously no good in a crisis. I could have killed him.

'And then,' he said, throwing his arms up in the air and beginning to pace, 'he refused to stop when some poor inexperienced member of the force tried to pull him over.'

'So where is he now?' I asked kindly, which was very nice of me as I just wanted to cry with frustration and slap Joe in the face.

'That's just it. I don't know. He kept on going and he's not answering the mobile phone. What am I going to tell Mr Ryan? He'll go mad!'

He can get in the bloody queue first, I thought, smoothing my hair with my hands so that I didn't strangle Joe on the spot.

That little predicament took up the next two hours and my entire lunch break. Half of the men on site took up the challenge to find Martin. There was lots of ringing around and cursing until eventually he was found fast asleep in the JCB up a concealed alleyway not five minutes from where the lads were working. While the men were busy searching I was left with a hysterical project manager to comfort which took several cups of tea, half a bag of sugar and the very very last drop of patience I could muster.

Finally I found myself putting on my jacket with spent arms, ready to make my escape. My plans to abscond were going very well. (Alarm set, answering machine on, no appliances exploding or sudden appearance of Mr Ryan.) Just as I shut the door, The Legend and Bear (I know, don't even ask) yelled at me from behind what looked like a clapped-out camper van and warmly invited me to join them in a drink. Sure wouldn't it be great crack altogether if I went to the pub with them instead of going home?

I was very troubled by their invitation (OK repelled and horrified if you must). I didn't really want to go to the pub with them but I didn't want them to think I was being a horrible unsociable cow either.

'Ah come on, don't be a granny about it!' The Legend shouted at me. 'I'll even buy you a drink. How about that? And if you're really lucky I'll bring you home with me. What do ya say, come on.'

Jesus, I was terrified. I'd love a cigarette, I thought wearily, berating myself for not being a happy smoker who always had a friend to turn to when being coerced into going to the pub with a bunch of intimidating and seriously misguided men.

But do you know what? I really fancied a drink. I won't kid you any longer by saying I really really wanted to go home and spend yet another hour packing and sorting for the morning, when I could be relaxing over a scoop or two. I deserved it. I was so drained. Sod the packing! I could always call in home for the bits and pieces I had shamefully neglected to bring with me because I had given into temptation instead.

'OK, count me in!' I said shaking off my fatigue with a twinkling smile.

The two of them nearly died with shock. So did I. Me go to the pub with them?

'You're serious? You'd come drinking with us? Haven't you a fella waiting for you somewhere then?' asked The Legend cocking an eyebrow and obviously trying his best to look coy.

'That,' I laughed, 'is none of your business.' Maybe he wasn't so bad after all.

I was pissed by eight o'clock. Isn't that disgusting? Here was I, the office clerk, of the 'has recently dumped her fiancé' fame having a ball of a time. I couldn't believe it as I sat squashed in between Martin (who had sobered up enough to come back to the pub) and Alan (another RTP all the way from Scotland). Just think this time last week I was all in a heap over Ralph and now look at me. Surrounded by dozens of men. Wasn't it gas?

While The Legend went to the bar to order me yet another vodka and as I sat chatting to Martin I realised that I hadn't really taken much time to assess the loss of said almost-husband of mine and how it might affect my future. Which was a bit cold of me really, wasn't it? I mean Ralph could have said all those awful things because he was simply smarting from my drunken outburst, couldn't he? Let's face it though and be honest, shall we? I didn't care. And you don't blame me either, do you?

I mean who wouldn't rather be squashed in the corner of a pokey pub with a dozen fellas all under the age of thirty and enjoy watching them practically beat the shite out of each other in a desperate race to buy you your next drink? Instead of, shall we say just for argument's sake, attempting to have a one-sided conversation with a wimpy, tight-arsed fella (i.e. Ralph) who makes you feel it was about time somebody invented a vibrator that could kill spiders and open jars of pickle so you wouldn't have to bother with him in the first place? Well, me for starters.

OK maybe I should be mourning the loss of Ralph the Accountant, just a little bit. Normally, after I've just broken up with my boyfriend I'm devastated. I spend at least a fortnight weeping hysterically at the slightest hint of a love scene on the telly and curse every couple I know. I spend days ripping their relationship to shreds because I am so lonesome and at a loss as to how I couldn't keep a fella interested for more than a week. Why was everything in my life so wrong and out of proportion? And I don't just mean my bum or shade of lipstick. But this time I really felt different. Everything felt right.

Normally when everything feels right I panic and get hysterical, convincing myself something must be wrong because everything is great. And you know what that means? Oh yes. Hands up if in your darkest hour you have spent like me hundreds of hours inspecting every single inch and orifice of your body. Probing, rummaging and pinching in your search for sneaky bits of cellulite which might be hiding just under your skin or under the roots of your hair? (Well, you can't be too careful.)

Waiting and watchful, these cute little bastards are like a bloody SWAT team suddenly jumping out of nowhere (usually when a potential mate is happily feeling one's bum) all ready to take a bow, flash a beaming smile and wreck your next relationship. I used to think that I would gladly die on the spot if anyone became intimate with my lumpy bits. Well not just anyone, I mean a man. Imagine if a possible boyfriend caught a glimpse of them! Or even worse, what if they saw my stretch marks – and I couldn't even get out of that one by saying I'd had a baby.

Unless, of course I tied rings around myself and spouted a long and detailed yarn about becoming pregnant then being forced by my barbaric and heartless parents to go and 'live down the country' until the poor child made its entrance into the cruel cruel world. Oh, how I had suffered before my thirteenth birthday. Maybe that would work?

My all-time favourite pastime when feeling suicidal and ugly used to be locking myself in the loo for ages and making appalling faces in the mirror. So while Dad nearly took the door off its hinges before it was too late and with Mother hollering and giggling up the stairs at him: 'That's what you get for drinking fourteen pints of Guinness, you stupid fool!' I'd happily ignore them both as I vainly searched for lines and wrinkles that simply weren't there but had to be there hiding somewhere. Why else had boyfriend number twenty dumped me?

When I would eventually return to normal sociable life (where I'd be forced to converse with people who were lucky or gorgeous enough to have lovers) and I'd take great offence at those who paid me thoughtful and kind compliments by allowing my self-esteem (which had barely risen to its knees, since some mean and abominable ex-boyfriend had trampled all over it) to convince me they were only taking the piss. But you know what? I wasn't going to bother with all that utter madness this time. And I didn't care one bit that Ralph's mother hated me. Why should I?

I was no longer 'Gina Birkendale engaged to Nauseous Ralph'. I was now 'Single Gina Birkendale having a ball in the pub with heaps of blokes one week to the day since dumping vile and ugly accountant Ralph'. Now that was something to celebrate! And celebrate I did. With virginal enthusiasm.

And then I celebrated some more when Danny

turned up by dedicating my next cocktail to him. So by the time Jason made his appearance I was oiled. Lashed. Plastered. My kidneys were about to vote on strike action, demanding overtime or else they'd pack in and go home. Which was really something I should have done.

I didn't, needless to add. Instead I happily ignored the searing pain in my back and had another drink. This one being essential, an absolute 'must have', as Jason, I realised with nervous shock, was making his way through the crowded tables towards me.

I hardly took the time to thank The Legend as he stood on a nearby stool to hand me over yet another drink. I grabbed it, hastily poured in the mixer and taking a large mouthful eyed up Jason who was now trying his best to squeeze past Danny so he could sit beside me. Dear God, his bum would be next to mine!

The romantic side of my sodden brain went into overdrive. (All right then maybe not the romantic side. Call it the 'getting ready to pull' side if you have to.) It really is a curse being a woman in love (or in lust). And isn't it amazing how in the presence of someone you're desperate to snog you can suddenly sober up in a short thirty seconds and become fixated with your appearance? You know, is your best leg the one in view?

But then I remembered Marlene Dietrich saying something about fellas being more interested in women who are interested in them, than a woman lucky enough to have beautiful legs. Trust a successful and gorgeous woman to come up with something like that.

Speaking of sumptuous and dazzling women, there was a very leggy blonde at the bar and her legs looked like legs. The kind of legs women are supposed to have. Legs any bloke would love to knot around his neck, if you don't mind. Whereas I got Dad's legs so they're more like something you'd find hanging off a weary bar stool than the alluring pair of pins Miss Bubbly and Bright at the bar was sporting. The cow! I'd have to keep my eye on her.

And what about my face? Would he notice that my mascara was being far too lazy and negligent to make me look enticing? That he'd have to settle for making eye contact with a twenty-something woman looking more like she's desperate to get herself to bed, than get him to bed?

I hurriedly fiddled with my hair which was a complete waste of time as I knew it looked like a neglected shrub which had been trampled on and overlooked consistently by its hapless owner. I tried to plait it but it refused point blank to co-operate and I swear I could hear it sniggering at me for forgetting that a woman's first job in life (along with owning at least one cleavage-enhancing bra) is to choose the right shade of hair colour. If I wasn't so distracted I'd have shorn every inch of it off there and then and bought a bloody wig.

But I was tormented. Jason was waving his

denim-clad arse right in my face as he struggled to put down his pint and find room to squash in beside me. I was breathless and in need of a ventilator by the time he'd snuggled in and made himself comfortable. But I didn't have time for such dramatics because another more vital thought was pulling at me, yanking at my slightly sobered up responsible side and begging for attention. I was quite shocked I suppose when I finally growled 'What?' to myself as I was quite happy squashing up to Jason.

And then it hit me. Jesus! Was I ready for sex? I mean that's what was hopefully going to happen. Squash first, then sex. My mental checklist started to whirr and grind into action just as Jason turned to face me.

'Gina, you're looking well!' he bellowed, his knee rubbing off mine. Oh bliss! (Had I taken my pill? Did I have clean knickers on?) 'I hope the lads are behaving themselves tonight,' he smiled.

My heart leapt, so did my hand and I spilt vodka all over my top. 'Fuck off,' I hissed to my inner wisdom, none too silently.

'Now who are you telling to fuck off?' Jason asked with a sharp intake of breath and pretending to sound hurt as he dazzled me with those amazing eyes. (God, what I wouldn't give for his lashes.)

I exercised enormous restraint. I told myself I wasn't pissed. Or desperate. Who was I kidding?

'No one,' I replied with a small baby laugh.

'Just talking to yourself again. Jesus, you're a weird one. Do you know that? You're mad,' he announced, winking at me. The dirty flirt! 'Are you enjoying the job then?' he continued, taking a slow sip from his pint.

God, now I wished he would just feck off and leave me alone. How was I supposed to hold a rational conversation with him if he insisted on looking at me when he was speaking? It was bad enough that my inner thoughts were ganging up on me insisting that I keep my bum well out of sight in case he caught a glimpse of it. He could have at least had the courtesy to address the table instead of twinkling and squashing and letting his arm brush off my knee all the time. I swallowed and decided I'd better say something in case he thought I was a loony.

'It's great, I'm really enjoying it,' I muttered, still on the far side of incoherence and trying not to sway and fall in a heap. I was so drunk.

The Legend all of a sudden decided to join our table and insisted on having a robust conversation with Jason about the weather. In particular the wind which was 'cold enough to dry the shite off a dog's arse'. And speaking of which, most of the lads now had frostbite after working in polar conditions all day, he happily told the entire pub.

I in the meantime was dying for a wee. I grabbed my chance and was shocked to find myself flashing Jason a filthy drunken smile (which I hoped would render him gagging for my return) while I hurriedly dashed to the loo in an effort to fight off a wretched bout of motion sickness, easily accounted for by my not having any lunch and then assaulting my body with far too much alcohol.

My poor kidneys were reeling from the onslaught and were insisting via a shrieking pain in my lower back that they had whiplash. The bastards! How dare they let me down at a time like this.

I went to the loo and allowed my kidneys time for a quick euphoric dance then eyed up my cleavage in the mirror. I got a terrible fright. It wasn't there. I couldn't find it. Who did I think I was trying to tempt a fella with my boobs? Boobs that had gone into hiding and refused point blank to bloom and look pert and delicious? I got busy shuffling and pulling. It was very embarrassing not to mention potentially catastrophic and I hoped to God no one would come in and see me.

Why hadn't I got into the habit like Roisin of wearing sexy underwear all the time? Even if I was only going out to buy a packet of firelighters? I could almost hear Roisin shrieking: 'Have you learnt nothing, you never know who you might meet!'

I made myself imagine I was Roisin. Now what would she do if she were here? Oh what the hell, I thought, I'll ring her. I yanked out my mobile phone from my bag and dialled as quickly as I could.

'Hello?' I was saved. She was there. (I pictured another tenner floating from my hand into a waiting

Trocaire box with a gentle whish.) 'Roisin, it's me,' I giggled down the phone

'Gina? Is that you? Where are you?'

'I'm in the ladies in a pub near work. Listen, I need some help and quick. '

'You're drunk!' she hollered a bit too loud, leaving my poor ear singed from her screeching.

'I know. Isn't it mad? I'm sooo pissed!' I said, ignoring the pain in my ear and the strange looks I was getting from the other women in the cloakroom.

I quickly filled her in on all the details, begging for any help she could give me on how a very drunk woman with no cleavage could attempt successful seduction.

'Right!' she said, obviously thrilled to be in charge. 'First of all, body language. Watch everything he does.'

'OK watch his body language, very important,' I babbled in reply. 'What if he keeps on squashing and licking his lips? Is that a good sign?' I continued, feeling out of breath and suddenly wrecked.

'That's brilliant! Oh I'm so excited. You haven't been on the pull since we were in Greece. Welcome back, honey!' she roared at me, nearly choking with hysterics. 'Oh, and when you're making your way back to the table, don't forget to pull in your tummy for God's sake,' she warned.

'OK. Pull in my tummy. Anything else?' I asked, realising I'd been in the loo for ages.

'Yes, you better ring me in the morning and tell me everything or I'll never speak to you again.'

I hung up and finally finished rearranging my cleavage. I had one more objective look in the mirror. Jesus, here stands a woman with what could only be two very overripe peaches stuffed up her blouse. However I had managed to manipulate my two ripe peaches in to a fairly convincing 36D bust.

I was just about to give myself a big congratulatory hug when something else caught my attention. My mascara! It had run down my face leaving me looking like a bloody panda. No wonder everyone had been staring. Ignoring the woman who had just come into the ladies, I cursed loudly and ripped through my handbag looking for anything I could use so Jason wouldn't think I had gone blind since he last saw me. I eventually gave in when all I could come up with was a shower cap and a squashed tampon. Instead I lovingly applied another thick layer of mascara and ruffled up my hair a bit to give me a dishevelled angelic air.

I was about to leave when another apparition kindly walloped me over the head. What if we ended up in his place? I stopped in my tracks. Where was his place? Feeling faint, I sat on the sink. Would it be some awful hovel which was only populated by a few vermin, all his cousins from the country and a couple of dog-eared carpets? I continued to sit, rigidly.

Even worse, he could be one of these fellas still

living at home. Visions of having tea and polite conversation with his mum, instead of having sex with him manifested themselves nicely in my mind, nourishing my decision to slide off the sink and dramatically pat cold water around my brow. Which one usually does when one is suffering from a mighty urge to keel over, agreed?

Or what if he shared his home with a million gadgets? You know, remote control for the kettle, dangerous self-flushing loo, lightweight mobile phone which he'd be feeling up instead of me!

I tried to calm down. It didn't work. OK, if he did live alone what would happen if by chance he possessed not one scrap of loo roll? Valid and very crucial point. I mean men and hygiene aren't the best of friends, now are they? How would I take my make-up off? I thought, gasping for air. He'd be waking up beside a woman with sticky mascara, bleeding eyes and four million spots.

And what about the smell, my distressed reflection shrieked grimly as I gazed at myself through a very streaky mirror. After a boozy night in the pub I'd end up smelling like an orang-utang's armpit.

Fuck it, I told my argumentative reflection. If we let paranoia and apprehension get a hold of us now, we certainly won't go forth to said filthy house and indulge in rampant sex, we'll only go home, I warned severely. I stomped out of the loo, and did exactly what Roisin had told me. I rebelliously yanked in my stomach muscles so far that they nearly went flying out past my spine.

It didn't bother me one bit, as I attempted my best supermodel strut back to our table, that Jason was staring at me. I wanted him to stare at me.

Feel free to scrutinise! I bellowed internally as confidence in my new 'Naomi Campbell eat your heart out' walk soared to indecent drunken heights. I flashed him another dirty smile, revelling in my success, thrilled that I hadn't gone flying on a stray and soggy beer mat and landed in a heap on the floor. Then my bloody phone rang. Which scared the living shite out of me and left me hanging for dear life on the first supporting beam that came to hand. Which just happened to be some poor fella's head. He got very pissed off with me and started cursing. I was petrified.

'Answer yer bloody phone, missus and stop hanging off me feckin' head, will ya?' he growled.

I obeyed instantly. He was after all bald, furious, pissed and had a tattoo on his face in the shape of a skull and crossbones. Which quite plainly meant 'Don't fuck with me and if I tell you to answer yer phone then you'll answer yer phone!' I answered the phone.

'Hello,' I squeaked, not sounding in the least like a woman who had just found her cleavage and could march Naomi Campbell under the catwalk. It was Ralph. I removed my hand from Baldy's head and grabbed hold of a neglected stool.

'Oh, how are you?' I asked, stunned.

'I'd be a lot better if someone matching your sister's description hadn't shoved a bloody big potato up the back of my car!' he seethed. 'I'll be sending you the bill. I've had to get the train to work all week!'

Poor Ralph. Imagine having to share a seat on the Dart? And having to put up with some nameless commuter trying to read the back of his beloved newspaper? God love him. What an experience for one so much more important than the rest of us.

The Ralphs of this world do have a purpose after all. My head cleared instantly. I threw a deep and blazing smile at Jason who was still staring intently at me. I considered very carefully what I should say to Ralph so he wouldn't be confused about my thoughts on the matter. The poor love. And he does so hate to be confused.

'Fuck off, Ralph,' I said slowly and sweetly. 'And leave my sister alone or I'll kill you.'

Believe me, I meant it. He was still ranting when I hung up. I on the other hand was amazed at my performance. Wasn't I brilliant?

I chucked the phone into my bag and made my way back to the table which was laden down with glasses and ashtrays. I was desperate for a drink now that Ralph had had the impertinence to sober me up. I took my final steps towards my seat, managing to maintain eye contact with Jason all the way, until eventually I was sitting beside him again. He gave me a cheeky smile. God, I love this man!

'Who was that then? Your mother wondering where you are I suppose?'

'Yes,' I lied, dipping into my bag of smiles and lunging a whopper at him.

'Fancy another drink then, unless you're in a rush?' he asked with a raised eyebrow. I nodded and flung another outlandish smile at him as he made his way to the bar. God, I felt great.

'I'd better be off so,' said a quiet northern voice interrupting my 'God, aren't I great' affirmations.

Jesus, I'd forgotten all about Danny who was sitting on my other side. I felt wicked all of a sudden for totally ignoring him from the minute Jason had turned up.

'See you Monday, Gina,' he said, picking up his jacket and shuffling past me before I even had time to say goodbye. I felt terrible.

'Have a good weekend!' I yelled after him, my words unable to catch him up as he whisked out the nearest door.

'Shit!' I thought. That was so mean of me. I promised myself I'd send him up a huge pizza at lunchtime on Monday. But I still felt aghast and sheepish especially after he'd been so good to me all week.

And he hadn't even said a word when I'd sent onto site a prescription for 'Preparation H' pile cream which was supposed to help soothe the sixteen itchy piles I thought he had. In fact I was actually supposed to have sent him sixteen piles (which are apparently eight metres in length and have nothing whatsoever to do with having a sore arse). I'd been shrouded in shame all that day.

'He fancies you like mad, you know.'

Jesus! Who said that? Who fancies me?

The Legend had craftily slithered across the seat while Jason was absent and was happily slurping from his pint as he made himself comfortable beside me.

'Who fancies me?' I demanded abruptly.

'He does, doesn't he?' came the reply. 'Isn't love a gas thing all the same?' he continued contentedly.

I'd better explain something before I go any further and totally confuse you. Our general foreman (i.e. the inebriated fella slouched beside me) was not only jarred, he was also slightly deaf. He obviously thought I'd said 'he' instead of 'who'. Which left me about to burst into tears. Jason was on his way back with the drinks, affording me a mere ten seconds to uncover the identity of this man who fancied me.

Shit! Did he mean Jason or recently departed Danny? I resisted the urge to grab him by the shoulders, shake him violently and yell: 'Tell me who fancies me, you deaf bastard.' It would be disastrous if Jason heard me. Not to mention the possibility of my skirt being suddenly concealed under a blanket of sixteen pints and four packets of cheese and onion crisps.

I'd just have to bite my tongue and play a little game of elimination. If I managed to become entangled in a stomach-churning kiss with Jason, then obviously Jason was my secret lovelorn hero. If not it had to be Danny. Please God let it be Jason, I begged.

'Shove up in the bed there man, will you?' Jason had returned. And he'd said 'bed'. The Legend reluctantly started to move and no, I didn't give him a helpful shove. I sat on my hands as they couldn't be trusted not to glide themselves under his bum and bulldoze him out of the way.

At last Jason was settled at my side and we started to chat. In no time at all I had forgotten all about making sure he didn't see my bum and I couldn't have cared less if my mascara had packed up there and then and sodded off in a huff. One by one the others limped home or to the chippie. I didn't really notice as I was enchanted. Captivated. Really enjoying the conversation, which was so disgustingly flirty and fun. I was thoroughly enjoying myself.

Jason was so not like Ralph. The novelty of being in the company of a real hunk, one whom you'd be quite happy to have sex with in the middle of the living room floor even if your parents were trying to watch telly, was overwhelming. Plus he was intelligent and imaginative as well as simply sexy.

In case you're worried, I didn't make a show of myself and act like a brassy common madam. But as the evening progressed and the barmen were offering us either a lease or a boot out the door, I couldn't help wondering when it would happen. You know, the 'How are you getting home, shall we share a taxi?' stage of the evening.

And let's face it, I didn't really want to bring him back to our house. Mother would frighten him into submission and insist on showing the poor chap every single photo of my First Holy Communion. Jessie would make him drink herbal tea and demand he let her read her latest poem to him before she'd even allow him to sit down. And what about Tommy? Would he muscle in and cramp my style? Would Jason have to sit through brother and sister slugging it out in the back garden?

The words calmly tumbled out of his mouth before I had a chance to catch them.

Had he said, 'May I take you home?' or had I dreamt it? Were those the words that were settling gently around me like shimmering snowflakes? Or was I simply langered? My legs started to shake.

I was too frightened to ask him to repeat himself in case he thought I was thick. I could hear Roisin shrieking: 'Body language, body language!' at me. With a start, I looked closely at him. He was smiling. How very inconvenient. Roisin was shrieking again: 'Say something before it's too late, you stupid cow!'

I shut my eyes, gripped my handbag and said a quick Hail Mary.

'Yes.'

Chapter 8

'Get up will you, it's lunchtime!' Some fucker was thumping on my bedroom door (or was it just my blaring hangover turning itself up a bit?). I stirred slightly. What was that taste in my mouth? I grimaced, trying to open one eye. Oh my God! Jason!

I sat bolt upright and yelped with shock as I realised too late that some complete psychopath had tied a very heavy brick to my head during the night. I shuddered. I heard Dad thump down the stairs yelling at Mum that I must be dead. I flopped back down on my pillow and tried to get my bearings.

How did I get home? When did I get home? Oh Jesus! Did I bring Jason home?

I took a deep breath and gingerly probed the bed with an unobliging hand. A hand not in the least bit willing to be neighbourly with any strange bucket-sized hands it might encounter on the other side of the mattress.

Had I lassoed him with my electric blanket? I thought, cautiously turning my head to peek under the duvet. Tied him to the headboard with my tights perchance? I wondered with dread as I pawed at sticky mascara which was holding my left eye hostage.

Oh Christ! I felt something furry. I immediately screamed and shot out of bed and onto the floor. The furry article was my age-old teddy and not a silky-haired chest or a silky-haired penis. I was so relieved. No, I wasn't – was I or wasn't I?

I think I was relieved because now I wouldn't have to explain to my inquisitive mother why there was a six-foot giant in her front bedroom. I'd probably pass out with my booming headache anyway. (Which was just beginning to enjoy itself by demanding a full Irish breakfast before it would even consider entering into negotiations to sod off.)

But, I was disappointed. And I couldn't even be disappointed in a luxurious and dreamy 'he hadn't come home with me, but sure we'd had a great shag in his house first' sort of way. Shit! I couldn't even recall if anything so delicious had happened.

Imagine me not capable of remembering if I'd had sex. It's one thing not to remember how one got home and it's quite forgivable to spend three weeks speculating if you've left your bag, keys and make-up in the back of a taxi. But not remembering if you've had sex! And not just any old sex, mind - sex with a hunk.

I checked under the bed just in case. And no, he wasn't there so I couldn't ask him. I was perplexed and annoyed.

I suppose I could have tried Roisin's trick of flinging my knickers at the wall. You know, if they stuck then we did, if they breezed wistfully onto the carpet then we didn't. Granted it was one way of finding out but I was so disgustingly groggy that any endeavour on my part to chuck my knickers anywhere other than in the laundry basket would unquestionably end in misery or a huge row.

I could just see it now. One half-hearted fling from me and they'd float lazily out my bedroom window and moor themselves nicely on Mr Markham's head (who was a great one for pottering in his garden of a weekend morning). And no, I didn't feel I could cope with explaining that one to him.

'Sorry about that, Mr Markham! Just trying to find out if I had sex last night. And while you're there, could you have a look and tell me if they're all gooey?'

I shuddered again, imagining him thudding on our front door with my crumpled knickers in a plastic bag. I felt myself wilt as I pictured him verbally swiping at whichever one of my innocent family greeted him at the door, our furious neighbour informing them (in case they didn't know) that a dirty stopout was in their front bedroom hurling knickers at the neighbours. Oh

God, I wasn't ready for that!

Come to think of it I didn't even know where my knickers were (which prompted me to scrutinise myself as I squatted on the floor). I hoped to God that I was still wearing them. What if I had decided to fling them into some stranger's back garden last night during, shall we say, wild intercourse with said giant. I had a discreet peek. No such luck. They were still there hiding under my tights. Dear Jesus, I had slept in my tights. You'll be pleased to hear I then managed to get myself into an appalling armlock as I attempted to get the bloody things off while forcing myself to get up off the carpet and into the shower.

Note: Do not attempt this at home. It is not clever to try and rip off your knickers and elevate yourself off the carpet when you're obscenely hungover. And can't remember if you've had sex.

Particularly when you're in a mad rush having just recalled that you're supposed to be moving house in a couple of hours. And are getting sod all help from a fuzzy brain that refuses to brief you on whether or not intercourse has taken place and instead allows you entertain the screaming possibility that you might be pregnant.

I bravely limped into the bathroom, averse to confronting my reluctant undies again.

'If you dare struggle this time,' I threatened, 'there'll be no boil wash for you, my friend. It'll be straight in the bin!' I snapped as I defied my knickers to resist the tuggings of one wildly exhausted woman. Which wouldn't gain them any brownie points as this woman was also suffering from inner turbulence and an unholy urge to wee. Thank God they eventually decided to behave themselves and slipped off nicely with the audacity to wonder what all the fuss was about.

I had the quickest shower humanly possible. I began to panic as I could swear our bathroom clock was jeering at me and having a great laugh as it reminded me I had less than an hour to go before I was supposed to meet the girls.

'Shit, fuck and bollocks,' I swore back as I lavished my smoky smelling hair with Mum's cleanser instead of shampoo. Another five minutes was wasted as I washed it out and tried yet again to remember what had happened last night. (Oh alcohol, you are a brazen bastard.)

I hastily scrutinised my vodka-hammered frame for any telltale signs that I had thoroughly enjoyed a night of raw passion with the gorgeous Jason.

I didn't find any hand imprints the size of a spade gloriously decking my willing flesh. Not one. Shit! And, no, there wasn't a single mark adorning any part of me to suggest Jason had consumed me with the desire of a debauched caveman. Bugger!

In fact I can't say I was engraved with teeth marks or any other emblem which might comply with mind-blowing sex having taken place.

My worn out body and I sulkily made our way

into the bedroom to attempt the next hurdle of getting dressed. And then we made our way downstairs to see if any member of our sober family would make us a nice cup of tea and perhaps throw light on the subject of how we got home. Did we arrive in a taxi? Did the milkman feel sorry for us and give us a lift? Had we simply passed out in the hall and some kind soul had put us to bed (and been far too polite to remove one pair of slightly small and very clingy tights)?

I sank into a kitchen chair wondering if Dad could be bribed into helping me move all my stuff to the flat. I didn't really want to ask Roisin, not now that I was floored with a vast and vicious sore head. She'd kill me.

I got the eye from Mum who was busy pretending to make toast.

'You're still drunk.' (Very rich coming from a woman not in the least bit chaste or spotlessly sober on an average Friday night.) I got up to put the kettle on. Mum, fed up now with making toast, had instead decided to clatter the crockery to within an inch of its life.

The toaster hadn't been in the least bit co-operative, its jaws declining to be prised open by my highly-strung parent even though she had brandished a bent fork threateningly over its head. Obviously Mum was still smarting heavily from the loss of accountant son-in-law, and the brass of eldest daughter to arrive home lush with lust and drink.

She continued to bang pots and clean down surfaces with uncharacteristic vigour. Her efforts beaming with the finesse of an elephant tottering in four-inch stilettos, if you don't mind. If I hadn't been half-asleep and still pissed I'd have been terrified.

'And just who was that fella that dropped you home?' she said sharply, flinging a saucepan into the nearest cupboard where it landed with a boom.

I made a lovely racket of my own as the kettle dropped from my hands and landed in the sink with a loud clank.

'What fella?' I demanded as I spun around a bit too quickly making my heart race which in turn almost caused me to faint from the thrashing in my head.

'That tall fella with the accent. He rang on the bell and handed you over to your father like a bag of spuds. I could have died.'

I nearly died myself. Instead I hung on to the sink to stop myself from quivering.

'It certainly wasn't Ralph,' she snorted. 'He'd be far too polite to arrive like that at four in the morning,' she tutted, wiping her hands on a teacloth and looking fierce. 'And you were so drunk you wouldn't stop laughing. It was disgraceful. I'm sure I saw the Markhams looking out their window at us. I suppose he was one of those eejits you're working with?' she snarled, yanking the kettle from my quaking hands and noisily filling it to the brim.

I nodded in reply as I tried to piece together the events of last night. Jason had walked me home! Had we kissed? Had he held my hand? Had I made an idiot of myself, I thought with a gasp. I made myself take lots of deep breaths. Contrary to what Mother was saying I was quite sure Jason wouldn't just simply thrust me in the front door and run away. Surely he had said something? Exchanged some pleasant four-in-the-morning chitchat with my father maybe? Enjoyed a brief but gentle bonding with him as I was passed from a set of muscle-bound arms to the nearest available chair perhaps?

I took a few more deep breaths and prepared myself for the noxious job of trying to entice and engineer all the outrageous details of my abrupt arrival home from Mum. Who let's face it was in a hot snot and she wasn't the only one. My hangover was now quite adamant that if I didn't stuff myself with everything in the fridge it would relentlessly enjoy making me suffer until I was forty. Or fifty. Which I could live with if it was a wine hangover or even a beer hangover but Mr Vodka Hangover is as we all know a bastard. And wouldn't be fooled into sodding off by my eating one slice of toast. Oh no, he wanted the entire pan. With four pounds of butter, a jar of marmalade and several pots of coffee. The unyielding uncompromising fucker!

I bravely chose to ignore the nausea in my stomach and persevere. I didn't need reminding that time was not on my side so my hangover would just have to sod off for now. The only way around Mum was to tell her what she was dying to know. (And she was dying — I could tell by the way she was scouring the inside of an empty coffee jar and giving me venomous looks.)

'That was Jason,' I mumbled, pretending to be engrossed in making a large pot of tea.

No reply.

'He's a civil engineer from Wales,' I continued, pouring boiling water into the pot and clattering around a bit myself.

Mum's only response was a loud 'Humph.'

'He's related to Tom Jones, you know.' (I said this very matter-of-factly knowing quite well that next to her beloved Frank, Mother would gladly feck off with Tom Jones if he asked her.)

'Really!' she squeaked, momentarily forgetting to look snarly.

One to me.

Information had been handed over as requested and may God forgive me for being such a liar. I remained silent as I poured the tea and watched Mum's face twitching with curiosity and a barely restrained urge to meddle.

'What a pity he couldn't stay for tea though I suppose it was a bit late, and he was in a rush after all.'

I immediately stopped all the pouring and clattering. What did she mean 'couldn't'? Why was he in a rush? I threw her the best smile I could radiate without locking my jaws.

It was my turn again as we sat at the table, both of us ignoring the tea and casting vengeful glances at one another through half-closed lashes. (Mine still being a bit sticky and Mum's bedecked eyes not in the least prepared to divulge or enlighten me just yet.) All the while we smiled and pretended to be enthralled with the washing which was hanging half-heartedly on the line.

'He's very well off, you know.' (May God have mercy on my deceitful soul but when needs must etc. It was worth a try as there was nothing my mother cherished more than a fella with cash.)

I waited patiently as I sipped my tea. Although inside I was itching to yell at her to speed up immediately and dispatch the goods, before my nerves exploded all over the table.

'Yes, well he was quite well-dressed, now that I think about it,' she said suddenly, fiddling with her hair. 'What a pity he had to get up so early this morning to collect his sister from the airport. I'm sure he was dying for a cuppa after carrying you home.'

At last! I sighed contentedly and closed my eyes. She had said the magic words, 'collect his sister'. I was so delighted that I wouldn't have to re-route the entire conversation from scratch to the colour of Tom Jones' boxers. My whole body relaxed. No wonder Jason hadn't been able to offer me an invitation back to his place. His sister was coming.

(Not his wife or his boyfriend, his sister!)

Nothing out of the ordinary there, I'm sure you'll agree? I mean it wouldn't be the done thing, would it? Me rushing around his place at six in the morning like a maniac, trying to locate my bra in case his sister found it swinging from his bedpost, for example.

A perfect explanation for Jason acting like a heartless fucker, don't you think? No holes the size of a crater waiting to be examined and poked at there, wouldn't you say?

I greeted my brother as he came into the kitchen and rummaged around looking for something to eat. I smiled pleasantly at Dad and Jessie as they fought for the remote control. I positively ignored the nasty thought that was worming its way into my head and whispering loudly at me.

'Maybe he's only a filthy liar.' (Naah!) 'And he didn't actually fancy me at all.'

I'm being idiotic, aren't I? Allowing the consequences of drink and my fascination with the size of my own arse to scream 'deluded hussy' at me: 'And he just couldn't wait to dump me home.' (Oh My God!)

Isn't it a pain in the arse when a seed of doubt has been broadcast? Sprinkling itself casually upon you. Ruffling you lightly at first then dusting you effortlessly before finally punching you into submission with roaring success. Shit! You fucking bastard!

I sprang up from the table and immediately rang

Roisin to tell her my conquest from last night was nothing but a lying toad fucker who had heartlessly dumped me home with some pathetic excuse about his sister arriving at the crack of dawn.

'You're being ridiculous,' Roisin replied with a frustrated tut.

'I'm not!'

'You are! Now pull yourself together. I'm on my way and I'll be there in half an hour. We'll talk about it then.'

'OK,' I whimpered.

Just wait until I see you on Monday, Jason Ward, I thought bitterly, as misery adhered to me like quick-drying cement.

I would love to tell you that the rest of the day passed me by in a hazy blur, that the move to the flat went without a hitch, and I was finally allowed to snuggle up and spend the evening holding hands with my two new companions. No, not Roisin and Lotty. I was thinking more along the lines of Self-pity and Loathing. A huge batch of Self-pity and Loathing, which had been dumped on me by one wretched bastard who got me drunk and left me on the doorstep. (I thought it was only taxi drivers that did that. How humiliating!)

I was quite content at the thought of having one 'friend' on either side of me as I sat on the sofa and stuffed myself with greasy chips and a family bag of Cadbury's best. I would have been quite happy indulging the three of us for at least a week. I was suffering terribly from a good old dose of the hangover blues mixed with those appalling feelings you're battered with for free when you know you've made an idiot of yourself.

I found myself physically unable to join in the festivities of moving house. There was far too much good humour floating around for my liking. Lotty's excitement positively irritated me. Roisin's enthusiasm and non-stop chatter, which accompanied her in bucketfuls nearly finished me off.

My entire family helped with the move which I thought was very unsympathetic of them. Mother passed around cups of tea and cake when the girls arrived to collect me and Dad came home early from football training to lend a hand. The bastards! They couldn't wait to get rid of me. All I wanted to do was disappear back up to bed and mope, thoroughly indulge my grief at being hard done by and tell them all to get stuffed.

Before I knew it I had kissed Mum and Dad goodbye, promised Jessie I'd ring her that night and allowed myself to be coerced into going for a meal with Tommy some evening that week.

I hardly noticed that we had pulled up on the hard shoulder of the motorway until Roisin started cursing. (She's very good at cursing and along with being able to apply fake tan to her entire body in less than thirty seconds it's a talent in which her creative powers are at their most innovative.)

'I don't believe this!' she yelled, banging her hands off the steering wheel.

I stirred slightly in my self-indulgent 'all men are fuckers' trance.

'Oh shit!' boomed Lotty.

Her voice reverberated inside my heavy head and made me feel like slapping her. Instead I forced myself to glance out over her bobbing head so I could see for myself what all the fuss was about. Steam was hissing loudly from under the bonnet of the car. I closed my eyes and cursed silently. Then I opened my eyes and cursed very loudly.

Roisin in the meantime had flung open her door and was attempting to prise up the bonnet without burning her fingers or ruining her make-up. Neither of her attempts was successful. Five minutes later she stuck her damp bushy hair back in the window and gave the two of us despairing looks.

'I can't get it open!' she hollered, all sweaty and wiping her forehead with the back of her hand. 'Jesus! Is my mascara everywhere?' she asked with a pant, inspecting her face in the wing view mirror. The wind from passing cars nearly took her eyelashes off not to mention her very short skirt.

'Let me have a look.' (The shock of hearing my own voice almost sent me back to unconsciousness.)

Grumbling loudly I pulled the inside lever which apparently is supposed to release the bonnet (not that I'm a mechanic or anything) and hopped out of

the car. Lotty followed my lead and we both piled
out onto the motorway. The wind whistled up our
bums and whipped through our hair leaving the
three of us looking like we had hairstyles that
belonged on top of a cake. My headache got worse,
Roisin's language became even more flowery if that
were possible and poor Lotty simply looked her
usual useless woebegone self. Any minute now a
seriously good row was going to break out, I could
feel it. The bloody bonnet was still refusing to
budge.

'Have you got an umbrella?' I demanded.

'What do you mean, have I got an umbrella?'
Roisin snarled back.

I bit my tongue. 'In-the-car. Have-you-got-an-
umbrella-in-the-car?' I said this slowly and
deliberately not to eliminate the possibility of a
misunderstanding but to give myself time to calm
down so I wouldn't let a roar and try to pull her hair
out.

'I think there's one in the boot,' she replied with
slit eyes.

'Right!' I snatched the keys from her hand and
marched towards the back of the car ignoring some
passing motorist who was beeping at us and making
rude gestures out the window. Another wanker. I
then made my first attempt at rooting through
Roisin's car boot which was chock-a-block with all
my gear.

Five minutes and a lot of foul language later I

produced Roisin's pink polka dot rather elegant umbrella from underneath a dishevelled plant Mum had insisted I bring to my new home. I made my way to the front of the car which was still steaming and gurgling as if trying and failing to digest an extra spicy vindaloo. I brandished my weapon menacingly at the bonnet. Roisin and Lotty sensibly backed away from the actions of a recklessly emotional woman flaunting a once harmless umbrella, which had suddenly taken on the unnerving likeness of a scud missile, and hovered beside a windblown mass of nettles and bushes.

With terrific zest that nearly floored the two of them I forced the tip of the umbrella under the bonnet. Roisin and Lotty started having a whispery conversation under the foliage about how I had obviously gone mad since last night. I ignored them even though I felt like yelling 'Feck off and let me be deranged, you bitches, and I'm damn well going to enjoy it as I have fuck all dignity left anyway.' (I was still draped in anguish and embarrassment after being unloaded on the doorstep like that.) 'And Jason,' I wanted to holler, 'thinks I'm as significant as a boil on a dog's bum!'

But instead of hollering I rolled up my sleeves and did a lot of twisting, turning, effing and blinding until at last with a little 'ping' the bonnet flew open, nearly taking the skin from my chin with it as the car belched more hot steam into the air.

Triumphant, I flung the umbrella to the ground

where the wind elected to pick it up and deposit it in the middle of the fast lane. I closed one eye and watched in horror as right on cue a German freight carrier thundered past and zoomed over it, splattering the poor thing like a marrowfat pea all over the motorway. It didn't look like a very elegant umbrella now.

Speechless, Lotty and Roisin quietly made their way back to the car and stared at the debris littered on the road. Bits of pink polka dot fabric flitted here and there. The two of them eyed me up. The danger was over. I was exhausted so there was no chance of me letting loose at either of them. In fact I felt great. I gave Roisin a big smile.

'I'm sorry about the umbrella. I'll buy you a new one tomorrow. '

'Jesus, you're a mad bitch, Gina, do you know that? Dangerous!' She smiled.

Lotty did a little dance on the side of the road. So did I. Our good humour restored didn't change the fact that we were still stranded in the middle of the motorway with a clapped-out car.

'Will we flag someone down?' suggested Lotty.

'Well we could,' commented Roisin, 'but what if some loony stops? That's the last thing we need.'

'What about the AA?' I asked Roisin as hailstones began to batter the three of us.

'Oh, Jesus no!' replied Roisin looking sheepish. Lotty and I stared at her. 'It's just I forgot to set up the direct debit with the bank.'

I shut my eyes and prayed for inspiration and a few buckets of patience.

'What about a taxi then?' said Lotty who was now shivering dramatically, dancing on the spot and rubbing her hands together uneasily.

'Lotty you're a genius!' bellowed Roisin. 'Let's get back in the car first before my tits fall off from the cold. Now who's got a phone with them?' she said, ushering us towards the car which was now swaying from side to side in the wind.

Why don't we live in the Caribbean, I thought as a huge gust of wind caught my hair and yanked it sideways, a bit like the hairdresser does while she's informing you that your locks are in bleedin' tatters and are split right up as far as your eyebrows. We could be sitting under a tree, eating mango in the sun and not stranded here in the pissing rain and freezing cold.

Huddled in the car we made ourselves as comfy as possible, though Roisin's shivering body was still vibrating like a tuning fork as I pulled out my phone.

'We should get two taxis. One for Lotty and me, and one for you and your gear,' suggested Roisin. 'What do you think?'

Jesus, I wished I'd stayed in bed. 'OK,' I said, dialling the number of our local rank. 'What about the car, can we leave it here?'

'Oh, fuck it! I'll send Jack out to pick it up later. He'd do anything for me,' Roisin replied with a satisfied smile.

I got through to the taxi rank. I have only one thing to say. Why are men so thick?

'You've broken down, have ya?'

'Yes!' I replied, realising I was talking to someone with the IQ of a bar of soap.

'I tink you've got de wrong place, missus. Dis is a taxi service not de bleedin' AA ya know.'

'I know!' I yelled, barely restrained as the last drop of energy seeped out of my weary body and evaporated in front of me there and then. 'I want two taxis if that's not too much trouble.'

There was a silence as he started working on the mathematics. Trust me to ring a fella who wasn't blessed with intelligence or manners. I shook my head despairingly at the girls. Roisin immediately grabbed the phone.

'Now listen here, do you want our money or not?' she demanded in a Mafia-style tone which was very impressive and guaranteed to cure the most stubborn case of constipation. 'If you do, then get your lazy arse over here now you stupid fucker. We're freezing!'

It must have been something she said because two taxis rolled up behind us fifteen minutes later. I was so appreciative I could have kissed them. Thank God I didn't. The first fella, who had no hair on his head but a forest protruding from his nostrils, emerged from his car and started poking at the steaming engine when he should have been unloading all of my stuff into his car.

'Yiz have a hole in de radiator, what d'ya tink, Dermo?'

Dermo, whose brain was virgin territory when it came to thinking and who obviously enjoyed a loving relationship with his local chippie, if the size of his trousers was anything to go by, sauntered over and stuck his head under the bonnet.

'Jaysus, Frank, wimmin can wreck a car quicker dan a bleedin' crusher,' he said sucking in his breath and nodding his head rapidly in agreement with himself.

'Excuse me!' I roared, interrupting their profound observations that 'all women are utter liabilities and as thick as shovels' conversation. 'We'd like to get moving please, now!'

Fat Bastard and Baldy stared at me. Then with a 'who's the snotty bitch' shrug of his shoulders, Baldy instructed Lotty and Roisin to 'Ge' in da car'. Which meant I was left with shoulder-shrugging Fat Bastard to see me and my worldly belongings safely home. At least the two of them packed all my gear in the car.

Baldy yelled 'Good luck' at his mate, threw his eyes to heaven and sped off with Roisin and Lotty casting me a few 'poor bitch' looks from the back window as they disappeared up the motorway.

I was about to burst into tears. I quietly climbed into the back seat of the car while Fat Bastard wiped his brow from the exertion of all the loading. Christ. I bet he'd have a heart attack in the middle of the motorway simply to spite me.

'Where to den, missus?' he said with a discernible snarl. I gave him the address and prayed he'd leave me alone for the twenty-minute journey. No such luck. He insisted on informing me that 'wimmin and cars don't go' and we should know better at our age not to be 'feckin' around wi' tings we know nu'in abou''.

I pretended to be asleep. I was sure that somehow this was all Jason's fault. If he hadn't acted like such a pig last night I wouldn't be in this taxi in the first place. Instead my brain would have been elated and brimming with post-coital desire for him. And it definitely would have instructed me to enlist the help of Dad and Tommy and a decent car. Instead I had been lumbered with this social fuck-up thrilled to flaunt his lack of intellect (which had such an uncanny resemblance to a plumber's toolbox) and wave it around at everyone.

I flew out of the taxi when we finally pulled up beside the flat, flung the fare at Fat Bastard and snatched hold of poor unsuspecting Jack who had just roared up behind us in his car and instructed him to help me shift all my boxes and bags. He was so obliging. Roisin you fortunate old cow, I thought. I was never so glad to sit down.

'Weren't they a couple of eejits. Did he say anything to you on the way here, Gina? Our fella just grunted and picked his nose,' said Lotty with a tut.

Lotty typically had been busy in the flat since

early morning, and delighted in showing off what a brilliant job she'd done in cleaning the place up. She'd even hoovered, and swept the path. I felt even more inadequate. Couldn't score with a bloke to save my life and certainly wouldn't dream of hoovering up the leaves on the doorstep in a fit.

'He was horrible,' I said nearly bursting into tears. Honestly, I'd have to get a hold of myself. 'He went on and on about the car and women. It was terrible.' I slumped further into my chair, resisting the urge to lock myself in my new bedroom and sleep for the rest of the day.

'The bastard! We should complain. And our fella overcharged us,' yelled Roisin from the kitchen where she was busy making coffee and snogging Jack. The two of them were so lovey-dovey I felt like screaming. It was so unfair.

'So what happened last night then?' asked Roisin gently as she passed around the coffee and ripped open a packet of biscuits.

'I'm not really sure.' I started feeling a bit squeamish about the whole thing. I didn't want Jack knowing that I hadn't a clue whether I'd had sex or not, that I'd been shamefully delivered home in the middle of the night and had nearly thrown myself over the banisters trying to get my undies off. But there was no way he was going to leave, he was too busy fiddling with Roisin's hair and playing with her earrings.

'This is the fella from work who abandoned you,

is it?' enquired Lotty from the top of her coffee
mug. How could she!

'Yes,' I snorted, embarrassment flooding through
my veins.

'Well, did he say anything to you before he
scarpered?' she continued, oblivious to the fact that
I was about to die with shame.

'Not really, no.' What else could I say? He'd raced
off home with some pathetic excuse about his sister,
and I only knew that because my mother told me.

'He had to run because his sister was allegedly
arriving today. Isn't that right, Gina?'

I threw a red-hot scowl at Roisin. She'd said
'allegedly' so it sounded like 'alleeegedly' which
really meant 'Gina was dumped and yer man is a
bare-faced liar who delivered the first excuse he
could think of and legged it.'

'So,' started Lotty (God, I wished she'd shut up),
'you went to the pub, he fancied you like mad, you
drank yourselves rigid and then he walked you
home and couldn't stay or bring you home to his
place because his sister was coming today, is that it?'

Oh, rub it in, I thought giving her an exasperated
smile. 'In a nutshell, Lotty, yes.'

'That's grand then.'

'What's grand about it? He obviously doesn't like
me and couldn't wait to get rid of me!'

I shouldn't really have shouted at her, but I
couldn't help it. A rotten silence pulled up with a
screech and parked itself nicely beside us.

Lotty put on her best 'I was only trying to help, you ungrateful cow' face. I felt awful. The two lovebirds stared at the floor, and the only noise audible was my grumbling stomach and the dripping of the kitchen tap.

'Look, I'm sorry, Lotty. It's just that I feel such an utter idiot about the whole thing.' I gave her a small smile. It did the trick. I wouldn't have to spend the rest of the day feeling guilty for being a horrible bitch as well as a stupid one.

'I just think you're overreacting,' she said gently, twiddling with her hair. 'Maybe he wasn't lying. Maybe he does like you. Why not wait and see what happens on Monday?' Lotty looked at Roisin and Jack. They nodded in agreement then they all looked at me, their stares ganging up one by one. Was I being ridiculous?

'I've got an idea,' boomed Roisin, 'foolproof and guaranteed to find out what he really thinks.'

Oh God, she was suddenly looking very eager to sort my love life out. Lotty joined in her excitement and Jack gave her the thumbs up. I cringed and wondered if it were possible to drown oneself in four inches of lukewarm coffee.

'Jack,' she said giving him a puppy-eyed look, 'I'm sorry but I can't make it tonight, Lotty and I are needed here. You'll have to go to the pub on your own.'

Jack did look slightly miffed but nodded in agreement nonetheless.

'Why, what are you up to?' (Did I really have to ask?)

'We,' she said pointing to herself and Lotty, 'are going to sort you out. Make you so beautiful and sexy that this Jason will faint from the pain of a large erection before Monday is over, that's what!'

In helpless anticipation of whatever mischief Roisin was planning for later I spent the rest of the day stabbing open box after box of packing, channelling my anger by hanging up pictures and sorting out the kitchen. I resisted the urge to sling myself into bed with a large bottle of wine and lay siege to my body by throwing the contents of a small supermarket at it. That, I can tell you, wasn't easy.

I screamed internally as I thrashed the sofa cushions, nearly breaking three of my fingers. Honestly, beating the shite out of the furniture and causing a whirlwind is no way to exorcise those negative 'I never want to speak to anyone with a willy again' feelings unless of course you think it's fashionably therapeutic to spend the day in casualty and six weeks with a sling around your neck.

'Oh, don't put anything in there!' Lotty hollered at me when I then attempted to jam five large saucepans into the nearest cupboard. 'That's the gin press!' she informed me with a sly smirk. 'The drinks cabinet is in the living room but this one's just for us, our private stash,' she finished with a whisper and a very exaggerated wink.

Maybe she did have a brain after all, I thought, which was quite horrible of me really and made me interrupt my insane clearing up just for a second. I looked at Lotty as she lovingly made the lot of us big salad sandwiches. How could I be so awful to her? In her own way she was only trying to help and here I was acting like a right cow.

Something clicked inside my head and instantly relief thundered through my body wiping away and sweeping up all the vile fallout from last night. I felt like me again and sagged into the sofa I had nearly annihilated.

Maybe Lotty was right, I thought, for the first time allowing the possibility that Jason did in fact like me to rear its head. I decided to give the idea ten seconds to make its case before the jury of one. 'He sat beside me in the pub all night. This is an indisputable fact,' I snarled at the sofa, waving my finger at it, daring it to deny it. (One to the defence. I was beginning to feel things were going my way.)

I didn't have time however to become prematurely elated and pat myself on the back. The bastardly prosecution stood up with a cocky smile which suggested there was enough evidence stuffed up its sleeve to convince any jury, no matter how prejudiced or hungover. I held my breath and reluctantly suspended the congratulations for the moment.

'Maybe he was horny,' the prosecution roared. 'He changed his mind when he realised with an erection-withering gasp that your hair is the wrong colour.' (He probably preferred blondes, like the one at the bar.) 'Your legs are too short.' (True! He'd have to stand me on a barstool if he wanted a snog.) 'Your cellulite hides the fact that you do have nice thighs somewhere if only he could find them.' (How many men carry a vegetable peeler in their back pocket to help get rid of all the orange peel stuff?) 'And as for your nose!' (Shit! The prosecution are on the ball. Definitely one to them. I have a nose you could hang half a cow off.)

I picked at Lotty's furry handbag as I returned to my manic-depressed mode. However more flashbacks nudged themselves shyly forward and into focus.

'The Legend said 'he' fancied me.' (Contentment had again claimed its rightful place in the argument and stuck its tongue out. I sighed happily. And OK, I thought calmly and retrospectively, we didn't have sex. No need to get hysterical over that one.) 'But he did bring me home and everyone knows that if a guy walks you home and doesn't simply try to palm you off on the first stranger he sees outside the chippie then he fancies you like mad.' (I learned this one in sixth class, along with you can't get pregnant if you eat a large bunch of fennel after having sex.)

'So what if his sister was coming,' the defence added to bolster up my already convincing case. 'For God's sake, you can't convict a fella for doing the dirty just because he has a sister, now can you?' the defence argued urgently. (I was now feeling full of vim even though I was being absurdly childish.)

'It was obviously a blatant lie,' interrupted the prosecution scathingly before the defence had a chance to continue. 'If she was arriving on Aer Lingus flight 787, why hadn't he said so?' it demanded with a nasty smirk.

I practically ducked as the words flew by me like cannonballs. I had to admit, I didn't have an answer for my defence. I conceded and opened my arms to welcome Misery and Torture back into my life. I hardly had time to accept my fate before the defence bounced back into the thick of it, full of conviction and energy.

'Surely,' it bellowed, clamouring to be heard and completely ignoring me, 'there was no need for him to even mention his sister was arriving?' (Good point, I thought. I mean we were both ridiculously drunk and had hardly reached the rank of 'first date'.)

The defence was now well into its stride. 'Taking his sister out of the equation completely,' it hollered, 'maybe he was simply a real gentleman.' (I hadn't thought of that.) 'Therefore, he was much too polite to initiate sex with the secretary.' (I had to agree, I hadn't thought of that one either.) 'A secretary who,' came its bellowing interpretation gathering momentum at an alarming rate, 'he hardly knew.' (Naturally, he had to take into account that she was utterly langered and suffering from a hazardous lack of oxygen to the brain because her tights were holding her hostage from the knees up.)

The defence sat down, clearly elated and wearing an 'up yours, mate' look on its satisfied face.

Of course! I practically yelled, doing a little dance around the coffee table. I know! I've heard this word before. Respect. Maybe Jason was overflowing with respect for me and was far too wholesome to try and lower the tone by shagging me senseless. I had to consider (whether I liked it or not) that we'd consumed enough alcohol to fuel a Boeing 787. He might only be petrified that I'd think he was nothing but a chancer, I happily informed the new curtains Lotty had so lovingly hung up this morning.

The worst over I practically hugged the sofa as I flung myself back down. Guilty or not? I pondered as I fiddled with my jewellery. For the moment, not. Jason, I decided, had one chance to make his case. Naturally I was quite willing to take full advantage of this near certainty by arriving in on Monday morning looking as much like a raunchy hussy as my credit limit would allow. I was now a woman with a calling and a mission to complete. There was work to be done. I was going shopping.

Yes, I do love shopping. It's a guaranteed crowd pleaser as far as I'm concerned. It revives me and never fails to inject me with sweet addictive jabs of happiness that no man can plunder or steal. And I will admit that if I had buckets of money I'd spend every single day delighting and wallowing in the naked rush I get when I've found 'it'.

You know, the trouser suit that makes you look like you have legs. Skinny legs with perfectly shaped knees. And of course the unforgettable once-in-a-lifetime pair of jeans that you have to buy because they actually flatten your arse and don't make you look like you have a hippo living in your knickers.

Or the perfect bikini (granted you wouldn't be seen dead wearing it in the back garden in case the neighbours saw you) but it's perfect for prancing around on a continental beach. Why? Because you don't care who sniggers at your flabby behind as long as you don't bang into them on the flight home. Imagine the last minutes of your holiday being spent diving for cover under the nearest conveyor belt because you're convinced they'll all scream loudly at you, 'Remember what Miss Piggy said,' (followed by lots of hooting laughter) 'don't eat more that you can lift!'

It's a pity that men don't understand why women adore shopping. I know they can't do two things at the same time and they're a bit thick when it comes to not buying you a galvanised bucket for your birthday when you really wanted a Gucci watch. But why is all the fun in traipsing from shop to shop lost on them?

You can't leave them outside for two minutes while you go in and buy your knickers without them buggering off to find some electrical store or

other which is showing Sky Sports on the display
TVs. You emerge not ten minutes later to find your
fella has evolved into an eleven-year-old (he's now
doing a nail-biting embarrassing jig because
somebody scored) and you have to pretend you
don't know him.

Believe me even if you're a saint and unruffled
enough at that point not to kill him there's still no
chance you'll be able to encourage the possibility of
the two of you actually doing something together
(like buying him a revolting football shirt he can
wear to the next two matches, if you have the
strength). I mean, how many blooming relationships
have ended in a blazing row in Bewley's because
'our' cherished time in the stores is nothing short of
'a waste of damn good football-watching beer-
drinking time and money'? Millions. Apparently
nobody but a nutter would want to travel the length
and breath of town shopping until they pass out.
Even if there is a sale on in A Wear. Sure you might
as well be at home watching *Football Focus* which is
a lot more fun and won't send your credit limit
soaring sky high faster than the speed of sound. It's
just desperate, isn't it?

Speaking of men, Ralph was probably the worst
shopping partner ever. And I don't only think it was
because he was a bloke. I think it was as simple as
him being a complete doorknob. He was a bit on
the miserly side as well. I didn't actually realise it at
the time. I was daft enough to think he was the

more sensible one, practical and very good at not actually paying for anything.

I couldn't count the amount of times I came home with fifteen bags and an elated heart. Whereas Ralph would have bought a stapler and a cup of coffee. And if we went out for dinner afterwards I'd get a lecture on money management and 'going Dutch'. Apparently paying for my own meal would instil in me some drop of discipline which I lacked when it came to spending money. And paying for all our drinks over the meal was the least I could do to show I did in fact know when enough was enough and when to call it a day. The shrewd bollocks! When I think of what I could have bought in Boots with all that extra money instead of wasting it on endless meals and gallons of chianti. I felt sick. And annoyed. And then sad.

Why did I ever want to be with him on those terms? Was I as daft as a brush or did I actually think I couldn't find anyone else? Maybe I would never know. I was however desperate to learn from the experience. I would never again go out with a fella who got up at six in the morning to iron his shirts. I would never go out with a fella who made me buy my own meals all the time (including my last birthday). And simply to be on the safe side, I would never go out with a fella without first having lunch with his ex-girlfriend.

Except Jason of course. I was fairly confident that he wasn't a stingy old bastard like Ralph. I'd hardly put my hand in my purse on Friday night and for once had had enough money the next morning to buy a pint of milk and some loo roll.

Shopping is such a personal thing as well, isn't it? I can remember hundreds of times, millions even, feeling positively wicked. It usually happens to me when by some vile twist of destructive karma I find I'm stuck at the train station, perplexed and clueless as to why in the name of God I'm having a conversation with the weirdo slouched next to me.

Or when I've been dumped and left tragically bereft with only an unnerving and wilting excuse to comfort me. (Does 'I love you, but it's not going anywhere' said through pleading-for-understanding eyes sound bone-crunchingly familiar?)

So while you're left reeling, and desperate to give someone a bash with your handbag, commotion and confusion direct you cunningly to their first port of call: that nasty filing cabinet in your head, the one that catalogues with frightening accuracy the details of your first love/bra/bank statement and other personal disasters. The one that laughs as your heart plunges with elevator-dropping speed prompting you to get langered, suicidal or fan yourself down with a large and scathing curtain of self-doubt.

Well there's only one thing for it. Throw on your best gear, pile on the make-up, sell the offending male's car/golf gear or signed Man United T-shirt for a fiver to the milkman and frogmarch your abandoned heart through at least three massive department stores spending until you faint.

Unfortunately it's not something to be taken on lightly when you've just moved house. I was quite put out as I knew there was no way that I was going to be able to shop myself silly until the following morning. I was wrecked.

Instead I patted my credit card fondly and promised it a full day's fun tomorrow before making myself trawl through the millions of bags of clothes that had arrived with me. I haphazardly flung them on hangers, picture hooks and any nails that were peeping out from the wall and looking lonesome. By the time that was finished I looked about ninety and my bedroom looked like a charity shop. That was all I could do. I didn't care. I didn't even make the bed. I'd wait until tomorrow when I'd be normal again and wouldn't need to pee every ten minutes.

Lotty and Roisin felt much the same (not that their bladders were doing the Riverdance or anything) but Lotty wanted to stay home and chill out. She'd had a dream last night, she told us very enthusiastically, about a gin bottle sprouting legs and arms and running amok around our new flat which obviously meant that destiny intended us to relax for the night and get squiffy. So we were staying put. I would be the subject of Lotty's make-up skills for the night and allow Roisin practise putting knots and colour in my hair in the hope that I'd look dazzlingly fab for Monday.

We got busy around seven o'clock, after I had

miraculously managed to cook a very passable dinner for three. (For once my garlic bread didn't look like it had arrived with the coal and my pasta dish oozed authenticity, nicely disguising the hard bits.) Even though I had to postpone the shopping spree until the morning you couldn't have wiped the smile off my face with a Brillo pad. Not only was I about to reinvent myself, I could also cook. Doors of opportunity hurled themselves open as Roisin and Lotty devoured the first proper edible thing I'd ever cooked that didn't make them want to puke. I fantasised long and hard about Jason doing the same thing. I'd finally be able to bring a man home for dinner. One he wouldn't have to cook himself (unless of course he didn't mind bringing an extra large box of Rennies with him or a stray dog if he preferred. It certainly wouldn't go amiss if he fancied shoving it under the table and feeding the poor thing a frozen chicken breast).

I felt fresh and alive. I had been airlifted to a place where Jason would be frantic to ask me out. I would let him chase the new me around for a bit (I quite fancied a mixture of Darina Allen meets Melinda Messenger) before finally allowing him to catch me. Then I would pay Lotty and Roisin a fortune to bugger off for the night and presuming I didn't hack off any fingers or toes with Roisin's huge blender I would seduce him with my new pasta-making skills before letting him drag me off to bed.

The transformation began. We were all excited.

'I've only ever tried this colour stuff on the dog.' Roisin was engrossed mixing and pouring. I couldn't have cared less. 'But it came out lovely.'

'Do your worst!' I hollered, thrilled and aflame with visions of the 'new me'.

I was amazed. The whole thing only took twenty minutes. So while I sat with a plastic hat on my head and with Roisin burning the scalp off me with a very hot hairdryer ('It'll help it take!' she roared, with a big smile) Lotty pulled out her vast supply of make-up and started plastering.

Lotty loved make-up. She wouldn't be seen dead without it. It was her friend. Often and especially with her last boyfriend (who was a blatant fucker who had a nasty habit of standing her up only to arrive unannounced several hours later, usually about four in the morning) poor Lotty would be applying mascara and lip liner with enviable speed and precision simply so the guy wouldn't see the horrors of her white exposed face and make a bolt for the back door. Which in my book made her as mad as a hatter. I decided absolutely to set her up with one of the more hunky RTPs at the Christmas Party. It would do her the world of good to be with a scruffy fella who wouldn't know the difference between a bucket of foundation and a gallon of diesel.

Within the hour the two of them were finished. Thank God! I couldn't stand the excitement and non-stop chatter that accompanied the creating of my new image.

'No, don't look yet!' tutted Roisin when I attempted to make a grab for the mirror. 'I'm not quite finished,' she continued as she arranged, rearranged, shuffled and fiddled with my new copper locks. I sighed, realising there was no point in making a sly grab for the mirror as she'd kill me. Lotty was too busy trying to poke my eye out with an eyelash curler anyway.

'Now. You can look now.'

The two of them stood back, hands on hips, evidently happy now that all the haggling and conferring over colours and textures had finally been settled. I immediately snatched the mirror off the table. There was complete silence as I became enthralled with the image reflected back at me. For a second I thought my hangover was having the last laugh and I was experiencing some sort of apparition. Or that Roisin had somehow managed to glue a photocopy of an elegant but slightly outrageous model to the frame. I couldn't believe it was me. I was gorgeous, re-born, beaming!

My thatch of lanky brown hair had gone. In its place was a shimmering coppery curly mane that glistened teasingly under the lights as it practically exploded with colour. You could have sworn I had taken each individual strand and polished it until it glowed. And to totally thrill me senseless my new hair perfectly framed and paid homage to the wonderful job Lotty had done on my face. I had a button nose. The twenty-three-year-old with the coat hanger lounging around on her face had gone. If Ralph saw me now he'd faint. All of a sudden I wanted to march into his office and roar at him, looking all gorgeous and angry and flirty, simply to piss him off (and hand him an invoice for all those meals).

I didn't join in the 'Gina looks like sex on a stick' celebrations that followed. I was much too excited to get drunk as I was now resolute in ripping through my clothes as part of an elusive search for a flattering one– or two–piece, which would match the colours I was now proudly displaying. It was a disaster. My supply of raunchy clothes was in the red range. I wouldn't be stomping into anyone's office wearing the only thing I owned that blended in with my beautiful hair and face. I'd be arrested, floating around the place wearing nothing but a dark green pair of leg warmers and a matching woolly hat (which I think belonged to Dad).

'Did you find anything?' asked Roisin, swigging from a pint of what I presumed was gin and tonic. I hung my head in anguish and grabbed a glass.

'Brilliant, I'm thrilled!' hummed Lotty as she filled it up, toasted the air, and lit a cigarette. 'That means we can go mental tomorrow!'

We flounced into the first store at ten o'clock, three women laden down with large handbags and enthusiasm aplenty. I immediately homed in on and began to stalk a display of dresses that would only fit a five-year-old or someone with no hips. I should have known better. My embarrassment and shame was instant. I backed away as each individual dress hissed contempt and spat ridicule at me. 'Look at her! Thinking we'd actually fit!'

I belted before any stigma fastened itself to me permanently and instead lurked unhappily for a few minutes in front of the twelve to fourteen size section of slinky dresswear. I tried to comfort my slightly battered and tearful ego which was smarting as if slapped with a wet rag. It didn't work. Then I had to face the barbaric humiliation of plastering a huge smile on my face in an effort not to seethe, pout or vomit as Lotty pulled a dress from the five-year-old section and held it up to her while she did a little twirl. The bitch! Any normal fella would happily die in an effort to jump in there with her. It wasn't fair. I strained in an admirable attempt to keep a hold on my 'You look gorgeous!' grin, reminding myself sharply that it wasn't her fault she was beautiful and so skinny that I could practically see her internal organs every time she stood under the lights. I grabbed the first dress I saw, strode into the changing rooms with my sulking ego lamely following me and stripped hastily before irrefutable envy caught up with me.

'You can't go to work in that!' Lotty looked horrified as she stood staring at me.

'Oh put your eyeballs back in, she looks brilliant!' Roisin gave me a huge thumbs up.

I looked down at the little purple mini dress I had just yanked on. It was very little as in barely-covered-my-bum little. And yes I had yanked it on (pulled, wrenched and cursed if the truth be known). My efforts to look stunning almost caused my shoulder to pop out of place while I struggled to haul the damn thing up past my ankles. I did feel a bit like a pre-packed turkey and I was confused. I looked at myself in the mirror.

Should I slink away and say a few Hail Marys in penance for trying to look like a brassy tart, I wondered, as I did a little twirl and scrutinised my bum. Or should I allow myself to be influenced by Roisin and throw a party because I now looked like a brassy tart or at least someone who could get away with looking like one if Roisin's reaction was anything to go by?

I did another twirl. God, I loved this dress! But there were various points I was forced to consider even if I did look good in it, I thought realistically.

I could only wear it weather permitting. (One gust of wind, I realised with genuine panic, and my arse would instantly freeze. Rendering me unable to walk. The last thing I wanted was Jason offering to wrap his fleecy jumper around my legs. I would of course, refuse, he'd think I was mental and I'd be left feeling like a right thick with my bladder on ice wishing I had a hot water bottle sellotaped to my bum.)

Worse than that, I'd have to detoxify myself for at least three months or (and I didn't like the sound of this one) face the hardship and shitty ordeal of being on a permanent diet (just in case an opportunity landed in my lap out of the blue requiring me to look like a brazen and extravagant hussy on a sunny day. You never know!)

It was a bit tight around my waist and I hated to admit it but I was terrified I'd need a scissors and three firemen to get me out of the bloody thing as it was. I certainly couldn't wear it any place where I'd have to sit down for more than five minutes (for example, in a restaurant with Jason). In that event I'd need a crane to lift me off the chair because my tights and bum would have fastened me to the bloody thing. I'd be like Spiderman laden down with suckers except they wouldn't be on my arms and legs. I'd have a home-made one planted on my arse composed entirely of overactive sweat glands mixed with a good dose of nervous energy, all nicely gluing me to the nearest surface.

I shuddered. I didn't fancy not eating for a week either. All that drinking pints of lukewarm water and feasting on cottage cheese. I shivered and felt all goose-bumpy. Was I prepared to go through all that deprivation just so I could devour my main course with a clear conscience, only to suffer the indignity of being hoisted out of the place with the aid of a cherry picker? I didn't think so.

But I adored this dress. I could have screamed. I reluctantly began the process of peeling it off, devastated that it had the power to become the fabric of my worst nightmares. To think my future had been plundered and pillaged by twelve inches of expensive material barely held together with a single button. I was desolate.

I gave Roisin the thumbs down. She looked as shattered as I felt and immediately went hunting for a sales assistant to see if she had it in a bigger size. She didn't, the bitch. I returned the dress to its hanger, vowing one day to come back for it when I had lost six inches off my hips and thighs and was a Weightwatchers gold member. I fondly waved it goodbye and marched out of the shop not giving myself a chance to change my mind. I wasn't beaten yet.

We called it a day after the security guard in Marks and Spencer threatened to call the police if we didn't go home. I couldn't blame him, I suppose. We had been there for two hours. We lumbered back to Roisin's rented car (courtesy of Jack) and piled all our stuff into the boot. There was hardly room for the spare tyre which we had to tie to the roof rack in the end with a pair of tights.

I slept soundly in my new bed after stuffing myself with a huge bag of chips and a mug of hot chocolate. Tomorrow was Monday. I couldn't wait.

Chapter 9

I didn't realise I looked like a Christmas tree until I caught my reflection in the vending machine which was minding its own business as it quietly sat beside the exit barrier on the platform. I indulged in a sneaky laugh and thought, Jesus, who's yer one? About fourteen people then banged into my back as I held up the queue of bodies trying to emerge from the train after realising that 'yer one' was me.

I panicked. Absolutely and utterly. I felt nauseous as I hurriedly glanced at my watch and felt my mouth go dry. Everyone was staring. It was far too late to go home and change. I barely managed to mumble 'Sorry,' and grin stupidly at the other commuters who were about to skin me as I ran through the gate and into the ladies loo.

I heard a muffled shriek, dropped my bag with fright and backed away from the reflection in the mirror. I had become the epitome of all things festive. Or to put it another way, remember *The*

Incredible Hulk? Well I looked like the hulk's sister. Frighteningly green although I wasn't bursting out of my clothes. Instead I looked like someone who was about to burst out crying. I caught sight of some graffiti splayed in big red letters on the left-hand side of the wall just above my head. 'Stupid whore' it bellowed. I had to agree. My hair was flowing and sexy. My face the picture of beauty and health. The rest of me? Oh my God! All I needed was a few fairy lights and a scrap or two of tinsel to make me the perfect candidate for the top of any traditional tree.

I had bought two jackets, you see. I fell for them both hook, line and sinker. One red and one brown. I had intended to wear the brown one with my new dark green fluffy cashmere jumper. ('If you want to get a fella, wear cashmere,' Lotty had advised me yesterday.) But I had picked up the red one by mistake as I pawed sticky sleep out of my eyes this morning and shivered from the cold as the gas meter had mysteriously blown itself out during the night.

I glanced at the dark green gaping slit up the side of the skirt, which had looked divine in the shop mirror but now taunted me and my new suede boots. I wouldn't mind so much looking like a mixture of Ms Haemorrhage meets Ms Snot. I could live with that. But I had grave doubts about my resemblance to a conifer with legs. I took the jacket off. It was freezing. I put it back on. I had to go, it was eight-forty, which meant I was seriously late, but with a bit of luck only Joe would be around. Dear

God, I beseeched, please let them all be down a hole somewhere.

'The Christmas party's not for another bit yet, Gina!'

I blushed profusely. The Legend was just pulling into the compound. I pretended I hadn't heard him and flew into my office to hide my legs under the desk. To think this morning I had bounced out of bed quietly confident that Jason would arrive into the office and trip over his tongue when he saw me, desperate to pick up where we'd left off on Friday night. Now I was terrified he'd choke on the vision.

Joe wandered in. He was all smiles as he faxed an order off somewhere. Jesus, why hadn't I taken a sickie?

'You're looking very festive, Gina!'

I wished one of us would die on the spot.

'For November,' he continued admiring my top.

I plastered a pleasant smile on my face.

'Mr Ryan will be in shortly. You'll meet at long last.'

I felt bile curdle in my stomach. I could just imagine the boss asking me if I kept a crib and a few wise men under my desk. He already thought I had the intelligence of a fork and now he'd probably saunter in and crack loads of stupid jokes about reindeers and the Virgin Mary. I didn't care, I decided, as thoughts banged into each other racing around like lunatics inside my head. I could cope with anything Mr Ryan might say, any lukewarm attempts he might make at taking the piss, just as long as Jason didn't see me.

If the place had been empty I would have beaten myself up with a chair. How could I have been so thick? I know I'm not great in the morning but mistaking this little three piece for a black trouser suit and a brown jacket is usually something Lotty would do. Not me.

'It serves you right.' Oh shit! Ridicule was paying me a visit, all ready for action with a good old dose of 'what goes around comes around' to fling at me. 'That's what you get for whacking Ralph in public and praying his mother would be run over by a herd of stampeding elephants.' (Apparently she's on safari at the moment, and yes, I had enjoyed playing and replaying at the back of my mind how fast she could run with a crowd of pissed off and very large animals trumpeting after her.)

'After all the Sunday meals the poor woman cooked for you.' Ridicule was gearing up for a long stay. I really didn't need this. I was panicked enough as it was. 'You should have been up at the crack of dawn baking cakes for her, you selfish cow, instead of wishing her house would blow down overnight so you wouldn't have to go.' Very true. I had frequently wished her house would disappear with her in it. 'And maybe I should have stuck my head up the chimney and given it a good clean while I was there,' I argued back.

Thank God the phone rang, and didn't stop for a

further two hours. Ridicule thankfully slithered off but promised to be back. 'Ah, feck off!' I whispered when it turned around to dump on me a final biting grin.

Every time the office door opened I jumped. Word had got around, 'Gina looks like a Christmas fairy.' I really was distraught. Then Danny rang apologising for buggering off like lightning on Friday night but I hardly listened to a word he said as I could hear two cars pulling up outside. I said something generic to him, hung up and decided now would be a good time to escape to the loo/post office/Mars. I thought that staying in the loo for the rest of the day was my best option and legged it just as I heard the car doors slamming shut and Joe yelling, 'Here he is!' to me.

I couldn't believe it. Here I was trapped in the chemical bog beside the kitchen and listening to Mr Ryan laughing horrendously loud at his own jokes as Joe clattered around making them tea.

'Oh she's around here somewhere!' I heard him reply when Rottweiler Ryan asked where I was. He was dying to meet me. The woman who had to work with all these mad fellas for five days a week.

'She must be a bit mad herself!' he roared at Joe.

The brass neck of him! I felt like flinging the door open and telling him to sod off but if I did he'd take one look at me and keel over with mirth. I waited wishing they would hurry up and move into Joe's office with the tea. I had a great plan concocted.

I would sneak very quietly into my own office and hopefully they wouldn't discover me until it was time for Rotten Ryan to go.

I waited. They were discussing some match or other. Then I waited some more while Joe deliberated on whether or not I had got lost on my way to the post office. Then I needed to go to the loo for real but I was terrified rigid that they'd hear me and wonder what the hell I'd been doing in there all that time so I ignored it. I was bursting. It was hell.

Eventually they sauntered into Joe's little office. I sagged onto the loo nearly fainting after holding onto my bladder for so long. What now? I decided I'd follow my original plan. I'd sneak into my office and pretend I was just back from the post office. Then I'd make a big palaver about a queue as long as my arm and hopefully that should do it.

Another two seconds and I would have been sussed. My back had hardly hit the chair when Joe tumbled into my office with Mr Ryan in tow. I'd got away with it.

'Gina! Here you are! We thought you'd been kidnapped.' God I wish. Yet another smile somehow fastened itself to my gob.

'This is Mr Benjamin Ryan,' Joe bellowed as if I was meeting royalty. 'Benjamin, this is Gina.'

A large stout hand extended itself to me. It was very hairy and quite brown. I was pleasantly surprised to see a smile and a flash of white teeth. In fact he didn't look at all scary and I would never have thought in a million years that this was the same fella that sounded as if he had a lot in common with a bag of spanners every time he growled down the phone at me. We shook hands like old friends. I was intrigued enough by him to forget the immediate panic about the 'me looking like a Christmas tree' crisis. It didn't last. Paranoia craftily muscled in on the conversation.

'About time!' he bellowed, giving me the once over. Joe only stood there looking daft and fidgety. 'You certainly brighten this place up a bit, Gina.' (Was that a reference to my attire? I wasn't sure.) 'Anyway, better be off. See you before the Christmas holidays I hope!' (What did he mean, 'see you before the Christmas holidays?' I still wasn't sure if he was being a cocky git or not.)

Thank God, the two of them drifted off towards the front door chatting away about cash flow and the price of a decent pint. I caved in with relief when the cabin door finally shut and he was gone. He wasn't that bad. Certainly nothing like the demon I'd been expecting. In fact he was quite nice for a boss and had the decency to keep any comments about his on-site clerk looking like a Yuletide log to himself.

Joe looked ecstatic as he danced back into my office.

'Mr Ryan was very taken with you Gina. He certainly appreciated your dressing all Christmassy, thought it was gas in fact,' he finished as he made his way into the kitchen to put the kettle on again. I shut my eyes and cursed.

It was just after five. No sign of Jason. I had calmed down a bit during the day. The lads had done their worst and I had survived the humiliation of them buying me a vibrating Christmas Santa Claus that danced if you shouted at it and wiggled around on my desk wearing nothing but a furry hat every time the phone rang. I put my jacket back on as soon as half-five chimed, said my goodbyes to Joe and sneaked out the main door. I could always jump into a bush if Jason arrived now, I decided (as if I was perfectly adept at leaping into soggy foliage). I'd blend in ideally, I thought with utmost confidence. I would just look like another out of control bunch of weeds and not at all like a mad one hiding in the undergrowth, I persuasively promised myself as my eyes examined every moving thing in the compound.

'Gina!'

I recognised his voice instantly. It pulsated through me, but instead of purring deeply in return I nearly wet myself. At the same time my stomach lurched like a ferry out of control, righted itself momentarily and finally sank with a crash at my feet. Jason strolled out from behind the offices wearing huge waders, a hard hat and not much else.

My poor brain revved itself up for the ordeal of actually having to reply to the six-foot giant. I was devastated to realise that he looked like a stripper, a slippery gorgeous stripper. I felt very sorry for both of us as I heard popping in my ears and couldn't help myself from swallowing or convince my legs to stop throbbing with nerves. I was also being bombarded with very confusing and contradictory messages. Any hope I had of my poor brain copping itself on and providing me with an itinerary of 'what to do when you look like the missing ball off the Christmas tree and are faced with the ride of the century (whom you almost snogged) approaching you at breakneck speed' was gone. Fecked off like a wounded animal leaving me to fend for myself.

I didn't know whether to fan myself down which I was itching to do at the sight of him or march back into the office mumbling something about forgetting to set the alarm. The man was a ride, no doubt about it. And I was floored. Not a fibre of rug left under me. Incompetent and nearly incapable of stopping myself from yelling 'Fuck!' and booting it.

'Those bloody telephone lines are a curse. Sogging wet. You'll have to call in an engineer tomorrow to have a look.'

I think I nodded though my head felt cemented to my neck. I lowered my handbag in front of my skirt in a paltry effort to hide as much of it as possible and instinctively prepared myself for his rejection. And when it came (and it would, he could still see my knees) I would smile as if I didn't give a monkey's, march out of the compound and crawl onto the train. Piece of cake. No problem. I'd done it hundreds of times before when faced with inevitable rejection by a wanker.

I looked at him. He was dying to laugh. I knew it. The way he was staring at me began to make me feel woozy. Just wait for the shitty remark, I told myself, then leg it. He opened his mouth to speak. I relayed precise instructions to my legs on how to run as if fifty mad bastards were chasing me.

'If I'd known Christmas was coming early, I'd have brought in some mistletoe. See you tomorrow, so.' There was a tiny silence where he sported a flashy nervous grin and I stood looking at him with an expression you'd only find on a corpse.

My left leg moved first. It did exactly as it was told. My right leg followed as I shot out of there at twice the speed of sound. I saw Jason pull a funny 'she's nuts' face as I managed to just catch sight of his bum as he jumped into one of the on-site transit vans while I flew past him.

At four hundred miles an hour, with my hair following me like a kite and my bag bashing off my hips I was half-way to the train station before my epidemic embarrassment suddenly ceased its mad run around my brain and collided head on with something totally unexpected and surreal. I stopped dead and waited while a quick checklist issued itself to me. Something wasn't sitting right. I felt uneasy like I had forgotten something. Had I ingested any copious amount of heroin, coffee or chocolate in the last twenty-four hours? No, the only mind-altering substance I could think of was my own pasta.

I tried again. Had I just imagined it or had a definite case of flirting just taken place? Yes (which was obviously sod all to do with my pasta). Had Jason basically just suggested he'd like to snog me? Yes!

There was a weird silence then I heard a little giggle. A grin appeared out of nowhere and assigned itself to my face. I still hadn't moved. I replayed the entire scenario a couple of more times in my head simply to make sure I hadn't gone mad. I mean look what happened the last time Jason had spoken to me. I'd spent an entire day wondering if we'd had sex. But this time I was quite sure. He wanted me. It took a while for this new revelation to sink in. He hadn't suggested I should be the new Christmas Barbie. He'd been nice. Floored by my new hair colour. Hooked on my new look. Yes!

Unexpectedly the little smug smile suddenly froze on my face. I became aware of something new but as familiar as my own name. Aware in a horrible nasty 'Ah, no' sort of way. Instantly and without warning I felt like a blockhead. A first prize blockhead. The sort of blockhead that makes you want to melt into the pavement and never have to speak to anyone ever again. Particularly himself.

Jason had plucked an opportunity out of thin air, I realised, wishing I were physically able to kick myself up the bum. He had been wonderfully careful treading the water and had made a decision to suss me out. A fella make a decision? He'd said 'mistletoe' for Christ's sake! And what had I done? No, I hadn't giggled suggestively and gone all girlish and coy. I hadn't engaged in playful conversation leading to a pub or my bedroom. I'd run like a lunatic. He'd think I was a lunatic, a real one.

I crawled onto the train, flustered uttering 'Stupid bitch' to myself a hundred times on the journey home. I had painted a perfect picture of myself as a mad nutter to the man I had lusted after for weeks. My heart nearly stopped as I realised that I might never get the chance to explain. To brief him on the fact that I was perfectly rational most of the time except when faced with having to converse with the man I was crazy about and me looking like an extra for the Christmas panto. The thought of it nearly killed me. Even worse than that, I thought closing my eyes, how on earth would I ever show my face in the office again?

The answer was easy. I didn't go to work for a week. In fact I would never have gone near the place again if I weren't lumbered with paying the rent on the flat at the end of the month not to mention having to do my Christmas shopping. I went home to the folks for the first two days. I finally told Jessie and awaited the non-stop slagging that was sure to follow.

'Ah, no, you didn't!' she replied after I spilled my guts about the whole episode to her in the pub. I nodded.

'Oh, Gina, that's desperate. You poor cow, you.' She wasn't making me feel any better.

'He thinks I'm mental!' I shrieked as I ran my fingers through my hair realising I was dying for a fag. Jessie looked at me and I was devastated when she didn't disagree.

'Tell him you had your period. It'll be fine. You'll just have to learn to forgive yourself for being as daft as a yard brush. It's the only way to move forward,' she continued sipping her beer and smiling at every fella that brushed past.

She looked stunning which made me feel even more worn out. No fellas were giving me the eye. Then again I wasn't wearing a slinky top and a very stylish pair of 'God they make you look so skinny' trousers. I looked at my shoes and my inexpensive jeans while I contemplated what Jessie had just said. She made it sound so easy. So trivial.

'But—' I started.

'But nothing!' interrupted Jessie. 'Look,' she said obviously getting annoyed with me, 'it's not the end of the world. I know you feel like a pathetic useless not to mention embarrassed thicko, but if he's the one for you he'll understand. Bring him out for a drink and explain. Ten to one you'll end up in the sack.'

I stared at my shoes again and thought about it. As

if! I really couldn't see myself tapping Jason on the shoulder and sprightly saying, 'Sorry for legging it like that but I was so in awe of you and terrified you'd laugh at me that I ran like a mad thing before I realised you weren't going to act like a jerk.' I knew at once that I'd rather drop stone dead.

I felt sick.

Two gorgeous fellas came and sat beside Jessie. They were obviously American, loaded and prepared to fight to the death over her. Jessie indulged them completely and forgot all about me. I felt unwanted and so obviously the 'older boring sister' that I was desperate to dash the hell out of there. I was so lost in my own misery that I honestly didn't notice the sudden extra weight on the seat as someone sat down beside me.

'You're supposed to be sick in bed, not living it up in the pub!'

My heart nearly stopped. Honestly, I'm not messing. I got such a fright I nearly slapped him. Danny smiled at me.

'I am sick! I'm drinking whiskey, medicinal and all that,' I mumbled and nearly fell off the chair from the force as waves of pure embarrassment washed over me. I'd been caught.

I became infected then with a case of the jitters, brought on by bouts of paranoid embarrassment. My inner thoughts were cringing and yelling, 'What if he knows! Suppose Jason told him all about our little tête-à-tête?' I tried to swallow but my tongue was glued to my teeth. I was convinced he knew. Knew that I wasn't ill, that I was only messing and not coming to work because I couldn't face Jason. Jason who thought I was mad. Which meant Danny thought I was mad too.

I fiddled with bar mats and Jessie's empty crisp packet while I willed Danny to feck off back to the bar or wherever it was he had come from and leave me the hell alone.

'You're very jittery,' he said ignoring the fact that I was ignoring him.

'It's a symptom,' I replied defensively.

'Of what?' he said, taking a sip from his pint.

'What do you mean, of what?' (He wasn't supposed to ask that.) 'It's a symptom of my illness!' I retorted, downing my short in one and planning to grab my coat and excuse myself.

'Well if you're that sick I'd better get you another so,' Danny replied rather sourly as he grabbed one of the fourteen-year-old bar staff and ordered me a hot whiskey.

I was furious. I didn't want another drink. I wanted to go home and eat. Watch re-runs of *Dynasty* with Mum and cuddle into the bucket-seat sofa and eat myself under the damn thing with whatever goodies Mum had hidden in the biscuit drawer. I didn't want another fecking hot whiskey.

'Really, there's no need.'

He wasn't listening. The impertinence of him! I put on my coat. Danny looked at me and pulled out his wallet.

'I'll thank you to indulge me and enjoy your drink, then you can go home if you like.'

I looked at him, with one hand in my coat sleeve and the rest of the coat hanging around my ankles. Who the hell was he to tell me what I could and couldn't do? Even though I was horribly flustered, some bit of me that was still functioning normally realised I was cornered. I didn't want him to get annoyed with me. I certainly didn't want him yelling, 'I don't care if you have the bloody drink or not, sure you're as daft as a brush anyway!' No, I'd stay put, throw the damn drink into me, say I was dying and then leave. Ten minutes I reckoned. Tops.

Reluctantly I whipped off my coat and decided I'd better be nice. This man held my life in his hands. It wasn't a hot idea to provoke him unless I wanted the whole pub to know my shameful secret. The fourteen-year-old came back with our drinks and got very confused over his float and Danny's change. I was delighted as it gave me a chance to order my paranoia into the furthest corner of my head and threaten it with a lobotomy if it dared even squeak. Our bullshit conversation began.

All smiles I asked Danny if he was geared up for the Christmas party. It seemed the most obvious road, one that should lead me out the exit as soon as my drink was cool enough to down. Five minutes later he was still harping on about how much he was looking forward to it. The man was animated, full of chat and oblivious to the fact that I was bored and at this stage desperate to get home. It also became clear to me that I couldn't be blatantly nasty to him, look at my watch, sigh loudly, mumble something about rushing home to take a few pills and simply march out of the pub. We'd both be hugely embarrassed.

I looked over at Jessie who was having a whale of a time as a further two Americans were hanging around the periphery of our table. It was like one of those nature documentaries that are always on the National Geographic Channel. Any minute now they'd lock horns/wallets/willies as the real dual began.

I had no idea who Danny was even here with. A sister? A girlfriend? His mates? I felt utterly downcast. Here was Jessie having a brill evening and look at me. Stuck with him. Don't get me wrong, he is lovely and we work very well together. In fact right now he's blabbing on about how much he's missed me today and he'll be made up when I'm well enough to come back. Apparently Joe is no good at ordering take-out pizzas for lunch and buying last-minute birthday presents for his sisters.

'I'm boring you, aren't I?'

Oh shit! I hate it when fellas say that. I immediately felt guilty when I saw how flushed his face was. In situations like this a good lie is always better than the truth.

'No! It's my head, it's killing me,' I said in a very

over-the-top tone patting myself on the head and pulling an 'I'm in mortal pain' face. I couldn't bear the thought of hurting his feelings, I realised. He beamed. God love him, I thought, he's having a great time here with me and I feel sick.

'Who are you bringing?'

I hadn't the faintest idea what he was talking about.

'Sorry?' I said flashing my winning smile.

'To the party, who are you bringing to the party?'

A touchy subject. I was bringing Lotty and Roisin so that they could square up Jason. I tried to bypass the question so he wouldn't know I was being evasive.

'Oh, I'm not sure!' I lied with a little laugh.

'A boyfriend, maybe?'

Another smile etched itself onto my weary face, the whiskey nearly choking me. I hadn't expected that.

'Maybe,' I replied.

The last thing I wanted was Jason to know I didn't have a fella. It would ruin everything. Just be nice and misleading I told myself then Danny can't tell him whether I'm bringing anyone or not. It worked. Danny's face fell as he at last tired of me and my company.

'Anyway, better be off. The lads are waiting for me.' I didn't argue as he stood up and put his wallet in his jacket pocket. 'Shall I walk you to the door?'

Feck! I didn't want to go home at all now. Jessie's

Americans had fought it out and she was hanging off the arm of a muscle-bound tall one. In fact he didn't look like he even had normal arms and legs. His limbs could have been displayed on hooks in the butchers shop. Prime cuts, premium joints. Get them while they're hot. And he was. Which meant I felt like another drink and a walk to the chippie so I could stuff myself and feel utterly miserable all the way home.

But Danny was waiting for me. I hissed at Jessie to be careful and not come home with a baby that looked like a pork chop and reluctantly walked to the door with my unwanted escort.

'Are ya all right, Gina?'

Christ! The Legend and a good shower of new and old Ruffty Tuffty Pipeliners were downing Guinness in the corner. I shuddered and felt another surge of panic ring in my ears. I had no idea they were here. What if Jason was here too. I waved over and tried to make myself look ill. You know, pull a face, force myself to look pale and then swallow four-letter profanities because I've plastered on enough make-up to tile the loo with.

'See you Monday, then?' Danny was staring at me with his eyebrows raised.

'Yes, better go. Thanks for the drink,' I mumbled.

He nodded and held the door open for me. All I could hear echo behind me was The Legend and the lads roaring at Danny, 'You're sucking diesel now, lad!'

I legged it.

I was desperate to buy two bags of chips and walk home at a mad pace devouring my food like a rejected orphan. As usual in situations where I feel like an unconditional twerp my first instinct is to eat. And I did feel like a twerp. All that palaver about Christmas parties and me pretending I was dying. Christ! I quivered and clutched my handbag against my stomach trying to squash the butterflies that were dizzy inside me as I remembered Danny asking what was wrong with me, and telling me how much he missed me. I now felt as ill as I had pretended to be in the pub. He knew I was lying and I knew he knew. So that was now two fellas I never wanted to see again.

At once I wanted a huge bag of chips, four battered sausages and a mammoth lump of cod to quench the rotten fiery feeling in my stomach brought on by the shock of me slap-banging into the lads like that. I was utterly mortified. That was strictly the last time I'd ever go out with my younger sister. I could still hear The Legend and the lads slagging Danny in Dolby stereo. Damn it!

I flounced in the door of the chippie, ready to order everything on the menu including the salt and pepper dispenser. But at the last second the engine that had been driving me along suddenly went into reverse, coughed, choked, spluttered and finally went limp. I was horrified not to mention livid to discover   I   was   embarrassed.   Wickedly inconveniently embarrassed and self-conscious. I took in my surroundings.

Jesus, I could just hear the fella behind the counter telling everyone about the fat miserable cow who was in and bought the whole place because she obviously spent her Friday nights having an intimate relationship with a battered sausage and three dozen greasy chips (or fat sticks as Jessie calls them). I shuddered. Typically I was the only customer. Feck! The only fat miserable cow in the place so there was no way I was going to buy the entire stock and prattle on like a daft old dear about how I was bringing home the dinner to my husband and seven children.

I stood there neither in nor out of the doorway sussing out the joint and making myself ignore the nasty looking man behind the counter. I was desperate to get my hands on a massive piece of cod, snuggle up with it, wrap my tongue around its comfy duvet of batter and loll with it as it soaked up pints of vinegar and bathed itself in salt. Instead I huddled in a corner and squeaked at the frighteningly large red-haired fella that I'd like a small chips, then read the menu about forty times while I waited for my order.

Eventually after said scary bloke had battered a few cod relentlessly and yelled at someone to get peeling more spuds I scampered out with my one small bag of fat. I began to stuff myself as soon as I had a toe outside the chipper's door.

'Fucking fantastic,' I muttered sarcastically, ramming about six chips into my mouth at once. All the lads think I fancy Danny. My stomach tightened. What if they told Jason? I stopped chewing. An unsettling flurry of 'Christ, what now?' tickled my spine and trickled unaided through my central nervous system. I couldn't bear it. Danny telling Jason, Jason never looking crossways at me again and The Legend and the lads slagging me until I was forty. I threw the chips into the first bin I passed, flew home feeling ragged and eventually found myself putting the key in the door.

I got an awful fright as I threw my coat on the sofa all prepared to raid Mum's biscuit cupboard and wallow in my bedroom. There was a strange woman in the kitchen, her silhouette gracefully moving from sink to kettle. I was confused not to mention slightly terrified. I stood absolutely still as the unknown woman clattered around, making herself a cup of tea.

Christ! It wasn't Jessie. (She was probably in full swing, *Dirty Dancing* mode, with her American outside the pub.) It definitely wasn't Mum (unless she'd dyed her hair a bizarre shade of red). Surely it wasn't a burglar? It was possible but what sort of woman tries to rob your house wearing four-inch stilettos and a mini skirt? There was no way she'd be able to stick our stereo up her jumper as she wasn't wearing one. I had another squint. No, not a jumper in sight only something that looked like a handkerchief that had been generously powdered with glitter.

Ever so slowly I inched my way from the sofa and tiptoed across to the double doors, my brain doing a dance as it tried to work out if Mum and Dad had some strange visitor they had forgotten to tell me about. Jesus, maybe Dad had a fancy woman! Mind you she was a bit tall for Dad and anyway Mum had dragged him off to the theatre for the night.

I screwed my eyes up against the glass. Yet there was something familiar about her. It was the way she was sitting. Not all legs crossed flashing a bit of thigh as you would expect from a woman who dared walk the streets wearing such an array of provocative and sexy clothes. The bitch! Oh no, this one was sort of sprawled in Mum's favourite chair her legs hanging loosely at either side like . . . like what? Like a bloke!

'Don't be so thick,' I whispered to myself. 'I know she looks like the irritating type who takes up the whole seat on the train and leaves you with about two inches to make yourself comfortable, but a bloke? Besides what sort of fella wears mini skirts and sits in your kitchen helping himself to tea and biscuits?' I tutted and continued to stare at the loose-legged lady of the night until some kind person switched the light on for me. It wasn't one of Mum's hysterical friends. Of course not. How could I have been so stupid? It was Tommy. It had to be.

With shaking legs I pushed open the double doors and as an afterthought grabbed the fireside poker. You know just in case it wasn't Tommy but some weirdo stealing our digestive biscuits.

Tommy and I both screamed at the same time.

'For fuck sake, I thought you were Dad!'

'I thought you were a burglar. What in the name of God are you doing, Tommy?'

I had to sit down as my legs were about to give. I almost wished it had been a thief. I would have got less of a shock. All my plans to call the police and enjoy being fussed over and being hailed the heroine of the night were forgotten. I stared at my brother utterly astounded. Jessie had made me feel underdressed, horribly ugly and about as fanciable as a plate of raw mince. I was now staring at my brother. He looked amazing!

My feeble shaky-legged ego threw in the towel immediately and stomped around shouting obscenities. How on earth was I supposed to cope with THIS? My brother! Looking more gorgeous than I ever have. It was crucifying. Embarrassing. Devastating. Unfair. I was in awe of how he managed to apply his eyeshadow with such utter perfection while I simultaneously tried to cope with the physical sight of him in front of me.

Believe me it's not every day you see your only brother in this unnerving light. I was flustered and shocked in a terribly defensive 'fuck you for looking better than me' nasty way. Which was unfair and totally immature. I should have been supportive. Taken control in those two seconds where he looked like he was bricking it and instead I only stared. Jealous beyond words because far from being the heroine of the night I had been demoted to the envious sister wearing a less effective bra than my brother and smelling like a big fat chip.

I forgot all about Jason and Danny as I stared at Tommy. He had always been a hunk. Not in a rocks-for-biceps way, but in a tall-toned-dark-and-stern manner. He'd had women stalking him since his first birthday. It was his face you see, chiselled and structured to perfection and masked with jet black hair. It all added to his intrigue. He even had the cheek to be blessed with beautiful blue eyes. (Mine, let's face it, are a yucky brown. Mum keeps insisting they're 'dusky brown' whatever the hell that is. But they're not swamped with suggestive bluey green shadows like my brother's and they sure as hell don't promise nights full of heavenly intimacy and loads of sex either. They're more like two pools of dirty dishwater.) His stared at me now. Shocked, afraid and hopeful. I stared back wide-eyed and thought it was about time I copped myself on.

It wasn't easy to know what to do next. I was waiting for Rikki Lake or Oprah to pop out of the pantry laden down with microphones and miles of wiring to ask me how I felt now that my brother had come out and liked to dress up in the same tights as me. I refused to let the situation get that bad. My brother had no part to play in some American trashy show. But even so I felt weird. Stop being so irrational! I yelled at myself over and over as Tommy sat down nervously on the edge of his chair. I wouldn't have known it was him except he continuously rubbed his left eyebrow with a shaking hand, a little quirk of his since God knows when.

'Stop doing that will you!'

He jumped.

You rotten bitch, I thought. I could have killed myself for being so mean.

'I'm sorry, Gina. I didn't mean to frighten you, I thought you were gone for the night.'

'So did I.'

There was silence and a lot of staring.

'Look, I'd better go. I'm late.' Tommy stood up, smoothed down his skirt and put on a black jacket, his eyes refusing to meet mine.

'No, wait, Tommy. I'm sorry, I'm being ridiculous. It's just such a shock that's all.' I grabbed his hand and felt like cringing at his perfectly painted nails and glittery jewellery.

'It's not as bad as you think, Gina. I got a job!'

Now I really was perplexed. What was he on about?

'In the club, I got a job. It's what I do now. I dress up like this,' he said, pointing to his mini skirt, 'play a few CDs, tell a few jokes and that's all. It's just a job.' His words calmed my preposterous mood and I instantly felt shitty for being such a cow.

With shaking legs, I forced myself out of the chair and put the kettle on. After a few minutes the atmosphere at last returned to normal. Well as normal as it can get when you're met unexpectedly by your brother looking a lot like Cher.

We chatted for ages. It was a slow process but it felt brilliant. Somewhere along the way I forgot my jealousy and my awkwardness. Tommy opened up to me like a new flower on a spring morning. He had found someone, he told me in an excited tone. A fella of the dishy hunky type and he wanted me to come along to the club some night and have a look. I promised I would.

I shut the door after him as he left for work, and sat down. Funnily enough I felt wonderful. Tommy had the guts to sort his life out, make decisions and confront the world. The last thing I had expected to feel tonight was motivated and inspired but I did and I was grateful.

It didn't last. I tried but I really didn't feel in the least bit inspired or brimming with self-love as I sat on the sofa in the flat a few days later murdering a pizza Lotty had ordered for me. The whole thing with Jason still smarted like a kick in the chops and yes maybe I was being self-centered and acting useless but I couldn't help it. Anyway the pizza wasn't the only distraction on the menu tonight. There was something funny going on with Lotty and Roisin. Something very funny.

I looked again at the kitchen door as I devoured a thick slice of pizza the width of a brick. Behind the door Lotty and Roisin were doing a lot of whispering, the sort that's really loud and hissy. I hadn't a clue what the two of them were up to and I was quite offended that I wasn't invited in there to hiss with them. (I mean I'm not one to pass up on a good old bitching session, they know that.)

'Won't be a second.' Lotty's wiry blonde hair appeared from behind the kitchen door. 'Pizza OK?' Somebody had stapled a smile to her face. I gulped a huge lump of ham and pineapple down, while I eyed her up.

'Fine!' I retorted indifferently and she vanished without another word. The snidy cow!

What were they up to in there? Were they fighting over the fifty-pence jar again? Was Roisin having a go at Lotty for putting all our coins in the gas meter last night so we were lovely and warm while sitting in the pitch dark? As soon as the kitchen door shut again I hopped up reluctantly from my warm patch on the sofa and fastened my ear to the door, pizza box at the ready.

'You tell her, you're more assertive than me.' Lotty sounded desperate. She must have been fighting with her mother again, I decided. But why wasn't she asking me for advice?

'She's going to hear us if we don't hurry up.' Now the poor girl sounded utterly distressed. I didn't know what she was worried about. Her mother lives in Cork for God's sake and her new hearing aid isn't that good. I shrugged my shoulders, grabbed

another meal-of-four slice of pizza from the box and
began stuffing myself as Roisin began to speak.

'Now look, you.'

Lotty let out a squawk that echoed around the
kitchen. I didn't blame her. Roisin sounded
ferocious.

'Get in there and tell her with me. She's our
friend not just mine. You're such a chicken at times,
honestly.'

I stood back from the door suddenly alert and
oblivious to the pizza topping that was dribbling
down my chin. I heard some weird shuffling noise
waft from the kitchen and immediately hopped
back on the sofa just as Lotty and Roisin emerged
all smiles and eyelashes fluttering. OK Lotty didn't
really emerge it was more like she was shoved. The
look on Roisin's face filled me with dread. She had
her Mafia hat on again. What the hell was going on?

'Gina, we need to talk something over with you.'

Roisin looked very serious and I was naturally
dubious. I tried to work out what was going on. I
looked at Roisin. She was seething quietly. Jesus, I
know I hadn't hoovered and I wasn't great at
cleaning the loo, but surely she wasn't going to have
a dig at me over that? How the hell could I do all
that normal day-to-day stuff after all that had
happened with Jason? I immediately felt all
defensive and self-righteous. Who was she to have a
go at me? I put on my 'Go on throw it at me, you
heartless cow' face and looked straight at her. Roisin

gave Lotty a shove.

'Yes,' started Lotty looking at my pizza box, 'We've been a bit worried about you, since, eh you know, you haven't been at work all week and all that, haven't we, Roisin?'

'For Christ sake, Lotty!' Roisin looked disgusted.

My eyes followed Lotty as she withered and sank into a beanbag.

'What Lotty is trying to say, Gina, is that you are being a complete pain,' stated Roisin. 'We are fed up with you whingeing all day and leaving piles of crap sprinkled around the apartment, like that pizza box for instance. It has to stop. Now!'

I looked at Lotty baffled.

'There's no need to humiliate her, Roisin. Now come on.' Fair play to Lotty I thought, fighting back tears from Roisin's completely unexpected attack.

'Why not?' snapped Roisin. 'I do everything else around here. Hoovering, cleaning, picking up empty crisp wrappers.' She threw me the most dire look.

Then there was silence. I was so shocked I didn't know what to say, so I looked at the carpet instead. Roisin began to calm down a little bit but she was obviously really fed up with me as her eyes were burning in their sockets making her look horribly possessed.

'It's been bloody murder living with you these last few days, hasn't it, Lotty?' Roisin bored a hole through Lotty's head as she waited for her friend to pipe up.

Lotty shifted awkwardly on her beanbag. I sat there simply staring at her.

'I think what Roisin means is, well, why not go back to work and get it out of the way? Probably Jason has forgotten all about your little, eh, outburst and it will stop you eating like a horse and walking toast crumbs into the carpet!'

I winced. My head began to boom. I was gagging on a snowball-sized lump of pineapple and cheese which had started somersaulting halfway between my throat and my stomach. My two best friends were ganging up on me like a hit squad. How could they?

'But I'm in mourning,' I whimpered,

'What in the name of God are you on about now?' Roisin was rocking from side to side. Unrepentant. That chillingly cutting and cynical glare of hers had returned. I felt the pizza sag in my hand as we both acknowledged her foul mood.

'I knew you wouldn't understand,' I started. (I thought this was my best defence — act like a heartbroken puppy and not give in to the desire to punch her lights out.) 'Just because you and Jack are all over each other non-stop doesn't give you the right to be spiteful to me. I'm in mourning for what might have been.' (I thought it was best if I combined fluttery hands with rolling eyes as if high from my inner sorrow.)

Roisin didn't budge. Instead of calming down her whole face turned purple. I tried another tactic.

'Instead of Jason and me having great crack, he thinks I am cracked. And look at you trying to kick me when I'm down. You're a horrible cow!'

Roisin's lips narrowed into a straight line. All the same I made myself cry though I really wanted to yank her bloody hair out. She didn't go for it. Feck! I thought.

'If you don't get yourself sorted out, go back to work and stop using our, yes our, flat as a mortuary, then Lotty and I are going to boot you out, aren't we?' Roisin kicked Lotty's foot.

'Well, Roisin does have a point, Gina. We're only trying to shake some sense into you and make you face up to the consequences. You're acting like a raving loony over some daft bloke. You'd never have done this before!'

I shuffled around a bit on the sofa feeling utterly distraught. She was right, I wouldn't. I've never spent this long having hysterics. No fella had ever caused me this much turmoil. And we hadn't even had a snog. Well I do remember that one boy Richard who ran off with my best friend in first class, and what was his name, the other guy? Fergal. He'd stolen my virginity and told everyone the next day. But that was it. I'd only suffered for maybe a day or two at the most and there had been nothing a long sunny afternoon spent shopping didn't fix. I was being daft. I was being oversensitive. I was eating and drinking enough for a family of six and their dog. I looked up sheepishly from the cold pizza which was now glued to the side of the box.

'OK,' I said in a very tiny voice. 'I'll go back. I'll face him.'

Chapter 10

'Get away, will ya, you're nothing but a cheeky fucker!'

I stuck my head under the plant list on my desk and bit my lip as The Legend's irate yelpings at Matt reverberated past me. I could have shot myself in the foot for ever having mentioned it.

'It' was the Christmas menu for our office night out. 'It' was causing a scene Stephen Spielberg would have paid millions for. Right on cue, the dancing Santa on my desk responded to The Legend and Matt shrieking at one another and started doing a jig across my paperwork.

'Turn that fucking— Sorry, Gina. Turn that stupid thing off, PLEASE!' The Legend glared at me, his hard hat slipping down over his brow and in front of his eyes as he waved the faxed menu at me. He looked hysterical and I tried not to grin.

'Now listen, you! (He said 'you' so it sounded like 'yuuuuuu'.) Stop yer messing. I'm not eating rabbit food for Christmas and if you don't like it you can fu— sorry, Gina – you can get stuffed, right!'

Matt was livid. He was a committed vegetarian and wanted everyone on the site to opt for the veggie selection on the menu. Needless to say The Legend wasn't having any of it.

'I'll give you my salad and that'll do ya. So ya can stop pestering my crew to eat that crap. Do ya hear me?'

Matt, who was swaying dangerously from the explicit torrent of hostility flying past his ears, stomped off in a huff embracing his veggie menu and cursing like mad.

'Sorry about the flowery language, Gina.' The Legend cleared his throat and nodded profusely to convey his sincerity. 'Book sixty-five of us in for the full whack and none of that veggie stir fry stuff, if you don't mind. Thanks.'

I glanced again at my plant list. It was nice to be back. I had missed everyone while I'd been hiding in misery and making Lotty and Roisin act as lookouts everytime the doorbell rang. I had prepared myself for the daunting task of 'returning to the work place when you feel like a gobshite' as best I could. With the aid of an aromatherapy bath provided by Lotty I had salvaged just enough self-respect to get me onto the train that morning.

'Put in a drop or two of this and relax,' Lotty had instructed. I'd poured in the entire bottle. Apparently lavender oil would grant me an unbroken night's sleep so I'd be as fresh as a daisy in the morning. Then I'd lashed on some ylang ylang oil, which would supposedly act as an aphrodisiac and make Jason dissolve into a crumbling heap as soon as he saw me. I'd practically drunk it. As I'd emerged from the bath a reconciled Roisin had jumped on the side of my bed and given me a lecture on assertiveness.

'Don't take any crap from him and stay in control.'

I'd promised to try as I snuggled into my duvet, full of dread but feeling like a Turkish Delight from all the baby powder that Lotty had insisted I sprinkle all over me. In spite of myself I did sleep. And in the morning, when I'd tiptoed across the site compound and let myself in, Joe put on the kettle and told me four hundred times how ecstatic he was to see me. He had even left a huge bunch of flowers on my desk with a little note saying how happy he was now that I had returned. I felt awful but at least I looked fantastic.

Lotty had got up fifteen minutes earlier to do my make-up. I couldn't have put a foot outside the door otherwise. I felt ready for action as long as Jason didn't come anywhere near me. I had to remind myself constantly not to launch out of my chair whenever the office door opened and I still suffered appalling flashbacks to that frenzied moment when I had run like a mad woman out of the compound. But Lotty and Roisin were right. I had to move on. Yes it had been a distressing experience and I had been ruined for days afterwards but it was imperative

I kept going. I was fed up being painful company for my friends.

My best defence was to look bone crunchingly beautiful and act completely sane. ('Mad people don't look gorgeous,' Lotty had promised me earlier as she lathered my eyes with mascara and blended in eyeshadow to match my suit.) Then Jason would gradually forget that he thought I was a loony and I could get back to the business of making him fall for me. Estimated time left for me to sneakily woo him to his knees, five weeks. Preferred location for our inaugural wanton coming together, the Christmas Party.

Manipulation of Jason was in full flow and I was planking myself. It's not easy acting lucid and composed when you're bricking yourself especially when you know, really know in your heart of hearts, that he still thinks you're round the bend.

As the morning progressed to afternoon I was ragged from catching up on my paperwork and having Danny on the phone every two minutes. I knew the sooner Jason came and went the better. I couldn't think about anything else. The earlier we faced each other for the first time since 'my loony episode' the sooner I could unwind. My stomach was in a constant knot and even though I knew I was being a bit over the top I couldn't eat. Sure he's probably forgotten all about it anyway. I thought about this one for awhile. He has in his backside! I was torn between chanting 'Please God, don't let him arrive now' to 'Please God let him pull up in his van and get this over with.'

I was in the middle of deciding which chant to go for when, bang, a van door slammed outside quickly followed by shuffling, gritting noises. Feet on gravel sort of noises. My stomach nose-dived to the floor. It had to be him! Danny and Joe were on site, The Legend and Matt were off at the hire centre. That left only me and the cleaning lady in the cabin. Shit!

I braced myself. It was very difficult not to stamp on a last-second urge which was trying heroically to make my legs flee for the loo. I continued to force myself not to wriggle in my chair as the gravelly foot noises got closer. I would prefer, after all, not to give Jason the impression I was sitting on a washing machine in full spin. I looked at my legs dithering under the desk. Stop it! Stop it! The growling didn't work. My nether regions weren't listening and my legs refused to act like my legs any more. I suppose it was a blessing and I should have been grateful but I wasn't.

Everything below my waist had instantly turned to liquefied slush as soon as I had heard that van pulling up. I was now the proud owner of a pair of pins that were behaving as if they belonged to an unstable nine-month-old baby. Frantic to dash headlong across the room at breakneck speed, only to be instantly thwarted by limbs that were shaking their heads and shouting, 'No, feck off. We're not going anywhere!'

I calmly tried placing both my hands on my knees in an effort to cease the jigging but it didn't work. My left shoe popped off my foot instead and landed under my desk. Bloody hell! What now? I could hear the key in the door. Should I crawl on all fours, retrieve the rebellious footwear and dash back to my swivel chair? 'Not enough time!' I panted to myself.

Typically my upper body had decided to join in the fun and was jigging riotously from one side of my chair to the other. I looked at my shoe bobbing up and down in front of me making me feel seasick. I simply knew if I made a grab for it now Jason would saunter in and catch me crawling along the carpet, not in the least composed, and wobbling like a big bowl of Granny's blackcurrant jelly. Puce from embarrassment. Grinning like a complete imbecile. Babbling from the floor about my mutinous shoes that liked to zoom all over the place at the drop of a hat. I couldn't take it. My self-respect was battling like mad to scramble on top of me as it was. It simply wouldn't hear of it. Me clambering all over the place like a half-wit? Hadn't I enough ground to cover with Jason without adding this to the fecking list?

The door abruptly flew open and slapped off the cabin wall.

'Hi, Gina!'

I nearly passed out from the intense shock of feeling warm blood whoosh through my poor legs again. I felt euphoric as naked relief surged through me drenching me with a glowing sensation of release as I looked up and registered a smiling Nicola. All my internal organs which had been taut, strained and complaining loudly only two seconds ago slowly began grinding and pounding themselves back into action. I must have looked exactly like that soggy fat piece of cod I had wanted the other night. Battered. Ruined. With two legs doing a brand new jig under the table to celebrate their renewed lease of life. Fair play to Nicola, I thought. If she did notice my psychotic air she never said a word. Instead she shrieked and gave me a big hug as we hadn't seen each other in weeks.

'Are you better?'

Oh Christ, she was wearing her demented motherly face which was nearly as scary as her 'Don't mess with me' scratchy one.

'Joe said you were dying! I had to call in and see you. Is everything OK? Danny said he met you and you looked awful.' (I raised an eyebrow in disgust.)

'It was nothing, I'm fine.' I think I said this with a little bit too much oomph. I could have kicked myself.

Nicola gave me a quizzical look. Rule number one, other women always know when you're lying your head off. A new expression carved itself on her face while I smiled like mad and prayed for the phone to ring.

'You're not pregnant are you?'

'Jesus, no, it was the flu!' I was horrified. The bitch!

And even worse I don't think she believed me. She stared at me for the longest time, her face all knotted with silent disbelief. Just as I really began to panic her eyes shifted, her face relaxed and thank God she was back to normal. All smiles she breezed out to the kitchen to make us some tea and shouted in at me that she wanted to spend the afternoon tying up the last few details for the Christmas party. I sagged. Drained and cursing I got up and recovered my missing shoe. Me, pregnant? Was the woman mad?

An unwelcome sensation warmed my stomach as the tiniest whiniest little thought ushered itself silently into my head. I ignored it while I busily told my bungee-jumping shoe how bloody cheeky Nicola was as I screwed it onto my foot.

'Get away, willya!' I roared when the thought didn't immediately respond and feck off. Instead it lightly tapped me on the shoulder and waved.

'What now,' I hissed.

A placard shouting 'You are what you eat' suddenly appeared in front of me. With a stomach-churning jolt I remembered the chips and the chocolate and the pizza and the wine that had kept me company while I'd been off work. I heard my breath being sucked in, whistling horribly as it flew past my teeth. Jesus, I'd practically forgotten. We had had a great time together with me watching every conceivable trashy show on the telly. You know the type: 'I've lost twenty-seven stone and need a makeover!' Myself and the curried chips had really got into that poor woman.

'My sister thinks she's all that but she's really a fat cow.' Oh yes, I'd shovelled hundreds of Danish pastries into my gob as I sniggered my way through that particular show. I glanced with one eye at the button on my trousers. It was about to pop! No wonder Nicola thought I was pregnant. No wonder Danny said I looked awful. I was getting fat. Me about to try and lasso the ride of the century was getting fat. I was floored. I struggled with an unholy urge to slink off home and shoot myself.

I stared again at my button and winced. At this rate all I'd need to do would be to wallop Jason on the back of the head with my stomach and drag him off to bed. He'd never know what hit him. A harsh gritty voice suddenly let a roar, 'Let me remind you!' Oh Christ, I couldn't stop Shame from beleaguering me. It had taken on an uncanny resemblance to my first primary school teacher, Mrs Daly. She had been a weapon and I had been terrified of her.

'Fourteen Danish pastries,' she began, boring holes into me with her piggy-small eyes. 'Twelve stone of chips,' she took a deep breath, her chequered skirt inhaling with her so she looked like she was wrapped in multi-coloured cling film. 'A lakeful of coke! Do you want me to continue, Miss Birkendale?' Another deep breath. My head was spinning. 'Don't tell me you've forgotten the two boxes of handmade chocolates you bought for Lotty and Roisin but devoured yourself?'

'Oh get lost will you, you tyrant!' I tried to disregard the roll call, but Mrs Daly wasn't having any of it.

She continued yelling, 'Toast!'

How many slices of toast had I eaten last night? Millions. And crisps! What do I say when I've scoffed and shovelled four bags of crisps into myself? MORE!

I heard a little shriek and felt a quiver run down my spine as I realised that I had finished off the last chunk of brie in the fridge last night. Neatly washed down with four glasses of coke when I'd emerged from the bath. And that was after the crisps episode. Fuck!

Mrs Daly had done her job and marched smartly off the stage. Now Guilt made a grand entrance and snuggled up beside me bringing Anguish along with it for the laugh. Shit! I tried to excuse myself by pretending I was obviously suffering from an eating disorder. A new type of bulimic, that's what I was. Just forgot to get sick, that's all. It didn't work. The brutal truth remained. I was putting on weight quicker than an athlete on steroids.

The phone rang abruptly. Still draped heavily in my 'I'm ugly and fat' trance, I answered it with a growl. That horrible guilty after-shock was still clinging to me.

'So, how about it then?' Danny's northern lilt filled my aching head.

'What?' I hadn't been listening. I'd been concentrating on my trouser button that was now only a whisper away from pinging to the floor.

'Lunch, do you fancy some? Thought you might like a break away from the cabin on your first day back?' My hair tightened as I grimaced at the thought of more food.

'Don't be ridiculous, Danny. I'm far too busy for that.'

I hung up, mortally wounded by the audacity of the man to ask me out to lunch when I was experiencing the worst 'fat day' ever known to woman. There was only one thing to do and I hated it. I picked up the phone and prepared myself for what lay ahead (surgically removing if necessary every redundant pound cushioning my hips). I squeezed my eyes shut and rang 'Trim Slim'.

'Of course it's none of my business, Gina. If it was, it wouldn't be any fun.'

Nicola was poking me with one of her 'Ah, go on! Tell me!' faces. We were sitting in her office and she wanted to know who I was bringing to the Christmas party. I shuffled the list of names and numbers in my head and wished for the hundredth time I'd ignored Roisin's threats that she'd burn my credit card if I didn't go back to work today.

Not that I said, 'Sod off, it's none of your business!' to Nicola regarding my 'date'. But I thought I did a great job of rabbitting on about it and not actually telling her. But the curiosity was eating her.

'Don't you have a man hidden away somewhere then?' She was very excited.

For some reason sitting in front of this beautiful creature feeling as fat as the spare tyre on a JCB I felt horribly embarrassed. I wasn't sure if Nicola was pumping me because she was thoroughly convinced I was up the pole or if she was simply being nice. The button on my trousers shifted and tried to take a chunk out of my tummy. I was persuaded; she was fishing.

'Surely you fancy someone? One of the lads perhaps?'

There was no stopping this woman. I looked at her as she tapped her pen on the desk and prayed she hadn't noticed how quiet I'd become in the last ten seconds. Did she somehow know I fancied Jason? I realised that I'd have to say something and quick. Nicola was flashing a smile that would curdle petrol. 'Just tell her,' some part of me roared, 'and stop being so effing paranoid!'

'Just a friend, two friends actually,' I mumbled.

'Oh!' Nicola looked devastated. 'Women friends?'

I nodded.

'Not a fella then?'

I shook my head.

'Oh, I see.'

There was a funny silence and I gingerly observed her. Then I wished I hadn't bothered. I knew what that look meant. Now she thought I was a lesbian. A pregnant lesbian! I was drowning in a panic that was instructing me to rectify the situation immediately. I could tell that Nicola's brain was ticking over at a hundred miles and hour and it was terrifying.

'I don't have a boyfriend at the moment, you see.'

'You don't have to explain a thing to me. Live and let live I always say.'

What in the name of God did that mean? I felt very flustered as Nicola abruptly changed the subject back to hiring a bus for the party.

'You cheeky cow,' I felt like yelling, 'hang on one bloody minute!'

A tap at the door infuriated me even more. I didn't want Nicola telling anyone she thought I was a lesbian. Or pregnant.

'Yes.'

Nicola had switched on her office face. Now I'd have to wait to clear my name. Wait in a horrible sweat until I could grab the first opportunity to fill her in on the details of my pathetic life. I found I was in an awful hurry to stand on my chair and yell loudly at her, 'I am suffering from the after-effects of eating the entire contents of a Cash and Carry because I am in love with a man. Not a woman! And I'm bloody well not up the pole either!'

Nicola's office door was opened gently while I steamed quietly to myself.

'The lads need to hire a crane.'

Jason towered above me all sweaty and dirty and

topless. I could smell diesel mixed with aftershave as he stood right beside me, his hair flitting around his eyes from Nicola's office fan.

'Yes, well make sure this one is sound!' barked Nicola. 'That means it has to be in good mechanical order and accompanied by the correct documentation. Do the terms 'roadworthy' and 'inspected regularly' mean anything to you, Jason? The Health and Safety hounds will be here in the morning, so if I find anyone sleeping, sunbathing or eating burgers in it there'll be murder, OK!'

Jason flinched and quietly shut the door. He didn't even look at me. Not once. I was devastated! I forgot that Nicola thought I was a pregnant fat lesbian. I didn't care if she thought I was some sort of sorry excuse for a woman. I only wanted to die on the spot. Then I felt angry. Boiling angry. Who the hell was he to stroll in here and not say a word to me?

'So, you'll be accompanied by your 'lady friends' then, will you?'

I fired a furious stare back at Nicola who was smirking away.

'Yes. Friends. And for your information I'm not pregnant. I'm not a lezzy. And I do fancy men, OK!'

I got up from my chair in a huge huff and began to storm out of Nicola's office. She was laughing.

'I'm only joking, Gina. Fancy another cup of tea?' I could have killed her.

Chapter 11

I stood in the queue like a mouse. My left hand which was hugging a mangled tenner quivered noiselessly as the line of chatting and giggling women ahead of me moved briskly and chartered me ever closer to the scales. We were like a line of penguins, rocking from side to side. Nobody else seemed bothered to be here, I noticed. Only me. I seethed behind the back of a lady sporting a vile blue rinse and wearing a dress that looked like my granny's knickers. She looked so thin, I observed, that I was quite sure I could fold and rip her in two with my little finger. What in the name of God was someone as skinny as her doing here. Maybe I should ask her? Maybe she thought this was the queue for the bingo bus? I sighed.

I had promised myself that without doubt the place would be black with really fat people making me look like the really skinny one. No such luck. As I handed over my tenner and collected my change I realised with horror that most of the women were thinner than me! Jesus, what I wouldn't do to look as scrawny as yer one. I was now acutely pissed off and more than happy to consider the notion of spending my hard-earned tenner in the café with Lotty and Roisin where they were waiting patiently for me. But it was too late.

I stuck my head out past Mrs Blue Rinse to see what was happening at the scales. I was at once irritated by the constant 'ping' as one after the other the party of babbling woman hopped on, waited for the ping, squealed, hugged the lady grinning beside the bloody thing and jumped off. I felt sick. I wanted to run but I knew I had to stay. Anyway, I consoled myself as Mrs Blue Rinse's hair bobbed in front of me, it can't be any worse than what happened yesterday with Jason. The memory of it nearly cut me in two.

We had finally met. It had happened in the kitchen. He'd sauntered in glazed with sweat and smelling as if he had been sautéed from head to toe with some potent oily substance or other. (No doubt from fecking around with his beloved crane, I'd decided, as my eyes explored his gorgeous body and my brain notified my hands to mind their own business and steer well clear of his chest.) I was floored when he actually spoke to me.

'All right, Gina?'

My brain had kicked in straight away. 'This is

your chance! Take it quick while he's forgotten he thinks you're barmy,' it had howled at me all in a raving frenzy. I had tried to appear sane and yes, I had actually replied.

'Fine thanks,' is what I had wanted to say. 'How's it hanging?' is what I'd actually said.

Then I looked at his crotch and got a whiff of his dreamy toasted scent. My hormones detonated and the next thing I knew, boiling water that was destined for my cup slopped all over my hand.

'Shit!'

I forgot about Jason's crotch and ran my blistering fingers under the cold tap saturating the two of us and practically flooding the kitchen.

'Are you OK?' Jason was staring at me looking concerned, his crotch nice and damp from the jet of water.

'I'm fine!' I snapped. And so did my button.

The next twenty seconds took place in slow motion. This is what it must feel like to drown, I decided as Jason and I stood staring at my dancing button for what seemed like yonks. A surreal silence and a gentle tremor accompanied us as I shuddered from barbecued embarrassment and felt the lino quiver under my feet. My trouser button was putting on a great performance.

Some part of me which was close to the edge felt like clapping as my button did a little twirl and a graceful pirouette before deciding to land with a refined roll and a happy sigh on the kitchen floor. It had escaped. It was thrilled. I was hysterical. I swallowed a shriek and squirmed as a cold sweat cascaded down my back. Now would be a great time to kill myself, I decided. Then I heard a voice, and realised it was mine.

'Right then. Just off to Spar to buy a few razor blades.'

I sauntered out of the kitchen light-headed and giddy. Jason stood, perfectly still with a first aid kit in one hand and my button in the other.

'Beat that!' I yelled at the scales tauntingly when there were only two trim slimmers ahead of me. 'I am perfectly capable of whipping up a round of self-humiliation all by myself, without your help,' I jeered, feeling miserable. All of a sudden it was my turn.

The scales loomed ahead of me scornful and teasing. 'Come on, Gina, let's see the damage, you big fat cow.' My eyes began to roast in their sockets as I stared at those effing scales. I hardly heard the lecturer when she spoke.

'Gina, is it? Up you come then, don't be afraid. We're here to help!'

I looked up, all guns blazing, to scrutinise this woman who was 'here to help'. A name badge with 'Annabelle Bloom, Trim Slim Leader' was the first thing that caught my eye. Then her power suit and her Jennifer Aniston figure charged at me. I was devastated to realise that she wasn't even that much older than me. The fantasy of a frumpy half-wit weighing me in, telling me how underweight I actually was and sure there was no need for me to be here at all, collapsed with a bang. Denial ran for cover. I felt like murdering somebody.

Why hadn't I been told someone more gorgeous than me was doing the business of the day? Or that I would feel sheepish and inadequate in a short four seconds? And that was before I'd even got on the bloody scales. I was fuming. Aniston-Annabelle hiked her eyebrows up as far as they would go and with a gentle push of my elbow guided me onto the electronic pinging machine. It pinged. I didn't hug anyone. Instead I gave Aniston-Annabelle an obscene look for having the nerve to be so lovely and fantastically good looking.

'OK, Gina, that's fine. Only a stone to lose. Take a seat and have a good listen to what's said during the meeting. Next!'

I marched past the line of bobbing penguins towards the door but somehow didn't end up next to Lotty and Roisin in the café as I had intended. Much to my distaste I found that I was sitting in the back row, legs crossed, flicking through some booklet or other Aniston-Annabelle had shoved into my hand. Posters hanging from every conceivable corner of the room promised me the Millennium figure to die for if I drank skimmed milk and ate lots of fruit. I don't give a monkey's bits about the Millennium, I thought, still seething. I've got five weeks from now to shave fourteen pounds off my thighs in time for the Christmas do, if you don't mind.

Suddenly we were all hushed into silence and Annabelle Bloom, Trim bloody Slim Leader, chucked us all a welcoming smile and congratulated the class on how many pounds they'd lost since last week.

'Well done, ladies! We've lost Roseanne Barr and half of Homer Simpson since we last met!' Everyone cheered. I slithered further into my chair and prayed for the end of the world.

Aniston-Annabelle chatted happily about polyunsaturated fats and cottage cheese while I stewed frantically. A stone! A whole stone to lose! Obviously the scales were wrong. I'd never been overweight in my life and now really wasn't the right time to start. She'd obviously made a mistake, I decided emphatically. She simply wanted to get her hands on my hard-earned cash so she could spend it during the January sales. I glanced at my watch and wondered how much longer I'd have to sit in this place where I really didn't belong.

'Does anyone want to tell us their story?'

I sneered inwardly as a wafer-thin twenty something waved her hand at Aniston-Annabelle and smiled a big red smile.

Peh-lease! I thought, rolling my eyes. Miss Skinny is probably going to bore us all to tears with her story about losing two pounds so she could fit into a size six bikini.

'Fire ahead so, Kim!' Aniston-Annabelle handed the stage over to Skinny Kim, who then eagerly stood up.

I nearly tripped over my eyes as they rolled down my denim shirt. She was wearing MY MINI DRESS! The one I had wanted so badly that day we all went shopping. My jaw dropped and I felt like jumping up from my chair and whipping it off her. Instead of leaping up or slapping the person sitting next to me I bit my lip and sank even lower in the chair so my bum was almost on the floor.

'I used to love my fifteen minutes in the car every day,' Skinny Kim started.

I shut my eyes. Here we go, I thought, bring out the violins.

'I'd drive down to the beach and chomp my way through a dozen bags of crisps. Then when I got home I'd have my dinner and start on the chocolate digestives.'

I gulped down a strong urge to snarl 'Sad bitch' at her. So, she'd had a few extra bikkies in the evening. Who cares?

'It was only when I had to go to my sister's wedding that I actually began to worry. I weighed sixteen stone.'

Skinny Kim began to look embarrassed and I reluctantly began to listen. Visions of my good self chomping through those hand-made chocolates while sprawled in the bath bounced around the corners of my head. She was still yapping.

'I stopped my secret eating and lost five stone in less than a year.'

The line of penguins bobbed enthusiastically in front of me and cheered relentlessly for her achievement. I stared a sulky glaring stare at the floor.

When the meeting finally ended I didn't join in with the post weigh-in excitement and chatter. I wasn't ready for all the togetherness and bonding that was happening before my eyes. I wanted to kill someone. I'd had a terrible shock, two shocks really. Not only did I have the equivalent of fourteen tins of beans living contentedly about my person (sagging off my hips and my arms to be precise) but I'd had been forced to look at another woman wearing my mini dress. On top of Jason witnessing my button pop (which has to be the most traumatic incident I've ever suffered and I really feel I need counselling to cope with the shame) the mini dress incident ruined me. It felt a hundred times worse than Nicola thinking I was pregnant.

'It's not fair,' I sobbed as I slunk my way towards the pub, fiddling with the little *Week One* diet booklet Aniston-Annabelle had given me.

'Well then do something about it!' A surly Mrs Daly was back, brandishing a weighing scales and a tape measure.

I hung my head despondently and profaned loudly. Just to really piss me off, standing beside her was a mannequin, wearing MY MINI DRESS.

'OK,' I yelled, 'I'll try.'

I did try. I spent a bloody fortune. I practically slipped a disc carting bag after bag of high-fibre low-fat boring food home from the supermarket.

'What ya got there?'

Lotty was cleaning the kitchen lampshade when I fell in the door practically tripping over a five-litre container of water that had somehow vaulted out of its shopping bag.

'Seventy-five quid's worth of tasteless and vile food,' I replied, feeling dejected and fat. Then I saw out of the corner of my eye the fabulous short dress Lotty was doing the cleaning in.

'Ferfucksake,' I mumbled, grabbing the shopping and dumping it on the counter.

'Let's have a look then.'

Lotty skipped over to me with a feather duster in one hand and a spray bottle in the other. She smelt of lavender oil and reminded me of a flower bobbing in the wind. Not a care in the world. Not a single pound of body fat to lose. Men throwing themselves at her daily desperate to get into her knickers. Where was the justice in that?

Simply looking at Lotty got me going. I went into overdrive. For the first two days I was great. I was thoroughly motivated by my desire to look better than any of those skinny cows on the front of *FHM* or *Loaded* magazine. Then I ran out of puff.

I suppose you could say I started going through cold turkey (including the one in the fridge). I had to have chocolate. I even started dreaming of it. Within thirty-six hours I had changed from a fairly rational twenty-something into a chocolate-obsessed woman. During my worst spell Lotty and Roisin had to sit on me so I couldn't race down to Spar and buy up the Christmas stock of Dairy Milk.

'Stop being so pathetic!' Roisin was roaring at me, but I could barely hear her because I had my head stuffed under my pillow. 'Being dictated to by a bar of chocolate, you sad thing. I'm off to get a curry, are you coming or what?'

I yanked my head from under the pillow and spat out a lump of hair that had got caught in my mouth while I'd been fermenting on the bed.

'I'm not sad and yes I am coming with you.'

'Well, don't think I'm going to sit there and listen to you whinge all night. You can only come if you're going to eat.'

'But I can't eat, I'm on a diet.'

I fumbled with my alarm clock while Roisin admired herself in my full-length mirror which I now hated and hadn't looked in for three days.

'Fine, I'm meeting Jack anyway. See you later so!' She only offered me one miserly 'Are you or aren't you coming?' look before bounding out of my room.

'Cow!' I yelled after her.

I would have grabbed Lotty and frogmarched her

down to the pub but she was working. With a mixture of loneliness and rage to drive me I forced myself into the kitchen, made a fibre-filled packed lunch to bring to work, said a quick prayer that it wouldn't give me the scutters and went to bed.

I am skinny and gorgeous, I affirmed over and over. I am going to the Christmas party, I promised myself as I plumped up my pillow, in that mini dress IF IT KILLS ME. Before sleep wrapped itself around me and made my eyelids heavy I realised with a sigh that IT probably would.

Life is funny sometimes, but I made a point of yanking myself back from the depths of self-indulgent despair. I was being a pain around the flat and at this stage even I couldn't stand my own company. The first thing I did was shop. Hours of sympathetic shopping to console myself over how bad I'd let things get. But that was it. I'd spent enough time acting like an eejit. From now on I made sure I continued to go every week to Trim Slim. The only slightly annoying thing that had happened since then was the pandemonium this morning.

Typically the electric meter had run out during the night leaving the three of us streaking around the flat and partaking in communal hysteria as we realised we were all late for work.

Lotty was in a wicked state. 'Maria will gut me!' she groaned as she flew around the flat collecting and chucking bottle after bottle of aromatherapy oil into her bag. Maria, her employer, really wasn't the least bit interested in stories about lost fifty-pence pieces and burnt out meters.

I felt for Lotty but I had enough to worry about myself. No electricity meant no shower and certainly nothing as luxurious as a cup of tea before facing the world. I was furious and made a mental note that today I would absolutely and without fail phone that bloody excuse of a landlord and get the whole thing sorted out.

I wasn't the only one who was furious. Danny was hopping mad by the time I got into work.

'Jesus, Gina!' he yelled at me as I streaked in the cabin door. 'I had to race back from the site to order the cement. Where the hell have you been?'

'I'm so sorry,' I began, ripping off my coat and scarf. 'It's our new flat. We have a bit of a problem . . .' I told him about the meters and how the gas had an odd habit of blowing itself out, and how the electric meter had refused to offer us credit during the night. I hoped that if I told the truth for once that it might stop him from murdering me. Then I made him a cup of tea. That seemed to do the trick.

'Forgive me?' I asked in a shy voice. I was amazed when he actually blushed.

'Ah, sure forget it,' he said, 'but give me your phone number. If it happens again I'll ring and collect you, OK?'

I agreed and gratefully threw myself into my chair

allowing myself to calm down and enjoy my tea.

'Your father's gone mad!'

I was up to my neck in paperwork and Mum was on the phone giving out stink.

'I told him quite specifically that I wanted a day-return ticket for the ferry so May and I could go shopping in Liverpool next Wednesday and the stupid man bought me a forty-eight-hour return. I think he's losing it, Gina. Has he been acting daft in front of you?'

I continued to write out the timesheet while I wondered what on earth my parents were going to do when Jessie and Tommy finally flew the nest. My mother had a PhD in driving Dad crazy. My father didn't need one. He was simply a control freak with some serious addictions to deal with. Once the house was empty I just knew Mum would want to come and live with me.

'Anyway, how much weight have you lost then?'

I cringed. I knew fine well that Mum had probably told everyone how well her daughter was doing at Trim Slim. 'Best in the class. Should be a leader.'

'Ten pounds and counting,' I replied smugly.

If I was acting smug, I didn't care. I was very proud of myself. I couldn't deny it. When Aniston-Annabelle had shrieked with delight at my first loss of four pounds, I had grinned for a week solid. I'd even let her hug me, just a small one though. I still

couldn't allow myself to get into this communal
show of affection that went on after every meeting.
The urge to vomit lingered but even so I didn't
quite feel like the outsider I had done initially. Once
or twice I had even contributed not 'I'm really into
this' speeches like Skinny Kim but small offerings
about how I was still persecuted by chocolate-
rampant dreams and flashbacks to the old me.

The Old Me. I felt a flush rise on my cheeks
merely thinking about it. Gina Birkendale Serial
Eater. The one who gobbled the last of the fruitcake
before it went stale. The one who gorged on chunks
of cheese with the paltry excuse of 'I'm just levelling
the block off.' The one who kept Tayto in business.

But thank God, I thought, escorting the reluctant
and extremely unwilling Old Me out of my head, at
least I hadn't become obsessed with food to such an
extent that I'd gone barmy and decided not to eat
any.

I was particularly thrilled to find that I could still
drink coffee even if it didn't have skimmed milk in
it. But best of all I had learned that I could go to the
pub, enjoy a drink or two and still lose weight. No
need for me to become the religious one who lost
the plot and stayed in all the time because I was on
a diet. 'I'm not on a diet,' I told myself frequently.

But I had admitted to myself that I hadn't been
eating properly. I'd allowed myself to learn how to
get through the day without starving and by giving
my body what it needed. What it didn't need was a

six pack of crisps and three pounds of brie. It was working. Something had clicked. I felt good.

The backlash was even more amazing I realised, while Mum chatted away about Granny who had punched some fella's lights out when he'd tried to steal her purse. I was soaring through my day-to-day jobs in the office without batting an eyelid. Joe thought I was a genius. My bookwork was up to date and my orders went in on time. Even more amazing was the fact that I felt completely at home when I had to go up on site with Danny so he could show me 'hands-on' the things he needed organised.

Not that that had happened overnight. My first trip up to the motorway had been horrific. Even worse than my inaugural weigh-in. Me? Go on site? Were they all mad?

My cries of refusal were disregarded as Alan and Matt, under orders from Joe, had grasped an arm each and yanked a high-visibility jacket over my head. Ignoring my shrieks, they happily towed me to a site vehicle where they proceeded to assault my survival instinct and drive like lunatics to where the lads were working.

I was in bits by the time we got there. I felt the heels of my very expensive shoes leave grooves the width of trenches gouged in the gravel behind me as the lads then hauled my shaking frame from the van and insisted I wear wellie boots and a hard hat so that I could have a look at the job without being killed. Naturally I was fuming at their pitiless treatment of me but there was nothing I could do when they blatantly refused to pay any attention to the demented woman hopping up and down and giving out stink.

But later, after Danny had explained the ins-and-outs of this and that effing machine and when I had bucked up enough courage to partake in breakfast with the men in the on-site canteen, I was baffled to find I was actually enjoying myself. I grew to love the banter, the slagging and the fun, something I would have run a mile from six months before. But the best thing about the new improved me was Jason. At last I had been noticed.

'He even drove me to the post office so I wouldn't have to walk with all those bloody calendars!' I told Jessie very enthusiastically on the phone when I got home that evening. I snuggled up to the memory of it while Jessie told me all the latest about her and the American pork chop. It had made my day. Me and Jason cruising up the main street like that, him chatting away like crazy. (It certainly made a change from him thinking I was crazy.)

The bungee-jumping button incident had never been mentioned since. I even allowed myself entertain the possibility that he had forgotten about it. And even if he hadn't I made myself forget about it. It had been exiled to the furthest corner of my head and buried (along with that screeching recollection of me clobbering my skull off the desk on my dreaded first day).

The Christmas party was now only two weeks away and things for once were ticking along nicely. There was only one major thing left to do. It was happening this weekend. Lotty, Roisin and myself were all geared up for the 'shagging shop'. Or to put it more politely than that, we were off to buy our outfits for the big night. I had promised them a session to remember. After all there would be the guts of thirty single men at the do. The two of them were giddy with anticipation. Roisin had even told Jack.

'Told him what?' I asked, aghast at first that she would consider doing the dirty on this her longest relationship to date.

'That we weren't married and if I met someone at your Ruffty Tuffty party that he'd just have to cope.'

I couldn't get over her blasé attitude. Not that I'm a prude or anything but I did think she was really mad about Jack.

'Anyway, I'm off to work. We've got two flights to London today, and seeing as it's Friday, God knows the aisles will be full of revolting fellas off on some stag night. See you later.'

I laughed and waved her off. Roisin simply loved terrifying and threatening unruly passengers. In a way it was her defence system kicking in. More than once she'd had some repellent traveller who thought he was clever and would have a go at her because she mixed up left and right when she was acting out the safety procedure on board. Her usually nonexistent dyslexia became rampant when she was nervous and especially at the beginning of her employment. But now with the help of her support group there was no stopping her. Even I forgot her suffering unless she occasionally left a note on the fridge which instead of saying 'I'm off shopping with my plastic' read 'I'm off shagging with my plastic.'

I closed the door after her and for once felt sorry for those poor fellas. They'd be getting more than a hangover if Roisin had anything to do with it.

Jessie was bringing the 'American pork chop' home so he could be scrutinised, embarrassed and made to share a meal with the Birkendales while my Dad shot filthy looks at him.

'Promise you'll chat to him,' she had pleaded. 'You know what Dad's like.' I had promised.

The meal had been duly organised for Friday evening. Mum was in a heap and desperate to cook something spectacular that wouldn't kill the guest or leave Jessie so ashamed that she wouldn't speak to any of us for a month.

'What's his name again?' I asked, terrified by the fact that I had become far too fond of referring to him as a lump of beefcake. I was horrified at the distinct possibility that I might let it slip at the dinner table and Jessie would clobber me.

'Jordan Kelleher, he's a chef.'

We hadn't told Mum that he was a chef. It would finish her off. So come Friday I slipped into a casual pair of jeans and my favourite blue top and made my way home. I'd had another great 'Jason Day' at work. This time he'd sat down and showed me how to use a spreadsheet. Not that I gave a toss about spreadsheets but it had been another welcome opportunity to have a good look at him.

Danny on the other hand had been in foul humour all day. His mood had turned even more dangerous when he'd arrived in and found Jason and me 'fecking around and doing bugger all'. The spoilsport. I could have slapped him.

It doesn't really matter, I promised myself as I put the key in the door. The man is obviously bewitched with me anyway. I soon forgot all about either of them. I had hardly shut the door behind me when I saw out of the corner of my eye Mum's favourite vase fly past the telly, still with a spray of roses clinging to the sides of it. I sighed. My parents were having a roaring argument because Dad refused to wear his good shirt at the dinner table and Mum was yelling that he'd look like a 'dirty knacker' and show us all up. Jessie was sitting on the stairs bawling her head off.

'He'll be here in half an hour, do something!'

Jesus, I thought and flung open the sitting room door. Mum looked sheepish as soon as she clapped eyes on me. She was after all about to fling Dad's reading glasses in the fire. I hiked up my eyebrows and stared at the two of them.

'Jessie's very upset. Please stop acting like a pair of hooligans, you'll only make her worse.'

Dad grumbled and picked up the paper. Mum handed him back his glasses and tramped into the kitchen to see what was burning. An audible noise that sounded like 'stupid eejit' echoed behind her. I nodded at Jessie to come in.

'There's to be no fighting when Jordan arrives,' I warned. 'Promise?' They promised.

Things had barely cooled down when Disaster loomed again: Granny rang the doorbell just as Mum was about to dish up. Even though Jordan had been warned that his girlfriend had a barmy Gran, we had pulled out all the stops to make sure she wasn't around for the big meal. This was still a potentially catastrophic situation!

'What's she doing here, Mum? She'll spoil everything, I know she will!' Jessie had turned milk white.

I bit my lip and smiled encouragingly at Jordan who was looking a bit flustered from Jessie's outburst.

'I have no idea,' yelled Mum from the depths of the oven where she was inspecting the lamb.

Jessie looked like she was about to faint. I couldn't blame her. All her efforts to orchestrate this evening were unravelling like the stitching on a cheap suit. I saw Gran peering through the living room window. Thank God Jordan came up trumps just as Jessie was about to bawl her head off. He gave her a comforting wink and told her to calm down, that everything would be fine. Then he gave her trembling hand a reassuring squeeze. Jessie didn't look at all happy, but nodded in acceptance.

'Now, would everyone move up a place at the table please,' Mum instructed, 'and make some room for Gran!'

'Go and let her in, Jessie.' I hissed at my little sister, who was still rattling with fright. 'And be polite!' I warned her.

Jessie sulked her way to the front door to admit Gran, who immediately marched past her into the kitchen, her huge handbag slapping off her tummy as she walked.

'I'm not interrupting, am I?' Typically, I noticed, she was dressed for Mass. 'I was on my way home from Mass and thought I'd accept a cup of tea, if you've got the kettle on. I don't want to be a nuisance.'

Jessie's mouth opened to spit a reply so I immediately piped up. 'Of course not, come in and meet Jordan!'

All eyes swivelled sympathetically to Jordan like closed-circuit security cameras. Jordan, who was dressed informally in a T-shirt and jeans, instantly stood up to greet Gran. She completely ignored the rest of us, and was busy eyeing up The American while we all shuffled around the table in an attempt to make room for her. I went over to help Mum just as Granny graciously accepted Jordan's offer of his seat, much to Jessie's displeasure. In the kitchen Mum smiled and whispered: 'Tell Jessie not to worry. Gran's just here to make sure he's got his bible in one hand and his bank book in the other.'

Sure enough, there she was, bombarding the poor fella with rapid fire questions.

'So, you're from America, then, are you?'

Jessie stiffened as she put the kettle on for Gran's tea, while Mum and I got busy serving everyone with their main course. It was official. Gran had commenced her interrogation of The American. Granny hated Americans for one reason only: Las Vegas. 'The greatest den of iniquity ever built by man' was how she described it. She frequently fulminated about the chapels in Las Vegas where you could get married at the drop of a hat and have card dealers and cocktail waitresses act as ushers while the minister was dressed as Elvis. The whole thing outraged her pre-Vatican Two sense of morality and thoroughly convinced her that all Americans were heathens without an ounce of religion or respect for anything bar money.

With one shining exception of course: the late President John F. Kennedy. The first Irish Catholic President ever elected. He had money, looks and charm. If that wasn't enough to make you mad with jealousy, he had also stopped the Russians using Cuba as a nuclear missile base, not to mention stopping a third world war as the whole world held its breath. He was her hero and bless her, Gran loved him like a mother. I mean, his photo hung alongside that of deValera and The Sacred Heart, for God's sake. All three of them were lit up by an electric perpetual light in Gran's little front room.

'Yes, ma'am,' replied Jordan, very politely. 'From Boston, to be exact.'

He smiled as he spoke, all white teeth and deep tan, with an accent that could only melt the heart. Without taking her eyes from him, Gran handed her hat, bag and gloves to Dad with instructions to put them in the sitting room.

'I don't suppose you'd have seen any of the Kennedy's around Boston, by any chance?' she enquired, while she waited for her tea.

'I'm afraid not, Mrs . . . ' Jordan looked at Jessie and I for help.

'That's Mrs O'Connor,' responded Granny, looking straight at him.

Jordan threw her a beaming smile. 'Mrs O'Connor,' he continued. 'But I do have a few of the late president's speeches on record, it that's any consolation to you. An amazing man, I'm a great fan of his.' Then he smiled at her.

Well done Jordan, I thought, as I registered Gran's approval.

Jessie handed her a steaming cup of tea while we all watched, utterly fascinated. So far so good, I thought, but too soon to start counting any chickens. We all nearly choked when, without prompt, Jordan suddenly leaned closer to her and added, 'You know, he was very clever. His economic programmes launched America on its longest sustained expansion since World War Two. He was also a great champion and took action in the cause of equal rights. He called for new civil rights legislation. He was a man of intellect and courage.' Jordan paused. 'Don't you agree?'

Gran could hardly speak for happiness. Her little eyes filled with tears as she nodded and dabbed at them with the lace hanky she kept mainly for show. I'm sure she would have adopted Jordan if she could. When Mum brought in the dessert, Gran accepted some for the first time in years. Just as I was about to start celebrating the success of the evening so far, Dad, who had been left out in the cold, decided to add his tuppence worth.

'He was some man for the women though, wasn't he?' He patted his belly and burped loudly. Trust him to undo all Jordan's work, which had been charming and witty, not in the least bit disrespectful. Mum kicked Dad on the shin under the table and Jessie groaned into her plate. The spell was broken.

Gran refilled her cup from the pot and stirred it thoughtfully. She had that look about her we had all learned to dread. She turned slowly towards Dad. I held my breath. Silence reigned briefly. Then Gran spoke.

'You know, Ted, there are things that you will never understand about women. We love men who

have sex appeal and we forgive them for straying.'
She paused to gaze out of the window. Everyone's
spoon hung in mid-air, especially poor Dad's.
Mouths were open, jaws had dropped. Gran talking
about sex! Imagine it! And forgiving adultery!

As if she was discussing the price of butter, Gran
continued. 'I'm not condoning what he did, mind
you, it was wrong, but who knows what we'd do in
his place. All real men are attracted to women. Isn't
that right, Jordan?' She didn't wait for an answer. She
turned back to Dad who was red in the face with
pure anger. More was to come. 'And he loved his
own,' she turned the full blast of her indignation on
Dad. 'Whatever was wrong with them, I'm sure he
was never ashamed of his own flesh and blood.'

We all knew who she was talking about, except
Jordan. Tension hovered like a blanket, until Mum
came out of shock and asked if anyone wanted
coffee. Dad said he'd get it and slammed his way into
the kitchen. Before we had time to absorb the
possibilities of that little episode, Gran turned back
to Jordan and asked if he had settled into any parish.
Myself, Mum and Jessie exchanged 'here it comes'
glances. I felt sorry for Jessie's American. As soon as
Gran found out he wasn't a Catholic, she might
change her mind about him.

'Yes, Mrs O'Connor,' responded Jordan. But Gran
wasn't finished. 'It must be difficult to fit Mass in
with your job. A chef, isn't that right?'

'Yes, I do go to church, Mrs O'Connor, but not

as often as Jessie, I'm afraid.'

Gran nodded happily. It was nice to know her granddaughter was with a nice chap. A fine looking fellow, he was. Not a wimp. God knows, one was more than enough in any family.

Gran stood up and asked Jessie to get her hat and coat from the hall. Jordan held her coat and walked with her to the dining room door. Jessie was saying she was sorry to see her go. Jesus, the world had gone mad

'Isn't Jordan terrific?' Mum suddenly whispered behind me. I had to agree, he had brought out the best in Gran. Not only that, any reservations Mum had about Jessie's new fella had dissolved. Unfortunately, just as we all started to relax and wind down, Dad decided it was his turn to stir it up.

'Do you not think it was all a bit indulgent.' (He was off on a tangent and thoroughly enjoying his own exertions to put the wind up the guest.) 'All those swanky meals on board for the likes of Gerry Ryan and the Mayor.' (He was on about the Independence Day visit of the JFK carrier to Dun Laoghaire a couple of years ago.) 'A lot of ego-massaging really, what do you think then, eh, Jordan?'

Jordan kept on smiling as he and Jessie sat at the table once more. The poor chap deserved a Blue Peter medal for keeping his cool. Fair play to him I thought, feeling for Jessie who was cringing once again.

'Don't mind him, Jordan,' Mum said patting his leg. 'I won't have a bad word about Gerry Ryan said in this house!' She gave Dad a vicious stare as she sipped her coffee. Mum loved Gerry Ryan. He had a special place in our house alongside Frank Sinatra and Tom Jones. Dad didn't stand a chance. If only he knew it. Obviously he didn't.

'For Christ's sake, he's a woman! Overpaid, overrated and no use at all. In fact, I think I'll ring him up and tell him!' insisted Dad.

'You'll do no such thing,' Mum said stonily. 'He's kind, attentive, knows about the world. I learned more about contraception and potty training from Gerry Ryan, than any book!' (This was true. How often had I come home from work and listened to Mum quoting Gerry Ryan: 'Gerry Ryan said this morning that if any fella he knew came home pissed and tried it on with their missus, they'd be flattened! Dad had cursed. His efforts the previous night to amour my mother had ended with him getting a whack of her Argos catalogue.)

'I think he's great!' Mum finished. Dad's coffee cup landed with a furious slap on the table. The salad bowl shook from the impact. 'I thought it was a great way to celebrate the Fourth of July. What do you think, Jessie?'

I had to do something. Dad had turned a funny purple colour and looked like he was about to stab someone. Preferably Gerry Ryan.

'Bloody sailors,' Dad interrupted, flapping his

serviette around before poor Jessie had a chance to open her mouth. 'Sowing their wild oats around the east coast like that, there should be a law against it.'

I tried again before my sister cracked and went for Dad. She was very good at headlocks these days with all that defence stuff she had learned.

'Where's Tommy tonight then?' I aimed this question at Mum. She loved to talk about her only son, unlike Dad who was secretly ashamed that he was gay.

'Working, Gina. He won't be home till late. But,' she said lunging a smile at Jordan, 'he does apologise for missing you tonight, maybe you'll meet later.'

Thank God Jordan piped up yet again, and began telling us 'haven't been further than Bray seafront' lot about his home in Boston. Jessie at last calmed down while Mum oohed and ahhed at all his stories. Then he thanked Mum for the wonderful meal. Mum was chuffed, praise from a real chef! She wasn't going to gouge out my eyes or Jessie's for not telling her in the first place. Dad slunk back off to watch the telly, while the rest of us decided to go out for a few drinks.

I kissed Mum. 'Probably see you Sunday. We're going shopping tomorrow. Unless of course, you fancy popping down to the night club with us?'

Just as I was about to shut the front door and follow Jessie and Jordan down the drive, Dad appeared alongside Mum, presumably to wave us off.

'You may think he's a great fella,' he muttered obviously referring to Jordan. 'But make no mistake – the only set of balls going up those stairs tonight are Irish ones.' With that, he marched back inside and slammed the door. Mum and I burst out laughing. Thank God that was over.

Chapter 12

The nightclub was jammed. Jordan struggled back from the bar with drinks for the three of us. We were here to see Tommy in action. While Jessie and her fella had a quick chat, I realised I was nervous. Nervous for my brother and what I would think of his act. And nervous because the punters were a rowdy crowd and might not like the idea of being entertained by a strange fella donning a Madonna castoff. I sincerely hoped they wouldn't boo him or try to beat the crap out of him. I needn't have worried. I didn't recognise the person who got up on stage and told hilarious jokes and captivated the crowd with his gyrating hips and one-liners.

The atmosphere was brimming with pure excitement and mirth. After a while even I forgot it was Tommy as I allowed myself to enjoy his performance. I got an awful fright when out of nowhere Mum's head appeared as she made her way towards our table. I didn't really think she'd come.

'It's him, isn't it?'

I was flabbergasted and cornered. I fiddled with my glass and tried not to look sheepish. What should I say? I glanced over at Jessie who looked like she was about to faint and decided to bite the bullet.

'Yes, that's Tommy.'

She looked at me with a smile. 'Well, you don't think I was going to spend the evening with yer man at home, do you,' she yelled, straining to be heard, 'when I could be here to cheer on my own flesh and blood?' Without another word she flung her handbag at me to hold and wrestled her way to the bar.

I in the meantime still felt like someone had removed my spine. I must have had such a stupefied look on my face watching Mum cheer and clap on her way to the bar for the drinks that one of the bar staff actually came over and offered to get me a taxi home. Clearly I was suffering from some diabolical illness or other that might make me sick all over the place. I nodded a dazed refusal of the 'I'm about to keel over but I'll be OK after a long hot bath' kind and assured the poor girl that she wasn't going to be up to her knees in roasted lamb. Then I ordered a drink from her instead.

We had a great night. Jessie and I completely relaxed once we realised Mum wasn't going to take to the bed for a month because her only son was giving Tina Charles a run for her money. Mum had a ball flirting with Jordan and passing around baby photos of Jessie while Jessie was having a ball feeling up Jordan. So by the time Tommy was finished and had joined us at our table we were all fairly merry and Mum being Mum threw her arms around him. Tommy was instantly embarrassed to have his mother paw at him in the pub and slunk away from her emotional show of affection. But secretly I knew he was chuffed. And so was I. And so was Jessie. Not only because Jordan wasn't in intensive care suffering from Montezuma's Revenge à la Birkendale but because we were all as proud as punch.

'I'm so proud,' gushed Mum, 'that I think I'll ring up Gerry Ryan and tell him all about you!' While Mum and Jessie dived into four packets of peanuts with explicit willingness, I decided I'd head home and indulge myself with an earlyish night and a bath. I arrived back at the flat in great form and desperate for a wee. Lotty greeted me at the door.

'You'll never guess,' she blurted, all in a tizzy.

'What?' I yelled as I made a very unladylike lunge past her for the bathroom.

'You had a phone call,' Lotty shouted up the stairs, 'from Jason!'

What! I nearly fell headlong from the toilet seat and onto the floor. My knickers got nicely twisted on the way back up as I tugged at them vigorously while simultaneously trying to grasp what Lotty had just said. A frantic flapping of arms and legs ensued. Apparently my knickers weren't the only thing in a knot, I realised as I eventually caught my fingernail in the elastic, hung my head and stared hopelessly at my bullheaded undies which weren't going anywhere. My stomach was lurching and tilting like a mad thing.

Jason had phoned me! I couldn't get over it! I had to get to the bottom of it. His preferably. And maybe this was my chance. Cursing, I threw open the bathroom door so I could yell at Lotty to give me all the details of The Phone Call while I ploughed on with my efforts to yank up my jeans and my knickers so I wouldn't fall down the stairs with excitement. Which is not easy let me tell you when you're in shock and have just found out that the man of your dreams has phoned you while you've been off gallivanting with your family.

'Jason!' I panted. 'You're joking? What did you tell him? Did he try my mobile? Jesus!'

I hopped and skipped my way down the stairs while Lotty bounced at the bottom of them, excited for me but making me feel horribly dizzy. Or maybe I was dizzy because Jason had actually phoned me. Or maybe I was dizzy because while I was hopping up and down Mum's roast lamb was step-dancing along with me making me feel incredibly vile.

'Isn't it wonderful!' Lotty was gushing like a fatal wound to the neck. Which I thought was exactly what she was going to get if she didn't tell me immediately what Jason had said. I belted to the bottom of the stairs in record time and very calmly asked her when exactly did he ring.

'About seven o'clock.'

I did a quick calculation, that was about an hour after I left work.

'What did he say?' I said feeling out of breath and giddy. (I was, after all hoping for something like 'I think she's amazing and I'm dying to snog her, so where is she?')

'Em, something about the fax machine,' Lotty replied thinking hard.

I was very taken aback. The fax machine? Did she say fax machine? That didn't sound in the least like 'Your flatmate's a stunner and I can't wait till Monday to see her again.' And it didn't please one bit the part of my brain that was at this very second flicking through my wardrobe in a frenzied search for anything I could wear that would make me look like Rachel out of *Friends*.

'The fax machine?'

I looked at Lotty feeling wretched and utterly confused. Fine then. He didn't want to snog me. How could he let me get all worked up like this? Did he not know by now that suggestive phone calls (albeit about a dodgy office appliance) late on a Friday night would remind me that God dammit I wanted to snog him immediately? The cruel fucker! I hardly heard what Lotty said next I was so crushed by false anticipation.

'Yes,' she continued, still exhilarated on my behalf. 'He said it was playing up and he'd wait around for

a couple of hours for you to ring him back – so go
on then ring him.'

'Ring him? He's waiting for me to ring him!'

Lotty nodded so hard I thought she'd break her
neck. But wait a minute, I thought even though my
brain was insisting that I shouldn't wait at all but
should just get straight down to business. I didn't
want to give him the wrong impression. I mean if I
rang back now he might think I was easy.

Desperate and full of despair I became the victim
of corrupt hormones, nasty ones that began
badmouthing me and reminding me a dozen times
a minute that we hadn't partaken in sex for centuries
now that Ralph was gone. And to get it seen to. 'No
need to worry about your reputation, Gina,' my
reckless hormones bellowed, 'you haven't got one!'

I realised with sickening clarity that I couldn't
bear the thought of being mugged by my demoniac
sex drive all night. Listening to it giving out yards.
Being bombarded by its threats to put itself up for
tender to the first person who wasn't a frigid old
cow. So with Lotty shaking as much as I was, I rang.

There was no answer from the office. I bit my lip
not in the least bit sure if I was relieved or not and
shook my head at Lotty.

'Try again!'

I obliged with trembling hands. This time the
phone was answered. Keeping a lid on my quivering
stomach was murder.

'Hello,' some male said. Thank God, I thought,

sagging slightly. I had at least managed to dial the right number.

'Jason?' I squeaked, hopes ablaze, hormones churning. Hopes ablaze or not, the quiver in my stomach reminded me that it had now ferried itself up to my larynx. I was mortified to realise that I sounded like a budgie being strangled.

'Gina?' came the hesitant reply. I at once grabbed the chance to redeem my 'she's got a dead bird stapled to her throat' ranking in the conversation and bravely put on my 'I'm not that bothered' voice. 'Hi, Jason, having problems with the fax?' I think I succeeded in sounding like a person with vocal chords that worked and didn't let on that I was at that moment a prime candidate for exploding blood pressure.

'Yes, Gina and it's Danny. Jason had to head off.'

Booming silence. Hopes no longer ablaze. Hormones screeching to a sparks-flying halt. Woman on phone about to bawl her head off. Man on other end of phone about to be exterminated by a torrent of abuse from said distressed female.

What on earth was Danny doing there? I took a deep and enraged breath. And what did he mean, 'Jason had to head off'? Had I gone through a partial cardiac arrest for nothing? I squared my shoulders. I was going to kill him. And I was going to enjoy it.

Danny of course started prattling on before I had a chance to verbally murder and inform him that I could quite easily be spending the rest of the year in a wheelchair with two broken legs, a broken heart and an ego throbbing from undiluted brutal humiliation.

'. . . So, Gina, that's about the size of it. All the lights are flashing and I can't get this urgent order for steel faxed off.'

I was even more fuelled now. My brain busily conjured up images of Lotty and me in casualty trying to explain to the men in white coats what I was doing at the bottom of the stairs with my jeans and undies hanging around my ankles in the first place. The blatant brass of Danny to treat me like some sort of engineer when I was an open book of trampled-on emotion.

'Where's Jason?' I demanded. 'I thought he rang me?'

A funny silence flourished on the line.

'He had to call it a night. He's on early tomorrow,' was the very icy reply. The sort of icy reply that wants to stab you in the tummy. And under normal circumstances it would have succeeded but not this time. This time it was about to be lashed at the last hurdle by my boiling-point indignation. If only Danny knew. There was no chance of 'forewarned is forearmed' here. Oh no. Only lashings of ignorant bliss. Barrels of which poor Danny was drowning in while being nicely sidetracked by his own impatience.

'Can you help me or not, Gina?'

I realised at once that he was using his snotty tone

with me. I blew. My vengeance was extreme and not in the least bit apologetic.

'No I can not, Danny Stone. Who do you think you are, making personal phone calls to the secretary's home at the weekend?'

His response was dry and acrid. 'You rang me.'

I spat several bullets onto the floor, his rebuttal successfully stimulating my in-built Birkendale wrath.

'I did not,' I retorted with an audible snarl. 'I was simply returning a call from Jason Ward. Some of us do have manners, you know!'

I heard Danny draw breath slowly. 'Thank you for your time, Gina. I won't disturb you again. I'll tell Jason that you phoned back as obviously he was the one you wanted to talk to. Good night.'

He hung up before I had a chance to yell, 'Don't dare do anything of the kind.' But it was too late. The engaged tone buzzed in my ear.

'Shit!' I said to Lotty who had stopped bouncing and was leaning tentatively against the banisters. 'He knows.'

Chapter 13

Monday morning arrived not with the usual gentle hum of my alarm clock radio informing me that I didn't have to get up for another fifteen minutes. Nor with the clatter of Roisin and Jack making coffee in the kitchen with the stereo blaring while they waited for the toast to pop. But instead with me sitting bolt upright with curlers still idly lounging around my head, wondering why the postman had arrived so early. I mean this is Ireland for God's sake. The postman never comes before lunchtime. Which means the odds of hearing the plop on the doormat at seven in the morning are zilch. Unless of course it isn't seven. Unless of course it's more like somewhere after twelve, and the electric meter has run out.

I vaulted out of the bed with the inborn agility of a gymnast and almost made it to the other side of the room before my traumatised body reprimanded and reminded me that it is only small children and fitness freaks that go to the gym for three hours seven days a week who can leap out of bed from a comatosed state and get away with it.

I shrieked as my left calf buckled under a 'How dare you wake me up, you cheeky bitch' cramp. I hopped and moaned my way to the door and into Lotty's room. She was fast asleep. I yelled at her to get up and departed just as she opened her eyes and screamed at me to explain why in the name of God I was waking her up on a Saturday. I did the rounds of the flat on one leg in my quest to rouse the undead and wished not for the first time that I was a witch who could turn our landlord, Mr Tibet, into a bloody rat. He still had not managed to take out the gas and electric meters as he had promised the last time this happened and set up ordinary two-monthly accounts like normal people do.

Normal people do not hop around their abodes yelling at their flatmates to get a move on because the meter has run out. Normal people do not wildly shake empty coffee jars with 'meter money – not to be spent in Spar' scribbled on the label in a vain search for fifty-pence pieces.

Flinging the coffee jar onto the sofa I hobbled back to my room, jumped into the trouser suit I had planned to drop into the dry cleaners at lunchtime, hurriedly dragged a brush through my hair sending rollers flying in all directions and with one final shout at the remaining sleeping beauties to get the hell up booted it to the train station. My mobile rang just as the train pulled up. I cringed as I heard Danny's voice on the line notifying me that I was late – again. I mumbled something about a train strike and hung up feeling foul.

Danny had stuck to his promise and made a habit of ringing me if it looked like I was going to be unmercifully late. So he had now become my back-up alarm clock and the first voice I heard if Roisin and I had spent all the fifty-pences on a pair of tights or a big cream cake the night before.

Normally I was happy and chatty when the call came but normally I hadn't acted like a bitch the Friday before. Normally I didn't feel, dare I say it, embarrassed? I was so ashamed and self-conscious at how rude I'd been to him. He hadn't deserved it. He'd only wanted my help which I hadn't given. I was amazed he'd phoned me at all this morning. Now I'd have to say how sorry I was. And I was, honestly. But I was dreading it because now I'd be apologising to him knowing that he knew I fancied Jason. So my apology would be redundant before I even opened my mouth. I'd say all the right things but we'd both know that I had acted like a horrible cow simply because Jason hadn't been there to take my call. I didn't know if Danny would feel worse if I apologised or if I didn't.

Reluctant legs brought me to the cabin door. Nicola's car was parked outside. Brilliant! All I needed now was a lecture from my superior about the irresponsibility of my lateness. I felt too awful about Danny to care. Inside, Nicola was far too busy to let loose on me as she was thoroughly enjoying eating the head off Alan for his offering her a lift in his JCB last Friday when he had spotted her shopping during lunch hour.

'Don't you know that you're compromising all safety regulations? Did you stop to think that I might be having a bite to eat with the Health and Safety? Obviously not! And where exactly did you think I was going to sit?' (Fair question, Alan's JCB only has one seat.) 'You don't offer people lifts in a plant vehicle, Alan,' she spat, 'ever!'

Alan slunk away without even looking at me. I felt bad for him. After all he had rescued my aching arms hundreds of times when he'd spotted me struggling back to the office with shopping bags galore and a month's supply of hair mousse. He always pulled over, took my shopping off me and dropped it into the office.

Abruptly I forgot about Alan as I sank into my swivel chair and surveyed my desk. The day's post lingered unopened along with hundreds of orders to be collected. I wished I were dead. I wished today was over and I wouldn't have to bulldoze my way through all this mess. I wished I hadn't been so nasty to Danny. Feck!

Nicola and Joe interrupted my 'I feel rotten' trance which was rather insensitive of them as I hadn't felt this bad since Jessie had tie-dyed my favourite white shirt about four years ago when she

was going through her gothic stage. All the same I
pushed it aside for now and made myself perk up
and look interested in what Joe and Nicola had to
say. I mean I was over four hours late so I didn't want
to lose my job as well as my dignity and cash flow
in the one day. Nicola looked at me as she lit a
cigarette.

'Joe wants you to show him how to use the
computer, Gina. Just the word processor if you don't
mind and when you've done that, you and I have
some business to attend to.' Christ! She's going to
fire me.

Half-terrified out of my life I glanced at Joe. As
always he was full of smiles which was very
unhelpful of him. I mean the woman was going to
give me my cards for God's sake. He could at least
have looked sympathetic. I decided to pretend that I
hadn't copped on to her. A bit of enthusiasm might
just change her mind.

'No problem, Joe. We can start whenever you
like.'

Unfortunately for me Joe wanted to start right
then. So after about an hour and a half of divine
patience on my part he was at last semi-literate. As
literate as me, you could say. Which meant he could
now do my job if he fancied it. Which was obviously
what Nicola had planned all along. Get me to train
in the project manager so he can do the paperwork
and then boot me out the door for being
consistently late and now in love with one of the site

engineers and at odds with the other one. Joe confirmed my misery with a clap of his hands.

'Right, Gina, I'll bash away and you pop into Nicola so she can have a chat with you!'

I offered a snarly smirk in reply to his inadequate lack of compassion and even though I was horribly nervous I confidently rapped on Nicola's office door.

'Come in, Gina.'

I faltered. How could she sound so cheerful when she was about to ruin my Christmas? I slithered into a chair opposite her and hoped Joe meanwhile would somehow delete the entire payroll by accident. Serve her right, I thought despondently. The nasty cow!

Nicola didn't waste any time. 'I haven't spoken to Joe about this because I know he wouldn't approve.'

That's it, I knew I was finished. Joe wouldn't fire me. He loved me. I was his right-hand woman. The one who kept him in tea, chocolate digestives and the occasional straitjacket when it looked like the Health and Safety were going to shut the job down because one of the nightshift had fallen asleep under a twenty-two ton crane. I shuddered as Nicola raced along with her 'You've had it' speech.

'I've been keeping an eye on your performance over the last couple of weeks and have made several observations regarding your bookwork and general efficiency.'

My heart plunged and I felt a flush rise steadily to

my cheeks. I wasn't going to be at the Christmas
party, I realised, a lump forming with great gusto in
my throat. Never again would I have the
opportunity to pretend I was annoyed with Matt for
hanging his wet clothes off the outside telephone
cable or enjoy the thrill of being winked and
hollered at by the lads when I went up the Main
Street to buy a few stamps. Of course it was my own
fault, I realised bitterly. I had become so distracted,
what with trying to lose the famous fourteen
pounds in five weeks and indulging Jason all the way
when he paid me unnecessary attention. Not to
mention the worrying like mad about Tommy and
the fact that Mum and Dad were constantly trying
to find strange and novel ways of killing each other.

Somewhere along the line I had forgotten I was
actually here to work. I mean most people don't get
paid to flirt for eight hours a day and enjoy
themselves. Nicola was right I deserved this. I mean
I wouldn't employ me if all I was going to do was
size up fellas and their bank accounts for my best
friends. It didn't matter if I was always up to date
with my job when really what counted was I could
do it with my hands tied behind my back, leaving
me free to spend the rest of the time daydreaming
about having sex with Jason. It was simple really. I
was selfish. A no-good thief perfectly happy to
accept payment for a week's work when it only took
me three days to do it.

I started to say something. What, I really don't

know because I felt so emotional but Nicola
interrupted me.

'Which is why I think a change is as good as a
rest, don't you agree, Gina?'

I was cornered. What could I do, only nod
reluctantly and utter a few goodbyes?

'Right then, you might as well get your coat,'
Nicola instructed, standing up and escorting me into
my office. 'We're going shopping!'

When Nicola explained to me that we were off
up to town, just the two of us, to spend the petty
cash on Christmas decorations for the office tree
(which apparently The Bear had 'come across' on
the side of the road) I nearly caved in with relief.
Having to apologise to Danny when we got back
was the only thing that calmed my elation at not
finding myself in the dole queue two weeks before
Christmas.

I wouldn't have to take on the first toilet-cleaning
job I spotted advertised in the local rag, just to meet
the rent. Instead I would still be able to splash out
on the new Clarins range of make-up and Gabor
sandals to complete my 'seducing Jason' plans. Talk
about a close call. The whole episode prompted me
to hand over all the small change I had rattling in my
purse to a tiny child I had spotted minding her own
business robbing a pair of earrings off a street trader.

I don't know which one of us was more shocked.
The street trader certainly wasn't pleased. Accused
me of being 'a woeful mother letting my brazen

offspring run around like a mad thing whipping earrings off stalls and God knows what else when she should have been in school, the little git.' I didn't care. I was full of Christmas spirit and goodwill to all men especially six-foot tall ones with Welsh accents and sumptuous bodies.

My brand new sparkling good humour was wrenched from me as soon as we arrived back. Danny was in my office using the photocopier. Lunatic butterflies took off inside my tummy as they registered his body language. I was hoping for indications of 'Never mind, Gina, must have caught you at a bad time.' Unyielding and rigid stony silence was more like it. Even though I could only see his back, his hostility was seeping unseen into the air. If he had been a joint we'd all have been stoned for a decade.

I made myself shut the door and sit down. I had to do it, I had to say I was sorry. Suddenly it became the most important thing in the world. I realised that I couldn't bear his fertile indifference to me and the idea that he might forever think I was a nasty little bitch. I desperately wanted him to know I hadn't meant it. That I appreciated I had acted like a nasty little bitch but I wasn't really one. Honestly. That I had been up the walls that particular night, the results of demented longings leading to an unholy compulsion for sex. Of course I couldn't say that to him. He'd think I was bonkers as well as a deplorable waste of space. But I had to try.

Only one obstacle stood in my way. It was a big one. I hate apologising to anyone. I think it must have stemmed back to my early days with Tommy when Mum would insist I say I was sorry even when I wasn't. The words were always forced out of me usually by a lingering threat of no telly for a month or even worse no Easter egg, no Santa.

With a hesitant glance I realised Danny would very soon run out of drawings to copy. It was imperative that I get a move on. The waiting was terrible. Me sitting there engulfed by waves of guilt which were busily arguing the toss with oceans of stubbornness trying to spit out those two small words. He aloof and hostile. Just like Dad when Mum would insist from behind her *Woman's Way* magazine that Tom Jones probably had a bigger willy than he did.

Obviously I couldn't blame Tommy for the whole thing, I realised, feeling rather pissed off. I mean the nuns would have to share the burden too, I decided. All those special religion classes leading up to my First Holy Communion. A whole year geared at making us little seven-year-olds apologise to the clergy for the awful things we'd done. The nuns were mad for it making us write out lists of lies we'd told and stuff we'd stolen. Even if you'd never told a lie in your life you'd be scared witless not to have your list as long as the nun's habit. We forgot it was all about receiving a sacrament. So did the nuns. In fact by the time the big day came along and the First

Confession bit was over, the only sacrament I was interested in was a possible windfall from my Auntie Flora.

A disgruntled noise emanated from Danny's throat shaking me out of the memory of my snow-white Communion dress with the tenner stuffed up the sleeve, compliments of Auntie Flora who had at last come up with the goods. Feck! He was going to abscond at any second.

'You can do it,' I urged myself in a futile attempt to fire up a bit of enthusiasm. I mean was I really going to be dictated to by seven letters and an apostrophe? Apparently so. It became blindingly evident that these seven letters and an apostrophe required the services of some kind person who would happily belt me on the back so I would have to spit them out.

'You pathetic cow!' I scourged.

I tried again. No joy. They were still stuck somewhere between my diaphragm and my gob. Time was running out and Danny had begun to make his exit. I shut my eyes and imagined that a little spot between my shoulder blades was being pounded with a mallet.

'I'm sorry!'

There. I'd said it. Danny wasn't the only one who reeled from the aftershock. My head spun around as it tried to physically catch sight of the famous words as they tumbled out of my reluctant mouth. Wasn't it great? I'd said it. I'd apologised. Unfortunately I didn't get much of a chance to pat myself on the back and make indulgent plans to buy a huge cream cake after work for successfully encountering one of my nastier hang-ups. Danny had performed a super-fast swivel while I was engaged in trying to break my own neck so he was now facing me at point blank range. God, I nearly fainted.

His face was purple. He looked like several suites of furniture had beaten him up. Which of course they hadn't. It was pure rage that was making him look like he was about to blow. All courtesy of me, wouldn't you know. I was petrified. I lowered my lashes so I was only half-looking at him hoping it might calm him down. It didn't.

'What did you say?'

I froze. Who could blame me? Even my toes felt icy as they sensed the frosty brunt of his annoyance. I must admit, I hadn't expected such a blistering response from him. I knew he was fed up with me at the moment, but this? I decided it would be best if I gave the apology bit one more try. It was always possible he hadn't heard me, I told myself. After all he is a fella.

'. . . about the phone call, I wanted to apologise . . .'

I tried to keep eye contact with him while I spoke, positive it could only help. Wrong again. He wouldn't look at me. He was far too busy running his fingers through his hair and staring at the ceiling. Finally, I heard a mumble.

'Let's just leave it, Gina, OK?'

Without so much as a 'Thank you for putting yourself through the turmoil of apologising, something you haven't done in years', he was gone. Slammed out of the place like his backside was on fire. Talk about ungrateful. I was appalled. Never mind, I consoled myself, you tried and God loves a tryer.

Roisin was curled up on the sofa when I got home. Even though the apology to Danny hadn't gone quite according to plan I was radiant with joy and didn't mind one bit that she was wearing my favourite lilac top. I'd just returned from Trim Slim where Aniston-Annabelle had confirmed that the hideous fourteen pounds had gone. It was official, I was skinny again. Granted not anywhere as skinny as the female cast of *Friends* or the blonde one who reads the nine o'clock news but definitely thin enough to get into 'the dress'.

'Do you want *Coronation Street* on, Gina or will we watch that Mel Gibson movie on the other side?'

'Don't mind, don't care, I'm thin!' I replied, eyeballing her from the middle of the floor.

Roisin stirred from her cosy patch on the sofa. 'Hmmm, what, what did you say?' She was half asleep watching *Fair City*.

I chucked my Trim Slim gold card at her and flung myself onto the sofa.

'Jesus,' she said, grabbing hold of it. 'You did it, you did it! Oh, thank God, we thought you'd be a fat Antichrist forever. Well done!'

I hauled myself up from the sofa and jigged in to the kitchen to put the kettle on. 'Where's Jack then?' I hollered.

'Who?' she replied, her voice cracking just slightly. Switching on the kettle I had a reserved glance around the kitchen door. Roisin was bawling.

'Ah no, he didn't,' I said gently from the door. It's not like Roisin to cry. You might as well ask McDonalds to finance a sanctuary for worn-out cows.

'He did!' she sobbed while she hugged a cushion. 'I was showing him the new dress I'd bought to wear to your Christmas party, and he freaked. Said I looked six months pregnant in it. Then we had a big fight. Then he dumped me. Just like that.'

The kettle turned itself off just as Roisin really started to snivel and wail. I ignored it and sat beside her.

'You poor thing. Never mind, I'm sure he'll come around in a day or two, wait and see.'

Roisin flung her soggy cushion onto the floor. 'He can do what he likes, I don't care. He even had a go at me because I spelt his surname wrong the other day when I addressed his birthday card. I don't want that, Gina. I want someone who'll pat me on the back and tell me to try again when I make mistakes. It's not fair, sure it's not?'

I nodded in agreement all the while thinking I'd like to kill the nasty little fecker. 'What would make you feel better?' I asked quietly, pulling knotted and salty lengths of wet hair out of her eyes.

'Mel Gibson and a pizza,' was the scarcely audible reply.

'Coming straight up!' I replied, searching for the remote control. 'What sort of pizza do you fancy, then?' I asked as Roisin cuddled further into the sofa. We both roared laughing when she replied with a grin, 'A twelve-inch vegetarian.'

Jack may be old news, I thought as I picked up the phone to dial the pizza company and Danny might possibly still think I was a nasty bitch, but at least, I realised, I was a lucky lucky woman who had the best of friends to fall back on.

Chapter 14

Jack was mourned for exactly one week. One week in which a small holiday home in the south of France could have been paid for with the amount of money that clattered into the till at Spar. All of it spent on family-pack boxes of tissues and bottles of red wine for the three of us. Consolation for Jack not ringing to say how sorry he was for being a rotten toad. We practically needed a prescription for the wine, Roisin was downing it that fast. But it made her feel a lot better and Lotty and myself had so many hangovers as a result that we didn't know which way was up when we eventually found ourselves sober.

Even though Roisin was the one who had been dumped it was a welcome opportunity for all of us to re-assess our own lives. I got an awful shock about half-way through the week to find myself at last wondering what had gone wrong with Ralph. I mean I hadn't thought about him for ages. So I cried

a little bit over him and the fact that my overdraft
had nearly turned into a twenty-five year mortgage
policy without telling me.

Lotty on the other hand worried herself
backwards that she hadn't had a fella for nearly a
year. Roisin and I consoled her and unreservedly
promised it was nothing to do with the shade of her
hair or the fact that she failed Social and Scientific
in the Leaving Cert. It was a cold and blustery
evening as we regarded our communal single status
over another bottle of the red stuff with only the fire
to warm us as the gas meter had yet again refused to
work.

'Well sod the lot of them, I say,' commented
Roisin, flinging a log onto the fire. 'I mean it's their
loss isn't it?' she continued, prodding the life out of
a piece of coal.

'It could be worse, yes it could,' agreed Lotty,
tucking her duvet further around her socked feet.
'The three of us could be tied down to fellas with
no money, no hair or even worse, chronic body
odour.' We all nodded in agreement.

'Look at Linda Fairway for example,' Roisin
mused, topping up our glasses to the brims. 'Found
out her mechanic husband wasn't just servicing the
neighbour's Nissan Micra last month. Wouldn't you
just die?' There was a sweeping hush while we all
contemplated Linda Fairway and her bad luck.

'I'd kill him. Stone dead,' piped up Lotty.

'Me too,' I agreed wholeheartedly, taking a sip

from my glass. 'And what about Shelly O'Neill? Imagine being her?' A chorus of, 'Holy fuck I'd emigrate!' followed.

'The poor bitch,' Roisin wailed with a roll of her eyes to heaven. 'Finding out your fella is chasing another woman is one thing but another bloke? I'd lose it. Crack up there and then. And when I was finished cracking up I'd sell his car and sod off to Spain and find myself a nice waiter.' We all giggled in agreement.

'I like my men to be men,' declared Lotty. 'Strong. Independent. Huge willy,' she finished with a cackle. We all screamed the flat down laughing and when we finally found our composure again Roisin proposed a toast.

'Here's to finding fellas who don't boil their socks in a saucepan or take a fancy to prancing around in our underwear when we're in work and won't catch them,' she giggled. 'But to apprehending real men,' she continued sounding extremely serious and hoisting her glass into midair. 'Real men who'll have us singing 'Fever' before midnight, loads of whom we expect to find at Gina's Christmas do,' she concluded with a suggestive wink.

'I'll drink to that!' Lotty clinked her glass against Roisin's.

'Me too!' I resolved, polishing off my last drop of wine.

When all the wine had been consumed and we all tumbled off to bed I realised with blind terror that no matter how much I yanked and pulled at it, Jason's face refused to sit itself nicely on top of the cardboard cut-out fella in Roisin's Real Man speech.

I'll think about it later, I'm far too exhausted to think about it now, I decided, falling into the bed and knowing quite well that I'd probably never think about it again this century. I was like that you see, it was me all over. Yard brush in the wardrobe to whoosh under the carpet anything I couldn't face right now. Needless to say, I was asleep before my head hit the pillow. And when the morning came accompanied by blurry memories of the night before I whipped out my yard brush and got sweeping.

Talk about a mad panic. With only five days to go before the big night, I found myself in front of a sales assistant who was telling me that 'the dress' was gone. Sold out. But they did have a lovely tartan skirt with matching bag if I fancied it. After lunging a look at her that loudly exclaimed 'I'd rather wear a bin liner' I flew through the first café door available, ordered a hot chocolate and rang Jessie. She wasn't there so I had to talk to Tommy instead.

'I'm devastated, ruined. What the hell am I going to wear now?'

Tommy was very sympathetic but other than suggesting 'black and backless' he was no help at all.

'How are you, anyway?' I asked while my brain

started listing other possible boutiques where I could search for something fabulous to cloak my new thinness with.

'Great, Gina. Actually, I wondered if you were busy tonight?'

Was I busy tonight? I hadn't a clue other than being very busy going up the wall if I didn't find an equally hot dress to 'the dress' to tease Jason with. I might as well go up the walls with Tommy, I decided. Then there'd at least be someone to carry me home.

'That fella I like . . . well he might be out tonight . . . in the club.' Tommy was all excited, I could tell by the crackle of the phone line which meant he was jigging up and down on the spot.

'OK, but I might be like a nest of hornets if I don't find my ideal dress,' I warned, not wanting to let him down but feeling it was only fair to brief him on my state of mind. 'Listen, I'd better go, the shops close in six hours, see you later then?'

Tommy laughed. 'Go for it, girl. I hope he's worth it!'

Jesus, I thought, hanging up and throwing my jacket back on, so do I.

Fourteen boutiques, a lot of foul language and three espressos later I had 'it' in my hand. It was exquisite. More than exquisite. It was fabulous and dainty and sexy. I wanted to be buried in it. I was already buried in it if the truth be known. It had cost me a month's rent which I couldn't afford. I didn't care. Well I did I suppose but I refused to let that put me off. I had wrestled long and hard to find it and I was damned if money was going to stop me now. 'It's no use,' I had informed my screaming sensible side when I snatched a peek at the price tag, 'I'm having it, and that's final!'

I knew I'd done the right thing when later that evening before I headed off to meet Tommy I tried it on with my unworn brand-new sandals. A match made in heaven. Which I would pay for in hell when my bank statement arrived.

'Jesus, it's fab! If you don't get a snog now it'll only be because he thinks you're a lezzer,' whispered Lotty, her eyes out on stalks.

'What do you think, Roisin?'

'I'll give you twice what you paid for it and organise a freebie flight to Paris for you if you swap with me,' Roisin pleaded, sucking in her breath and walking around me in circles to have a good look.

'Never,' I laughed. (Mind you Roisin's dress was a stunner.) Reluctantly I made myself take it off and with the other two deciding to stay in for a change, went off to meet Tommy. I met him just inside the door of one of the more upmarket clubs in town.

'Is he here then?' I asked, my head bobbing around looking for someone in the crowd who fitted the description of 'tall and well endowed, not a stallion but certainly not a donkey either'.

Tommy was all flustered as he scoured the herd of heads nearest us, his make-up dabbed slightly with perspiration as it shone under the lights.

'If he was coming he'd be here by now. He's always here by now.' My transvestite brother sipped at his drink, quietly upset.

I was concerned not only that Tommy was feeling let down but also because I wanted a good look at something one doesn't come across every day of the week: a handsome man who is nice to women and nicer to fellas that dress like women. I hoped Tommy hadn't been hallucinating.

Tommy's mystery man was a no-show. We stayed for the rest of the evening just in case before finally walking home.

'Don't worry,' I said gently before we went our separate ways at the chippie, 'I'll meet him the next time, OK?'

Tommy put on a brave smile and clattered off in the opposite direction. I was amazed looking at him. Even I couldn't manage wearing heels like those. With a final wave I wrapped my scarf around me to keep the cool air at bay and home I went.

Chapter 15

'It was an accident. I don't get paid till Friday. I didn't realise – honestly!'

There was a stalemate boiling dangerously on the landing. Any second now I was going to kill someone. That someone was Lotty. I stared hard at her as she sniffled in front of me wailing about having spent the electric money and the gas money on her bus fare and a pint of milk. I in the meantime was being buffeted not only by her irresponsibility but the fact that I was late. Again! And let's face it I wasn't exactly Danny's best friend at the moment, now was I? Undoubtedly my phone would ring and he would reef me out of it. And worse, I wasn't in any position to defend myself and appeal to his good nature seeing as he was so fed up with me at the moment. I clenched my fists, bit my lip and tried to cool down. 'We'll talk about it later,' I snarled, realising that although I wanted to dismember Lotty, I'd actually better get a bloody move on instead.

Although I was dressed, I hadn't a scrap of make-up on me, so I looked brutal. Without any warning, which I thought very unfair, a furious rapping on the front door shocked Lotty and me from our duel, as we both looked at each other with 'who's that?' expressions. As quick as a whip, Roisin, who'd been poking the gas meter with a coat hanger to see if she could get anything out of it, all the while thoroughly enjoying Lotty and I putting down the ground work on how to maul each other before ten in the morning, flitted off to answer the door.

'Well, hello there!' crooned Roisin from downstairs.

Lotty hushed me as I was about to peer over the banisters to see who was causing such utter commotion with Roisin's hormones at this indecent hour. Regardless of Lotty, who was shushing me like mad, I nevertheless craned my neck at an awkward angle to see who was there.

'Gina! It's for you!' yelled Roisin as she belted back up the stairs wearing an animated smile before I had a chance to steal a proper look. 'He said he tried to ring you, but your phone mustn't be on. I must say, Gina, I wouldn't mind him in a sandwich. He's lovely!' she finished, disappearing into her bedroom.

Danny stood motionless at the bottom of the stairs. Jesus, I thought, grabbing my bag as I made my way down to meet him. This is going to be murder.

I wasn't wrong. The trip to work in Danny's vehicle was awful. As soon as it realised that nobody minded, Silence paraded around the car. It got a mortgage, moved in and brought all its relatives: Atmosphere, Bungling Embarrassment and Frenzied Awkwardness. I tried to make conversation, honestly I did. In the end, after explicity snubbing my efforts, Danny spend most of the trip with his hands-free phone kit.

Harbouring an etched frown, he ordered all the supplies that I should have organised at 8.30 this morning. Realising that he was never going to accept my apology, well not for a while anyway, I slipped quietly from the car and in to my office. Instantly, Nicola, who was chatting away about the Christmas party, cheered me up. I made myself join in with her discussion about what we all should wear for the big night. Feck Danny! I decided. I'd done my best and it was only two days to the Christmas party after all. If he wanted to act like a pig, let him.

The three of us couldn't think of anything else as we chatted over breakfast a couple of days later. Today was the day.

'I'm so excited!' shrieked Lotty. Roisin and myself grinned over our bowls of cereal. 'So excited that I forgot all about my three-thirty appointment yesterday with Mrs Murphy. She was coming in for her usual massage, and where was I? In Dunnes looking for knickers! Maria nearly lost her head with me. I don't think my advising her on the benefits of calming oils was exactly what she wanted to hear. Oh well.'

Roisin giggled. 'Well, I don't know what you're so worried about. I nearly boarded the wrong bloody flight. I could have been in Germany if the supervisor hadn't called me back!'

As I sat on the train my mind began planning furiously. The Christmas party was on tonight and there were preparations to be made by a desperate woman about to go on the rip. First, I had to make sure I could take my half-day from work. (This was of life-threatening importance as I had to start the business of getting ready for the eight o'clock deadline by three in the afternoon at the latest.)

I wasn't long in the office when I realised sourly that certain things are easier said than done. A major dilemma was dished up by The Legend just before elevenses. He was in a heap due to biting comments by fellow male employees regarding the necessary wearing of a suit. The man doesn't wear suits. Not even to his own mother's funeral.

Thankfully the problem was solved by Lovely Nicola who pointed out that no swanky ensemble of posh clothes meant no beer. Manipulation and guidance on her part resulted in The Legend swearing he'd wear a chicken suit if necessary. Unfortunately Lovely Nicola's persuasive ways did not terminate the flow of sarcastic comments from sniggering lads.

With the suit crisis temporarily halted I make an appointment for the hairdresser while flirting dangerously with Jason who's just strolled into my office. I bathe in suggestive comments regarding his anticipation of my appearance when dressed in something other than a trouser suit or a pair of wellies with cement stuck to them. And I ignore the unsupervised snarly looks thrown around by sulky Danny every time Jason and I bask in each other's gazes.

Needless to say I ring Lotty and Roisin every ten minutes to ensure neither is hitting the bottle too early unless it contains either hair colour or shaving foam.

Instead of doing the post, I race around to the chemists and suffer the indignity of having to purchase an unwanted bottle of vitamin C tablets and some safety pins, followed by mighty endeavours to secure a three pack of condoms via a game of charades where my mouthing 'birth control' about four hundred times falls on deaf ears. Literally. The man behind the counter is very old and as deaf as a post. He doesn't sell birthday cards or balloons. But they do in the newsagent around the corner, I'm instructed rather brusquely. Feck! I finally accept that I'll simply have to get them out of a vending machine in the hotel tonight, I leg it out of the shop.

Next stop, the knicker department up the road. Thankfully the procuring of a very fine pair of silky knickers and a bra plus two pairs of tights goes without a hitch. I make a mental note to ensure the same happens later when I'm putting them on. Crucial if I am to eliminate any possibility of a panicky race to Spar for ninety-nine pence support tights special.

Then I finally race back to the office and pretend to look busy for another half-hour. I enjoy an excited conversation with Nicola about the evening ahead before allowing myself a final glimpse of Jason's behind, abandoning my desk and heading for the train. I dream about him all the way home. 'Suffer with a smile the glory of having at last found The Right One.'

Arriving home with fifteen minutes to spare, I lounge on the sofa with a large cup of tea and two sugars. Then at last it's time for me to commence the transformation from 'Generic Gina' to 'Who's yer one, isn't she gorgeous?'

The 'suit' scenario (started earlier that day in the office) came to a head at the exact moment Lotty, Roisin and I stepped out of a taxi and made our entrance into the trendy hotel, all three of us looking like a million dollars, myself on a high (and I don't only mean my heels) gagging to see Jason. I glanced at Lotty and Roisin as my shoes sank into the piled carpet gracing the reception area. Both girls were beaming with expectation, desperate for a good flirt and high on a promise from me that there'd be a bounty of fellas, fine things to pick and choose from who'd die happy simply to sit beside them over dinner.

And I'm sure they would have, if most of them weren't about to start a riot in the corner of the bar.

'There's more brains in a used condom than in your head, Alan Commisky!'

Jesus, The Legend was all in a flap and about to light on Alan who was winding him up like a clock over the whole business of attire. Roisin and Lotty swapped horrified glances with each other. These were the fellas they were to spend the next ten hours with? I had completely forgotten that my flatmates were strangers to the constant colourful language I was subjected to daily. All the same I marched over, with Lotty and Roisin trailing behind in a cloud of appalled whispers. I got there just before the head barman was about to eject the whole lot of them out on the street.

'What on earth is going on?' I demanded of Alan, tapping the barman's shoulder and giving a promising nod that I'd sort out the rowdy bunch immediately so there'd be no need for the guards, or an ambulance for the old dear three seats away who was going into cardiac arrest from all the offensive language.

Alan immediately sat down and pointed at Fran, one of Danny's labourers. 'It was him, he started it!'

he insisted with a whimper.

I felt like a schoolteacher, pursing my lips and wagging my finger. 'If there's another word from any of you,' I threatened, flinging a harsh gaze at the sombre group, 'we'll all be out on our ears – got it?'

They got it. A sulky hush descended initially but it wasn't long before the chat resumed. Roisin and Lotty got over their initial shock and were more than thrilled when I squashed them in beside myself and Jason and two of the finest specimens of man I'd ever seen – Nick and James, our new site engineers who had just arrived in from Kent.

Lotty and Roisin both relaxed even more, and breezed through all the introductios that followed. I was astonished that neither of them flinched as they passed pleasantries with The Legend. He had made me look like a hanging liar, I realised as I observed Roisin leap into a conversation with him. He didn't look in the least like the serial killer in disguise I had described to them during my first week at work. After all the brawling in the office earlier about what he should wear, there he sat, not a bother on him in a Ralph Lauren suit! I had another sneaky look just to be sure. Yes, it was him, shaved and all. Then again, why was I surprised? He was paid a fortune each week to keep his crew out of trouble, so he could afford to look like Charlton Heston. I had to hand it to him – he looked fantastic.

Glancing around the table, I was shocked to see all the men looked completely different and good enough to eat. Not one of them tugged uncomfortably at their ties, and thank God, none of them had worn their filthy old work boots. In a funny way I felt proud of them.

Tonight was going to be my night, I decided emphatically, accepting with a broad smile a drink from Jason. I couldn't believe this moment had finally arrived!

The rest of the office gang turned up about five minutes later. Nicola and Joe squeezed in beside us. The two of them were in great form, and for once not trying to kill each other. Nicola had brought her fella, George, along for the festivities. He was a butcher from Sandymount and would have been quite happy to spend the evening jabbering on about how to pluck, stuff and joint turkeys if Nicola hadn't issued him a roasting glare that shut him up instantly. I was very relieved. I didn't want to know what my piece of turkey breast was doing the day before yesterday or partake in a conversation The Legend had started about what happens to all the feathers after they'd been plucked off the poor thing. Nicola ushered George off to the bar instead much to his disappointment.

'Where's the grub so, Gina? What time are they dishing up?'

I looked at Alan with a grin.

'I could eat the legs off the table,' I was informed.

So after another round we all sauntered into the function room. I was slightly dismayed to find Jason didn't walk with me and instead somehow I ended up falling into a trot with Nick. He was being very chatty and pleasant and I tried to smile politely while I looked around for Jason. It was OK, panic over, as I spotted him just behind me hopefully getting an eyeful of my dress as he strolled alongside Lotty.

I was quite excited as we entered the dining area. Acres of linen tablecloths all dressed with Christmas candles and rows of sparkling crystal wine glasses. I was immediately seduced by the dim intimate glow of the candles and the way they reflected themselves in the sets of silver cutlery. Fantastic! What a great place for Jason and me to fall madly in love. Naturally the band started up as soon as we sat down, their renditions of 'Good Lookin' Woman' utterly ravaging the atmosphere beyond repair. I'd be patient, I resolved. I'd wait. Sure hadn't I the whole night ahead of me yet? I could hardly expect the band and the other sixty-four people in the room to be nice and quiet allowing me to get on with my own personal business, now could I?

I sat beside Jason who sat beside Lotty who sat beside Roisin and James whom she'd lassoed the minute she'd set eyes on him. Matt sat opposite me wearing a suit that made him resemble a traffic light.

'Where'd ya get the suit, lad?' chortled Joe. 'That Liberace fella must be buried naked so, is he?'

The whole table rocked with laughter. Matt replied with a couple of very rude gestures.

'There'll be none of that in front of the women, you dirty looking eejit.'

Briefly my eyes met Danny's. We still hadn't spoken properly since the morning he had driven me to work. He settled down to his starter ignoring me. Fine! I'll bloody ignore you back, I thought. But the pit of my stomach felt unsettled by his coolness which had been dragging on forever.

I turned to Jason fully prepared to start the chat-up proceedings and was halfway through asking him with fluttering hands how he was when I realised he was talking to Lotty. Not your usual, 'Haven't met you before so I'm being polite' conversation but an established energetic, face-to-face discussion. Noticing too late that my mouth was still open I stuffed a forkful of melon in my gob hoping I didn't look like someone who'd attempted a premeditated flirt only to find the subject of the exercise was busily doing the same thing to her best friend.

The melon stuck in my throat and I looked sideways while I tried to swallow it. Confirmation that the happy couple were still at it boomeranged back at me.

She's just being friendly, I decided, ignoring Urgent Trepidation that was putting in a loud request for an oxygen mask to be provided with the main course. I've no reason to think otherwise, have I? Of course not, I assured myself as I was reluctantly dragged into a conversation with Nicola and George about rising house prices.

'What do you think, Danny?' asked George through a mouthful of melon and raspberry coulis, the conversation having now moved onto horse racing.

'Donkeys at the four-thirty, every one of 'em,' Danny replied full of chat as he devoured his melon and obviously in great form.

How dare he be in great form, I thought miserably, dabbing my mouth with a napkin and placing it on my shimmering silver dress. Tonight was supposed to be my night. I should be the one full of beans, soaking up the atmosphere and simply waiting to be lured into a fluffy bed with Jason. Instead I was forced to listen to Nicola, George and Danny as they continued arguing the toss over horses and houses. Leaving poor me alone with my glass to wonder when in the name of God I would be tipsy enough not to care that Jason was chatting up MY FRIEND and hadn't noticed I was wearing an AIB overdraft special for the occasion.

'You look great.'

My head without asking rotated full circle bulldozing its way through the umbrella of gloom that was trying to sabotage my evening. It stopped with a screech in front of Jason's nose practically dislodging it. I scolded myself instantly while I grinned gregariously at him. I mean as if, for God's sake. As if Lotty would flirt outrageously with the man I was prepared to die for! I felt wicked for even contemplating such a thing while I gladly drank in

Jason's immaculate appearance.

'Thank you,' I said demurely, pretending to look shy while enjoying him and the mulled wine I had thrown into me earlier which was now making me feel cosy and secure.

'I know I shouldn't say it but, ah no, I won't.'

Jason was playing with his fork and not looking at me. He was looking at my dress, I realised with glee. So I shifted slightly, carefully allowing my overdraft special to inch up my leg a tiny bit. A crumb from the cake if you like. I let on I didn't know what was coming next.

'Say what?' I encouraged. 'You can't start to say something and not finish it, now can you?' I taunted, pretending to be cross. Polishing my smile and dabbing my cleavage with a hanky.

'That dress,' he drooled. 'You look so . . . ,' Jason lapsed again and reluctantly exposed me to an uncertain if not fearful smile.

You'll be relieved to hear that I didn't at that point stab him with my knife and yell: 'Look like what? Spit it out before my blood vessels burst all over the damn dress!' No, I decided I'd put on my best performance ever of 'Oh stop you're embarrassing me but please continue' by fluttering my eyelids and casting sweeping glances at my hands.

At that moment the band decided they'd do a heavy metal version of 'Santa Claus Is Coming To Town'. I could have cried but I didn't have time as

Jason leaned towards me and cupped my ear with his hand. Goose pimples immediately rose on my neck and the urge to squirm was hastily pounded upon by breakdancing hormones which were yelling, 'Close contact at last, thank God.'

I breathed deeply absorbing his Armani scent and nearly fell off the chair. Then caught myself at the last minute, urgent hands propping me back up just in time. Just in time for Jason to growl, 'You're the most beautiful creature I've ever seen.' Then I did feel like I had fallen off the chair.

In the ladies there was a mad flurry of hands as we all rooted through our purses looking for change.

'I've got one,' Roisin panted, frantically digging out a pound coin from the bottom of her evening bag. 'What about you, Lotty? You always have buckets of change.'

Lotty scoured the depths of her tiny Next handbag. 'I've a couple of them in here somewhere. Hang on, here they are.'

Two one-pound coins appeared along with a scrunched-up tissue and a purple lipstick. We grinned at each other. A trio of cats who got the cream or who were about to get it more like.

The evening was going great. Roisin had clicked with James in a big way, Lotty, against all her own personal odds had been placed under surveillance by Nick for the duration and she was now ready to let him catch her and I was of course exhilarated that my efforts with Jason were finally bearing fruit.

We all giggled observing the condom machine in the corner of the ladies while The Spice Girls wailed 'Two Become One' on the stereo behind us.

'Just to make sure that two don't become three,' Roisin sniggered, dropping the first of her pound coins into the slot, hastily followed by another two.

A good pull on the little knob in the middle of the machine should have produced a neat little three-pack. One each. We rubbed our hands while we waited, big smiles parading across our perfectly made-up faces. Nothing happened. We stared at each other with horror and then at the offending machine.

'Ah, feck!' grumbled Roisin. 'I don't believe it. What now?'

'Let me have a go,' I insisted, elbowing the two of them out of the way. I pulled and yanked but again nothing appeared. The vending machine remained calm and composed, unwilling to give in.

'Will we leave it?' suggested Lotty, suddenly looking nervous.

'We certainly will not!' I spat, wishing I was as imperturbable as the machine was but then it didn't have half a dozen glasses of mulled wine coursing through its veins and zooming around its insides like shots of adrenaline, now did it? It didn't have to endure being clobbered by visions of Jason wearing nothing but a sprig of mistletoe either. I therefore decided that the situation warranted a bit more assertiveness. I couldn't help myself. Gina Birkendale, hot and horny, allow her night be undermined by a vending machine? I'm afraid it was out of the question. I shot a grin at the girls and gave the box a good thump.

The electronic alarm went off instantly and several cubicle doors flew off their hinges as a group of women raced for the door screeching 'Fire!' We were nearly deafened by the piercing wail emanating from the bloody thing.

Roisin groaned. 'Bloody typical, I knew this was going to happen, I knew it!'

The wailing continued and that was only from Lotty. 'Jesus, Gina, we'll be arrested. Do something!'

'Like what?' I screeched, fighting to be heard over all the noise.

'What's the problem, ladies?'

Lotty and Roisin cringed with embarrassment before streaking into the nearest empty cubicle leaving me to do a spin on my six-inch heels furious and determined to interrogate the person responsible for asking such a daft question.

'The problem,' I replied with a taut thorny snarl, 'is this bloody machine. It's not working!'

'Is it not?'

I gaped at the barman who was twirling a set of chubby keys between his fingers. I was flummoxed. Was the man deaf? Was it possible he was related to one of the taxi drivers who had caused us all that distress the day we moved into the flat? A brother, perhaps? A complete idiot? Definitely. The mulled wine kicked off its shoes, rearing to have a go at this grinning blockhead. It was all I could do not to snatch the keys out of his sweaty palms and dismantle the damn machine myself.

'I'd better have a look so.'

I exhaled loudly, throwing furious looks at his back. Roisin and Lotty decided it was safe to come out of hiding and joined me while Blockhead twiddled with the lock, finally managing to put a stop to the ear-splitting alarm. We all breathed a sigh of relief.

'Don't be messin' with it again, righ'?' Blockhead said, looking terribly cocky for one so utterly stupid. 'I'm the key holder so I don't want to be in and out of here all evening, OK?'

The audacity of him! Like all fellas he was oblivious to the torrent of filthy looks being chucked at him. In fact I think he thought he was in there with three beautiful women staring at him as if he was mad. Madly in love being his own interpretation if his roving yet 'void of any brain cells' eyes were anything to go by. Why was I surprised? God only knows.

'This piece of workmanship is constructed of all welded steel, a high security device, two millimetres thick, ya know!'

'A bit like yourself,' I wanted to growl but I bit my tongue willing him to hand over the goods so we could get the hell out of there and back to our three dishes in the function room. Blockhead grinned a toothy smile at his flabbergasted audience. That was it. Roisin flipped.

'Give me my three-pack NOW!'

Lotty and I suppressed giggles and had to turn our backs as, God love him, Blockhead jumped a good six inches then wilted under Roisin's evil eye before miserably handing over her purchase.

'Thank you,' she hissed, eyeballing him until the poor chap got the message and scooted out the door with his flattened ego.

'Bloody hell, what a complete pain he was!' Lotty said with a chortle, accepting her condom and hiding it in her zip compartment.

'Right, come on, girls. We've been in here long enough,' I instructed as we danced out the door and headed for our table, via the bar of course.

Chapter 16

There's nothing like a free bar and a few paranoid builders to get any evening on its feet. Roisin and Lotty were screaming the house down as they drank in every word of The Legend's story about 'Syphilis Sally'. I'd heard it in the canteen that first day when somehow or other I'd gathered enough courage to actually keep my bum in the chair and have breakfast with the lads. I'd been horrified.

Poor Sally had worked for Mr Ryan for exactly one month before hotfooting it out of there and back to the agency bawling her head off and demanding compensation. I didn't blame her. I mean, can you imagine it? A woman desperate for love and a plethora of fellas who were more than willing to show her a good night. In her four weeks on site poor Sally had been shown a good night by at least a dozen of them. They had loved it (no shame whatsoever) and my heart went out to this wretched woman even though we'd never actually met.

Then came that awful Monday morning when Sally was late arriving to work and informed Joe over three cups of tea that she'd been to the doctor. She was suffering with cystitis and was in the horrors. Joe, always a lover of a hot piece of gossip, told The Legend, who didn't know what cystitis was and so asked Alan, and Alan decided it must be syphilis. Syphilis! J-A-Y-S-U-S!

Within the hour the site looked like a ghost town. Plant vehicles abandoned with the keys still idling in the ignition, pumps switched off, hard hats and high visibility jackets thrown willy-nilly on the ground. There was murder. Fellas from Benjamin Ryan Construction were queuing up in emergency surgery to get themselves tested. It cost the company thousands of pounds in lost progress not to mention the humiliation which spread like wildfire. Poor Sally scarpered. (I'd have done the same myself.) The Legend never lived it down.

'It was her own fault, sure she was probably a feminist anyway!'

Roisin curled her lip at Alan. He was only twenty-one, and probably didn't even know what a feminist was, other then being a lezzy of course. Any woman who didn't love being whistled at from the top of the scaffolding on her way to work was a dyke. It was official. The lads had told him so. I was omitted from this definition mind you because I was a woman who believed all women should have equal rights, which wasn't the same thing at all.

Feigning laughter at Roisin who was telling a few jokes of her own, I slyly rested my back a bit further into my chair and closer to Jason's arm which was hanging around looking like it needed something to do. It worked, instantly it rested on my shoulder. I beamed and shuddered all at the same time. Then I pretended I had to shift my bum in a bit closer to Jason's thigh while I laughed at Lotty who was telling everyone how amazed she was that I hadn't turned into a six-in-the-morning chain smoker who swore profusely at the drop of a hat. His leg responded and latched itself to mine.

Everything was going swimmingly until I noticed Danny. I froze as I watched him slipping into the chair next to Roisin's. James's chair, James being absent and en-route to the bar. The hard neck of him. Muscling in where he wasn't wanted. My stomach did an unexpected cartwheel as it observed Roisin actually looking thrilled by his presence and talking to him. She looked chuffed. Had the woman gone mad? I was disgusted to find my insides certainly had. They now thought they were members of the Rapid Reaction Force, Danny's every move making them jump, skid and stand to attention for a full five minutes. I knew this feeling. I'd had too much to drink, there was no other explanation. Nothing to do with Roisin coyly touching his sleeve and engaging him in animated conversation, of course not.

By the time Matt had almost started a fire with the sparks from his hobnailed boots denting the dance floor, I knew it was time to head home. I'd been lavished with Jason's affection all night and I'd nearly passed out cold when he'd pulled me up for a slow one. Naturally I insisted I couldn't dance this one with him but I did. And I loved every second of it even though Lotty and Roisin were making rude faces at me from their table while Danny was watching my every move, his face as hard as Mum's last effort to cook a pasta bake.

Roisin gave me the signal – it was time to go. Shaking with nerves I whispered to Jason that I really ought to be making a move, it was terribly late and I had to be up early in the morning. (I nearly laughed when I heard myself say this – Gina Birkendale, up before the crack of noon on a Saturday? Never!) There was a busy gathering up of coats, a final cracking of disgusting jokes and promises of hair of the dog cures in the morning until finally we were on our way.

The night air was sharp and clear. As Jason linked my arm through his I realised that from this moment everything would be totally different. There was no going back.

Granny Birkendale was definitely an Irish Mother. She could have been Peig Sayers' sister as she was always on the look out for sinners, loved a good disaster and would murder to get her hands on the juiciest leg of pork for Sunday dinner. And of course there was also the Mass thing.

Few of the Birkendale clan had seen the inside of a church since Jessie's christening. Granted Mum popped in when she really needed something (like a new car for instance) full sure that a few Our Fathers would do the trick. Otherwise we were all considered a bunch of heathens in Gran's eyes.

But I had to admit, even if I didn't agree with her about most things, one small gem of hers had latched itself on to me. The same one Gran often mumbled as she knitted quietly in our sitting room, disgusted to find her whole family ignoring her because we were agog watching a taboo sex scene in *Eastenders*.

I gently examined her words as I lay on my bed. Then I reluctantly turned them over a few times, scrutinised them back and front, subjected them to a probing internal examination before admitting with a tortured sigh that they now had a place in my life. Even though I closed my eyes tight, they wouldn't bugger off. At this rate I'd be stuck with them for the rest of my life. I still couldn't fathom it. The one small detail where my Gran of all people had hit the nail on the head, so to speak.

I opened my eyes and stared at the ceiling thinking that would do the trick. Stare at the ceiling and they'll have to go away, I informed myself. It's painted magnolia for Christ's sake. I began to feel like a pop star being stalked by a lunatic fan. Of course I wasn't rich or lucky enough to bother any professional stalkers; even they'd have better things to do. They'd simply pass me on to the 'as thick as two planks of wood' department. And who could blame them?

Looking at the words that were now streaked across my ceiling, I certainly couldn't. There they were as bold as brass. My constant companions, 'A standing cock has no conscience.'

I mean what sort of a gobshite was I for God's sake? A huge one apparently. There I was swinging off Jason's arm while I waved goodbye to Roisin and Lotty. I didn't feel the time pass as we strolled contentedly towards his apartment and hardly noticed the ladder in my wearied tights as I accepted a nightcap and snuggled into his chest. In fact I might as well have been on a different planet until the moment I made my grand entrance from Jason's en suite loo as Gina Birkendale Sex Goddess. Poised, ready to tantalise and partake in a full twelve hours of debauchery. Make-up removed, fancy knickers on and my poor mind scuffling to gather its composure now that it was under siege from a potent mixture of trepidation and sickening delight at what lay ahead.

Only to find him snoring. Like a camel. Like my Dad after a belly full of Guinness. Not like someone who a mere two minutes earlier promised to ravish me senseless and leave me in an orgasmic heap for a week.

I dithered in the doorway for at least five minutes while I worked out what to do. I felt horrified, wickedly let down and freezing all at the same time. My own fault. That's what you get for larking around in the middle of the night wearing nothing but a little (and very expensive) two-piece. Heatwise it was not very practical. The equivalent of a serviette and a piece of thread you could say.

Then I encountered the 'what's the proper thing to do' issue which seemed extremely important as I gazed at Jason levitating off the bed with all the snoring. Jesus, should I jump on in there with him? (It might not be very polite.) Or should I jump in the first taxi passing and cut my losses? (It would definitely lessen the chances of me looking like a plonker.) I shivered while dithering in the doorway and tried to reach a settlement. I could hardly spend the whole night shuffling from one foot to the other outside a civil engineer's loo now could I?

I was too cold to delay things any longer. In a last-minute rendezvous attended by 'Frozen and exhausted Gina' meets 'Dubious, her confidence just streaked out the window Gina' a flurried compromise was met. Frozen and Exhausted Gina elbowed itself to the fore and wouldn't take no for an answer no matter what. I whipped over my head a loose shirt Jason had left on the back of a chair and quietly slipped into the bed beside him.

I knew at once that I'd done the right thing. A gigantic bicep wrapped itself around me before I even had a chance to close my eyes. 'Hi there, gorgeous!' Jason pulled me closer before the snoring started up again. He could snore all he liked. I was in a heaven reserved only for the very lucky and the very lucky. I fell asleep acutely aware that an unwavering hard willy had found a home pressed against my back. Maybe in the morning, just maybe.

There was no maybe about it. Gran was right. I'd spent a tortured two days not being able to think about anything else.

'Why don't you tell us about it?' Lotty looked horribly concerned. She and Roisin had enjoyed a brilliant night with Nick and James. And they were seeing them again. All the same even though I was sick with jealousy there was no denying that Lotty had been fantastic. Worried herself stupid all day that I might give in to whatever trauma had befallen me and revert to my old ways. She'd even put a lock on the biscuit cupboard. I sniffled and got up to put the kettle on.

'I'll be fine – in about a year, so let's just leave it, OK?'

Lotty said nothing but looked at Roisin. Roisin shrugged her shoulders and got on with the business of ringing James. How could I tell them? How could I say that early the next morning as Jason hugged me close, his hands running along my spine and delicious sleep still clinging to us, that it had been Lotty's name whispered into my eager ear, not mine?

Another week passed. I was going great guns.

'Where's the Spread Boss?' Joe anxiously poked his head out the cabin window. 'He should have been here ages ago!'

I looked up from my paperwork and smiled at him. 'Fancy a cup of tea?' I grinned.

'Gina, you're a star, I'd kill for one!'

I left Joe to hang out the window while he waited for Gerry. Gerry was our man-of-all-trades, the new 'especially recruited from the pub last Wednesday night' Spread Boss who was supposed to have stripped some machine or other this morning. And of course he hadn't, so poor Joe was once again left in the perilous position of trying not to crack up until either Gerry or a strong cup of tea arrived to salvage his sanity.

I meandered into the kitchen and filled the kettle. I thought I was doing very well. Hadn't lost it once this week not even when Jason had breezed into my office and as cool as you liked asked me out for lunch. I had resisted him and his wolfish grin. Wasn't I fantastic? I'd plastered a sterile cold smile on my face and nicely refused. It wasn't even a smile but more like jaws — a clenched acknowledgement simply for show so he couldn't call me a frosty cow. It was murder and I was tormented by doubts.

What if he'd simply made a mistake? After all my months of hard work was I possibly overreacting? He'd been perfectly civil and friendly when I'd vaulted out of the bed hurriedly thrown my clothes

on and made for the door fuelled by hurt and rage
and about a million other sensations. He'd even
offered to take me out for breakfast. Some part of
me, a huge part, refused to believe he'd actually
meant to say her name. I deserved him for God's
sake. After all those weeks of sweating it out and
praying for a miracle.

But it was no good. No matter how many times
I replayed that moment in my head and no matter
how many millions of times I agonised over it I
couldn't make 'Lotty' sound like 'Gina.' Unless of
course I stuck my tongue to the roof of my mouth
and pretended I had a speech impediment.

As for Jason, he hadn't even mentioned it. I clung
to this skinny little branch of hope. Had he
forgotten he fancied Lotty? Maybe he was mortified
and was trying to make it up to me? I liked the
sound of that. Sure why not let him crawl around
me for a few weeks and then see what gives? Perfect!

I handed Joe his tea and waited.

'You're mad. Insane. Off your head. Are you crazy?'

Jessie stared at me, disbelief engraved in her eyes
as she regarded me and my lunatic suggestion that I
should try again with Jason.

'After he called you Lotty?'

I shuffled in my chair. Yes, it did sound wicked
now that I was hearing it from someone else.

'It was the drink, Jessie – that's obvious.'

Now that I was far away from Jason, of course it

was obvious. A bit of space had dampened my initial anger and feelings of being an utter gobshite.

'If you do this, Gina, I'll – I'll never speak to you again!' Jessie folded her arms, daring me to call her bluff.

'But—,' I started.

'But nothing. So much as look at him again and that's it!'

I slumped in my chair. Jessie and I had met for lunch and we'd been having a grand time until I'd bucked up the courage to tell her about Jason. I mean I had to tell someone. Neither of us spoke for several minutes.

'How's Jordan then?' I casually asked, fiddling with my hair.

Jessie was still het up. 'At least he has the decency to remember my name!'

I felt the blow and reeled momentarily. Of course she was right, I knew it. I did. But I couldn't help wondering.

Danny was as cool as ever when he rang the office that afternoon looking for a locksmith to be sent up to the site.

'As soon as you can, Gina. It's urgent.'

A fumbling silence followed before he hung up. I was just about sick of it. 'Get over it!' I felt like yelling at the humming phone line. I hung up and sighed. Why had everything gone so wrong?

Chapter 17

'My black coat, my black coat! Where is it, Jesus!' Roisin was racing around the flat like a mad thing already twenty minutes late for her meal with James. 'He'll think I've stood him up. Oh shite, where is it? Gina, have you got it in your room?'

'No!' I yelled, burying my head back in my *Cosmo* magazine.

Lotty had already gone ages ago to meet Nick. Yet another night loomed ahead, the remote control and me all snuggled up with a low-fat pizza. Christ! No dishy fella breaking down the door desperate to woo me. No offers of a good night clubbing from Jessie who was still fuming with me over the whole Jason episode. Unable to stand my own company for another second I picked up the phone and rang Mum. Even she was out.

'Hasn't been seen since lunchtime yesterday. Probably shopping – again,' Dad informed me before hanging up.

I shut my eyes as Roisin finally found her coat.

'Don't wait up!' she roared before slamming the front door behind her.

Feck this! I thought. There was always one fella who'd happily keep me company for the night when all else failed. I slipped into my coat, threw my last two fifty-pences into the gas meter and headed off to the video shop. If it wasn't going to be Jason giving me the eye for the evening it was damn well going to be Pierce Brosnan.

It must have been Pierce. I'm holding him responsible. I awoke after my night in alone and felt marvellous. I never feel marvellous on a Monday morning – ever.

Monday mornings are always the same. I'm exhausted. I fall in the cabin door with Martin and Matt at my heels. I shut my ears to Martin's cranky complaints about 'needing a new bit for his drill' which in turn usually leads to a loud discussion outside my office door about sex. Not that I mind loud discussions about sex or anything but the laddish, macho rumpus that follows is enough to put any woman off her breakfast unless of course she's a horribly unattractive builder who lives in a pair of wellies.

But today was different. I couldn't put my finger on it, or explain it for the life of me. OK I'm lying. It might have something to do with the firm decision I made after my fourth glass of wine last

night. Call me a stupid cow if you like but, yes, it's
the one where I forgive Jason for accidentally calling
me Lotty and making me feel so awful that not even
the purchase of a new pair of Gucci sunglasses can
put a smile on my face.

The same one where I convince myself that
without a shadow of a doubt he fancies me rotten
and simply made a mistake. An oversight. A blunder.
Granted a blunder that merits nothing short of a
horsewhipping but a blunder all the same. And we're
all human here, aren't we? I'm quite sure I referred
to Ralph as Mel Gibson a hundred times but it
didn't mean anything!

Cheered up out of all proportion I flung open the
windows in the flat before floating into the kitchen
to put the kettle on. Thank God the meters were all
still running. And bless Roisin, she'd left me a little
heap of fifty-pences on the counter. Keeping an eye
on the time I shovelled a handful of them into the
coffee jar and sauntered into the shower.

I've a very busy day ahead, I informed myself as I
lathered shampoo into my hair. All the philandering
and vamping around I'm planning to do has to be
perfectly orchestrated. No hitches this time. It'll be
exactly the same as planning out my daily diet sheet,
I assured myself. Simple.

Now what was on the menu for breakfast? Gina
arriving to work packaged in a short black skirt,
complete with angora slash-neck jumper and fire-
engine red lipstick.

And for lunch? I thought a convoy of mind-altering perfumes coupled with a cleavage-enhancing shimmer stick might do the job.

And for afters? Well how does seven-denier nudey tights that make me look like I have Michael Flatley's legs, firm, toned and downright sexy, sound?

I felt so relieved, I realised as soft soapy water alleviated the wrath of last night's bottle of Rosemount red. Off the hook, full steam ahead. And OK I knew Jessie was concerned and why wouldn't she be? If I were her I'd have been frantic too. But I did think her worries were unfounded I mean the man was obviously taken with me.

So taken he called you Lotty!

'Shut up!' I snarled.

Typical, I thought rolling my eyes. Common Sense had decided to join me in the shower without being asked. I pretended I hadn't heard a word and turned the temperature up on the shower unit instead. I shut my eyes in a blatant show of 'Get lost I'm ignoring you' which I hoped would send Common Sense staggering from the room. It did, finally allowing me to get dried and dressed for my Big Jason Day.

I was still awfully sleepy though as I charged through my wardrobe searching for my favourite cashmere scarf. It refused to enlighten me on where it was hiding, so instead of heaving everything out of the closet only to dump it all on the bed I decided I might as well apply my make-up first then do the hair then find the damn thing.

I applied my foundation expertly (Lotty is a very good teacher) and still yawning like mad slipped into my tights and lay on the bed in an effort to zip up my skirt (one of my 'haven't been seen since I got skinny' skirts which fits me at last) and somehow couldn't get up again. Jesus, I thought, that Rosemount has a lot more punch than I bargained for.

Five minutes later, with the towel on my hair now tilting sideways, I was still flat out. But it was a lovely flat out. Peaceful, comfortable, dreamy. I shut my eyes and felt even more snug. Now I had a problem. Even though I really wanted to get up and get moving I couldn't arouse my legs into action. Five more minutes, I compromised with them, then that's it.

Now that we were all agreed I relaxed even more. I couldn't honestly remember a moment in the last year when I'd felt so tranquil (unless there was a bottle of ylang ylang oil involved) and even then my ability to unwind had never been this – this perfect.

I should do this more often, I decided, enjoying the sensation of sunlight stroking my eyelashes. God, isn't it great? I wondered if Lotty had left on one of her relaxation tapes somewhere, one of the subliminal kind she constantly harps on about. Try as I might I couldn't hear a single sound in the flat so instead I congratulated myself on my new-found talent by turning my head a little to the side so the towel now covered my left ear, drowning out the noise from the crèche next door.

My dreamy haze stirred slightly as it acknowledged a knock on the door. Even though it was quite a demanding knock, I couldn't have been bothered to move, my five minutes weren't up yet. Anyway it was probably the milkman looking for his empty bottles. Feck that, I thought. It wasn't worth getting up for.

I sank even deeper into my personal paradise and ignored it. By the time the second louder rap permeated my mind it was too late. Sorry, I thought to myself, I'm not getting up. Come back next week.

I grinned and allowed my mind to descend even further into this wonderful absorbing place it had just found. And you'll never guess what happened next? Pierce Brosnan kicked in the front door of the flat and manhandled me. I'm not messing, honestly. Even though I was sleepy and giddy all at the same time I acknowledged his arms around me, picking me up and touching my neck. Then I got a whiff of him as he gently kissed my lips.

Before I knew what was happening he had gathered me towel and all up off the bed. The last promise I made to myself as he pulled me into his chest was that no matter what happened I was buying a case of Rosemount at the off-licence tonight – for definite!

Granny was giving me a funny look so I shut my eyes even though I couldn't work out what she was doing in my flat. Had Roisin and Lotty let her in without telling me? Who cares, I decided and drifted off again.

'God, look at her, would you? She looks terrible!'

I turned my head not in the least bit willing to be pulled away from my dreamy Utopia. The voices continued relentless and concerned.

'It's my fault – I knew I should have come home last night!'

I could have sworn that was Lotty's voice. All the same I kept my eyes zipped shut.

'Don't be daft. If you had come home you'd be here too. Anyway was he good, then?'

Lotty's tone changed from utter despair to utter delight. 'Yeah, he was great. Jesus, Roisin, I think he's the one!'

In your dreams, I thought vaguely from my far off haven. Pierce Brosnan's the one and don't I know it!

Jessie's voice wafted into the conversation. 'She's going to be grand, the doctor said so.'

Even though my eyes were still closed, I registered the nodding of heads and sighs of relief.

'What's all that wet stuff on the bed?' I think it was Lotty again.

'Gran, wouldn't you know it.' Mum's voice. 'That's a pint and a half of holy water from ten Mass. The doctor said it was OK as long as she promised not to drench the floor.'

Then shuffling on the bed noises as someone got up.

'Look, I have to go to work. I'm on the lunchtime flight to London. Give her a kiss from me when she wakes up, OK?' That must be Roisin. Silence returned and I welcomed it.

Sunlight lazed across my eyelids coaxing me back to the here and now. I sighed deeply relishing the moment before being forced into a bolt-upright position in the bed by a vile urge to be sick.

'She's awake, she's awake! Get in here, Ted, she's awake!' I glared at Mum through one eye and felt the skin on my face ripple and crease into a ball thinking full sure this was it. But the nausea passed. Thank God! I sat back and looked at Mum.

'The doctor said you'd be as good as new. No need to worry, you're not dead yet.'

What on earth was she talking about?

'I knew there was something wrong. I felt it, honestly I did. There I was shopping myself rigid in Marks and Sparks with May when, wham, it hit me!'

What doctor? Where was I?

'I should have phoned you but I thought you'd be at work and I didn't want to ring the office and talk to any of those fellas. They'd only think I was mad. But then that Danny chap rang. Isn't he lovely? Anyway he told me he'd found you out cold and to come straight away.'

Danny! I grasped Mum's hand even though my head was spinning.

'Mum,' I asked quietly, 'what happened?' Her hand locked with mine and a single tear ran down her face.

'It was the gas meter, Gina. It leaked and nearly killed you.'

I made a face at Jessie as I sipped at the hot tea she had just handed me.

'It could have happened to anyone for God's sake, I don't know why you're making such a fuss!' I nodded my head in agreement with myself. Of course it could. Plenty of women nearly gas themselves first thing in the morning. Probably happens a dozen times a day. Jessie still looked cross.

'Didn't you know it wasn't working? Honestly Gina, you should realise by now how important it is to keep these things maintained.'

I snorted and returned to my tea. I'd never in a million years admit it but I was hugely embarrassed about the whole episode. Imagine. Being gassed! I thought things like that only happened in sit-coms. I'd been rushed to hospital but only kept in overnight. If it weren't for Danny I'd have been in big trouble. Pushing up the daisy's trouble.

Our gas meter wasn't merely wonky, it was extremely dangerous. Apparently the gas had filled the flat after the pilot light had mysteriously blown itself out during the night. Seemingly I couldn't smell or taste it but I had ingested so much of the stuff that it had nearly killed me. In a nice way of course, a nice, sleepy 'Pierce Brosnan is ravishing me' kind of way. If I hadn't opened the windows that morning, I'd be a corpse by now.

'Thank God you didn't fart!' Jessie smirked as she handed me a biscuit. 'Don't you think you should ring your hero then?'

I looked at the phone and my heart sank. What on earth was I going to say?

Mum raced to the door as an Interflora van pulled up outside the house. Awful as it sounds, I was hoping Jason would be in a right state once the news got around that I had almost gassed myself to death and that he'd whiz around to Mum and Dad's with a massive bunch of flowers and an envelope with two plane tickets to Montego Bay.

I pretended I hadn't noticed the van. Still perched on the sofa, trying to look like butter wouldn't melt, I flicked through the evening paper with one eye while the other was cocked towards the door. Mum snatched the flowers off the poor delivery man before he'd even managed to put one foot on the doorstep. I hurriedly stuck my head back in the paper as she flung open the sitting room door and thrust in my face the most amazing bouquet of flowers I'd ever seen.

'They're for you,' she shrieked. 'Hurry up, who are they from? Do you think Ralph might have heard the news and decided to forgive you?'

I curled my lip and looked at Jessie. She was trying not to giggle as she watched Mum hopping from one foot to the other, her eyes begging me to open the little greeting card and put her out of her misery. I could hardly contain my own excitement. Were they from Jason? Was I holding in my hand our first love letter?

Slowly I opened the envelope. A little card with 'Get well soon' slipped into my hand. Underneath it was written a single sentence: 'Sorry not to have made it sooner. Hope these cheer you up.' It was from Danny.

'Well?' Mum was on the verge of exploding with anticipation.

'They're from Danny,' I hissed, bitterly disappointed although I didn't dare show it.

'That's very thoughtful, isn't it, Jessie? First he saves your life and now he sends you flowers,' Mum finished with a wink. I nearly puked as I flipped the card towards the bin and immersed my head back in the paper. Mum sauntered into the kitchen, the excitement over.

'I really think you should ring him, it's been two days. He haunted the hospital, Gina, no messing.' Jessie was staring intently at me. 'And,' she continued, trying to conceal a smile, 'he's bloody gorgeous!'

I was horribly miserable over Jason but maybe Jessie was right. I could ring Danny and thank him and while I was doing it, sure there was no harm in pumping him a little bit, was there? You know, casually ask if Jason knew what had happened? What a brilliant idea, why hadn't I done it sooner? Calling myself all sorts of names, I ran out to the hall and dialled the office.

He wasn't there. Feck! Instead I ended up chatting to Joe for over an hour about the whole thing.

'I'll tell him to call you as soon as he gets back,' Joe finished before wishing me a speedy recovery.

I'd been so long on the phone I hadn't noticed the site van that had pulled up outside the house. Christ! Maybe it was Jason!

I bolted up the stairs and straight into the loo. In a stomach-churning frenzy I applied a fresh layer of foundation and a dab of lipstick. I counted from one hundred down to zero while I was doing it. Precisely enough time for him to hop out of the car and walk up the driveway. I snapped shut my lipstick case just as the doorbell chimed.

'Gina,' Jessie was roaring up the stairs at me. 'Gina, you've got a visitor!'

With one last fleeting look at myself in Mum's full-length mirror I counted to ten, exhaled loudly and ever so slowly strode towards the top of the stairs.

Voices trickled from the sitting room to greet me as I began my descent. I felt like a bride, I decided with a giggle, like a bride waltzing down the aisle. I cocked my ear, all my senses on alert. Yes, there was a man in the sitting room. Yes, his voice, sounding deep and husky from my stance half way down the stairs, definitely belonged to a fine thing. I entered the sitting room, my legs wobbling. My perfect smile froze. I fell into the nearest chair. It wasn't my beloved Jason. It was Danny.

Jessie disappeared into the kitchen to put the kettle on. Back in the sitting room the atmosphere was throbbing with an awkward tension. Danny perched on the sofa while I perched on my chair. I was grateful for his saving my life. I was. But by the same token, I wished he wasn't there. We'd hardly said a word to each other lately. And yes, I did want to thank him for what he'd done for me. But not here, not at home and not when I was expecting Jason at any moment.

I immediately launched into my 'I'm being very polite and thank you for saving my bacon now please leave' speech. He didn't leave, but my efforts at least shifted the atmosphere that had been clinging on to us and having a ball.

'Sorry about the door frame, did I get you into trouble?' For the first time in weeks, Danny looked me straight in the eye.

'No, not at all. Our landlord was so terrified I'd sue, he hardly uttered a word!' We both smiled. My smile camouflaging the fact that I was still struggling to get over the shock of Danny seeing me that day in what could only be described as not my finest moment. Legs sprawled all over the bed. Thank God I'd slapped on a bit of make-up first. Thank God I'd put on my angora sweater. Before I'd crashed out. Before several blokes in casualty got a look at me,

tights and towels all over the place. I still rattled from
the humiliation. And speaking of humiliation, there
was something I had to know.

'How come — I mean was I very late?'

Danny blushed and wiped his chin with a shaking
hand. 'It was after ten. You didn't answer your phone.
I put it off for ages and then I remembered the
meters.' He stopped explaining and shifted again. 'I
felt — I was concerned, you know, just in case.'
Silence.

'Well, thanks. I owe you one, I guess!'

Jessie came in with the tea and lovingly poured a
steaming cup for Danny. When she was gone I
approached the question. The big one. The Pierce
Brosnan one.

'Was it you — it's just I was a bit tired at the time
— did you . . .' I couldn't say it. I was raging with
myself! How could I put it? Were you the guy that
tenderly touched lips with me, sending me into
orbit? Jesus, there was no way. Danny cleared his
throat and put his cup on the floor.

'I'm a first aider,' he began.

Of course, you daft cow! Imagine thinking —
Jesus!

'I shut down all the meters first, then I had to
check for a pulse and basically get you out of there.
I rang an ambulance from my mobile, picked you up
and . . . em . . . that's how it happened.'

I had never felt like such an eejit in my life. All the
men on site were trained in first aid. I sank back into

the chair, wishing it would swallow me up. At least now you know, I comforted myself. Pierce Brosnan indeed!

I thanked Danny at least six more times before he headed back to work. Mum and Jessie fell into the room as soon as he had gone.

'Well, how did it go?' Mum was grinning so hard she looked like someone whose plastic surgeon had gone bonkers and inserted a coat hanger under her teeth.

I fumed quietly before answering, 'Fine, thank you.' Obviously this was the wrong answer.

'Isn't he something? Did you thank him for the flowers?' She elbowed Jessie and battered me with another grin.

'YES!' God! Why were mothers so intrusive? 'Look, I'm heading to the flat this evening so I'm going upstairs to get my things together, OK?'

'Only trying to help!' Mum huffed her way back to the kitchen leaving me alone with Jessie.

'You're still brooding over that other bloke, aren't you?'

I conjured up my indignant 'how dare you' expression. Jessie put on her coat and ignored me for a full minute.

'I am not!'

'Look,' she started, closing her eyes with frustration and facing me full on. 'He's a wanker. Danny is not. I'm going to say it again, are you ready? He's a w—'

'Shut up!' I roared, standing up and grabbing my own coat.

'No, Gina I won't and besides, are you blind? Danny's mad about you.'

I yanked a scarf around my neck.

'Don't be ridiculous, he only did what he was trained to do.'

Jessie pulled her famous stony face. 'He may be trained to do it, Gina, but he didn't have to do it.' She flounced out the front door.

I watched her leaving before yanking off my scarf and throwing it on the sofa. 'Ah, bollocks!' I roared to nobody in particular and stormed up the stairs to lick my wounds.

Chapter 18

Lotty impaled her Barbie doll on the top of the tree. Search as we might, there wasn't a single Christmas angel to be found in Dublin.

'Finished!' she proclaimed. 'What do you think?' The three of us took a step backwards, critically eyeing up the tinsel-laden doll.

'She doesn't look very comfortable – she looks pissed,' Roisin observed, her head cocked sideways.

'Will I straighten her up then?' Lotty asked, taking a sip from her glass of wine.

We all grinned at each other. 'Nah!'

The flat looked amazing. Christmas cheer shone from every corner. It was wonderfully cosy – and intimate, I suppose. I busied myself wrapping up presents while the other two opened another bottle of wine. I had a special gift for Mum, one she had been begging me for since she'd met some old school friends last week. Jessie put it down to mid-life crisis syndrome.

'She's already had her nose pierced and yesterday she told Jordan, quite seriously, that foreplay is the most important part of sleeping together. Something she insisted Dad knows nothing about. I nearly fainted! Dad ran out of the kitchen and Mum started laughing. I don't know what's got into her!'

I put a bow on Mum's present, deciding it was the perfect stocking filler for her and grabbed myself a glass of wine. I'd been back to work for a whole week and the excitement of the Christmas holidays stretched ahead of me. Everyone was in great form at work and the following night we were all going for a final drink before the break. I welcomed a shudder of pleasure that tickled its way past my shoulders and up my neck. Myself, Lotty and Roisin would all be going home for Christmas and the lucky bitches both had a fella to come back to in the New Year. I sipped my wine and started wrapping Lotty's present. I had a feeling, a warm feeling, that I would too.

'Will I put the kettle on?'

Jason stood in the doorway and fired a smile at me that bounded across the room, reminding me of the first time we had met. He'd been doing it all week. Flirting like a demon and asking me over and over how I was since the gassing.

'Someone was praying for you, someone was. God love you, are you OK now?'

Fluttering my eyelids, I'd replied: 'Just about. But

I still feel dizzy now and then.'

This time however I refused the tea. If I didn't make the post office before lunchtime Nicola would kill me.

I stood in the queue, quietly delirious. My stage-two efforts to impress Jason were going without a hitch, no matter what Jessie said. I'd chosen today's outfit with precision and attention to detail. And if I do say it myself, I looked fantastic. Even Nicola enquired with a jealous gasp as to where I had bought my powder blue boat-necked sweater. Then she'd offered me a huge Christmas bonus if I promised to lend her my knee-length Prada boots for the New Year. As for Jason, he'd been agog when I'd arrived this morning. If he wasn't licking my damn boots by seven-thirty this evening I'd gladly give up.

I danced my way back to the office, even stopping for a chat with the security man. Then I made my way to the canteen to see Margaret, the canteen lady, to wish her a Happy Christmas.

'The rats are gone!' Margaret looked chuffed. The canteen had been under siege by big ugly vermin for a week now. 'That nice fella with the explosives blew them to kingdom come,' she continued. 'Of course the only downside is I have to use the portaloo outside,' she continued holding her nose and making me laugh. 'My lovely porcelain toilet was detonated to smithereens!'

I had a cup of tea with Margaret and Curtis, the

blast engineer, who had just arrived to get his breakfast. Then I had a peek at the big hole in the canteen where the loo used to be and decided it was time I headed back to my desk. After all, I thought as my stomach did a flip, Jason was waiting.

Three site vehicles were parked in the compound when I arrived back. Thank God, that meant Jason was still here. The Legend's head was lodged under the bonnet of one of them and, yes, Jason's bum protruded from under another. It was hell itself trying to resist the urge to walk over and feel it.

'. . . terrible 'bout Gina. Thank God she's OK,'

I was unexpectedly touched by The Legend's concern for me and decided to make straight for him to say how much I appreciated it.

'. . . no thanks to you though, you stupid bugger. Lucky Danny was here, eh?'

My heart shuddered from the impact as reinforced steel shutters slammed down in an effort to protect me from what was coming next. I hardly noticed Jason's bum as it performed a little wiggle from under the bonnet.

What was going on? What did the Legend mean? Why was my heart belting along at four hundred beats per minute? Jason stopped the wiggling and started to talk.

'How was I to know?' His voice was careless.

'Danny rang you, didn't he? That's what he told me.'

Jason shifted his weight from his left foot to his

right foot while he considered The Legend's response. I stood perfectly still while my booming heart and I waited.

'I was having my breakfast, man, what do you expect? Though she's good for a ride, no doubt about that. The gas didn't do her that much damage!'

I acknowledged that The Legend didn't laugh laddishly at Jason's comment. He simply cuffed him around the head and told him to keep his dirty effing hands off me, sure I was a nice girl.

My legs remembered how to walk and somehow I found I was sitting at my desk. Shell shocked. A taste in my mouth. What was it? A coppery film that stuck like glue. I couldn't swallow it no matter how hard I tried. The taste of stupidity itself. I sat for ages. 'She's good for a ride.' His words trampolined in front of my face. They could have auditioned for the bloody circus.

I remembered sitting up in the hospital bed with Mum crying her eyes out and worried sick that I might die. Then, as if by magic, Danny's flowers seemed to appear on the desk in front of me. FUCK! My mind somersaulted as it worked out exactly what had happened. Danny had phoned Jason and told him to go and get me. Told him he was worried that I was late. And Jason hadn't budged.

I fumbled my way into the kitchen and put on the kettle. A large coffee with three sugars was needed. I sipped it quietly, ignoring Nicola as she laughed happily in the main office with Joe, the two of them cracking jokes and enjoying themselves. He hadn't budged. No major mathematics needed here. He hadn't bothered. He'd left me for dead even though he knew the meters were acting up.

Driven by that inner strength afforded to people who have just realised that the ride of the century is in fact the bastard of the century, I managed to wrap up the fifteen bottles of whiskey put aside for suppliers, which Joe had left on my desk. And no, I didn't drink a drop. My insides lurched at the mere thought of it. The job completed, I hugged and kissed Nicola and Joe and against all their protests lied my head off and said I couldn't go to the pub.

Before I headed for the door, Nicola caught me by the sleeve.

'Mr Ryan asked me to give you this – have fun spending it, OK?'

She knew. I knew she knew. Knew something horrible had happened. I accepted my Christmas bonus with a watery smile, gave her a hug and headed for the train.

I hardly heard The Legend who was busy telling Matt that his bald patch was a solar panel for a sex machine. I forced myself to walk past Jason without saying a word. His face registered something as he realised I was leaving the compound. He called after me but I blanked him. My two-week holiday loomed ahead of me. Barren and destitute. Two weeks to hate myself. Two weeks to spend admitting that yet again my sister was right.

'Come on, girl. You've been as miserable as shit for days now!'

It was out of the question, I wasn't going clubbing with Tommy. Miserable stupid women do not go out and get pissed. It only makes them more miserable and stupid, except that now they have a hangover and enough aches and pains to convince themselves that they've done three rounds with a woolly mammoth.

Tommy kept at me. 'I'll lend you my vibrant indigo top, slim-leg trousers and my ankle boots if you like,' he said persuasively.

I shook my head and continued to read my book.

'How about the dramatic red top then?'

I didn't reply.

Tommy stamped his foot. 'No man is worth getting this upset over!'

I sipped my tea and willed him to go away.

'OK, I'll go as far as offering my warm henna scarf and rich green jacket but that's it, no further!'

'No!' I snapped the book shut. 'I'm staying in, I'd be awful company anyway. Ring up Roisin, she'll go.'

Tommy sat beside me on the sofa.

'Please, Gina. I just know my bloke will be there tonight. Please!'

I stared at the telly.

'I'll buy you a Black Russian . . .'

I finally agreed to go if Lotty and Roisin came as well. Dressing myself proved time-consuming and by the time we arrived the club was jammed. We eventually got seats and Roisin headed up to the bar. Even though I was determined to be totally miserable, the two Black Russians Tommy bought for me did the trick. I could be happily miserable now. Within half an hour I felt human again. Barely alive, but alive all the same.

Christmas day had come and gone. I hadn't even bothered to get dressed and had mooched around in my tracksuit. Hadn't washed my hair. Hadn't put on any make-up. Simply sat in front of the telly, drank a glass or two of Dad's home-made coffee liqueur while watching *Top of the Pops* and wished I were somewhere else. Sunny St Lucia with Pierce Brosnan preferably.

The only time I'd felt any joy was when Mum opened the stocking filler that I'd bought her. Ten pounds worth of wacky backy. We'd spent the rest of the afternoon locked in the shed, getting stoned, devouring a box of Quality Street and laughing like a couple of witches. But I still hadn't felt any better. In fact, I'd felt worse. Jason's words and the way he had said them followed me around like a stray dog. In the end, I'd told Jessie everything. She'd been so lovely about it I'd wanted to cry.

'Fuck him. He's a waste of space.' She'd been very adamant about the 'fuck him' bit. 'Here, have a chocolate.'

So I did, then I had another twelve and three bags of crisps before I felt sick. In the end, I'd decided a good book would solve all my problems.

But tonight the Black Russians were doing a much better job. By the time Tommy hissed: 'There he is!' at me, I was plastered.

Boggle-eyed, I tried to focus on the spot beside the bar where Tommy was furiously wagging his finger.

'He's here, I can't believe it!'

Neither could I. Taking a deep breath and with the smallest tremble of my outstretched hand I hastily downed the last of my drink.

'Is it . . . the guy to the left of the barman . . . or the right?' I don't know how I managed to even speak but I had to be sure.

'The left, to the left!' Tommy was jigging up and down, his earrings flapping around like mad. 'Isn't he a hunk?' He sat down beside me, his face full of expectation. 'What do you think, Gina?' The coppery taste invaded my system again as I pulled at my brother's sleeve and pointed to the ladies room.

'I think . . .' I replied barely able to speak. 'I think I'm going to be sick!'

'I'm so sorry, Tommy.' We were swinging our legs contentedly as we sat by the sink. 'I really wish it wasn't Jason out there.'

Tommy grinned. 'Don't be mad, woman, I don't care. Plenty of donkeys in the stable yet, you know.'

I was amazed, I thought he'd be devastated.

'Are you sure you're not upset?' I asked.

Tommy pulled a dramatic face. 'Me? Upset? No, Gina, I'm not. If he isn't good enough for my sister, he's certainly not good enough for me.'

'So, what now?' I asked.

There was a companionable silence as we considered our options.

'Well, there is one thing we could do . . .'

I glanced up at my brother who was smirking like a lunatic. 'Follow me!' he instructed as he hopped off the sink to make his way outside.

'He's going to do what?' Roisin guffawed loudly, nearly falling off her stool. 'Fabulous!' she shrieked. 'Will he give us the nod, then?'

I grinned like a maniac as we all fell silent and watched. Watched and waited so that when Tommy finally waved us over it was all we could do to keep straight faces.

If Jason could have fecked out of there at a hundred miles an hour he would have.

'Jesus, Gina,' Jason said, spluttering his pint all over his hand. 'Didn't expect to see you here.'

I'll bet you didn't, you wanker, I thought vengefully. He was bricking it. Nervous now that we were face to face, he had the gall to put a bit of space between himself and Tommy by taking a step back, when only two minutes ago he'd had his arm around him.

He didn't want me to see, of course. See that after all the flirting and messing with my heart, which was now punch-drunk, he had someone else. A gorgeous someone else with legs longer than mine and a bigger cleavage. Even though Jason hadn't the faintest notion that his 'girlfriend' was a gay bloke, and had obviously never seen Tommy in action at work, I still felt wicked and not in the least bit compensated by the shock that was in store for him. I pledged to myself that I wouldn't sock him one. Even though we weren't an item, he looked guilty. The prick! I managed nonetheless to feign surprise and shock and then anger. Until I realised that I wasn't pretending and I really did feel like murdering him.

I pulled myself together nonetheless while Roisin and Lotty kept a safe distance, afraid they'd give the game away by laughing their heads off.

'So Jason, you know my friend then, do you?' I said this as light-heartedly as I could. Jason's face contorted as he squirmed. Then he hung his head.

'I was going to tell you, honestly.'

Tommy pretended to be shocked by sucking in his breath. 'You two know each other!' he proclaimed.

'Yes!' I snapped, very over the top and beginning to enjoy myself. 'In fact, would you excuse us for a moment?' Tommy obliged, and released his grip on Jason. I pulled him aside and whispered loudly in his ear: 'I sincerely hope that you'll treat my friend better than you did me!'

Jason pretended to look sad, coy and insecure all at once. But I didn't buy it and it made me feel ill.

'I will and I'm sorry, Gina—'

I turned on my heel and marched off, Roisin and Lotty running to keep up with me.

'Well, did he go for it?' Roisin asked, her eyes ablaze and full of mischief.

'Yes!' I roared, punching the air and doing a dance.

Chapter 19

'It was the best laugh I've ever had!'

Tommy sat on the floor of the sitting room drinking his coffee and filling us in on exactly what had happened when he'd gone home with Jason that night.

Lotty, her eyes wide open, clutched Roisin's arm before hissing: 'Did he see it – the lad, did he see it?'

The room exploded with laughter. Then we all stared at Tommy. Naturally, it wasn't only Lotty who wanted to know the answer. Tommy kept us waiting with an exaggerated glint in his eye.

'Let's put it this way,' he started, looking around for an ashtray. 'He certainly felt it!'

I couldn't speak for five minutes I was so hoarse.

'What happened then?' Roisin was agog and hanging on Tommy's every word, as we all were.

'Pour me a glass of wine and I'll tell you – this coffee is wicked,' said Tommy, handing Roisin his cup, mock disdain plastered on his face. A short time later, the wine poured and consumed, Tommy continued.

'Well, let's see . . .' he started.

Lotty giggled uncontrollably.

'Shush!' hissed Roisin, flinging a cushion at her.

'First of all, he tripped over his jeans trying to get them back on . . .'

I hung my head and laughed for the longest time.

'Then,' Tommy was so full of mirth he could hardly talk, 'then, he became savagely irate and ordered me to leave.'

'And did you?' I asked, tears rolling down my face and plopping into my wine.

'I certainly tried. But then poor Jason changed his tune, became quite upset, and begged me to give him my word that I wouldn't tell.' Deliberately Tommy stopped and eyed up his audience. 'Which I eventually promised to do under one condition.' He took a suck of his cigarette and remained silent.

'What, what did you say, you madman, you!' Roisin could hardly contain herself.

Tommy stretched out on Lotty's beanbag, placing his hands behind his head.

'Oh it was simple really. I promised not to tell everyone in Benjamin Ryan Construction if he agreed that I could tell just one person.'

'Jaysus, did he nearly faint?' asked Lotty. Even I was agog now and horribly curious.

'Naturally he was baffled that I even knew where he worked. In the end he had no choice but to go along with it. But he was such a snivelling mess by that stage I thought it only fair to name the person involved. So I did.' Tommy stopped for breath.

A sizeable hush hovered in the room as we all waited for the next instalment.

'I put back on my tights . . .'

At this, Roisin simply fell to her knees and grabbed her ribs.

'. . . and said "My sister, I'll tell her, I'll tell Gina."' Tommy started to vibrate on the beanbag.

'As I expected,' Tommy said when he was able to continue, 'he got severely agitated and muttered, "Gina?" a thousand times. Then the penny dropped, very slowly at first but eventually it did gather a bit of speed. Leaving poor Jason a ruined shaking heap on the floor.'

I looked at my brother, astonished at what he had just done for me.

'So, Gina,' Tommy asked slyly, while the others hooted with glee. 'Any other fellas you want me to terrorise? Sure, what are brothers for?'

Chapter 20

I filed away the latest batch of invoices, rang Mr Ryan to thank him for the very generous Christmas bonus he had given me, and pulled on my coat.

'Are you off then, Gina?' Joe sauntered into my office, for once not wired over something or other but quietly at ease. A bit like me, I thought, pulling on my gloves and grabbing my bag. I smiled at Joe, realising for the first time how much I actually liked him. I know he was highly strung at times but at the end of the day if he weren't there I'd miss him like mad.

He'd been so good to me – especially during the early days when I was constantly in a knot and at a loss at how to confront and cope with my appalling new surroundings.

'See you in the morning,' I said as I handed him a final bunch of letters to sign.

'Right you are,' grinned back Joe. 'I'll have the kettle on for you!'

I sat on the train and closed my eyes. A feeling of wellbeing tucked itself around me. I had thoroughly enjoyed the rest of the Christmas break, after those first few days where I had taken on an uncanny resemblance to a slug. I shuffled in my seat and looked out the window.

This was the first day, the very first day where I'd been to work and hadn't felt I was walking a tightrope. Beating myself up over what clothes to wear and applying make-up in an irrational frenzy every time I visited the loo. And guess what? I liked it. I liked this feeling of serenity and peace. Now I do realise how corny that sounds but when you've been on a rollercoaster with the bastard from hell you're allowed to feel bloody wonderful when you've jumped off without breaking both your legs – and your heart for that matter.

I had been slightly apprehensive the night before. Just a little bit. You know, in case Jason landed in the office door today ready to annihilate me with a baseball bat. But he hadn't. In fact, you could say he crawled in. He relinquished his position of Drop Dead Gorgeous God without a fight and accepted his new title of Corrupt Bastard without contesting it. How could he? He was a Corrupt Bastard who had been royally caught. Caught and hung out to dry. I doubted his ego would ever get over the shock.

For the rest of the day I suppressed giggles whenever I saw him. I couldn't help myself. Jason

Ward: caught in the dark with another bloke. There was a God after all, and it bloody well wasn't him. The train arrived at my stop and reluctantly I got up from my comfy seat and walked home to the flat.

Something else had happened over the holidays. Not for the first time this week I remembered Roisin's 'Real Man' speech. Men with standards (especially ones who put down the toilet seat after using it). Men who were kind (kind enough not to care when you've boiled their best suit in the wash so it now wouldn't fit a flea). Men who would love us (love us so much that when we've spent the mortgage on a new jacket they don't even blink).

I chucked my keys on the sofa and carefully picked up a single red rose from the coffee table. Lotty had dried it out for me in the hot press, so it looked as soft and beautiful as it had the day Danny had sent the bouquet to Mum's house. I'd done a lot of thinking over the holidays. You could say Jessie forced me into it but that wouldn't really be true.

'Do you like him?' she had demanded.

I'd bowed my head in reply. Of course I liked him.

'Do you like him enough to go out for a drink with him?' She was getting exasperated now.

I grinned at her short fuse and nodded.

'Is this the same man that has asked you out for lunch dozens of times and you've always said no?'

I laughed at her, and her red face.

'Well, what's the problem then?' she finished,

slamming her cup into the sink.

There was no problem. I had been plagued all through the holidays by those little incidents I had hardly noticed at the time. Like the evening in the pub where The Legend had proclaimed that someone fancied me. Of course he wasn't referring to Jason. He had been talking about Danny.

I reeled from the memory of my sending up to site the Preparation H cream. Danny had laughed, whereas Jason would have fumed for a week. I hung my head in condensed remorse as I recalled the 'come for lunch' phone call, made by Danny during my 'fat day'. How could I have been so rude? Then there was the late-night incident over the fax machine. Would I ever forgive myself? And after all that Danny had still cared enough to kick in the door of the flat and ensure I would live another day. Christ, I was eaten with remorse! But there was no time to dwell on my past mistakes. Now that I had finally made a decision, one set in concrete, the whole nine yards, it was about time I did something about it. I did want to be with Danny, that much was clear. Naturally, there was, alas, the smallest of hitches. How was I going to get him?

The first couple of weeks of January brought rain, sleet and snow – but no Danny. I saw him in the office of course, full of his natural good humour which I had always taken for granted but now appreciated. All to no avail. I had become the invisible woman where he was concerned! The shock of this after deciding he was the one for me was too much. The cold spell continued both inside and outside the office, my heroic attempts to beguile him were getting me precisely nowhere I realised, as Danny, always in a hurry, turned down yet another offer from me for a quick drink after work. It didn't seem to matter that I was smiling for all I was worth, holding my breath and generally looking desperate. Not even the sight of me parading around in my January Sales fabulous new suit dented him into submission. It was murder.

Then to make life even worse, Jason stopped crawling and instead began trying to lay on the charm. As in the laying on of hands, if you don't mind. He merely smirked when eventually I told him I'd seen better hanging off a dog's behind. Ironically enough, I had Danny to thank for my new found wisdom. Let's face it, this must have been the first time in my whole life that I was chasing the good guy. That awful instinct I was born with that enticed me only towards fellas from hell was gone. Utterly extinguished. I didn't know myself.

As soon as my working day was over, I rushed off to meet Jessie. It made perfect sense to me that she was the person to consult. After all, her fella was normal, had yet to abscond, break her heart or tell her he fancied her best friend, or her brother. Jessie was unusually quiet as she sipped her expresso and listened to me gush on about my change of heart.

'You were right,' I babbled, hands fluttering all over the place. 'How could I have been so daft? And he saved my life – how romantic! What do you think, Jessie? What should I do?'

I took a big smiley slurp from my coffee cup and sat back in my chair. Jessie only offered a listless grimace. No whoops of joy that for once I was taking my little sister's advice. No shouting of orders to the waiter to whisk over two huge cheesecakes so we could celebrate goodo before she sat back, assessed the situation and offered me inside information and tip-offs on what course of action to take next. I was amazed and horrified when after what seemed like ages, Jessie grabbed my hand over the table and with a comforting squeeze whispered: 'Jesus, Gina! I think he's got a girlfriend!'

I was distraught. 'What do you mean "he's got a girlfriend?" ' I demanded, disbelief hurtling itself at me. 'He can't have!'

Jessie instructed me to sit tight while she whisked off to order more coffee. I collared her as soon as she sat down.

'Hang on a minute, Gina and I'll tell you everything.'

And she did. All the wretched details of how she and Jordan had met Danny the previous weekend, just before the holidays had ended. But he hadn't been alone. What really rubbed salt into the wound was that Jessie couldn't even say he'd been with someone awful. Because he hadn't been. He'd been walking arm and arm up the main street with a really nice and very attractive woman. A sister of Jessie's friend, if you don't mind. They'd even stopped for a ten-minute chat! I registered the utter regret which was boring holes into me. I couldn't touch the coffee Jessie had bought for me. No wonder Danny had been skipping off home every night on the dot of six! He had someone to go home to! My stomach curdled. I had to get away, I decided there and then. Maybe Australia. Nice and warm and on the other side of the bloody world.

'Look,' Jessie grabbed my arm as I made my way out the coffee shop door, 'let me see what I can find out, OK? It may be nothing.'

I solemnly agreed and, feeling wretched, headed for home to beat myself up with the sofa.

You needn't worry. I didn't go completely off the rails. If anything, Jessie's revelation prompted me to despise Jason even more. Working with him was becoming intolerable. Obviously he didn't like being ignored (I worked that one out at last). I knew for certain that I wasn't imagining his new-found interest in me when the next day at work, as cool as you like and dressed to kill, he sauntered into my office and suggested that we go for lunch. Of course I declined, even though his denim shirt rolled up to the elbows, and jet-black hair furnished him with a cool sexiness any other woman would melt over. In fact, I was chuffed with the expert delivery of my refusal. Like a group of Vikings heading for war, it was direct, with no compromise offered as it screamed towards him waving a big axe.

As the next couple of weeks passed, bringing January to an end and a thousand rejections from me as I continued to rebuff Jason with a force as palpable as fire or ice, he still maintained an unhealthy interest in what I was doing at the weekends. If he was looking for a truce, I decided, he could bloody well fuck off. More than once, Danny passed us in the main office where he undoubtedly noticed my indifference to Jason, or at least I prayed he did. I realised this was the one way I cold use Jason, now that I had all but blown things with Danny. I felt it was the minimum I could achieve, to ensure that there was no room for doubt in Danny's mind, even if we never became an item. It was important to me that he understood my feelings for Jason were rancid. Roisin and Lotty were a great help, especially when I'd have a brief fling with Misery. There was as yet, no news from Jessie regarding Danny's mystery woman.

'If it's meant to be then it will,' declared Lotty as we all huddled on the sofa during the ad break on *Coronation Street*.

This might cheer you up,' offered Roisin flinging an Oxendales catalogue at me. 'Retail therapy!' We all laughed.

And of course, they were right. I threw myself

into indulging Lotty's new fascination with pound shops, or any kind of shop where you could buy ceramic rabbits and ash trays by the bag full. We spent hours furnishing the flat with as many artificial flowers one could buy for a fiver, then there was the best find of all. Lotty's favourite. A 'Made in Taiwan' hedgehog-shaped toilet brush and holder. Laugh if you like, but choosing pound shop cosmetics and body lotions kept my feet on the ground and stopped me from driving myself mad with 'What if'. What if I'd gone for lunch just once with Danny? Would I at his moment be lazing on a bed with him in Paris after a mad love-making session? Would he still want me after seeing my feet? Or what if I'd chatted to him at the Christmas party, made the first move towards an apology and a truce? Feck it! I mumbled as I rummaged through mascaras and lipsticks. Tomorrow is another day.

'I know it's a pain, but can you do it?'

It was a freezing and miserable week in early February and Nicola was desperate.

'I'll tell you what, take Monday off, how about that?'

I sat back in my swivel chair and crossed my arms in front of my chest pretending to be annoyed. Of course I'd do it! But I hadn't told her yet. Nicola was desperate to take Friday off, so she could jet off on a romantic weekend break with George. Which meant she wanted me to do a rake of VAT returns

for her and run the payroll. I wouldn't even have Joe
here to help me as he'd be busy running three
toolbox talks in the canteen for the men. Or in
other words, getting himself in a huge tizzy as he
delivered yet another lecture to a crowd of eejits
regarding on-site safety and the perils of pretending
fork lifts were go-carts. Then of course, there were
time sheets to be done, and a few hours of bookkeeping just in case I got bored. I tried not to smile
at Nicola as she became more and more uptight.

'I'll even throw in a couple of late lunches next
week, oh come on, Gina. I'd do it for you!'

I decided to relent. 'On one condition,' I barked
trying to wind her up.

'Anything,' jumped in Nicola with utter sincerity.

'Any chance of a cup of tea?'

Lotty, Roisin and myself basked in the sitting room.

'God, isn't this the life?' murmured Roisin with
her feet on the coffee table. 'We're warm, cosy and
I've spent all those leftover fifty-pences on a take
out!' A communal undertone of contentment
followed. Since I had almost, but not quite, been
gassed to extinction, Mr Tibet had decided to have
the flat over-hauled. Now we were proud customers
of Bord Gais as well as the ESB. The shrill ringing
of the phone shattered the moment.

'I'll get it,' grumbled Lotty forcing herself up from
the sofa.

'I'll put the kettle on,' said Roisin, 'the Chinese

will be here in a sec.' I nodded, half asleep with a copy of OK magazine on my lap.

'Gina, it's for you.' Lotty poked her head around the side of the sitting room door looking like she'd just won the lottery. 'I think it's Jessie!'

The news was bad. Jessie had passed Danny and the girlfriend as she skated home on the icy roads from the supermarket last night. Apparently, she was tall, clung to him constantly and laughed non-stop with him. I was eaten with jealousy. I made another quick bargain with the almighty that if I could have one more go, just one to make things right, I promised I'd help Gran for a month with her meals-on-wheels work. She didn't like asking Mum who made a big joke of it and brought the whole thing down to the level of meals-on-heels, or so Gran alleged. The next day was Friday, and although I'd be as busy as hell I decided to make the effort. One last try. I made another decision as Roisin and Lotty swapped gripes about the hard-up lives of cabin crew attendants and aromatherapists. If things didn't work out this time, and regardless of how much I adored my job, I was going to quit.

The Legend was pretending he was sick.

'I can't, Gina, honest to God, I'm dying.' Dying from drink, I thought. He swayed in front of my desk, which was littered with payslips, cheques and hundreds of invoices. 'Sure Joe will do it,' he offered

with a half smile. I shut my eyes and gave up. I had
asked the Legend to hand out the wages for me, I
simply didn't have the time to do it myself. The VAT
returns slept soundly in my desk drawer, untouched.
I was beginning to panic. The Legend skulked out of
my office and back to his van. I looked at the phone,
dithering, uncertain. I suppose I could ask Danny? It
was certainly an option. there was no way I was
going to get all of my workload cleared by the end
of the day otherwise. Shaking, I picked up the
receiver.

'No problem, Gina, but it'll be late before I get
there.' I was amazed at how friendly he sounded!

'Thanks,' I uttered quietly, not wanting to assume
anything. Anything along the lines of he still fancies
me rotten even though he has a girlfriend and has
forgiven me for being ungrateful and pretending I
wasn't indebted to him for rescuing me. I finished
the payroll and yanked out the VAT returns. Danny
was coming, and I was going to be ready for him!

It's at times like this that I think all office staff are
deranged. Two hours after I had started, I still wasn't
finished. My desk was piled high with sales and
purchases ledgers, neither of which would balance.
For a split second I though of ringing Ralph. Then
I decided I'd rather fling myself under the first
moving vehicle available. Outside in the freezing
fog, there were only a couple of the lads clearing up
the compound for the weekend. I knew there was
no point asking them. Unless of course, I felt the

urge to enquire about the price of a length of timber, or how to construct a lethal weapon out of a bag of cement. Just as I was about to give up, the door opened. Thank God, I was saved! I was fully prepared to grab whichever unlikely fella had rambled into my lair of panic and force them to help me. Then I recognised Jason. Ignoring me, he ambled into the kitchen to put the kettle on. Feck!

'Are you sure you don't want a cup of tea?' For the third time in fifteen minutes, I politely said no. This time, instead of leaving, Jason began to jitter just inside the periphery of my office.

'Oh, come on, Gina! You've been blanking me for weeks. What the hell is going on?' Jason was furious.

Initially, I was delighted that he was so rattled with me and prepared myself to blast him out of it. The bastard. I'd really had enough. Just as my brain caught up with my fury and I was about to let rip, I stopped. He looked different. Wound up and irritated. Ready to blow.

'Well?' he insisted.

In a short second I was acutely aware that it was just him and me. Alone in the cabin and I didn't like it.

'There's nothing to discuss,' I mumbled bowing my head into my paperwork. An uneasy, charged silence flourished.

'I don't accept that. I know you like me, Gina. You always have done.'

That was it. My warrior instinct took hold. By the

time I was finished with him he was going to wish
he'd worn flame retardant clothes before hitting on
me. I gripped my pen so I wouldn't stab him, and
quietly stated, 'I don't like men that swing both
ways.' I barely had time to catch my breath, before
Jason slammed the office door wide open and
marched in to face me head on.

Slithering towards me with what he obviously
considered his best asset, Jason wiggled his crotch
and whispered, 'You could hang a door off it, you
know.' He sounded like he was gargling gravel and I
felt faint. He was now so close to me that I could
smell his aftershave. It didn't beguile me any more,
like it had in the old days. Now it repulsed me and
I felt sick with nerves.

Jason inched closer, I was sure he was going to kill
me. I could visualise the headlines already: 'Site
clerk murdered by fella wearing too much
aftershave'. If I hadn't been so frightened, I'd have
burst out laughing. I gulped hard and forced a reply.

'If it's all the same to you, I'd rather slam a door
on it.' I stared him out even though he looked like
he was sitting on a stick of dynamite.

My fear level didn't reach crisis point until he
growled, 'You bloody prick tease.' I didn't have time
to gather my wits, and run for it. In a split second he
had flung me up against the wall behind my chair.

While Jason spat insult after insult at me, and
raved on about how I'd made a complete fool out of
him, the part of my brain which wasn't shocked out

of its wits hollered at me to find something, anything to defend myself with. The only thing within reach of my outstretched arms was a small desk that was home to the fax machine and my make-up bag. Fantastic, I thought, my breath coming in short bursts. Just the job. Gibbering with angst, I realised whacking him with a small bottle of Rimmel glitter nail polish wasn't quite what I had in mind. Now why didn't I keep an axe down there like any other person might, who worked in a lonely cabin almost in the middle of nowhere?

More to the point, had I learned nothing about chasing men? The first male I had ever fallen for was only seven and I was five. He ran off bawling to his mum that I was plaguing him into sharing a drink of 7-Up with me out of my Barbie cup. The next candidate, granted was a bit older and stuffed full of hormones, still almost passed out cold when I suggested we go away for a romantic weekend. As for the next guy? Well, what more proof did a girl need? He was trying to fecking kill me!

A sudden crash made us both jump. I began to sob. Not only was I in the process of being strangled, now the weather had obviously turned and with my luck I was about to be struck by lightning. Without warning Jason was airlifted. Well, that's how it looked to me, even though I was half-hysterical. I fell back into my chair hugging my throat, which hurt like hell. In front of me Jason was seven feet tall, with two extra limbs attached just underneath his arms.

His knees were level with my neck even though I was sitting down and I noticed, with the complete clarity permitted to those who have been scared shitless, that he had a muck stain on the right leg of his jeans. One second he was in front of me, the next he was gone.

'Keep your fucking hands off my woman or I'll have you, Ward, right?'

It was Danny roaring. Although I still don't remember actually doing it (I was after all trying to comfort my threadbare nerves which were still throbbing with terror) I got up and walked slowly from my desk to the open door of the cabin. Through hazy sunshine and a lot of dust, I saw Jason flat on his behind holding his jaw. Then there was Danny. His face chiselled into sheer cliffsides by pure anger, as he wiped his hands on the legs of his jeans. I struggled to get down the cabin steps. My coat hanging off one arm, handbag around my neck, I reached out my hand to Danny. He put his arm around me and carried me the rest of the way before helping me into his car and going back to Jason.

'Jesus, are you OK?'

I nodded stupidly at The Legend who was on his knees looking in the car window at me. Across the compound Jason stood up and wiped away a tiny trickled of blood from his mouth. Danny shoved him hard in the back and pushed him towards the Security Guard in his cabin who had woken up from all the noise.

Minutes later Danny came back and sat beside me in the driver's seat. 'Well, Gina, looks like we're off to the hospital – again!' I tried to smile.

'I always seem to be thanking you for saving my life,' I sniffled.

'Ah sure, someone has to do it. You're not safe to be let out alone,' he added, sounding deeply serious. 'And I only came back to collect the wages!'

I offered a diluted smile and wiped my nose.

'I didn't fancy him you know. He just wouldn't take no for an answer.'

Danny said nothing but started the car.

'I'm freezing,' I said truthfully, and I was. My teeth were chattering from the cold and the shock.

'I'll get you to casualty, that's a nasty mark on your neck. Then I'll get you home.'

Jesus! Isn't he great? I registered this even though I was in a heap. Heap or not, I saw my chance and I took it.

'What about your girlfriend, am I delaying you or anything?'

I held my breath.

'That's off. We finished last week.'

I tried not to squeal with delight. 'Oh did you?' I replied hoping he didn't see my excitement.

'Why?' I knew he was smiling. 'Are you interested?'

I was too shy to answer.

'By the way,' he continued, chuckling, 'make sure this is the last time I take you to casualty. I prefer drama of a different kind, like the Abbey for example, OK?'

The next couple of days flew by. I wasn't worried because I knew it would happen. I could feel it. Apparently, so could Nicola, who delighted in putting me through hours of torture by slagging me rotten and calling me a no-good hussy. So, when Danny, looking bashful and reserved, strolled into the office and asked me did I fancy seeing the new Pierce Brosnan movie at the cinema, I didn't have to watch his body language. Or have Granny courier over a pint of holy water. I wasn't drowning in a horrible urgency that insisted I investigate his dark eyes, in case, perchance, there was any ulterior motive sniggering behind them. Instead, I relished the tingling in my toes, and with an outpour of inner strength, somehow resisted the urge to whoop with delight.

Putting down my pen, we grinned at each other. There was no need for a quick Hail Mary this time, instead I shyly looked at my feet. For once I had landed on them.